LEGO NINJAGO
Masters of Spinjitzu

SPECIAL EDITION

PAPERCUT Z™

LEGO® GRAPHIC NOVELS AVAILABLE FROM PAPERCUTZ™

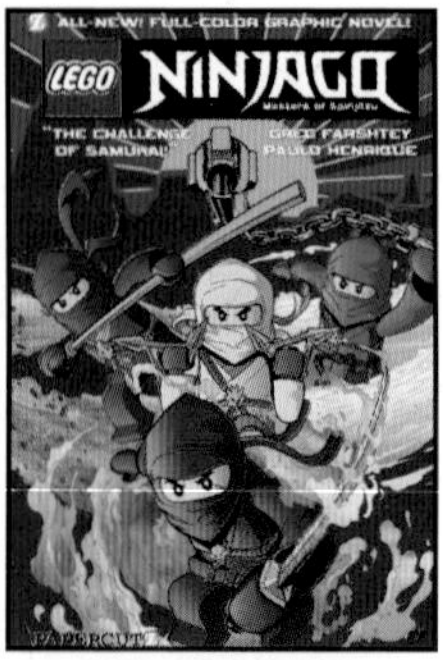
ALL-NEW! FULL-COLOR GRAPHIC NOVEL!
NINJAGO
"THE CHALLENGE OF SAMURAI"
GREG FARSHTEY
PAULO HENRIQUE
PAPERCUTZ
NINJAGO #1

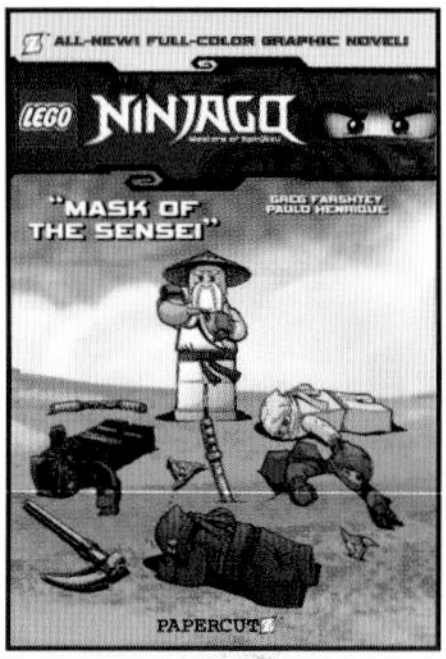
ALL-NEW! FULL-COLOR GRAPHIC NOVEL!
NINJAGO
"MASK OF THE SENSEI"
GREG FARSHTEY
PAULO HENRIQUE
PAPERCUTZ
NINJAGO #2

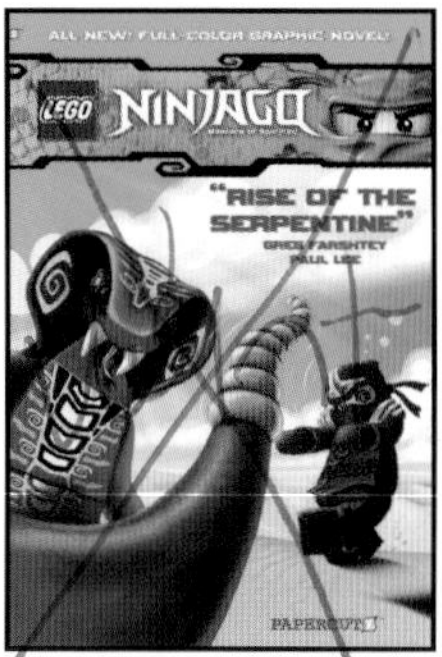
NINJAGO
"RISE OF THE SERPENTINE"
PAPERCUTZ
NINJAGO #3

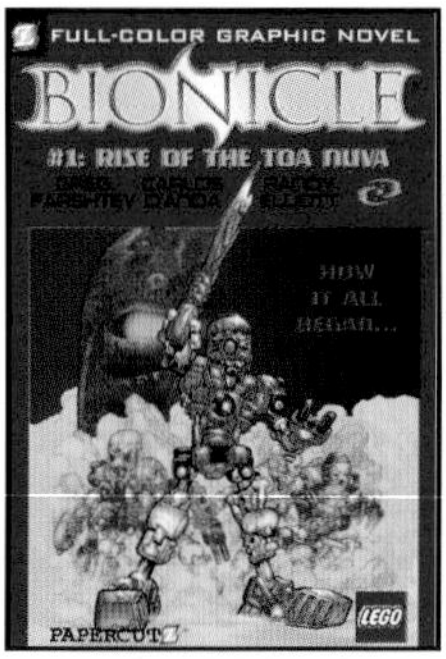
FULL-COLOR GRAPHIC NOVEL
BIONICLE
#1: RISE OF THE TOA NUVA
HOW IT ALL BEGAN...
PAPERCUTZ
BIONICLE #1

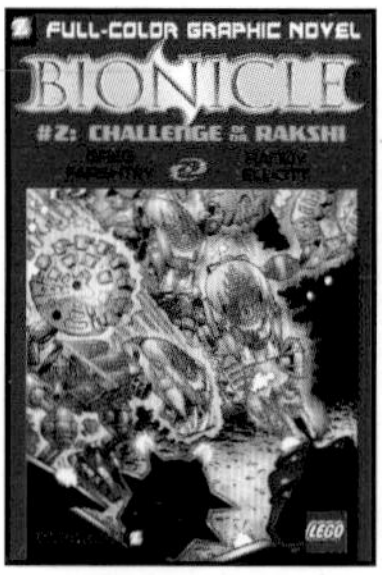
FULL-COLOR GRAPHIC NOVEL
BIONICLE
#2: CHALLENGE of the RAKSHI
BIONICLE #2

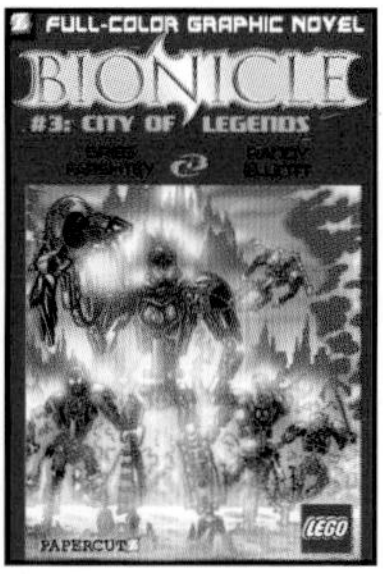
FULL-COLOR GRAPHIC NOVEL
BIONICLE
#3: CITY OF LEGENDS
PAPERCUTZ
BIONICLE #3

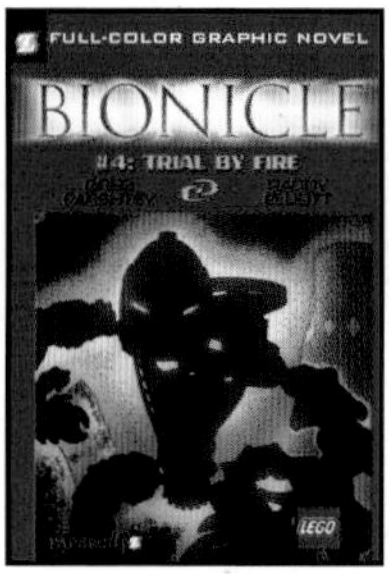
FULL-COLOR GRAPHIC NOVEL
BIONICLE
#4: TRIAL BY FIRE
BIONICLE #4

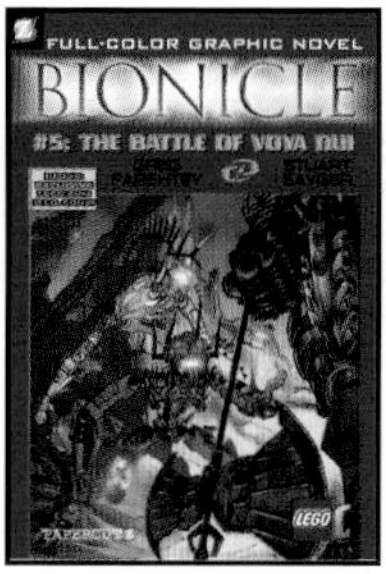
FULL-COLOR GRAPHIC NOVEL
BIONICLE
#5: THE BATTLE OF VOYA NUI
PAPERCUTZ
BIONICLE #5

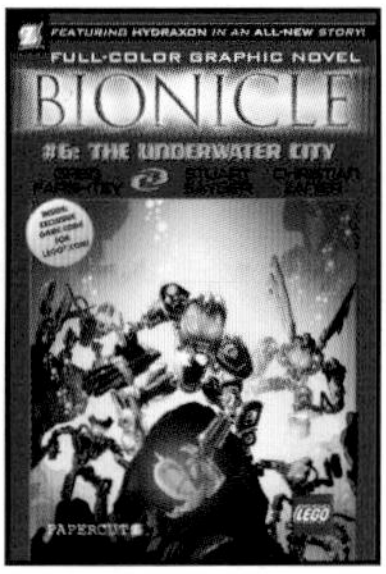
FULL-COLOR GRAPHIC NOVEL
BIONICLE
#6: THE UNDERWATER CITY
PAPERCUTZ
BIONICLE #6

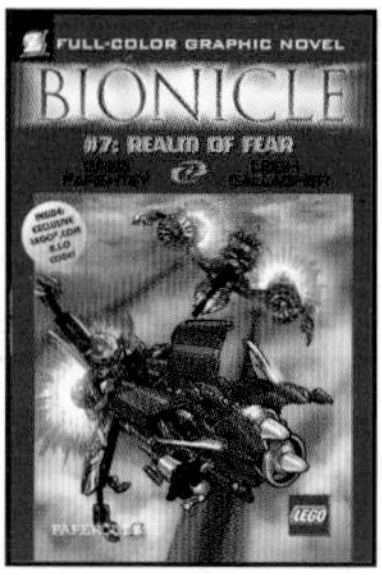
FULL-COLOR GRAPHIC NOVEL
BIONICLE
#7: REALM OF FEAR
PAPERCUTZ
BIONICLE #7

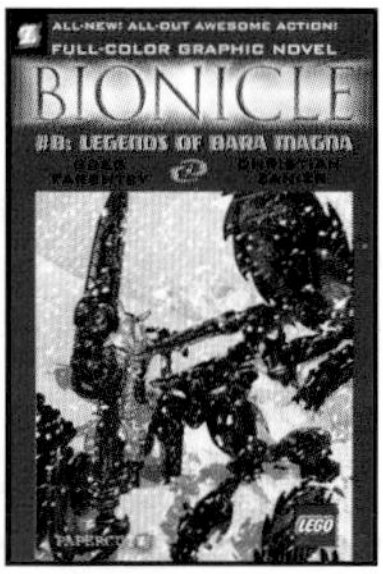
ALL-NEW! ALL-OUT AWESOME ACTION!
FULL-COLOR GRAPHIC NOVEL
BIONICLE
#8: LEGENDS OF BARA MAGNA
BIONICLE #8

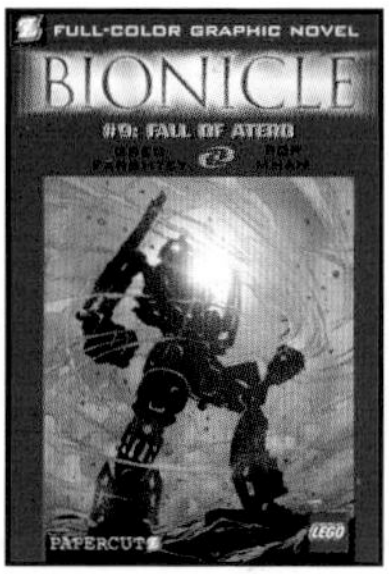
FULL-COLOR GRAPHIC NOVEL
BIONICLE
#9: FALL OF ATERO
PAPERCUTZ
BIONICLE #9

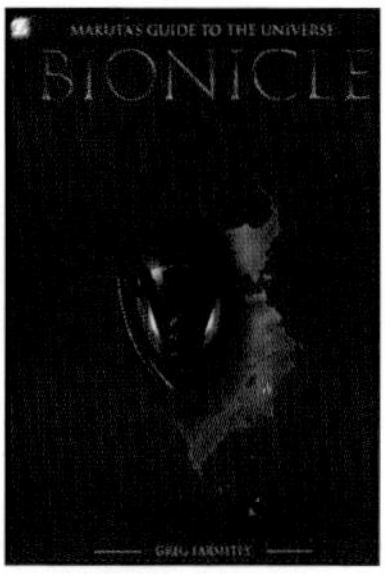
MAKUTA'S GUIDE TO THE UNIVERSE
BIONICLE
Makuta's Guide to the Universe

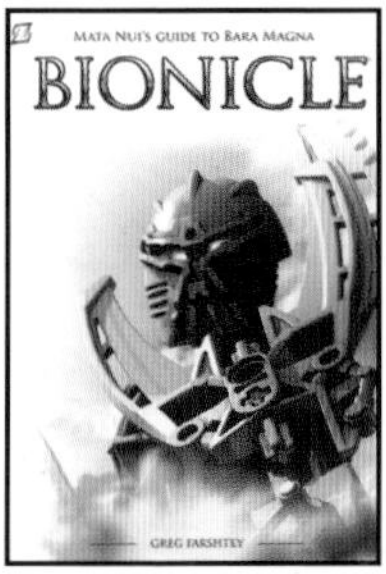
MATA NUI'S GUIDE TO BARA MAGNA
BIONICLE
Mata Nui's Guide to Bara Magna

NINJAGO graphic novels, BIONICLE® graphic novels, and guide books are available in paperback and hardcover at booksellers everywhere.

Or order from us: please add $4.00 for postage and handling for first book, add $1.00 for each additional book. NINJAGO #1-3 are $6.99 in paperback, and $13.99 in hardcover. BIONICLE #1-3, 8, and 9 are $8.99 in paperback, $13.99 in hardcover. Guide Books are $9.99 each in paperback only. Please make check payable to NBM Publishing. Send to: Papercutz, 160 Broadway, Ste. 700, East Wing, New York, NY 10038 • 1-800-886-1223

www.papercutz.com

LEGO NINJAGO
Masters of Spinjitzu

SPECIAL EDITION #1

"THE CHALLENGE OF SAMUKAI!" AND "THE MASK OF THE SENSEI"

GREG FARSHTEY • Writer
PAULO HENRIQUE • Artist
LAURIE E. SMITH • Colorist

PAPERCUTZ™
New York

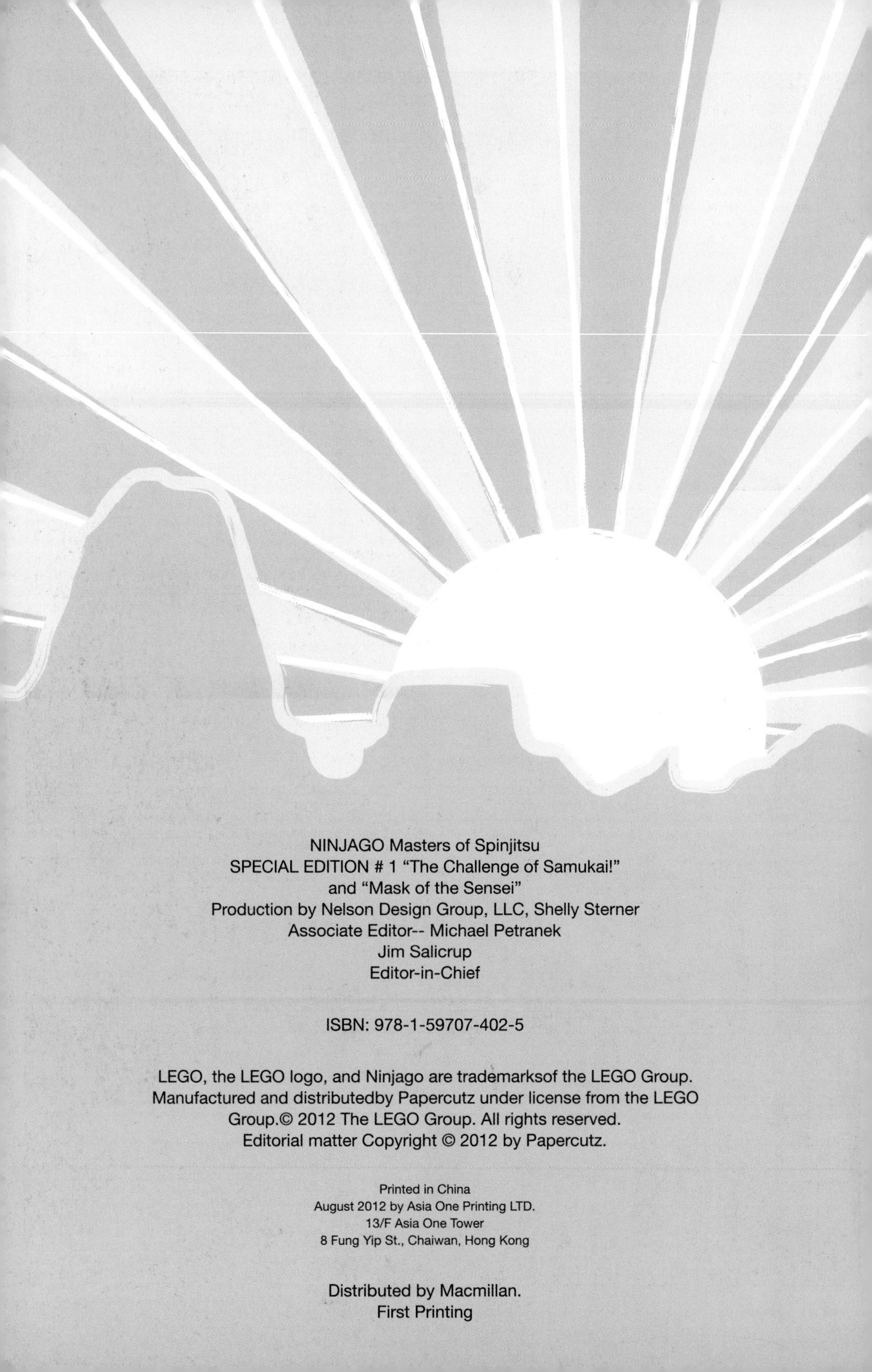

NINJAGO Masters of Spinjitsu
SPECIAL EDITION # 1 "The Challenge of Samukai!"
and "Mask of the Sensei"
Production by Nelson Design Group, LLC, Shelly Sterner
Associate Editor-- Michael Petranek
Jim Salicrup
Editor-in-Chief

ISBN: 978-1-59707-402-5

Printed in China
August 2012 by Asia One Printing LTD.
13/F Asia One Tower
8 Fung Yip St., Chaiwan, Hong Kong

Distributed by Macmillan.
First Printing

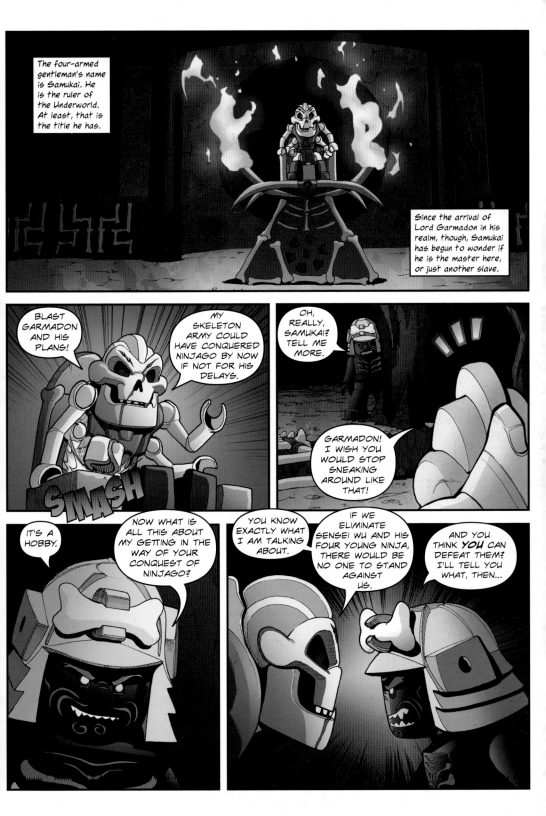

The four-armed gentleman's name is Samukai. He is the ruler of the Underworld. At least, that is the title he has.

Since the arrival of Lord Garmadon in his realm, though, Samukai has begun to wonder if he is the master here, or just another slave.

BLAST GARMADON AND HIS PLANS!

MY SKELETON ARMY COULD HAVE CONQUERED NINJAGO BY NOW IF NOT FOR HIS DELAYS.

OH, REALLY, SAMUKAI? TELL ME MORE.

GARMADON! I WISH YOU WOULD STOP SNEAKING AROUND LIKE THAT!

IT'S A HOBBY.

NOW WHAT IS ALL THIS ABOUT MY GETTING IN THE WAY OF YOUR CONQUEST OF NINJAGO?

YOU KNOW EXACTLY WHAT I AM TALKING ABOUT.

IF WE ELIMINATE SENSEI WU AND HIS FOUR YOUNG NINJA, THERE WOULD BE NO ONE TO STAND AGAINST US.

AND YOU THINK YOU CAN DEFEAT THEM? I'LL TELL YOU WHAT, THEN...

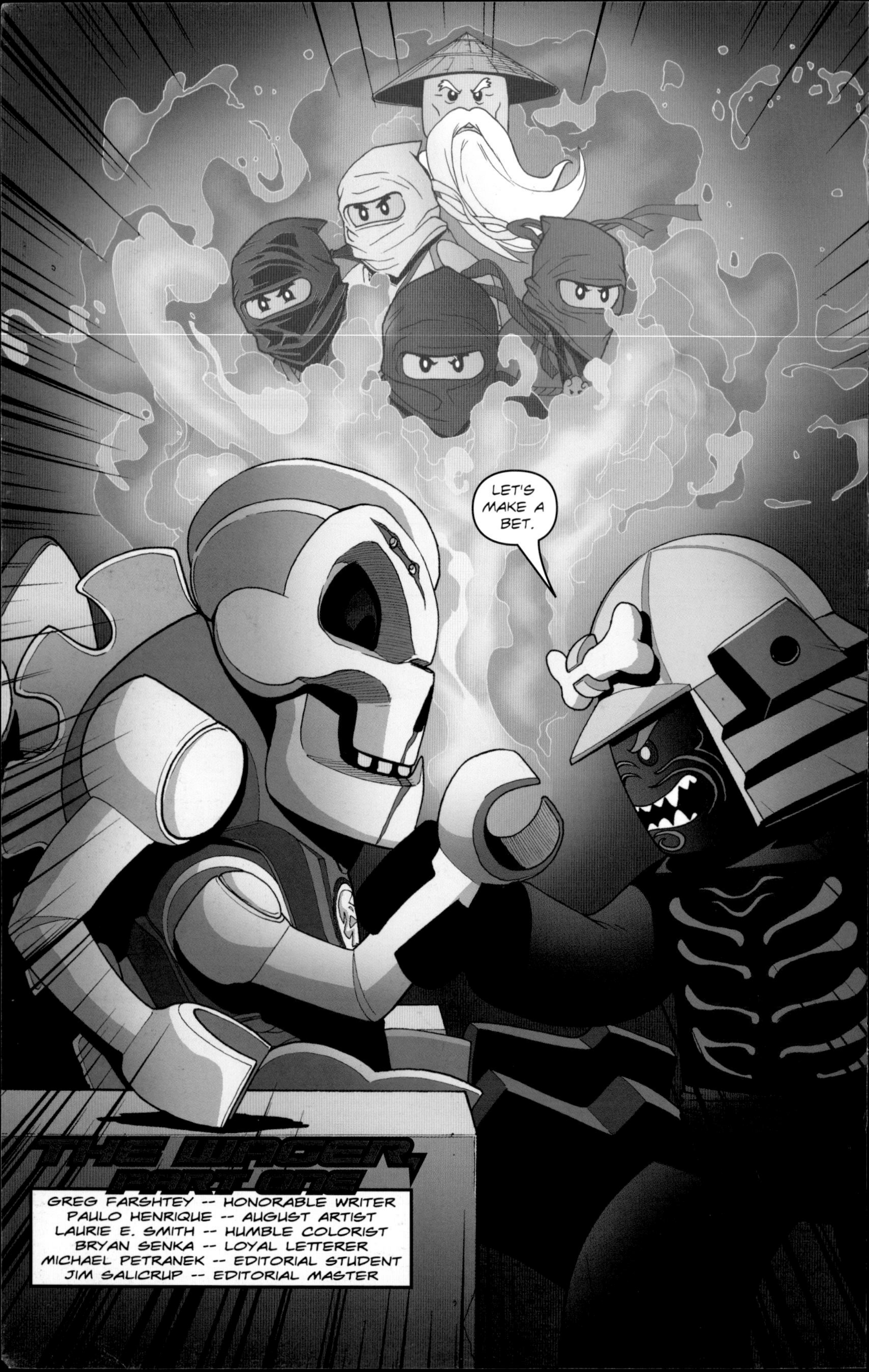
LET'S MAKE A BET.
THE WAGER, PART ONE
GREG FARSHTEY -- HONORABLE WRITER
PAULO HENRIQUE -- AUGUST ARTIST
LAURIE E. SMITH -- HUMBLE COLORIST
BRYAN SENKA -- LOYAL LETTERER
MICHAEL PETRANEK -- EDITORIAL STUDENT
JIM SALICRUP -- EDITORIAL MASTER

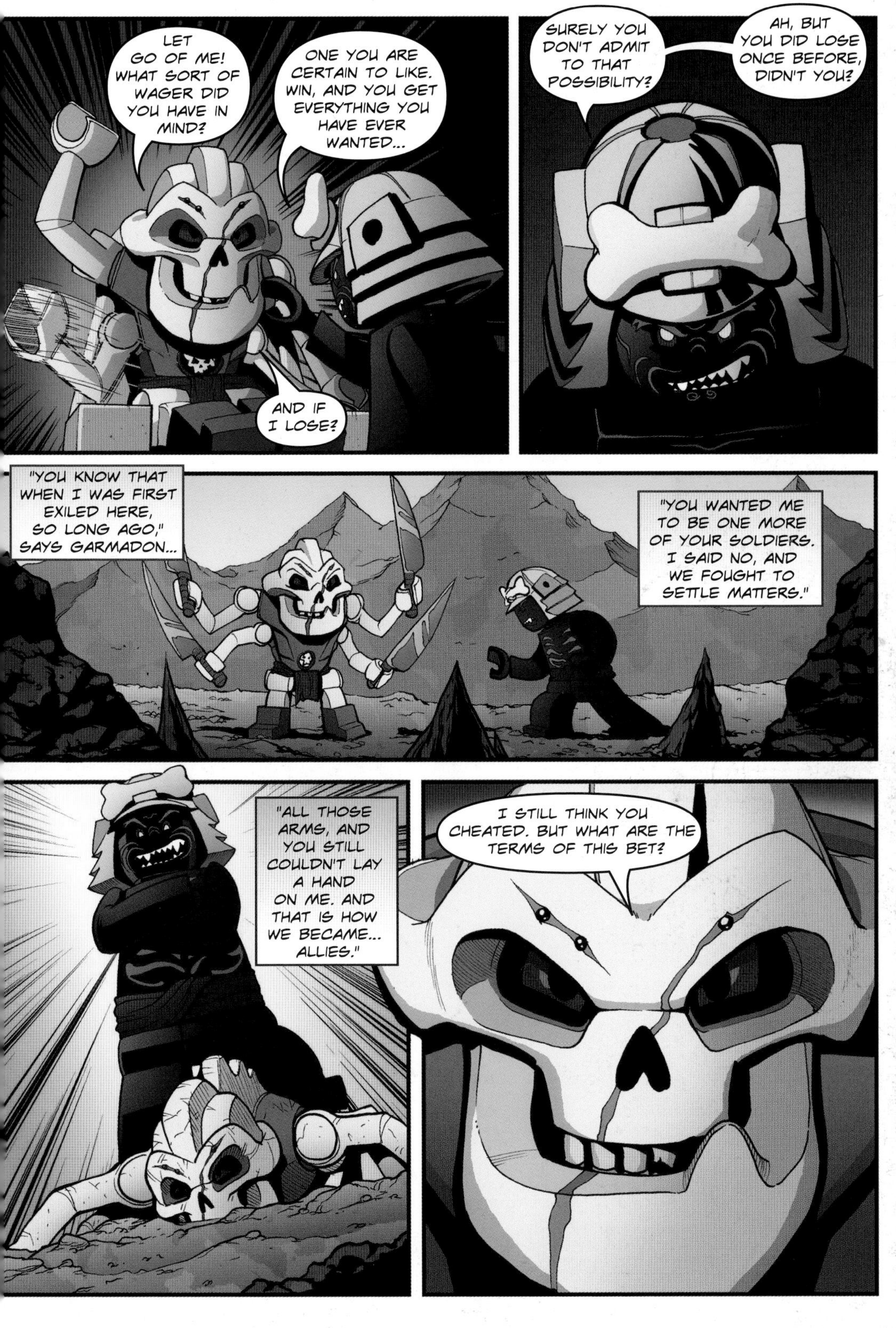
LET GO OF ME! WHAT SORT OF WAGER DID YOU HAVE IN MIND?
ONE YOU ARE CERTAIN TO LIKE. WIN, AND YOU GET EVERYTHING YOU HAVE EVER WANTED...
AND IF I LOSE?
SURELY YOU DON'T ADMIT TO THAT POSSIBILITY?
AH, BUT YOU DID LOSE ONCE BEFORE, DIDN'T YOU?
"YOU KNOW THAT WHEN I WAS FIRST EXILED HERE, SO LONG AGO," SAYS GARMADON...
"YOU WANTED ME TO BE ONE MORE OF YOUR SOLDIERS. I SAID NO, AND WE FOUGHT TO SETTLE MATTERS."
"ALL THOSE ARMS, AND YOU STILL COULDN'T LAY A HAND ON ME. AND THAT IS HOW WE BECAME... ALLIES."
I STILL THINK YOU CHEATED. BUT WHAT ARE THE TERMS OF THIS BET?

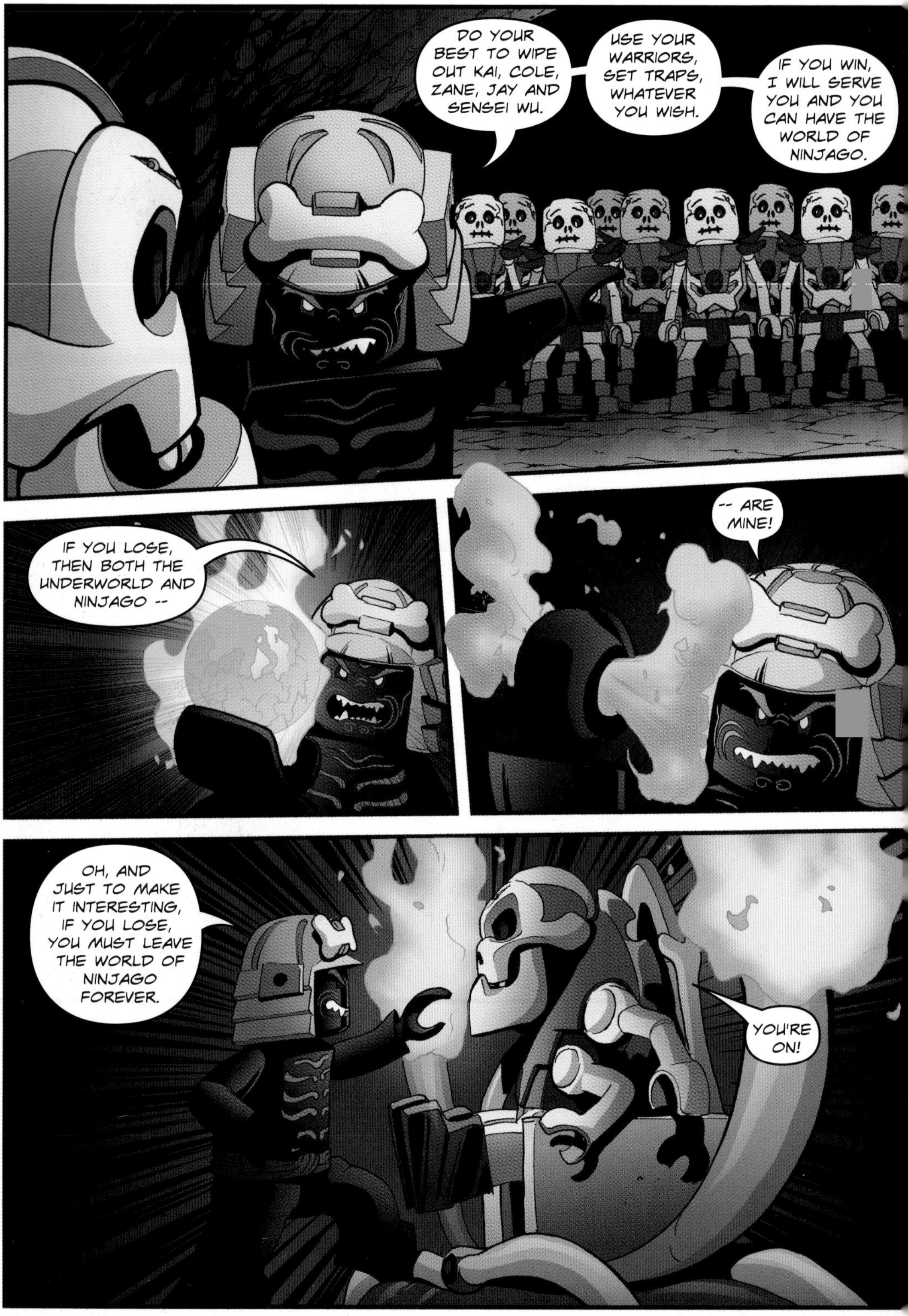
DO YOUR BEST TO WIPE OUT KAI, COLE, ZANE, JAY AND SENSEI WU.
USE YOUR WARRIORS, SET TRAPS, WHATEVER YOU WISH.
IF YOU WIN, I WILL SERVE YOU AND YOU CAN HAVE THE WORLD OF NINJAGO.
IF YOU LOSE, THEN BOTH THE UNDERWORLD AND NINJAGO --
-- ARE MINE!
OH, AND JUST TO MAKE IT INTERESTING, IF YOU LOSE, YOU MUST LEAVE THE WORLD OF NINJAGO FOREVER.
YOU'RE ON!

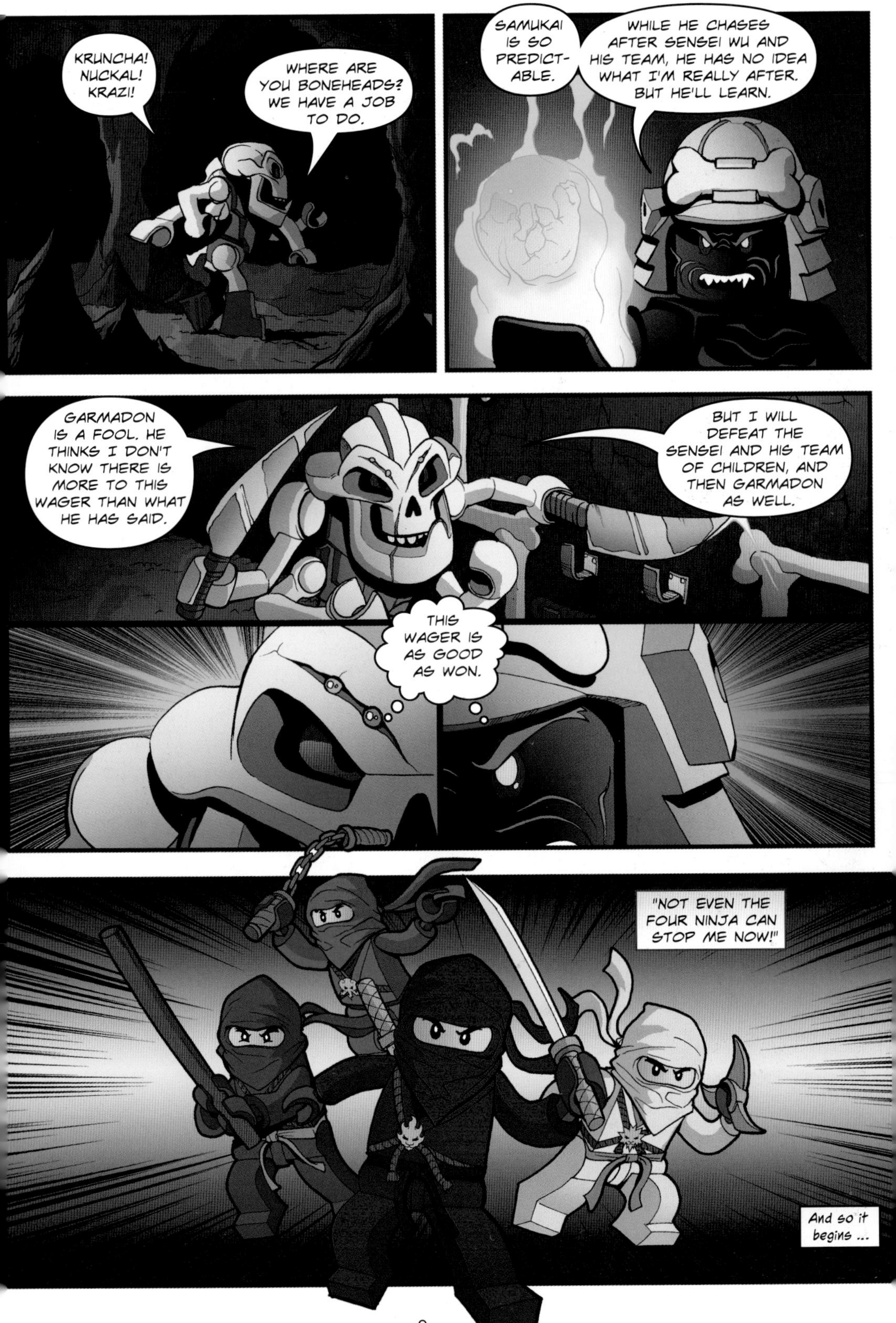
KRUNCHA! NUCKAL! KRAZI!
WHERE ARE YOU BONEHEADS? WE HAVE A JOB TO DO.
SAMUKAI IS SO PREDICT-ABLE.
WHILE HE CHASES AFTER SENSEI WU AND HIS TEAM, HE HAS NO IDEA WHAT I'M REALLY AFTER. BUT HE'LL LEARN.
GARMADON IS A FOOL. HE THINKS I DON'T KNOW THERE IS MORE TO THIS WAGER THAN WHAT HE HAS SAID.
BUT I WILL DEFEAT THE SENSEI AND HIS TEAM OF CHILDREN, AND THEN GARMADON AS WELL.
THIS WAGER IS AS GOOD AS WON.
"NOT EVEN THE FOUR NINJA CAN STOP ME NOW!"
And so it begins ...

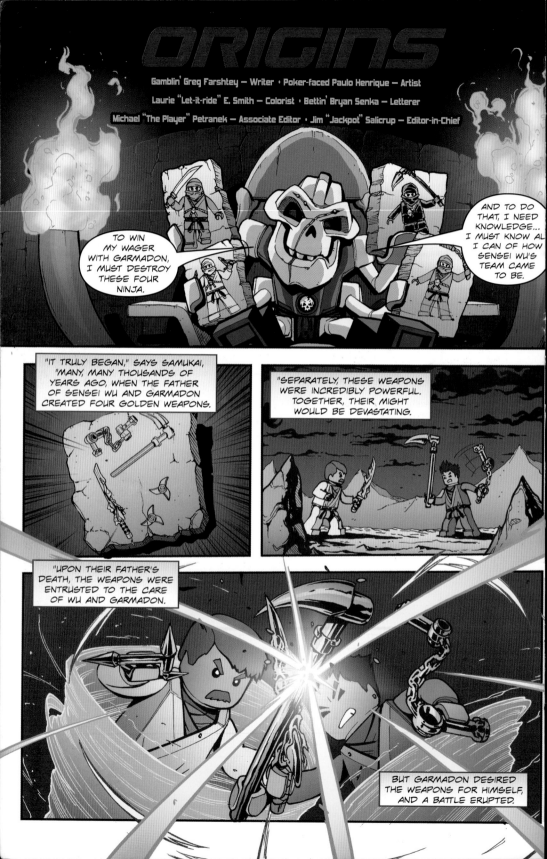

ORIGINS

Gamblin' Greg Farshtey — Writer • Poker-faced Paulo Henrique — Artist

Laurie "Let-it-ride" E. Smith — Colorist • Bettin' Bryan Senka — Letterer

Michael "The Player" Petranek — Associate Editor • Jim "Jackpot" Salicrup — Editor-in-Chief

TO WIN MY WAGER WITH GARMADON, I MUST DESTROY THESE FOUR NINJA.

AND TO DO THAT, I NEED KNOWLEDGE... I MUST KNOW ALL I CAN OF HOW SENSEI WU'S TEAM CAME TO BE.

"IT TRULY BEGAN," SAYS SAMUKAI, "MANY, MANY THOUSANDS OF YEARS AGO, WHEN THE FATHER OF SENSEI WU AND GARMADON CREATED FOUR GOLDEN WEAPONS.

"SEPARATELY, THESE WEAPONS WERE INCREDIBLY POWERFUL. TOGETHER, THEIR MIGHT WOULD BE DEVASTATING.

"UPON THEIR FATHER'S DEATH, THE WEAPONS WERE ENTRUSTED TO THE CARE OF WU AND GARMADON.

BUT GARMADON DESIRED THE WEAPONS FOR HIMSELF, AND A BATTLE ERUPTED.

"THE FUTURE SENSEI WU WAS THE VICTOR, AND GARMADON WAS BANISHED TO THE UNDERWORLD... MY REALM. IT SEEMED THAT THE GOLDEN WEAPONS WERE SAFE FOREVER.

"SENSEI WU HID THE WEAPONS AWAY. USING THE POWER OF SPINJITZU, HE FOUGHT FOR 'JUSTICE' THROUGHOUT THE LAND AND BECAME A HERO TO THOSE IDIOTIC MORTALS ON THE WORLD OF NINJAGO.

"STILL, HE NEVER RELAXED HIS GUARD. HE KNEW THE FOUR WEAPONS OF SPINJITZU HAD TO BE PROTECTED. AND ONE DAY, AS HE REACHED OUT ACROSS THE PLANET WITH HIS SENSES, HE SUDDENLY KNEW...

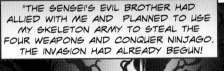

"GARMADON HAD RETURNED!

"THE SENSEI'S EVIL BROTHER HAD ALLIED WITH ME AND PLANNED TO USE MY SKELETON ARMY TO STEAL THE FOUR WEAPONS AND CONQUER NINJAGO. THE INVASION HAD ALREADY BEGUN!

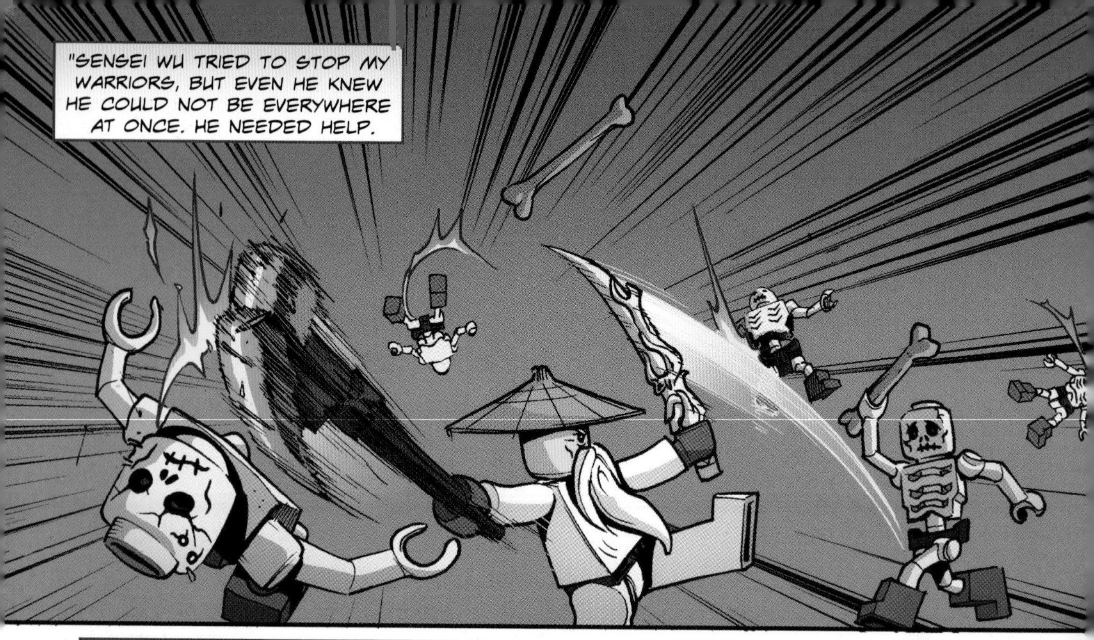
"SENSEI WU TRIED TO STOP MY WARRIORS, BUT EVEN HE KNEW HE COULD NOT BE EVERYWHERE AT ONCE. HE NEEDED HELP.

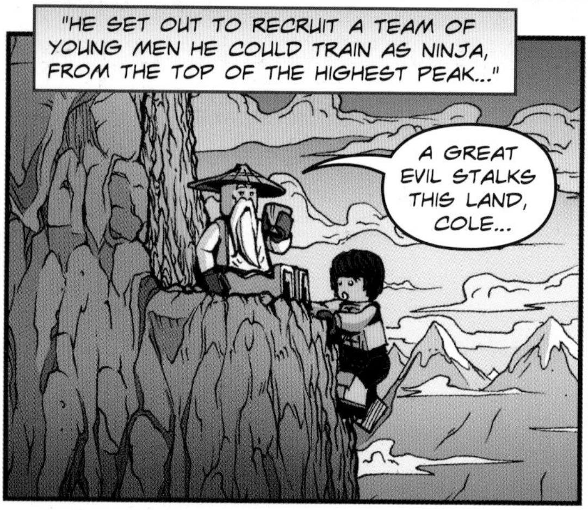
"HE SET OUT TO RECRUIT A TEAM OF YOUNG MEN HE COULD TRAIN AS NINJA, FROM THE TOP OF THE HIGHEST PEAK..."
A GREAT EVIL STALKS THIS LAND, COLE...

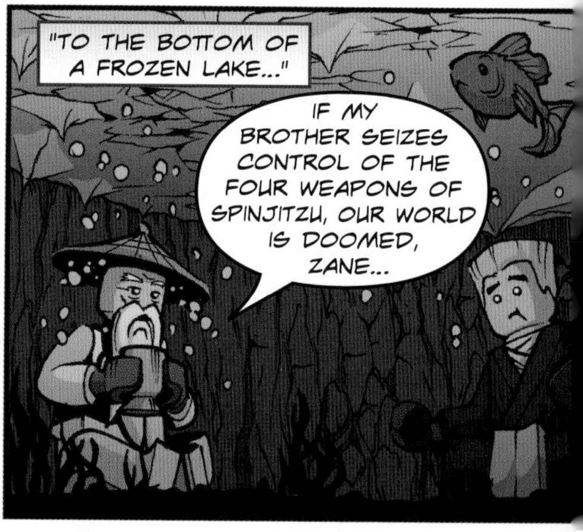
"TO THE BOTTOM OF A FROZEN LAKE..."
IF MY BROTHER SEIZES CONTROL OF THE FOUR WEAPONS OF SPINJITZU, OUR WORLD IS DOOMED, ZANE...

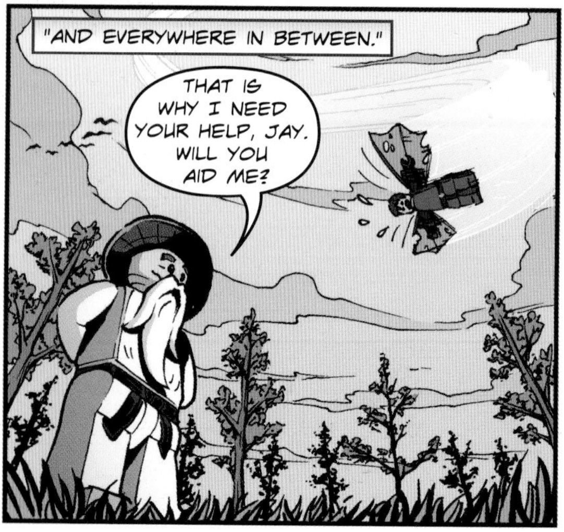
"AND EVERYWHERE IN BETWEEN."
THAT IS WHY I NEED YOUR HELP, JAY. WILL YOU AID ME?

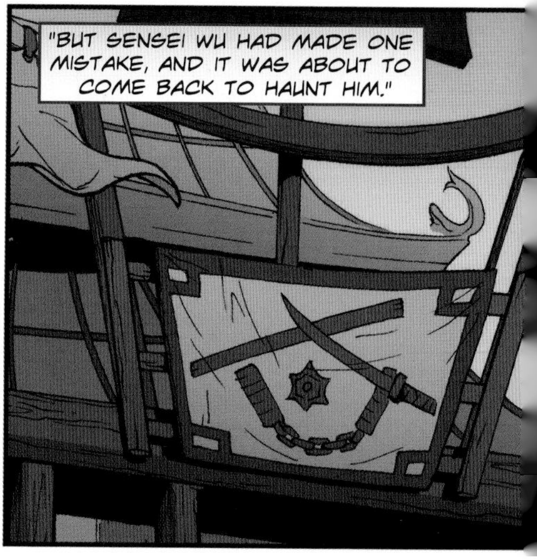
"BUT SENSEI WU HAD MADE ONE MISTAKE, AND IT WAS ABOUT TO COME BACK TO HAUNT HIM."

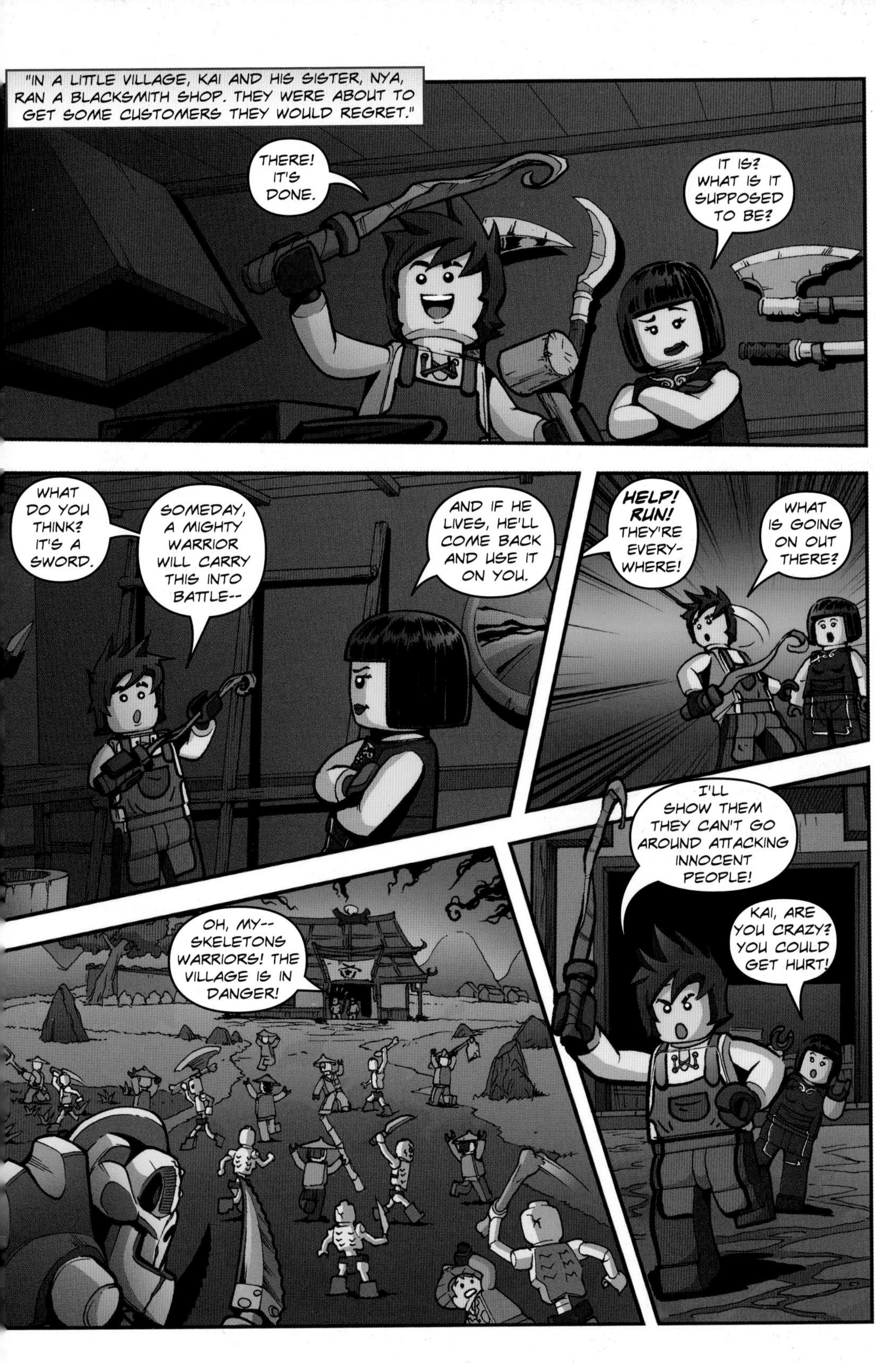
"IN A LITTLE VILLAGE, KAI AND HIS SISTER, NYA, RAN A BLACKSMITH SHOP. THEY WERE ABOUT TO GET SOME CUSTOMERS THEY WOULD REGRET."
THERE! IT'S DONE.
IT IS? WHAT IS IT SUPPOSED TO BE?
WHAT DO YOU THINK? IT'S A SWORD.
SOMEDAY, A MIGHTY WARRIOR WILL CARRY THIS INTO BATTLE--
AND IF HE LIVES, HE'LL COME BACK AND USE IT ON YOU.
HELP! RUN! THEY'RE EVERY-WHERE!
WHAT IS GOING ON OUT THERE?
OH, MY-- SKELETONS WARRIORS! THE VILLAGE IS IN DANGER!
I'LL SHOW THEM THEY CAN'T GO AROUND ATTACKING INNOCENT PEOPLE!
KAI, ARE YOU CRAZY? YOU COULD GET HURT!

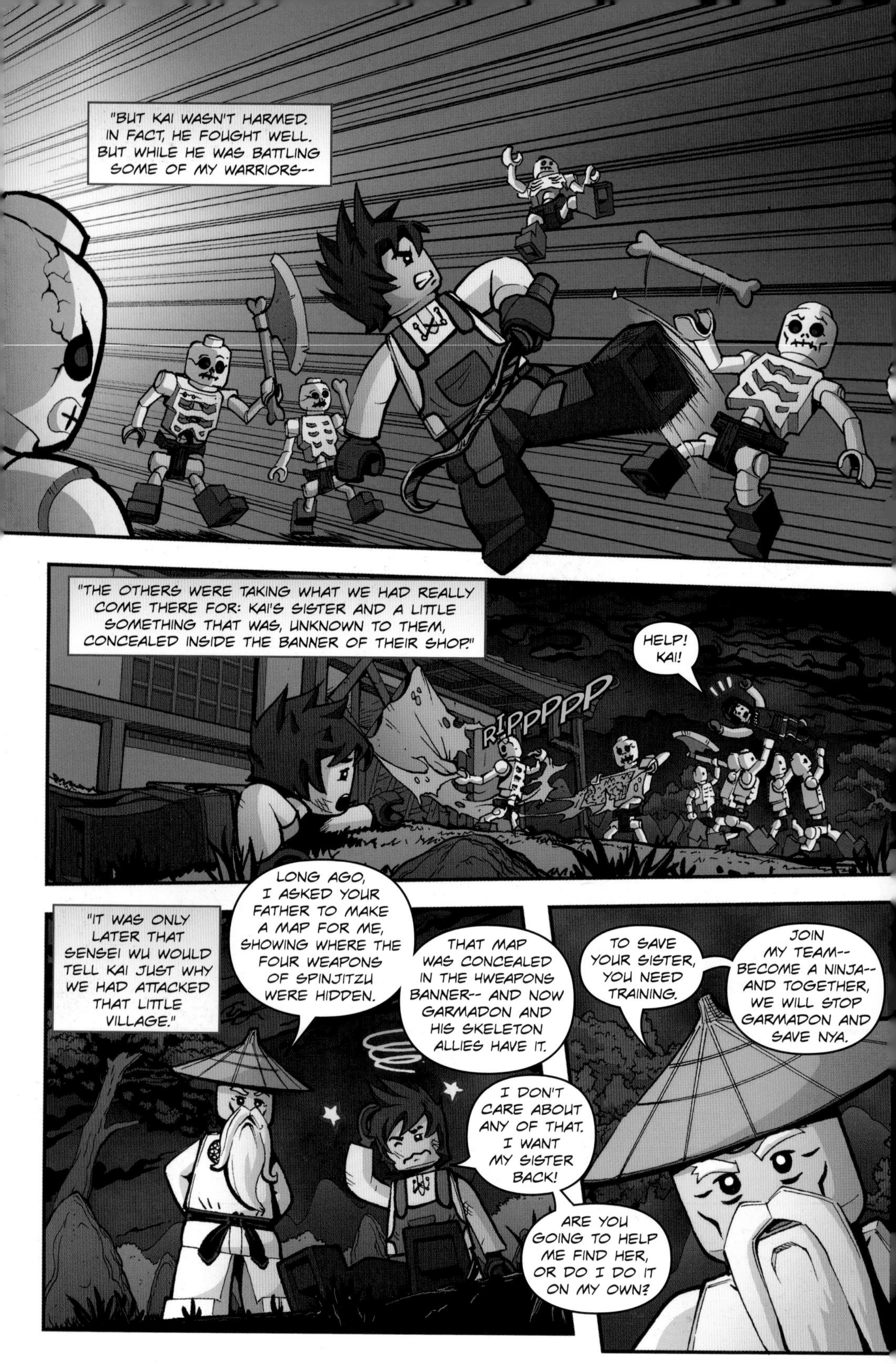
"BUT KAI WASN'T HARMED. IN FACT, HE FOUGHT WELL. BUT WHILE HE WAS BATTLING SOME OF MY WARRIORS--
"THE OTHERS WERE TAKING WHAT WE HAD REALLY COME THERE FOR: KAI'S SISTER AND A LITTLE SOMETHING THAT WAS, UNKNOWN TO THEM, CONCEALED INSIDE THE BANNER OF THEIR SHOP."
HELP! KAI!
RIPPPPPP
"IT WAS ONLY LATER THAT SENSEI WU WOULD TELL KAI JUST WHY WE HAD ATTACKED THAT LITTLE VILLAGE."
LONG AGO, I ASKED YOUR FATHER TO MAKE A MAP FOR ME, SHOWING WHERE THE FOUR WEAPONS OF SPINJITZU WERE HIDDEN.
THAT MAP WAS CONCEALED IN THE 4WEAPONS BANNER-- AND NOW GARMADON AND HIS SKELETON ALLIES HAVE IT.
I DON'T CARE ABOUT ANY OF THAT. I WANT MY SISTER BACK!
ARE YOU GOING TO HELP ME FIND HER, OR DO I DO IT ON MY OWN?
TO SAVE YOUR SISTER, YOU NEED TRAINING.
JOIN MY TEAM-- BECOME A NINJA-- AND TOGETHER, WE WILL STOP GARMADON AND SAVE NYA.

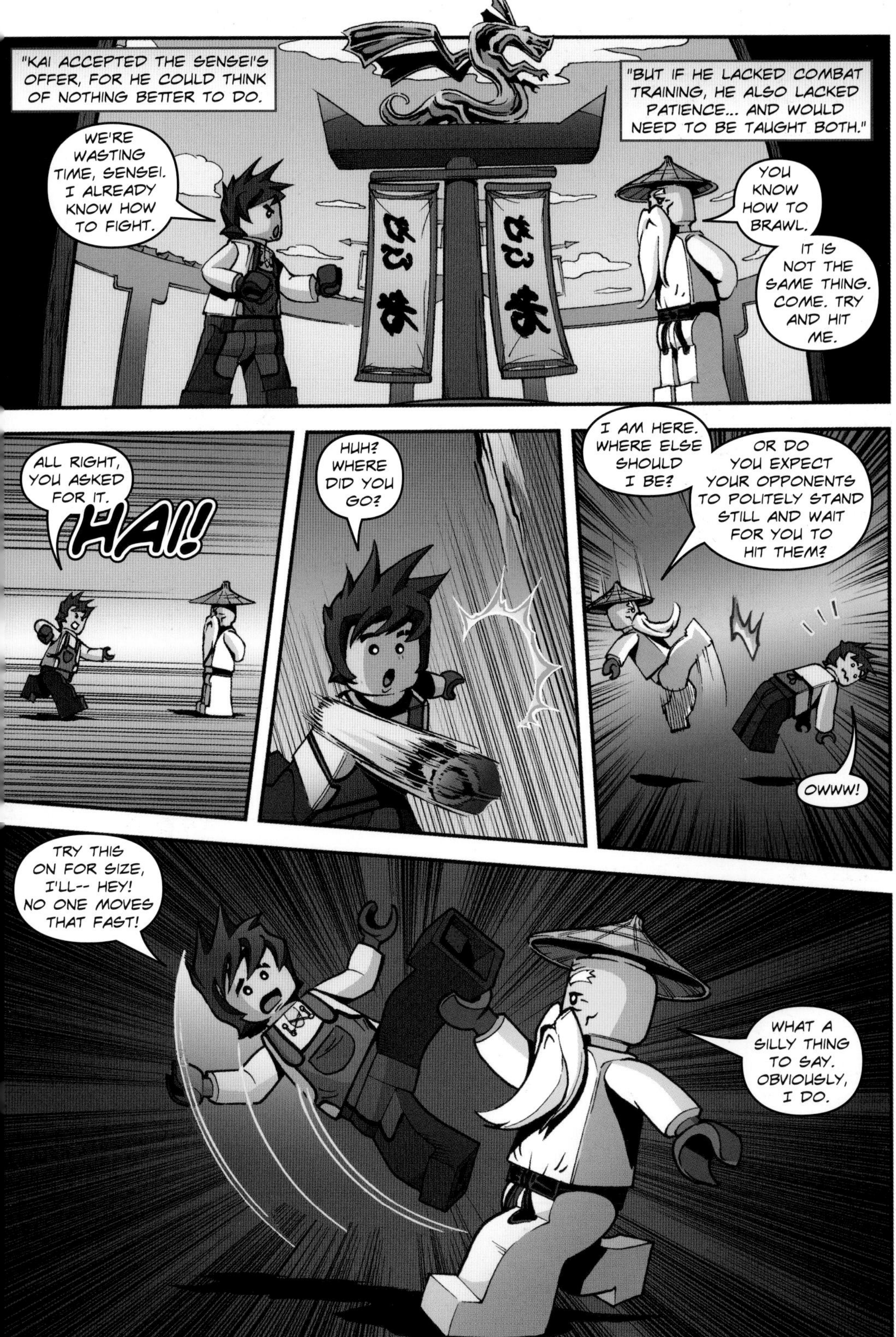
"KAI ACCEPTED THE SENSEI'S OFFER, FOR HE COULD THINK OF NOTHING BETTER TO DO.
"BUT IF HE LACKED COMBAT TRAINING, HE ALSO LACKED PATIENCE... AND WOULD NEED TO BE TAUGHT BOTH."
WE'RE WASTING TIME, SENSEI. I ALREADY KNOW HOW TO FIGHT.
YOU KNOW HOW TO BRAWL.
IT IS NOT THE SAME THING. COME. TRY AND HIT ME.
ALL RIGHT, YOU ASKED FOR IT.
HAI!
HUH? WHERE DID YOU GO?
I AM HERE. WHERE ELSE SHOULD I BE?
OR DO YOU EXPECT YOUR OPPONENTS TO POLITELY STAND STILL AND WAIT FOR YOU TO HIT THEM?
OWWW!
TRY THIS ON FOR SIZE, I'LL-- HEY! NO ONE MOVES THAT FAST!
WHAT A SILLY THING TO SAY. OBVIOUSLY, I DO.

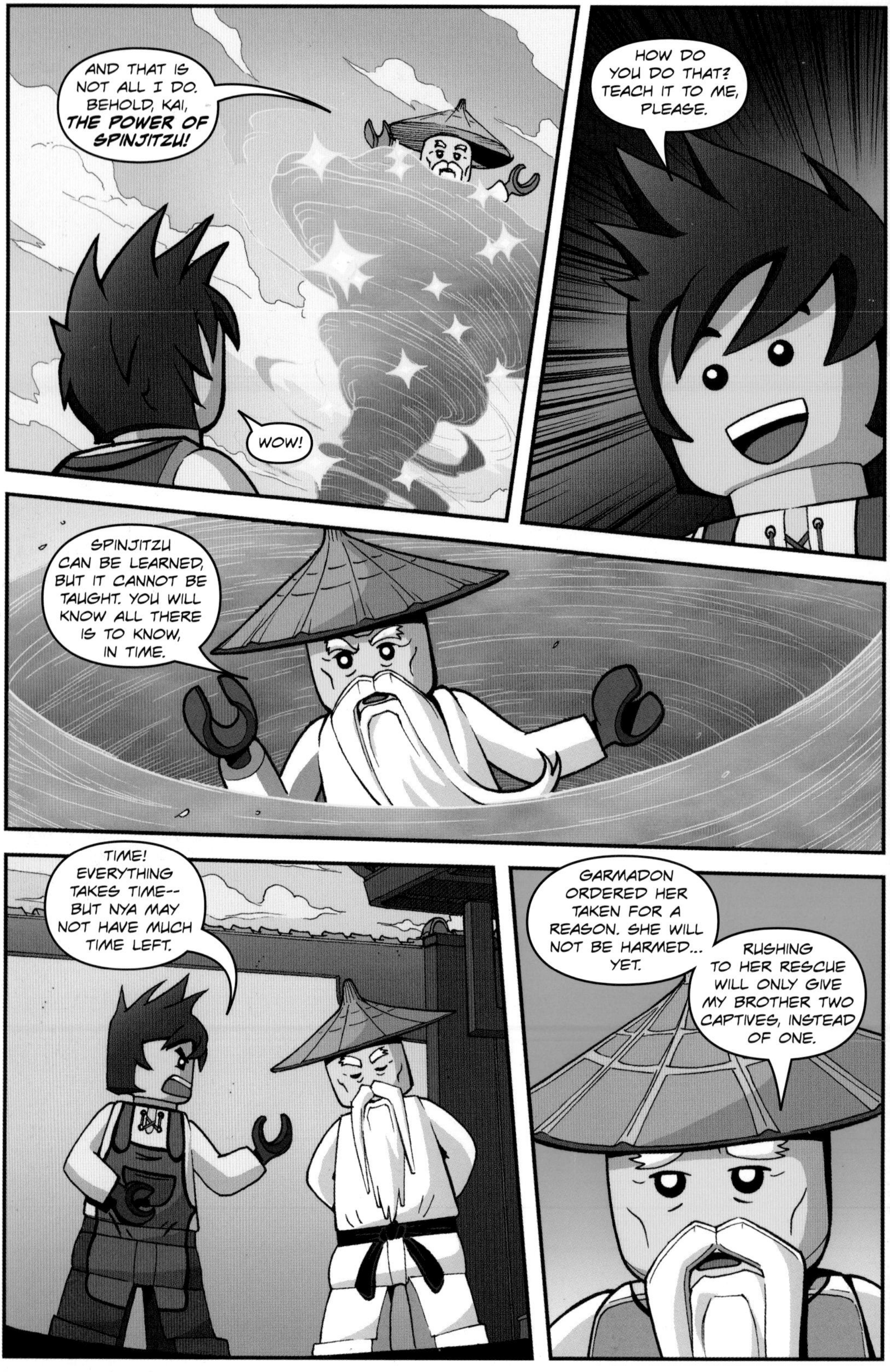
AND THAT IS NOT ALL I DO. BEHOLD, KAI, THE POWER OF SPINJITZU!
WOW!
HOW DO YOU DO THAT? TEACH IT TO ME, PLEASE.
SPINJITZU CAN BE LEARNED, BUT IT CANNOT BE TAUGHT. YOU WILL KNOW ALL THERE IS TO KNOW, IN TIME.
TIME! EVERYTHING TAKES TIME-- BUT NYA MAY NOT HAVE MUCH TIME LEFT.
GARMADON ORDERED HER TAKEN FOR A REASON. SHE WILL NOT BE HARMED... YET.
RUSHING TO HER RESCUE WILL ONLY GIVE MY BROTHER TWO CAPTIVES, INSTEAD OF ONE.

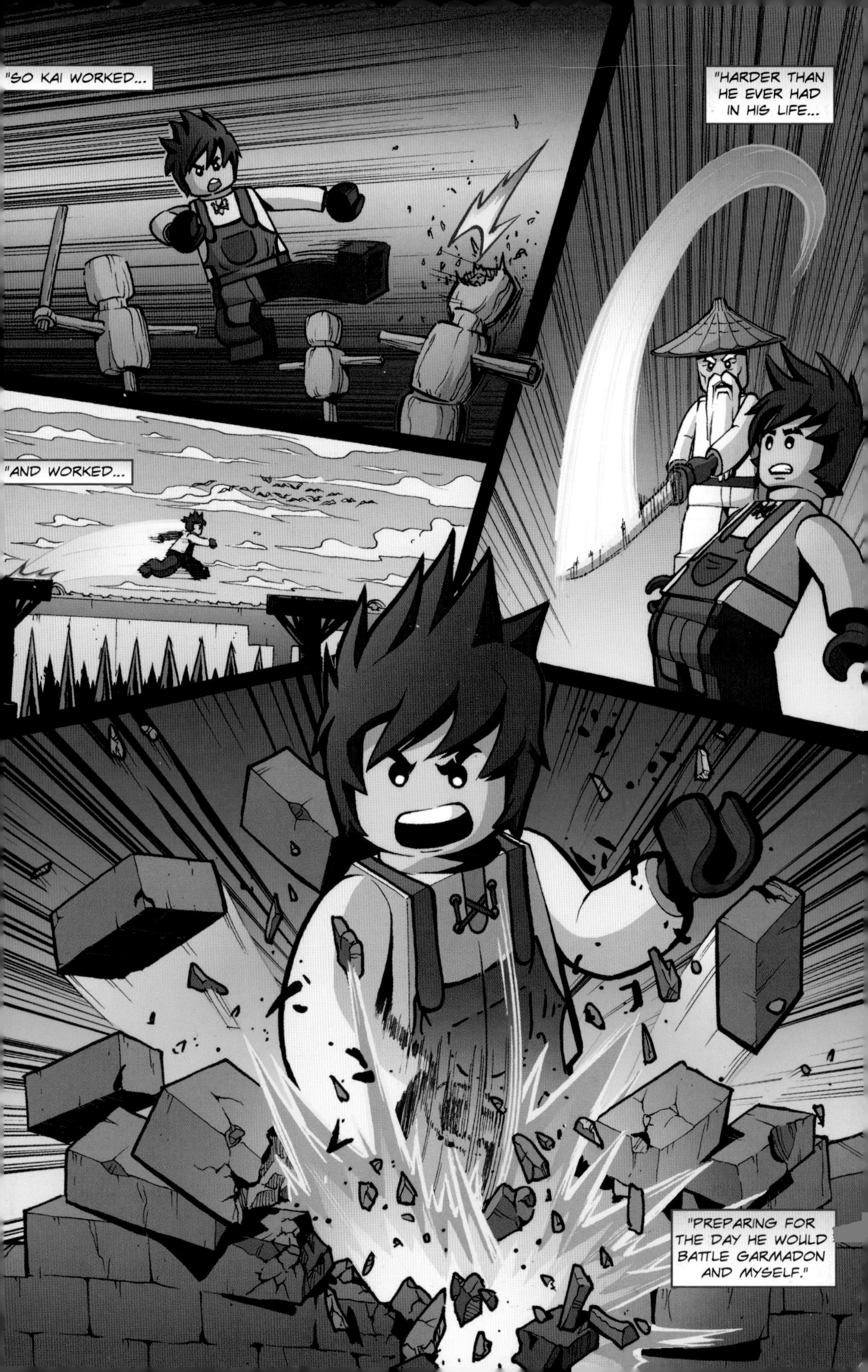
"SO KAI WORKED...
"HARDER THAN HE EVER HAD IN HIS LIFE...
"AND WORKED...
"PREPARING FOR THE DAY HE WOULD BATTLE GARMADON AND MYSELF."

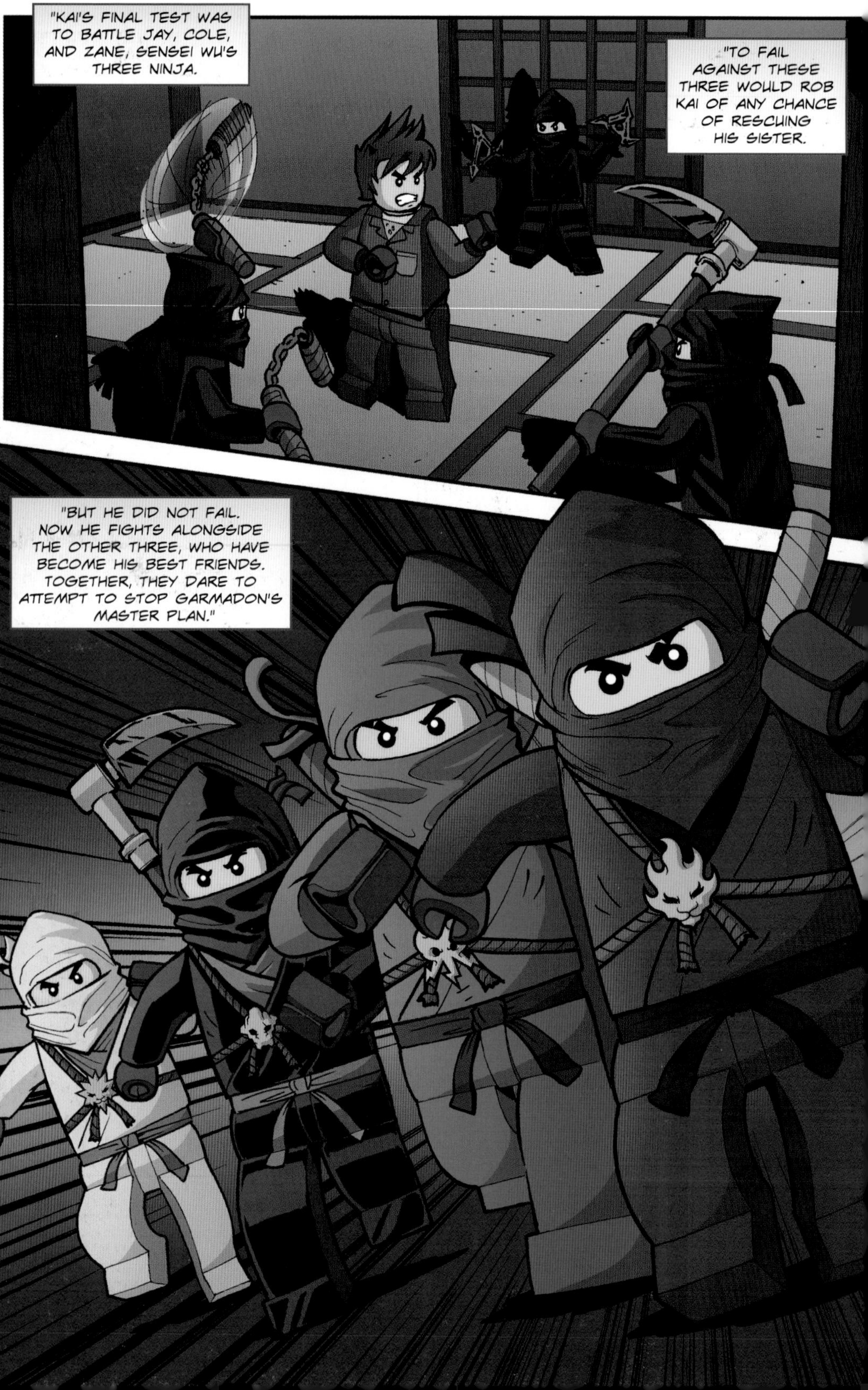
"KAI'S FINAL TEST WAS TO BATTLE JAY, COLE, AND ZANE, SENSEI WU'S THREE NINJA.
"TO FAIL AGAINST THESE THREE WOULD ROB KAI OF ANY CHANCE OF RESCUING HIS SISTER.
"BUT HE DID NOT FAIL. NOW HE FIGHTS ALONGSIDE THE OTHER THREE, WHO HAVE BECOME HIS BEST FRIENDS. TOGETHER, THEY DARE TO ATTEMPT TO STOP GARMADON'S MASTER PLAN."

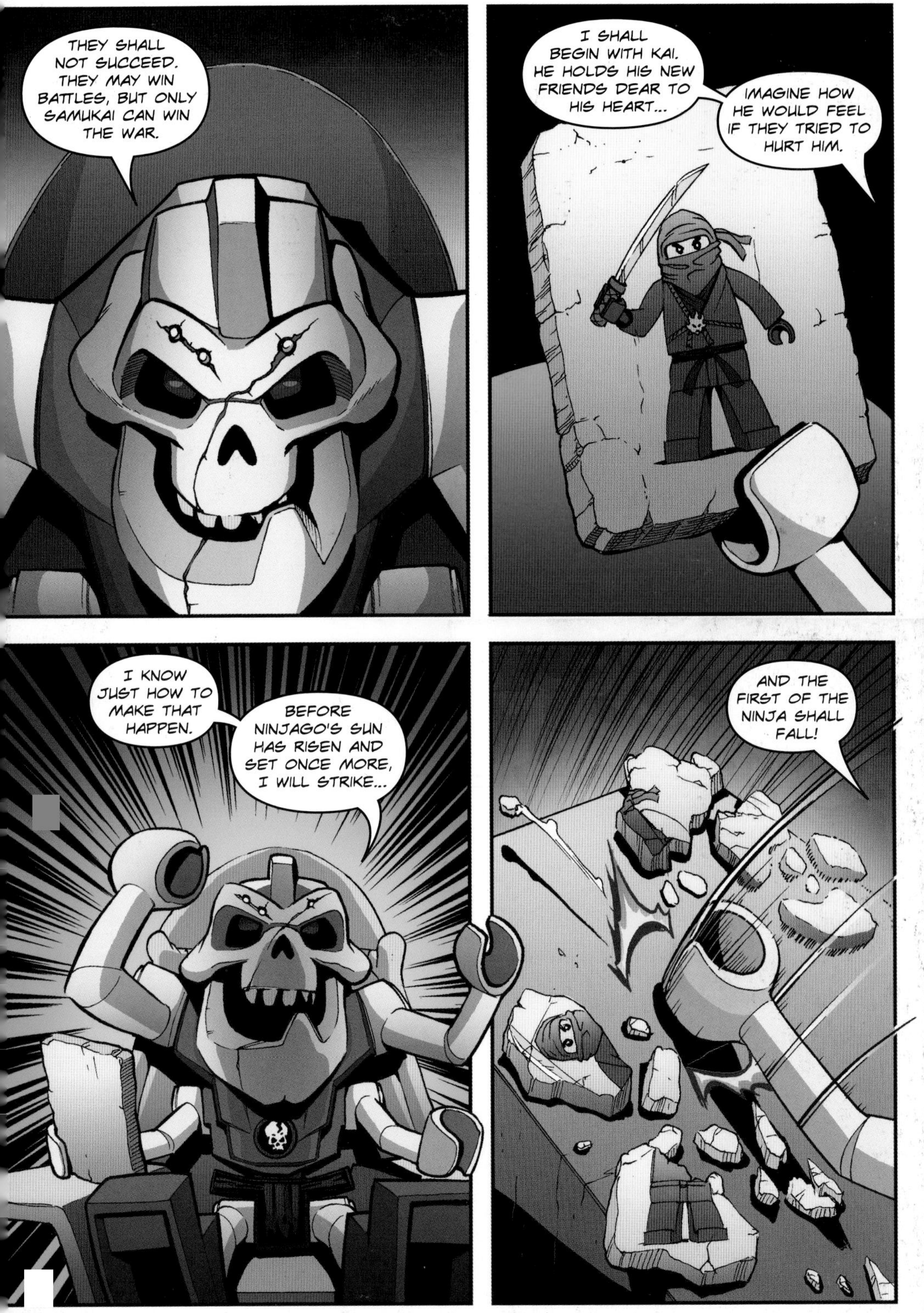
THEY SHALL NOT SUCCEED. THEY MAY WIN BATTLES, BUT ONLY SAMUKAI CAN WIN THE WAR.
I SHALL BEGIN WITH KAI. HE HOLDS HIS NEW FRIENDS DEAR TO HIS HEART...
IMAGINE HOW HE WOULD FEEL IF THEY TRIED TO HURT HIM.
I KNOW JUST HOW TO MAKE THAT HAPPEN.
BEFORE NINJAGO'S SUN HAS RISEN AND SET ONCE MORE, I WILL STRIKE...
AND THE FIRST OF THE NINJA SHALL FALL!

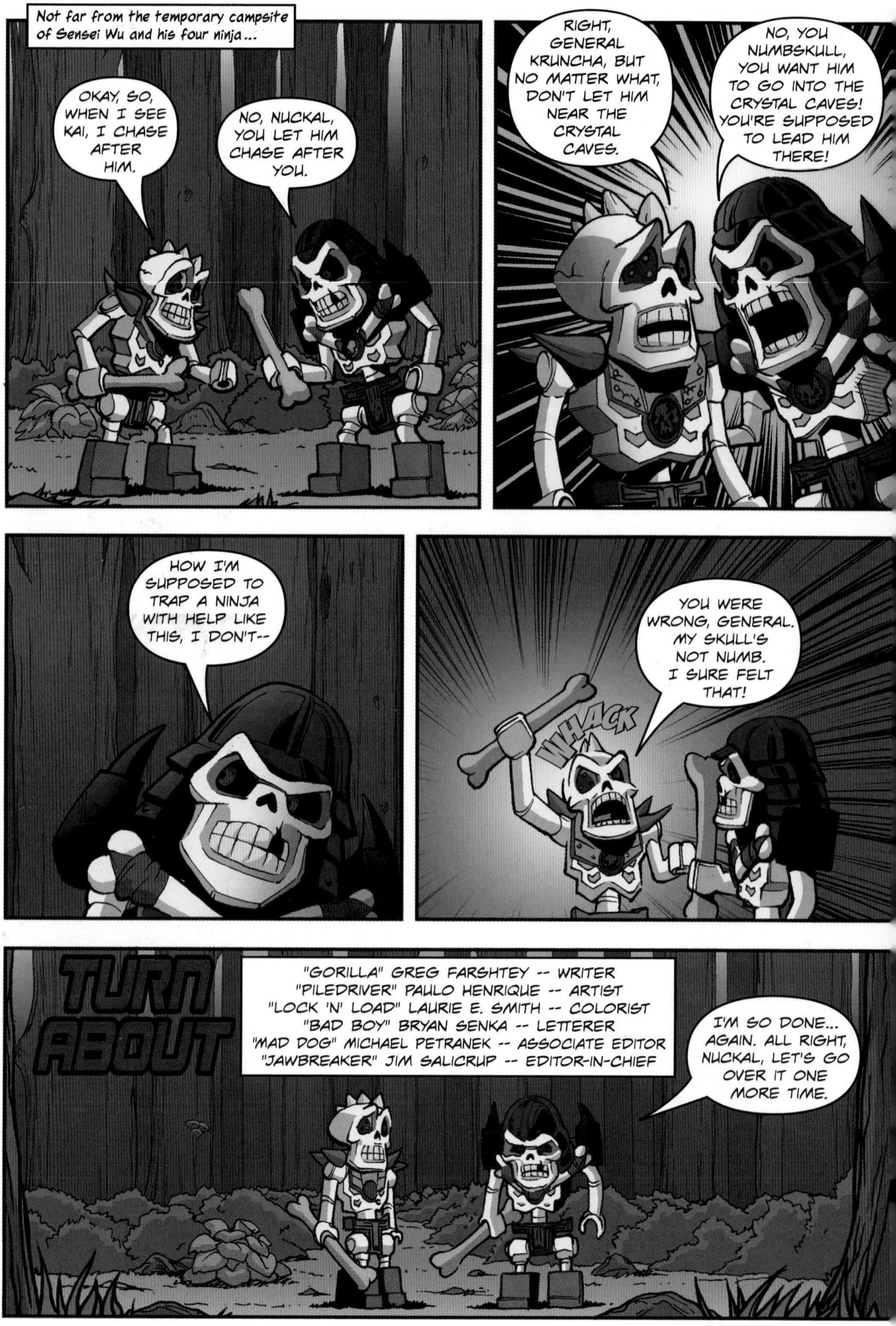
Not far from the temporary campsite of Sensei Wu and his four ninja...
OKAY, SO, WHEN I SEE KAI, I CHASE AFTER HIM.
NO, NUCKAL, YOU LET HIM CHASE AFTER YOU.
RIGHT, GENERAL KRUNCHA, BUT NO MATTER WHAT, DON'T LET HIM NEAR THE CRYSTAL CAVES.
NO, YOU NUMBSKULL, YOU WANT HIM TO GO INTO THE CRYSTAL CAVES! YOU'RE SUPPOSED TO LEAD HIM THERE!
HOW I'M SUPPOSED TO TRAP A NINJA WITH HELP LIKE THIS, I DON'T--
WHACK
YOU WERE WRONG, GENERAL. MY SKULL'S NOT NUMB. I SURE FELT THAT!
TURN ABOUT
"GORILLA" GREG FARSHTEY -- WRITER
"PILEDRIVER" PAULO HENRIQUE -- ARTIST
"LOCK 'N' LOAD" LAURIE E. SMITH -- COLORIST
"BAD BOY" BRYAN SENKA -- LETTERER
"MAD DOG" MICHAEL PETRANEK -- ASSOCIATE EDITOR
"JAWBREAKER" JIM SALICRUP -- EDITOR-IN-CHIEF
I'M SO DONE... AGAIN. ALL RIGHT, NUCKAL, LET'S GO OVER IT ONE MORE TIME.

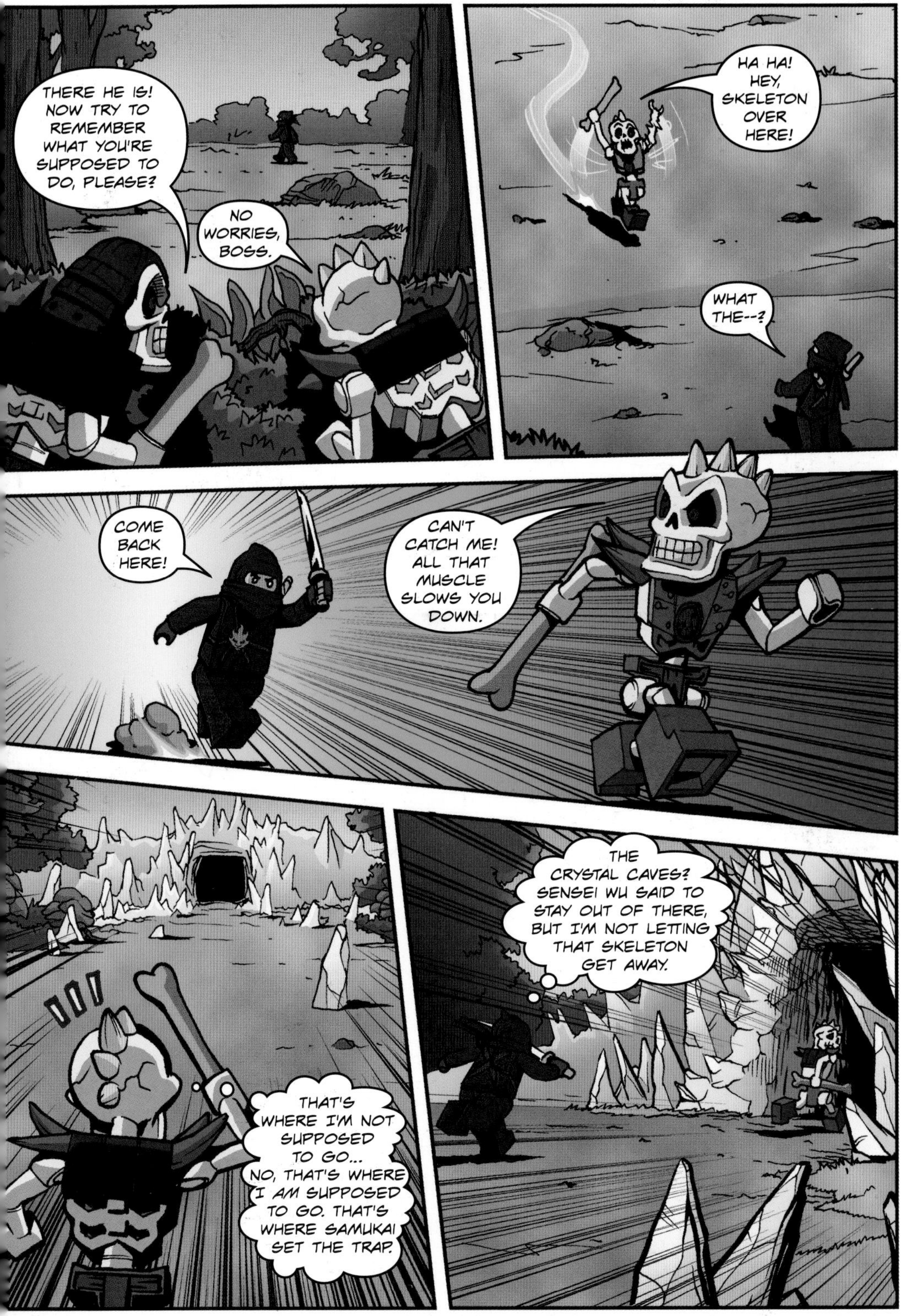
THERE HE IS! NOW TRY TO REMEMBER WHAT YOU'RE SUPPOSED TO DO, PLEASE?
NO WORRIES, BOSS.
HA HA! HEY, SKELETON OVER HERE!
WHAT THE--?
COME BACK HERE!
CAN'T CATCH ME! ALL THAT MUSCLE SLOWS YOU DOWN.
!!!
THAT'S WHERE I'M NOT SUPPOSED TO GO... NO, THAT'S WHERE I AM SUPPOSED TO GO. THAT'S WHERE SAMUKAI SET THE TRAP.
THE CRYSTAL CAVES? SENSEI WU SAID TO STAY OUT OF THERE, BUT I'M NOT LETTING THAT SKELETON GET AWAY.

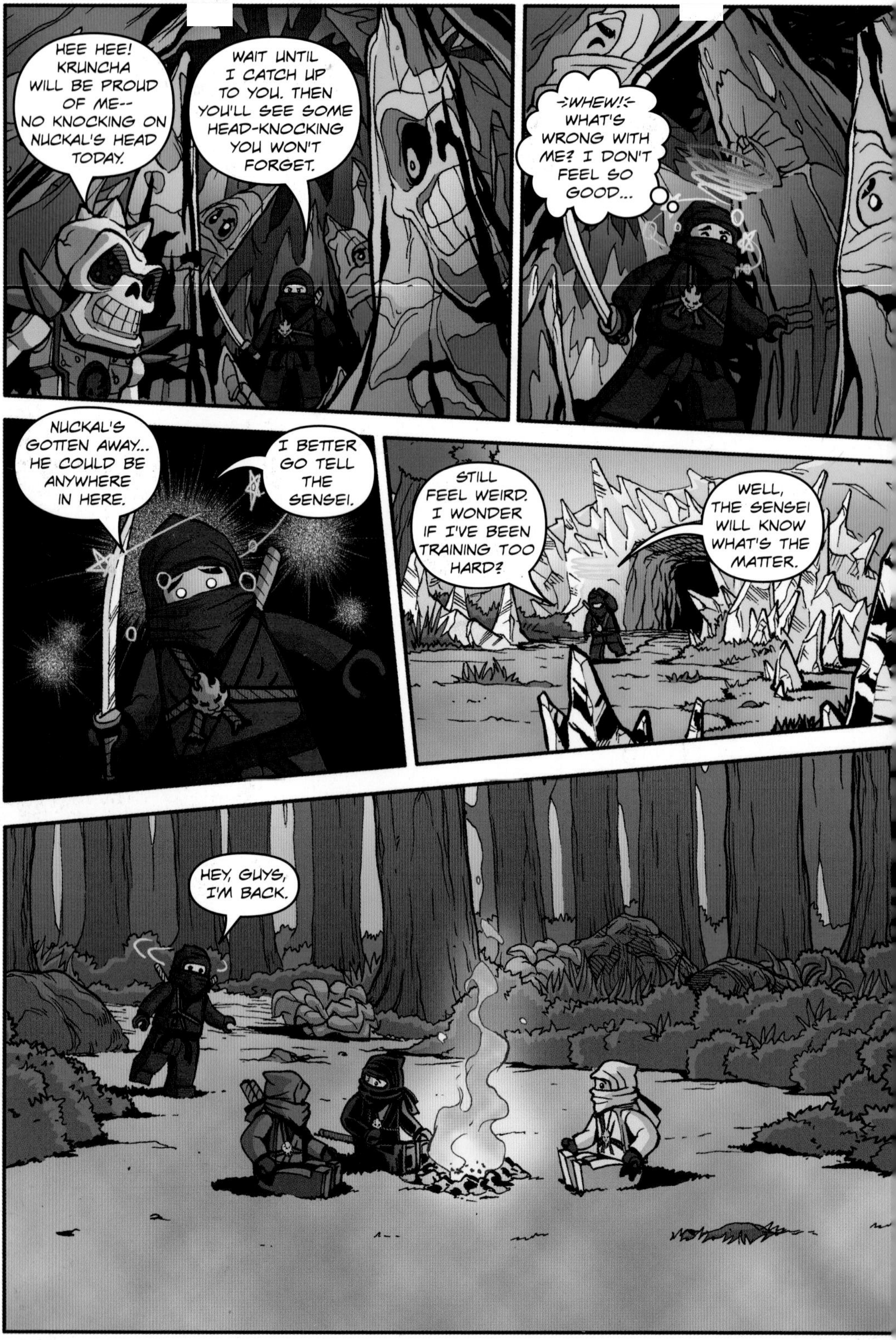
HEE HEE! KRUNCHA WILL BE PROUD OF ME-- NO KNOCKING ON NUCKAL'S HEAD TODAY.
WAIT UNTIL I CATCH UP TO YOU. THEN YOU'LL SEE SOME HEAD-KNOCKING YOU WON'T FORGET.
WHEW! WHAT'S WRONG WITH ME? I DON'T FEEL SO GOOD...
NUCKAL'S GOTTEN AWAY... HE COULD BE ANYWHERE IN HERE.
I BETTER GO TELL THE SENSEI.
STILL FEEL WEIRD. I WONDER IF I'VE BEEN TRAINING TOO HARD?
WELL, THE SENSEI WILL KNOW WHAT'S THE MATTER.
HEY, GUYS, I'M BACK.

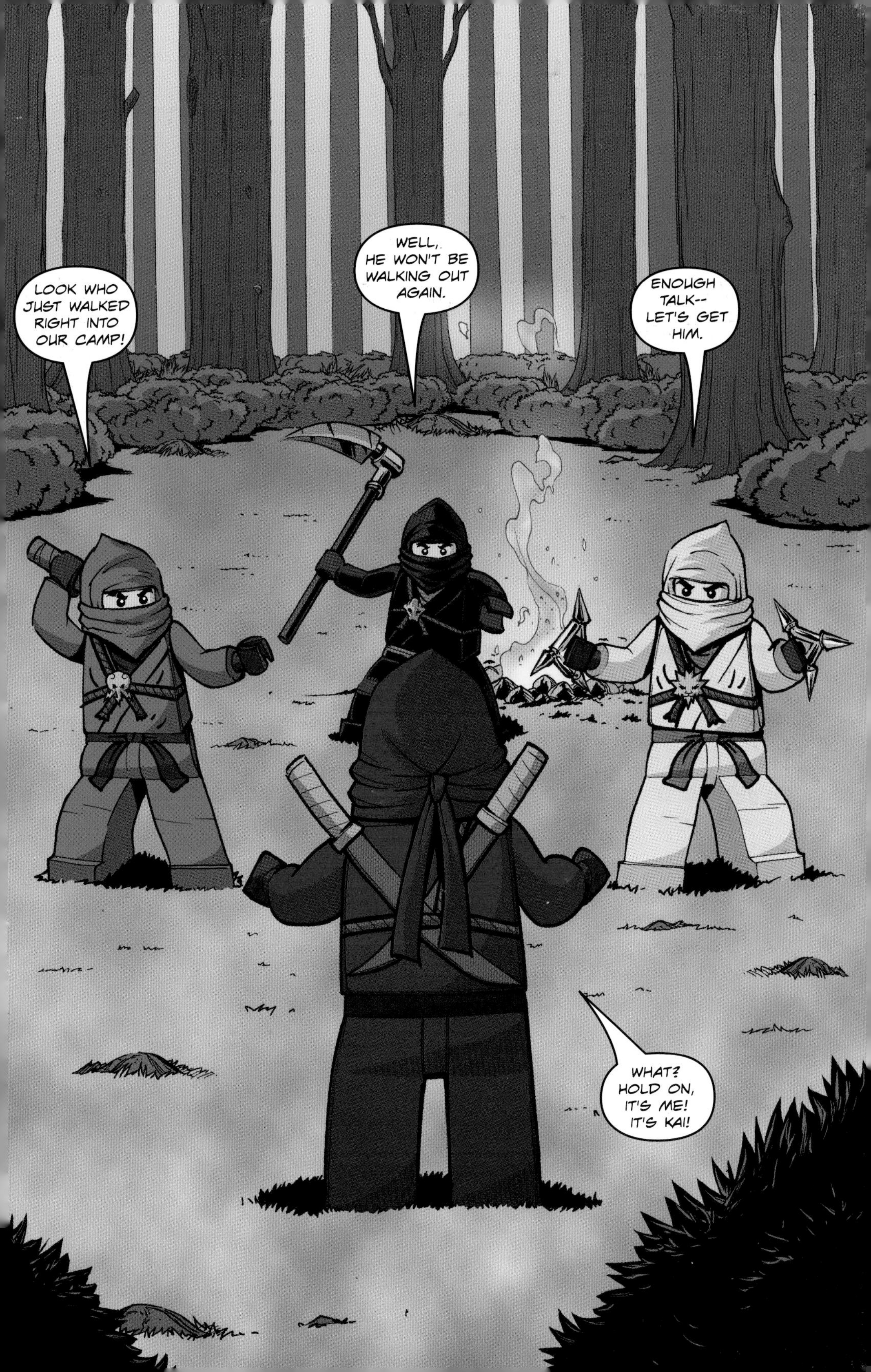
LOOK WHO JUST WALKED RIGHT INTO OUR CAMP!
WELL, HE WON'T BE WALKING OUT AGAIN.
ENOUGH TALK-- LET'S GET HIM.
WHAT? HOLD ON, IT'S ME! IT'S KAI!

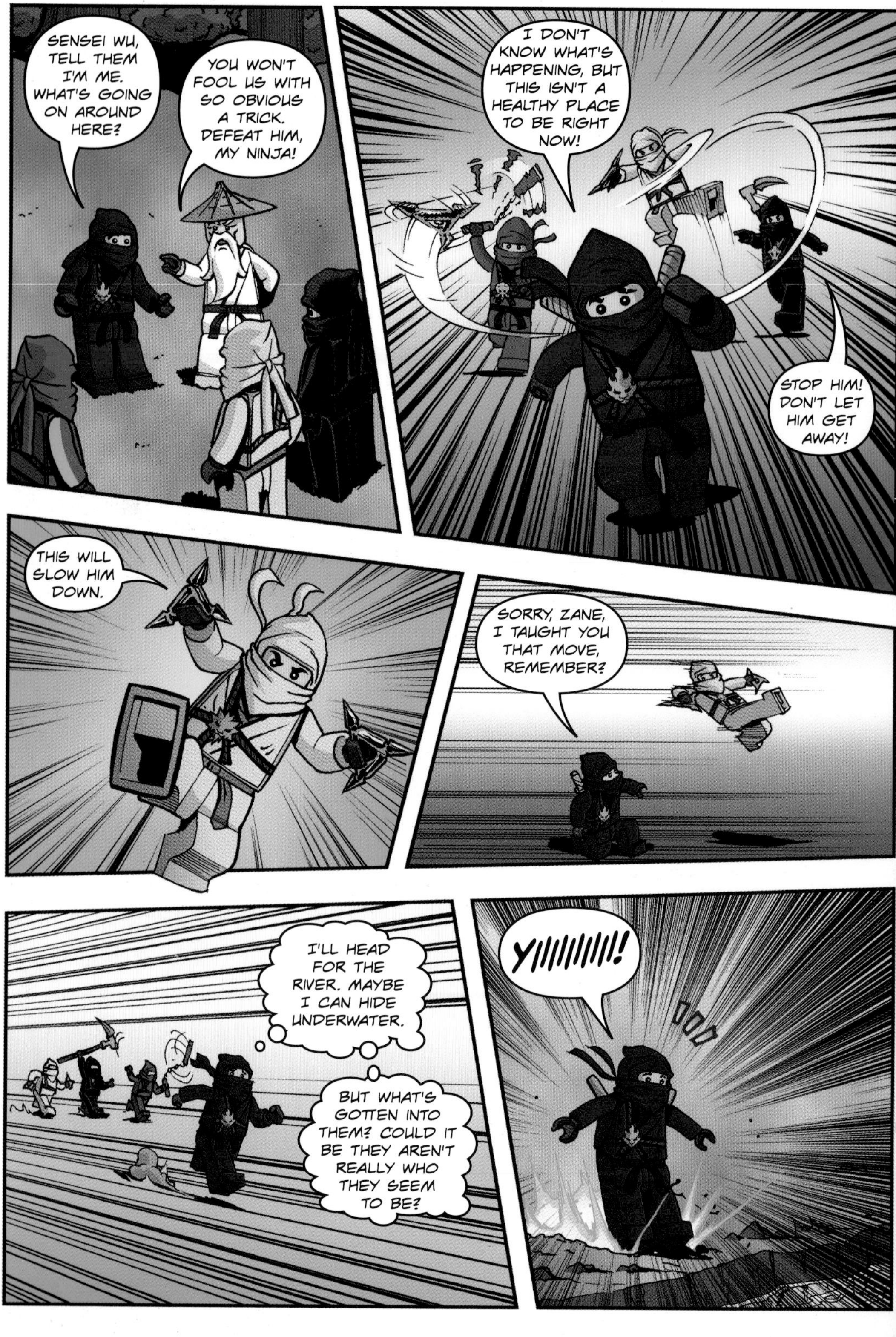
SENSEI WU, TELL THEM I'M ME. WHAT'S GOING ON AROUND HERE?
YOU WON'T FOOL US WITH SO OBVIOUS A TRICK. DEFEAT HIM, MY NINJA!
I DON'T KNOW WHAT'S HAPPENING, BUT THIS ISN'T A HEALTHY PLACE TO BE RIGHT NOW!
STOP HIM! DON'T LET HIM GET AWAY!
THIS WILL SLOW HIM DOWN.
SORRY, ZANE, I TAUGHT YOU THAT MOVE, REMEMBER?
I'LL HEAD FOR THE RIVER. MAYBE I CAN HIDE UNDERWATER.
BUT WHAT'S GOTTEN INTO THEM? COULD IT BE THEY AREN'T REALLY WHO THEY SEEM TO BE?
YIIIIIIIII!

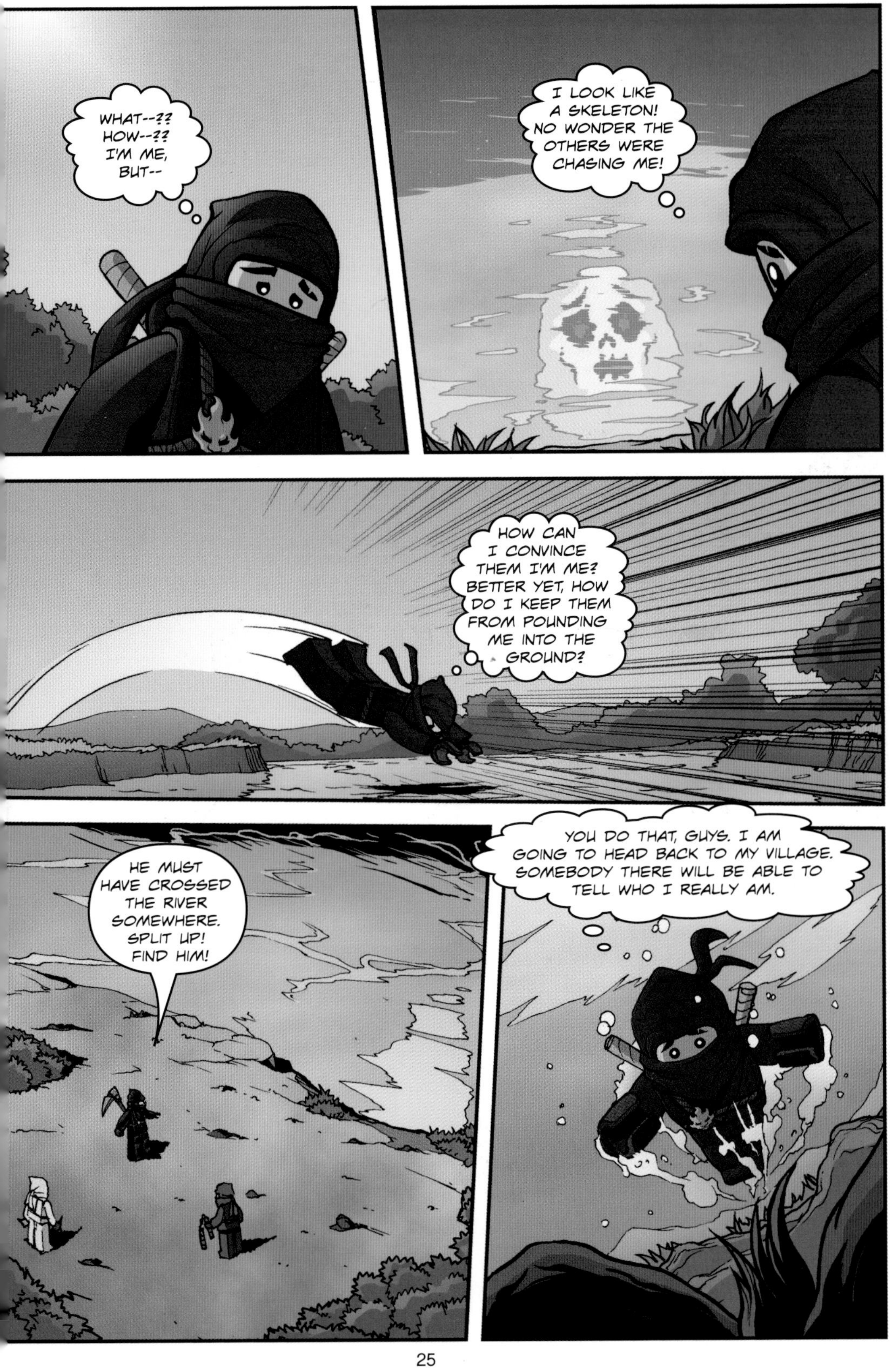
WHAT--?? HOW--?? I'M ME, BUT--
I LOOK LIKE A SKELETON! NO WONDER THE OTHERS WERE CHASING ME!
HOW CAN I CONVINCE THEM I'M ME? BETTER YET, HOW DO I KEEP THEM FROM POUNDING ME INTO THE GROUND?
HE MUST HAVE CROSSED THE RIVER SOMEWHERE. SPLIT UP! FIND HIM!
YOU DO THAT, GUYS. I AM GOING TO HEAD BACK TO MY VILLAGE. SOMEBODY THERE WILL BE ABLE TO TELL WHO I REALLY AM.

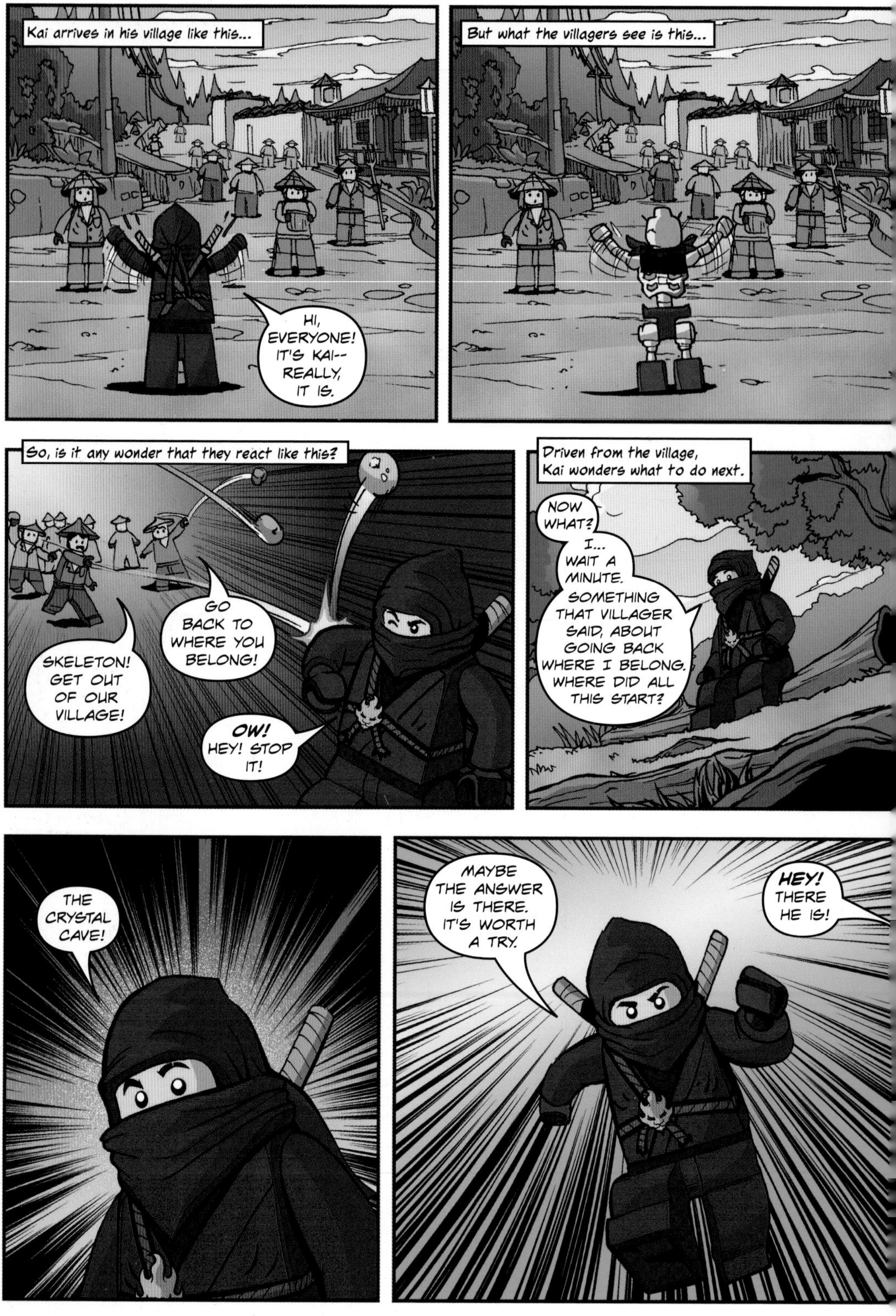
Kai arrives in his village like this...
HI, EVERYONE! IT'S KAI-- REALLY, IT IS.
But what the villagers see is this...
So, is it any wonder that they react like this?
SKELETON! GET OUT OF OUR VILLAGE!
GO BACK TO WHERE YOU BELONG!
OW! HEY! STOP IT!
Driven from the village, Kai wonders what to do next.
NOW WHAT?
I... WAIT A MINUTE. SOMETHING THAT VILLAGER SAID, ABOUT GOING BACK WHERE I BELONG. WHERE DID ALL THIS START?
THE CRYSTAL CAVE!
MAYBE THE ANSWER IS THERE. IT'S WORTH A TRY.
HEY! THERE HE IS!

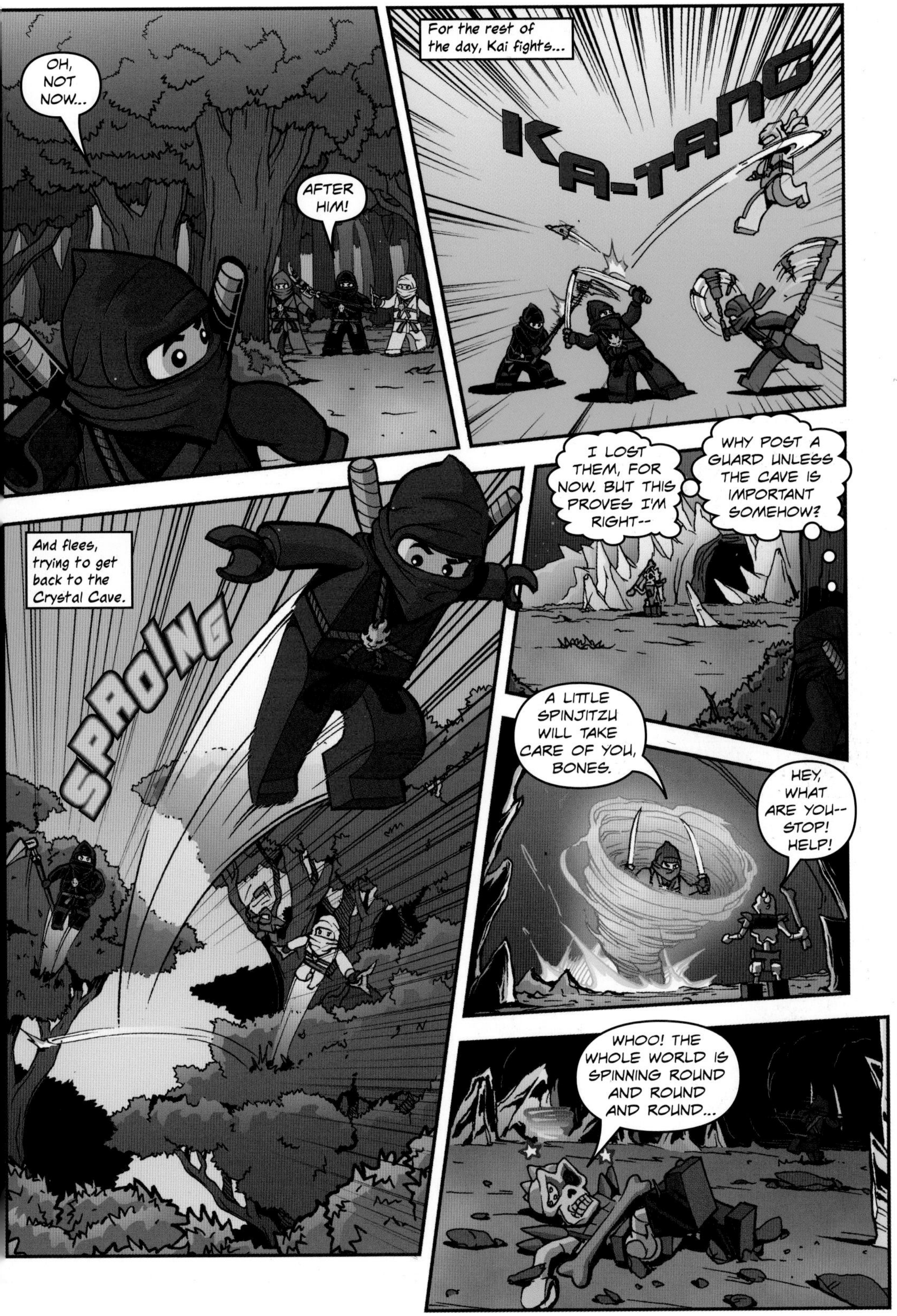
OH, NOT NOW...
AFTER HIM!
For the rest of the day, Kai fights...
KA-TANG
I LOST THEM, FOR NOW. BUT THIS PROVES I'M RIGHT--
WHY POST A GUARD UNLESS THE CAVE IS IMPORTANT SOMEHOW?
And flees, trying to get back to the Crystal Cave.
SPROING
A LITTLE SPINJITZU WILL TAKE CARE OF YOU, BONES.
HEY, WHAT ARE YOU-- STOP! HELP!
WHOO! THE WHOLE WORLD IS SPINNING ROUND AND ROUND AND ROUND...

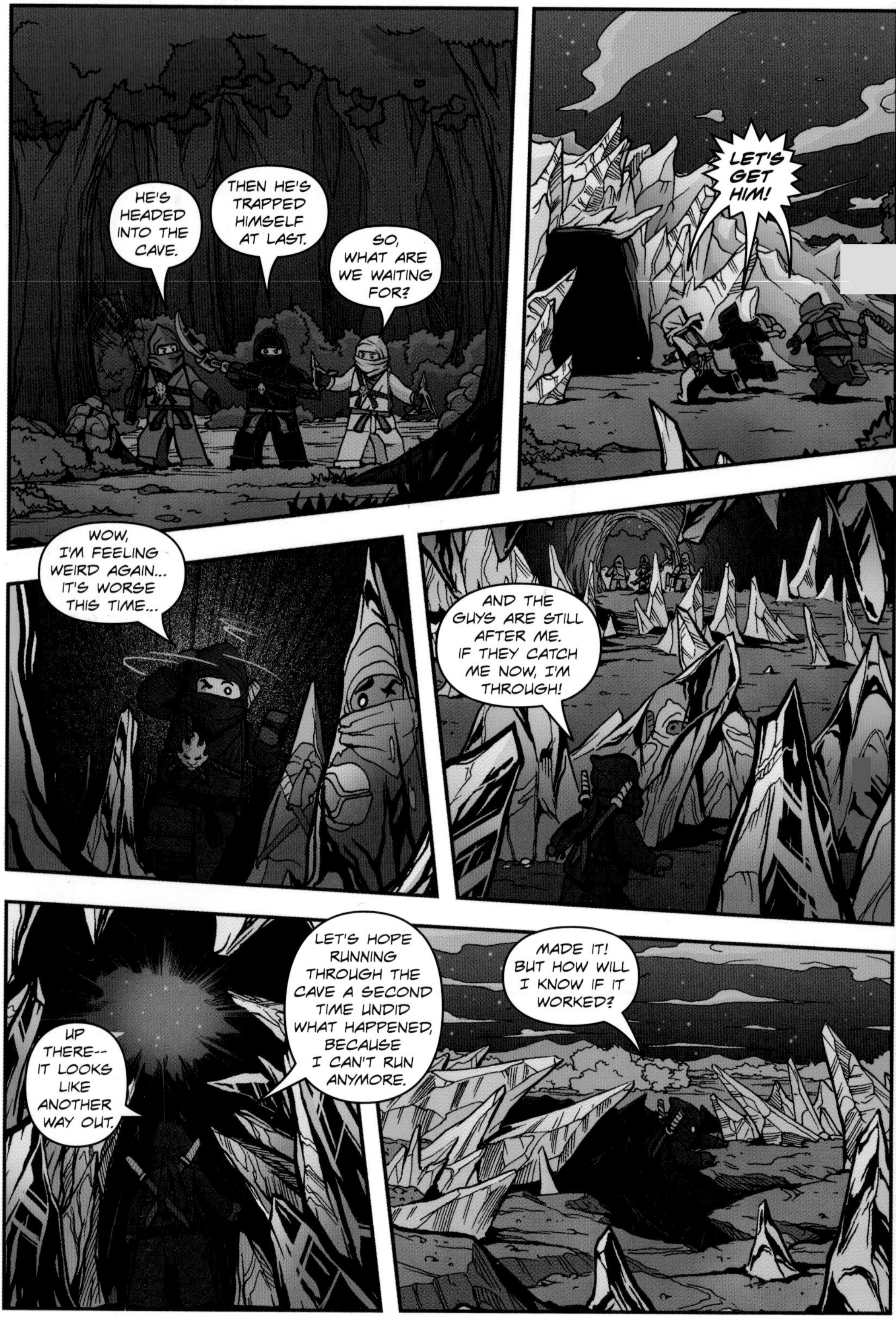
HE'S HEADED INTO THE CAVE.
THEN HE'S TRAPPED HIMSELF AT LAST.
SO, WHAT ARE WE WAITING FOR?
LET'S GET HIM!
WOW, I'M FEELING WEIRD AGAIN... IT'S WORSE THIS TIME...
AND THE GUYS ARE STILL AFTER ME. IF THEY CATCH ME NOW, I'M THROUGH!
UP THERE-- IT LOOKS LIKE ANOTHER WAY OUT.
LET'S HOPE RUNNING THROUGH THE CAVE A SECOND TIME UNDID WHAT HAPPENED, BECAUSE I CAN'T RUN ANYMORE.
MADE IT! BUT HOW WILL I KNOW IF IT WORKED?

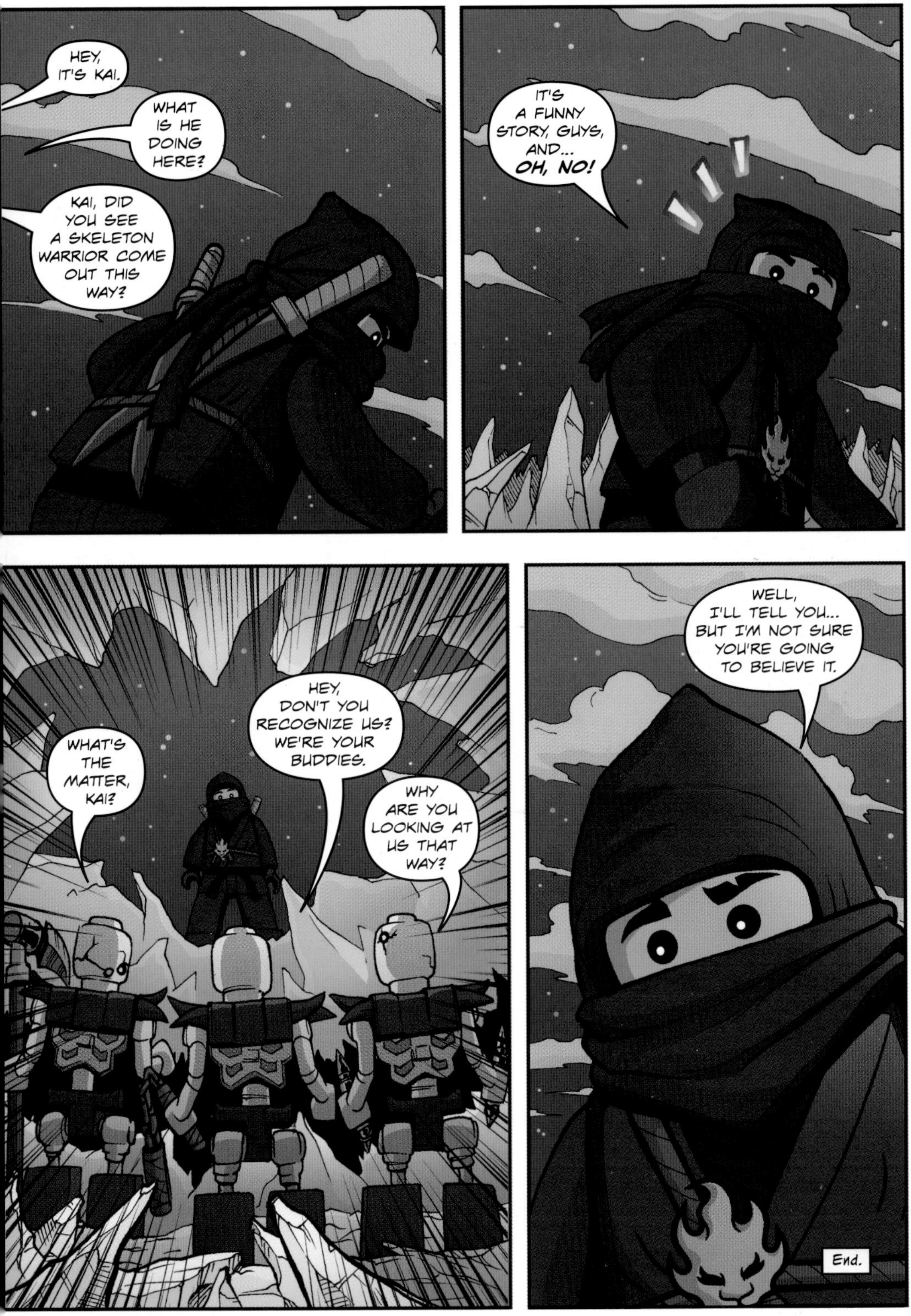
HEY, IT'S KAI.
WHAT IS HE DOING HERE?
KAI, DID YOU SEE A SKELETON WARRIOR COME OUT THIS WAY?
IT'S A FUNNY STORY, GUYS, AND... OH, NO!
WHAT'S THE MATTER, KAI?
HEY, DON'T YOU RECOGNIZE US? WE'RE YOUR BUDDIES.
WHY ARE YOU LOOKING AT US THAT WAY?
WELL, I'LL TELL YOU... BUT I'M NOT SURE YOU'RE GOING TO BELIEVE IT.
End.

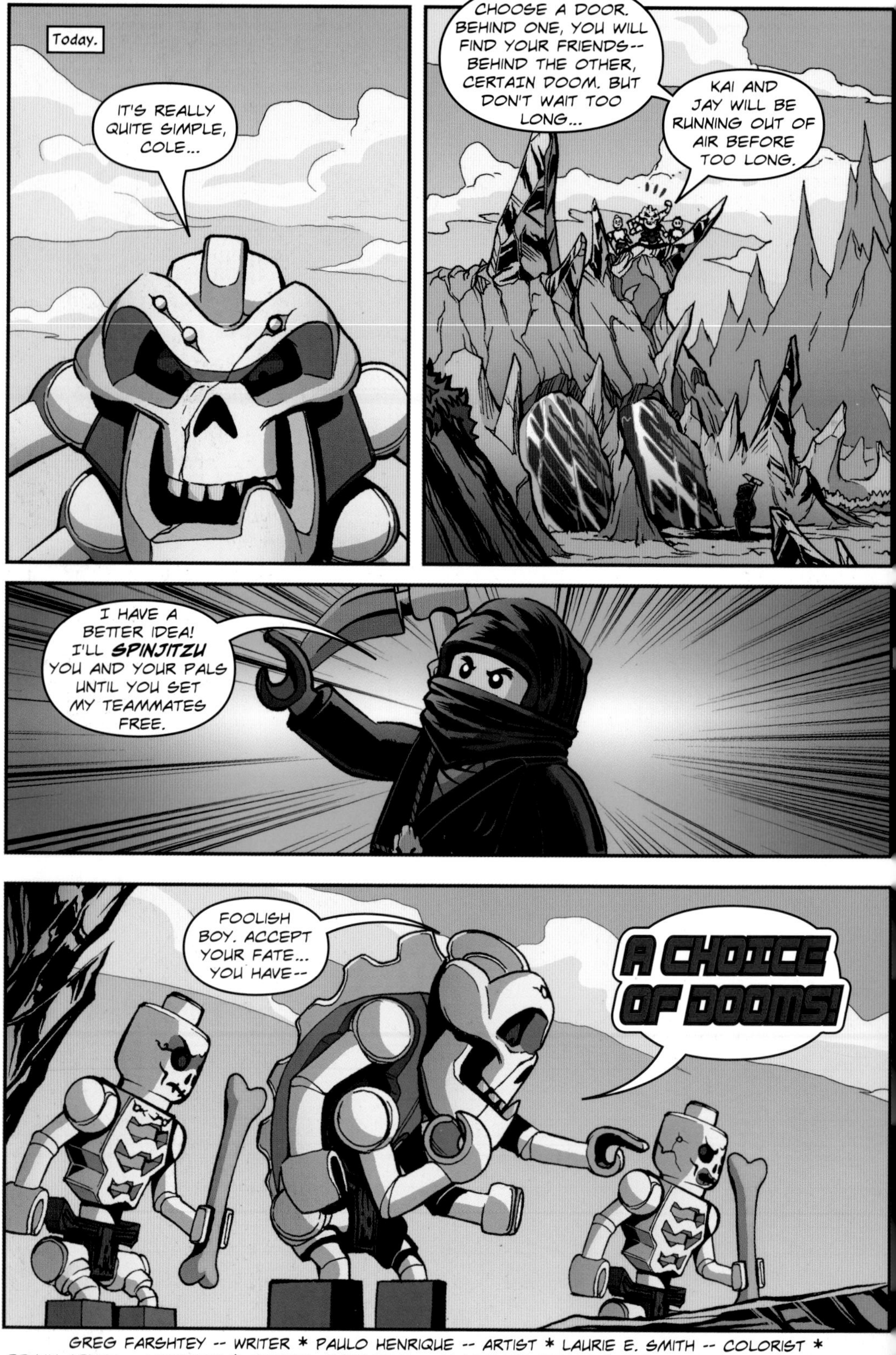
Today.
IT'S REALLY QUITE SIMPLE, COLE...
CHOOSE A DOOR. BEHIND ONE, YOU WILL FIND YOUR FRIENDS-- BEHIND THE OTHER, CERTAIN DOOM. BUT DON'T WAIT TOO LONG...
KAI AND JAY WILL BE RUNNING OUT OF AIR BEFORE TOO LONG.
I HAVE A BETTER IDEA! I'LL SPINJITZU YOU AND YOUR PALS UNTIL YOU SET MY TEAMMATES FREE.
FOOLISH BOY. ACCEPT YOUR FATE... YOU HAVE--
A CHOICE OF DOOMS!

GREG FARSHTEY -- WRITER * PAULO HENRIQUE -- ARTIST * LAURIE E. SMITH -- COLORIST * BRYAN SENKA -- LETTERER * MICHAEL PETRANEK -- ASSOCIATE EDITOR * JIM SALICRUP -- EDITOR-IN-CHIEF

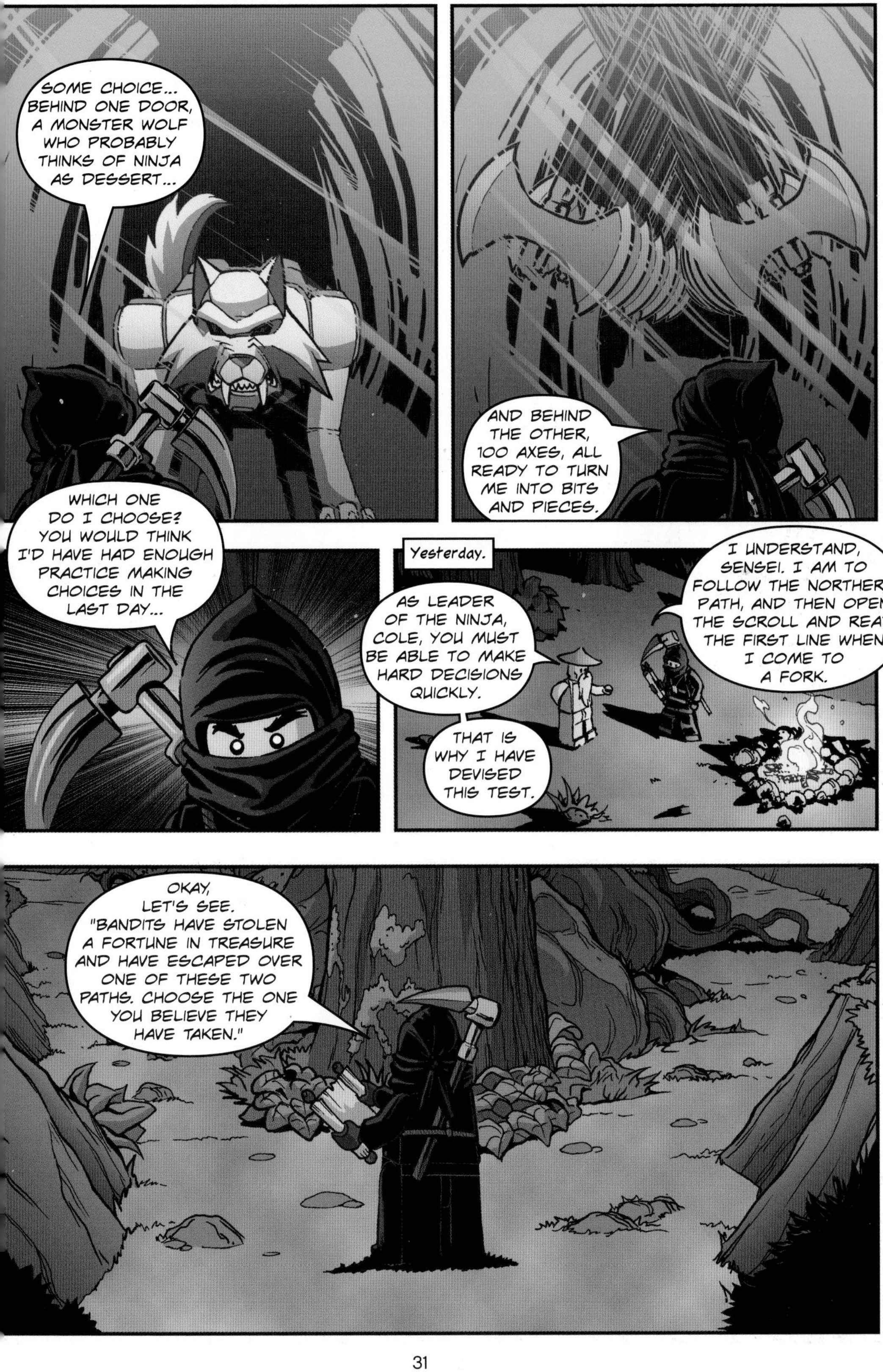
SOME CHOICE... BEHIND ONE DOOR, A MONSTER WOLF WHO PROBABLY THINKS OF NINJA AS DESSERT...
AND BEHIND THE OTHER, 100 AXES, ALL READY TO TURN ME INTO BITS AND PIECES.
WHICH ONE DO I CHOOSE? YOU WOULD THINK I'D HAVE HAD ENOUGH PRACTICE MAKING CHOICES IN THE LAST DAY...
Yesterday.
AS LEADER OF THE NINJA, COLE, YOU MUST BE ABLE TO MAKE HARD DECISIONS QUICKLY.
THAT IS WHY I HAVE DEVISED THIS TEST.
I UNDERSTAND, SENSEI. I AM TO FOLLOW THE NORTHERN PATH, AND THEN OPEN THE SCROLL AND READ THE FIRST LINE WHEN I COME TO A FORK.
OKAY, LET'S SEE. "BANDITS HAVE STOLEN A FORTUNE IN TREASURE AND HAVE ESCAPED OVER ONE OF THESE TWO PATHS. CHOOSE THE ONE YOU BELIEVE THEY HAVE TAKEN."

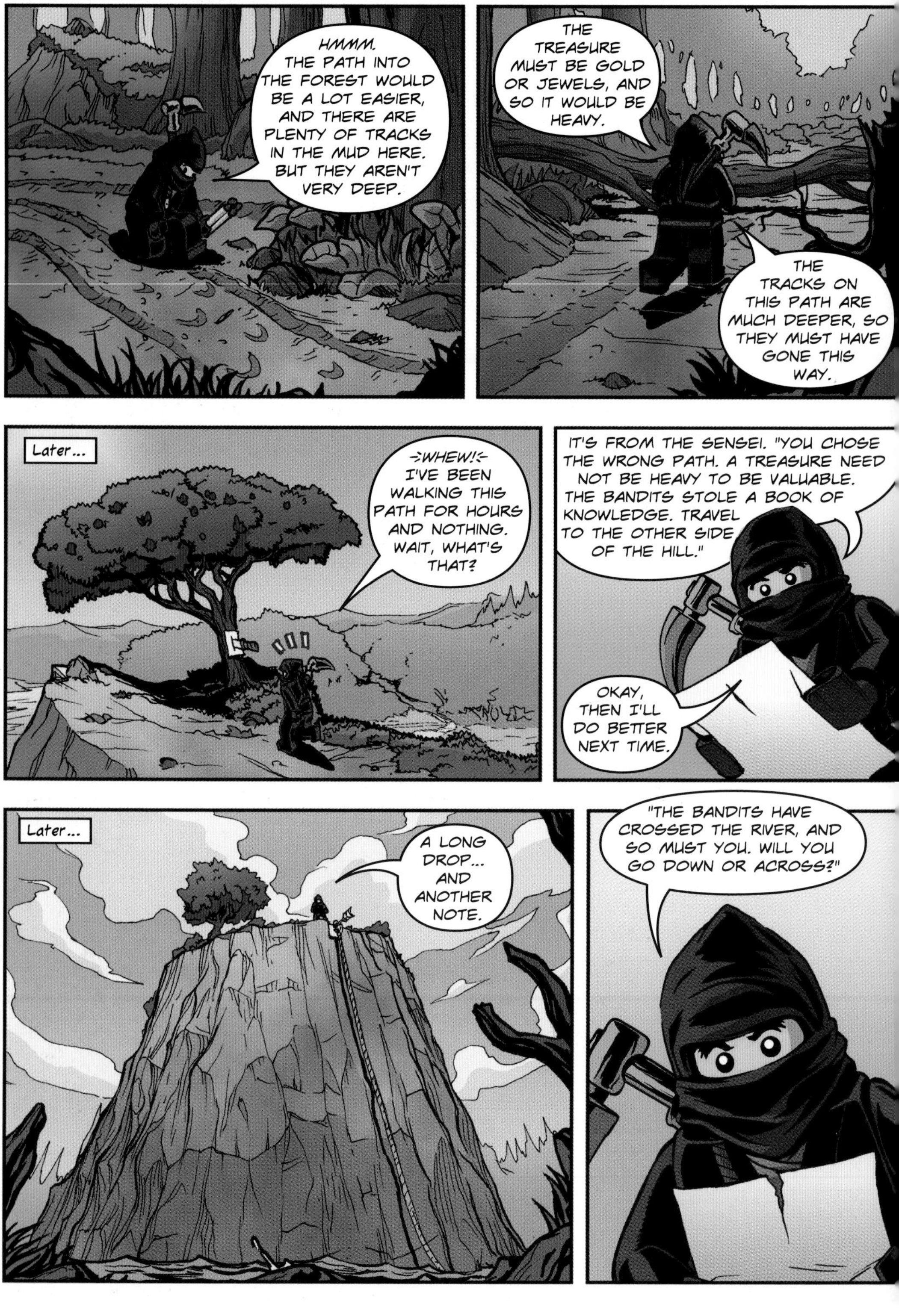
HMMM. THE PATH INTO THE FOREST WOULD BE A LOT EASIER, AND THERE ARE PLENTY OF TRACKS IN THE MUD HERE. BUT THEY AREN'T VERY DEEP.
THE TREASURE MUST BE GOLD OR JEWELS, AND SO IT WOULD BE HEAVY.
THE TRACKS ON THIS PATH ARE MUCH DEEPER, SO THEY MUST HAVE GONE THIS WAY.
Later...
WHEW! I'VE BEEN WALKING THIS PATH FOR HOURS AND NOTHING. WAIT, WHAT'S THAT?
IT'S FROM THE SENSEI. "YOU CHOSE THE WRONG PATH. A TREASURE NEED NOT BE HEAVY TO BE VALUABLE. THE BANDITS STOLE A BOOK OF KNOWLEDGE. TRAVEL TO THE OTHER SIDE OF THE HILL."
OKAY, THEN I'LL DO BETTER NEXT TIME.
Later...
A LONG DROP... AND ANOTHER NOTE.
"THE BANDITS HAVE CROSSED THE RIVER, AND SO MUST YOU. WILL YOU GO DOWN OR ACROSS?"

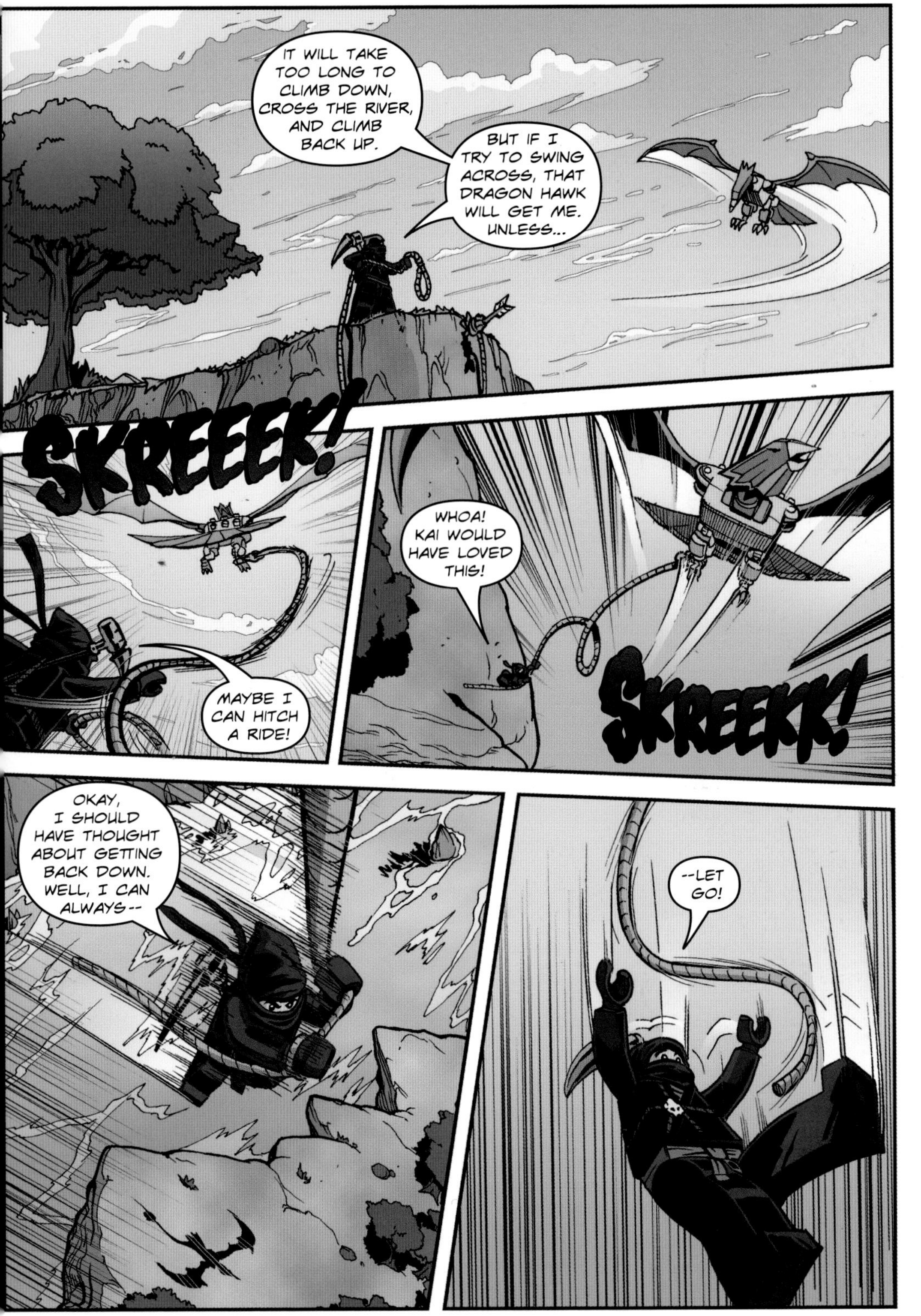
IT WILL TAKE TOO LONG TO CLIMB DOWN, CROSS THE RIVER, AND CLIMB BACK UP.
BUT IF I TRY TO SWING ACROSS, THAT DRAGON HAWK WILL GET ME. UNLESS...
SKREEEK!
MAYBE I CAN HITCH A RIDE!
WHOA! KAI WOULD HAVE LOVED THIS!
SKREEKK!
OKAY, I SHOULD HAVE THOUGHT ABOUT GETTING BACK DOWN. WELL, I CAN ALWAYS--
--LET GO!

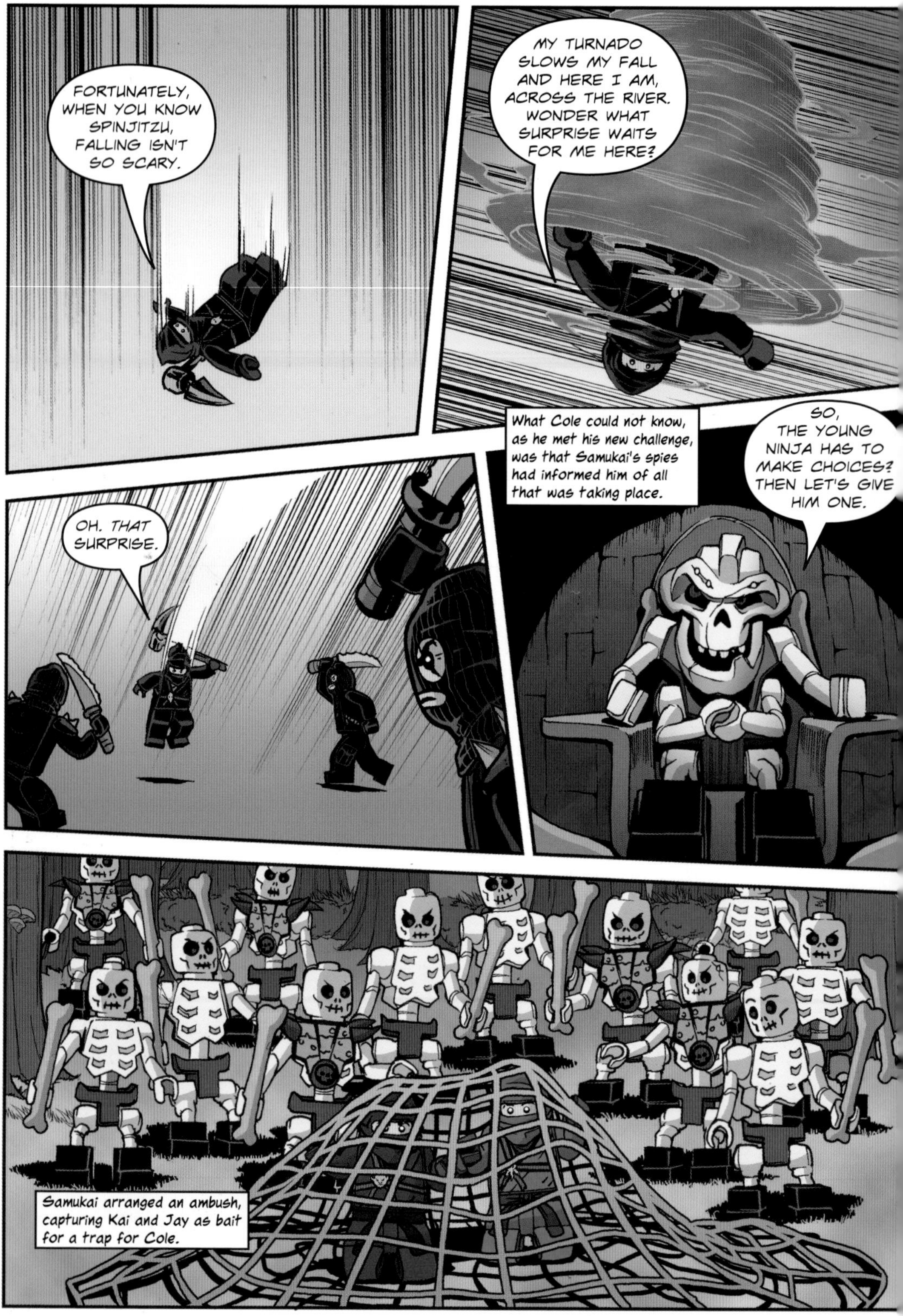
FORTUNATELY, WHEN YOU KNOW SPINJITZU, FALLING ISN'T SO SCARY.
MY TURNADO SLOWS MY FALL AND HERE I AM, ACROSS THE RIVER. WONDER WHAT SURPRISE WAITS FOR ME HERE?
OH. THAT SURPRISE.
What Cole could not know, as he met his new challenge, was that Samukai's spies had informed him of all that was taking place.
SO, THE YOUNG NINJA HAS TO MAKE CHOICES? THEN LET'S GIVE HIM ONE.
Samukai arranged an ambush, capturing Kai and Jay as bait for a trap for Cole.

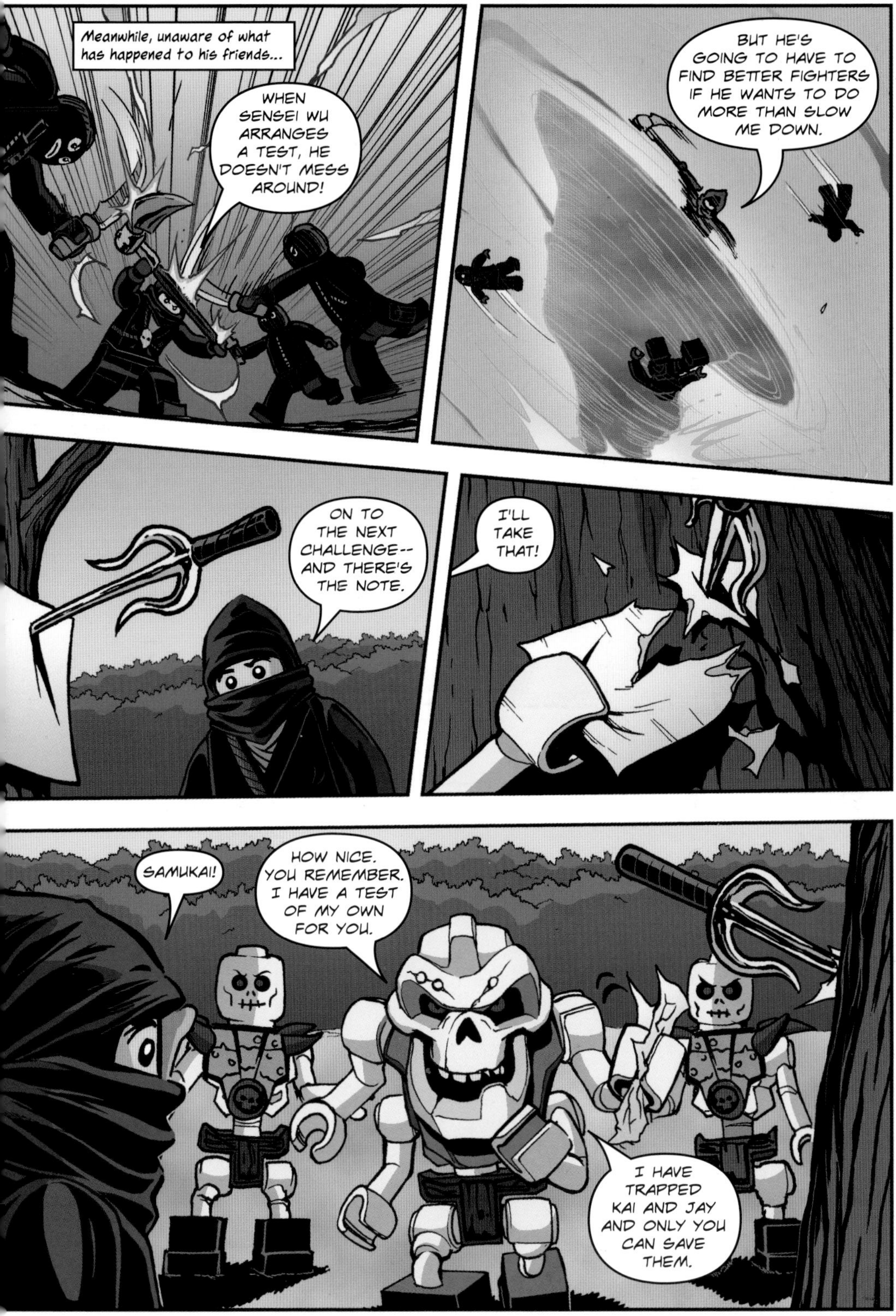
Meanwhile, unaware of what has happened to his friends...
WHEN SENSEI WU ARRANGES A TEST, HE DOESN'T MESS AROUND!
BUT HE'S GOING TO HAVE TO FIND BETTER FIGHTERS IF HE WANTS TO DO MORE THAN SLOW ME DOWN.
ON TO THE NEXT CHALLENGE-- AND THERE'S THE NOTE.
I'LL TAKE THAT!
SAMUKAI!
HOW NICE. YOU REMEMBER. I HAVE A TEST OF MY OWN FOR YOU.
I HAVE TRAPPED KAI AND JAY AND ONLY YOU CAN SAVE THEM.

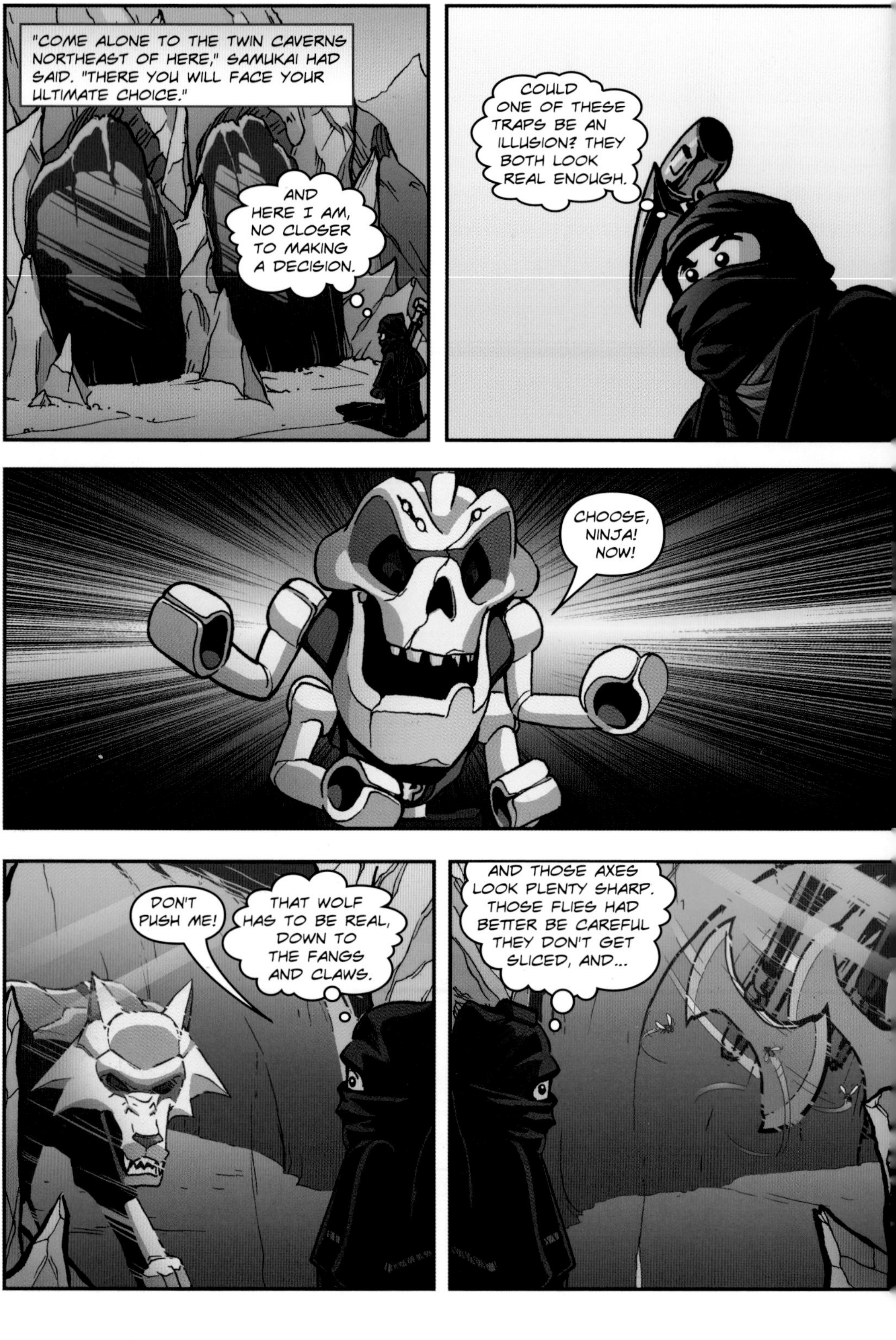
"COME ALONE TO THE TWIN CAVERNS NORTHEAST OF HERE," SAMUKAI HAD SAID. "THERE YOU WILL FACE YOUR ULTIMATE CHOICE."
AND HERE I AM, NO CLOSER TO MAKING A DECISION.
COULD ONE OF THESE TRAPS BE AN ILLUSION? THEY BOTH LOOK REAL ENOUGH.
CHOOSE, NINJA! NOW!
DON'T PUSH ME!
THAT WOLF HAS TO BE REAL, DOWN TO THE FANGS AND CLAWS.
AND THOSE AXES LOOK PLENTY SHARP. THOSE FLIES HAD BETTER BE CAREFUL THEY DON'T GET SLICED, AND...

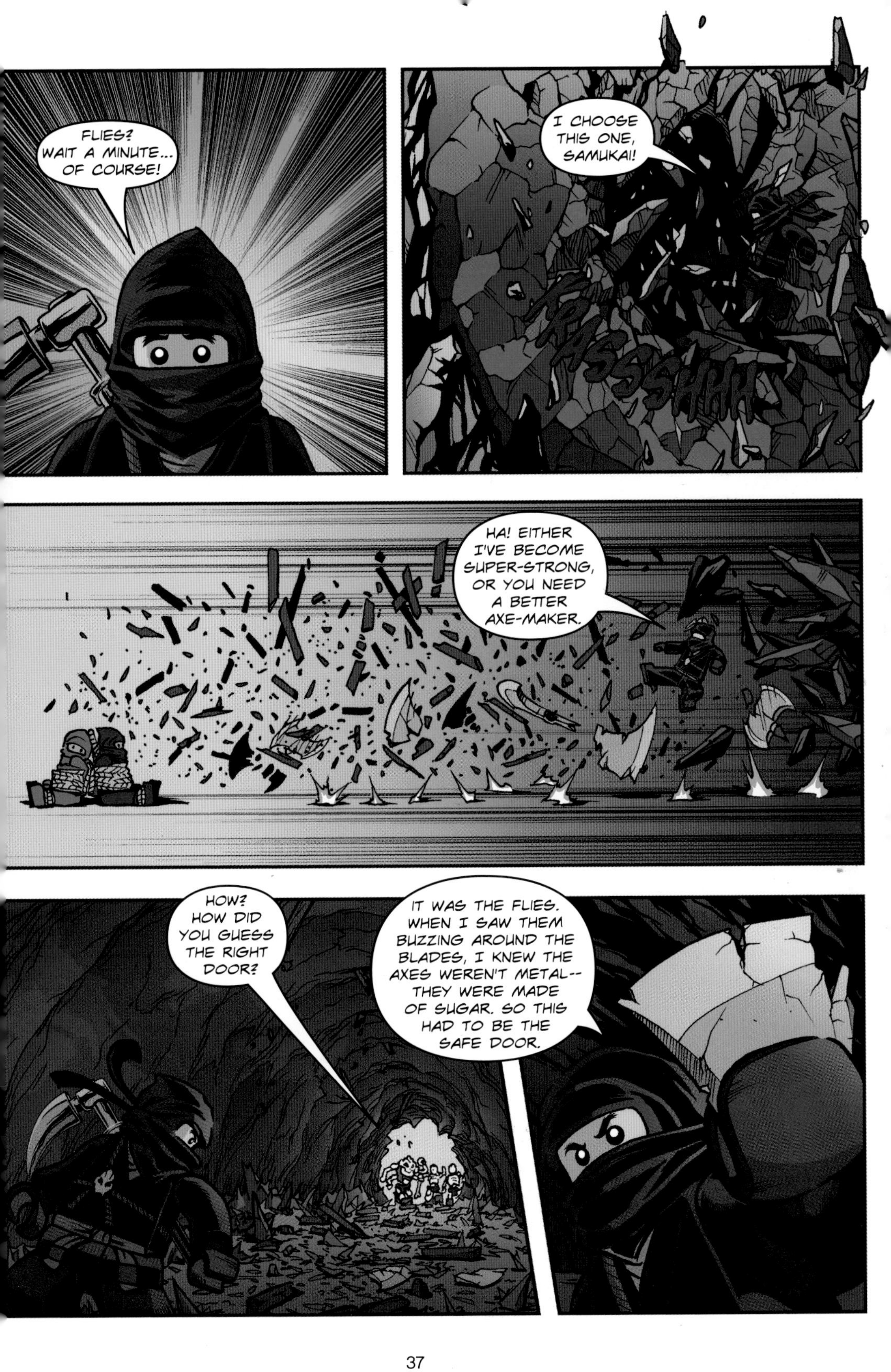
FLIES? WAIT A MINUTE... OF COURSE!
I CHOOSE THIS ONE, SAMUKAI!
KRASSSHHH
HA! EITHER I'VE BECOME SUPER-STRONG, OR YOU NEED A BETTER AXE-MAKER.
HOW? HOW DID YOU GUESS THE RIGHT DOOR?
IT WAS THE FLIES. WHEN I SAW THEM BUZZING AROUND THE BLADES, I KNEW THE AXES WEREN'T METAL-- THEY WERE MADE OF SUGAR. SO THIS HAD TO BE THE SAFE DOOR.

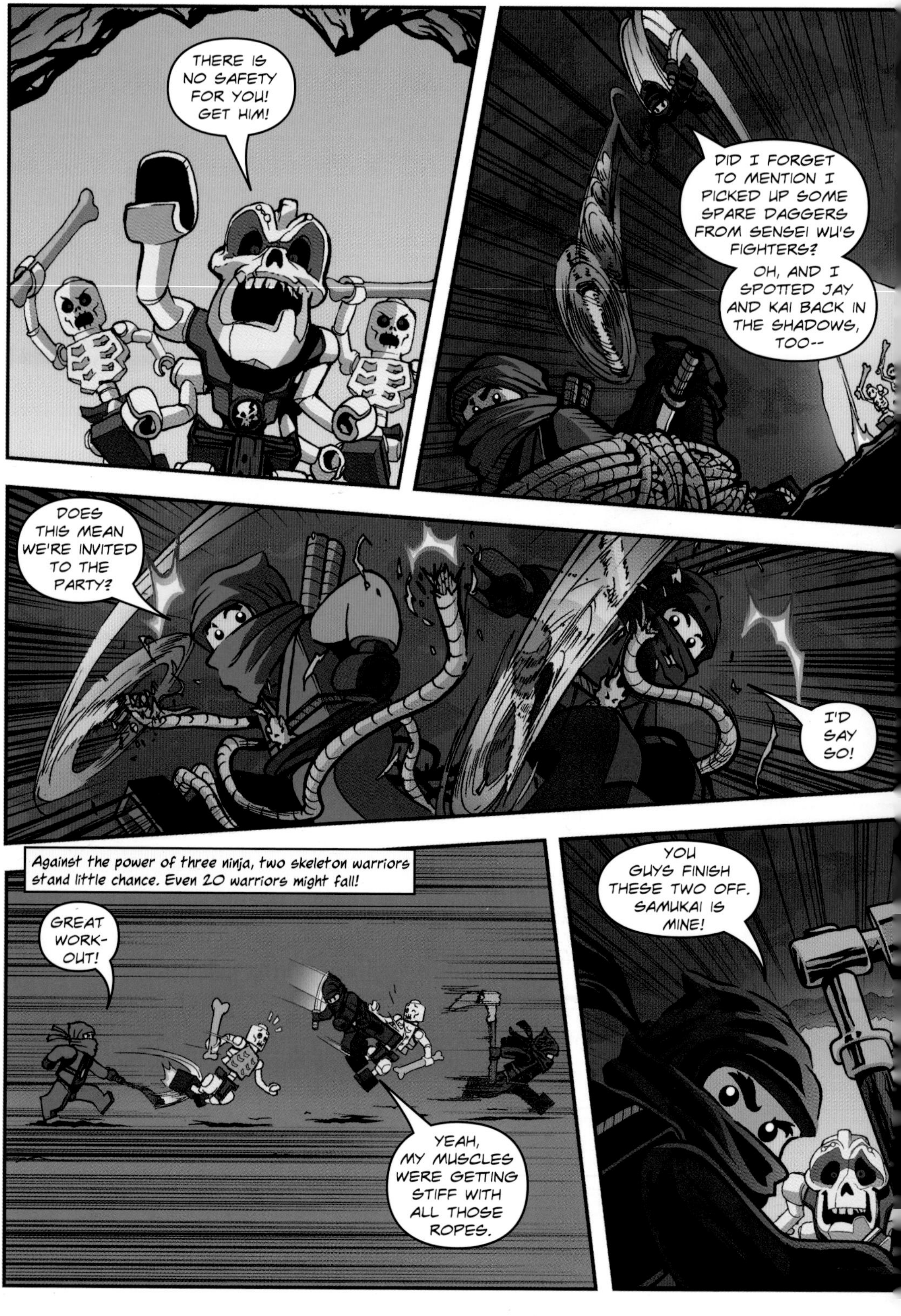
THERE IS NO SAFETY FOR YOU! GET HIM!
DID I FORGET TO MENTION I PICKED UP SOME SPARE DAGGERS FROM SENSEI WU'S FIGHTERS?
OH, AND I SPOTTED JAY AND KAI BACK IN THE SHADOWS, TOO--
DOES THIS MEAN WE'RE INVITED TO THE PARTY?
I'D SAY SO!
Against the power of three ninja, two skeleton warriors stand little chance. Even 20 warriors might fall!
GREAT WORK-OUT!
YEAH, MY MUSCLES WERE GETTING STIFF WITH ALL THOSE ROPES.
YOU GUYS FINISH THESE TWO OFF. SAMUKAI IS MINE!

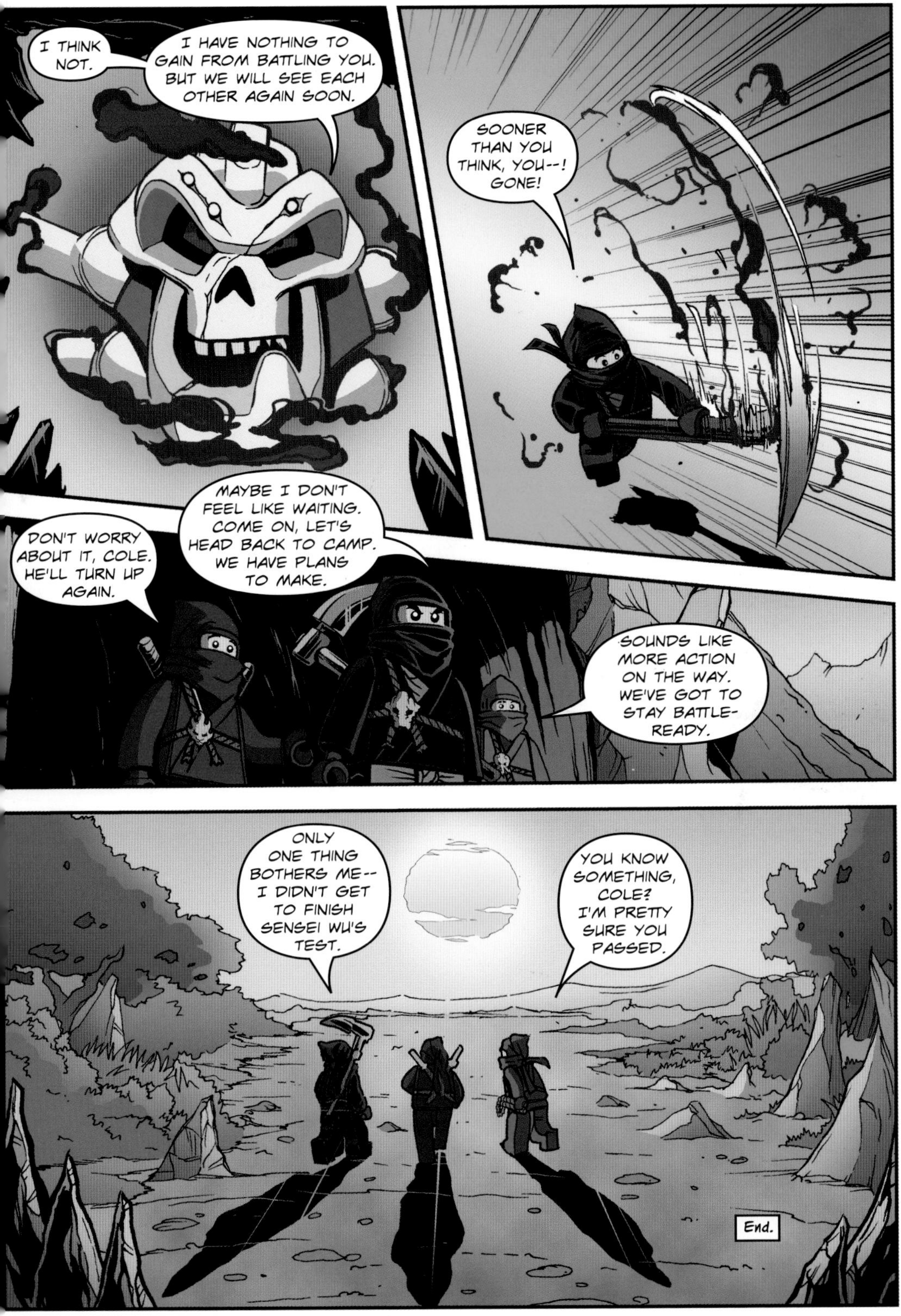
I THINK NOT.
I HAVE NOTHING TO GAIN FROM BATTLING YOU. BUT WE WILL SEE EACH OTHER AGAIN SOON.
SOONER THAN YOU THINK, YOU--! GONE!
DON'T WORRY ABOUT IT, COLE. HE'LL TURN UP AGAIN.
MAYBE I DON'T FEEL LIKE WAITING. COME ON, LET'S HEAD BACK TO CAMP. WE HAVE PLANS TO MAKE.
SOUNDS LIKE MORE ACTION ON THE WAY. WE'VE GOT TO STAY BATTLE-READY.
ONLY ONE THING BOTHERS ME-- I DIDN'T GET TO FINISH SENSEI WU'S TEST.
YOU KNOW SOMETHING, COLE? I'M PRETTY SURE YOU PASSED.
End.

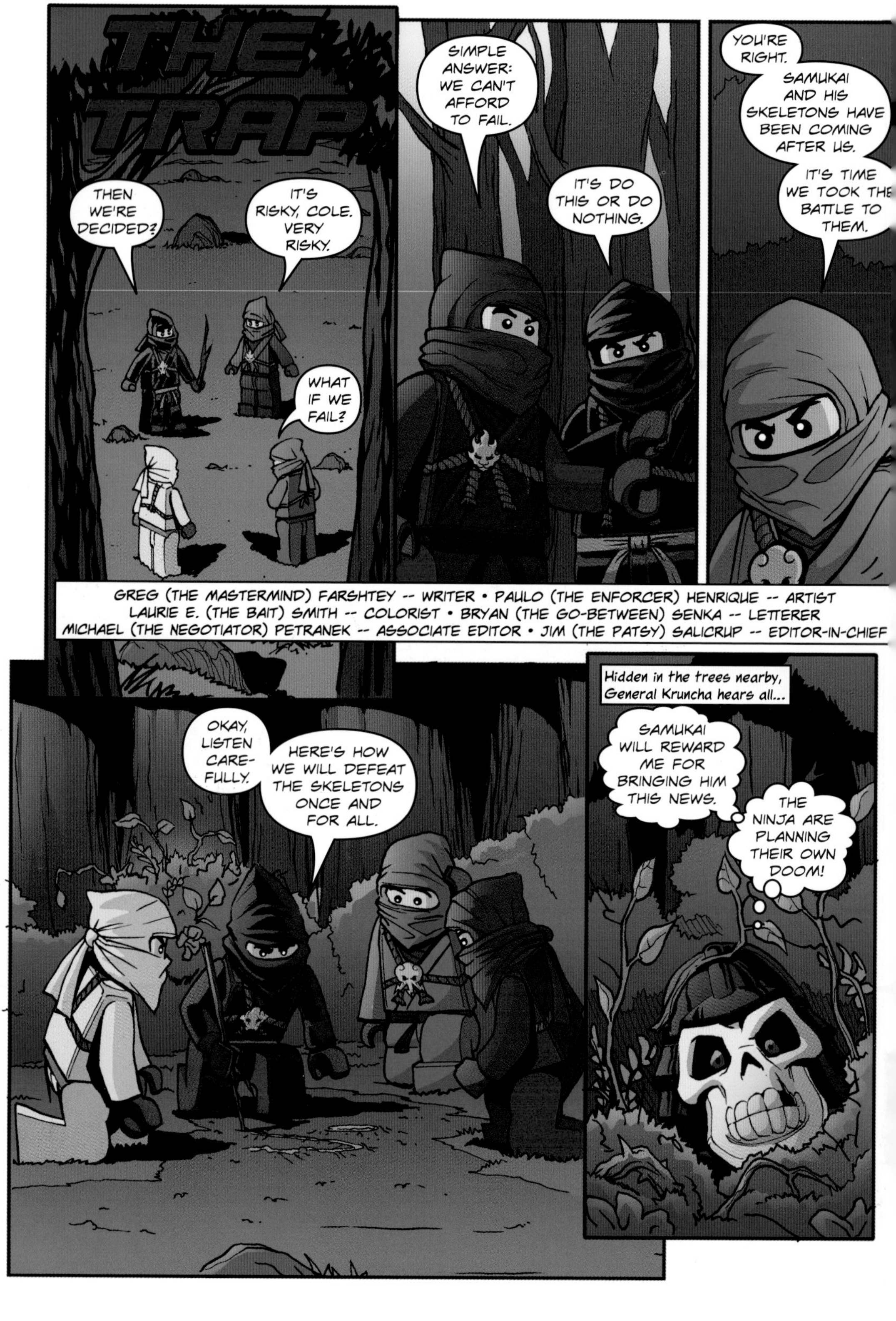
THE TRAP
THEN WE'RE DECIDED?
IT'S RISKY, COLE. VERY RISKY.
WHAT IF WE FAIL?
SIMPLE ANSWER: WE CAN'T AFFORD TO FAIL.
IT'S DO THIS OR DO NOTHING.
YOU'RE RIGHT.
SAMUKAI AND HIS SKELETONS HAVE BEEN COMING AFTER US.
IT'S TIME WE TOOK THE BATTLE TO THEM.
GREG (THE MASTERMIND) FARSHTEY -- WRITER • PAULO (THE ENFORCER) HENRIQUE -- ARTIST
LAURIE E. (THE BAIT) SMITH -- COLORIST • BRYAN (THE GO-BETWEEN) SENKA -- LETTERER
MICHAEL (THE NEGOTIATOR) PETRANEK -- ASSOCIATE EDITOR • JIM (THE PATSY) SALICRUP -- EDITOR-IN-CHIEF
OKAY, LISTEN CARE-FULLY.
HERE'S HOW WE WILL DEFEAT THE SKELETONS ONCE AND FOR ALL.
Hidden in the trees nearby, General Kruncha hears all...
SAMUKAI WILL REWARD ME FOR BRINGING HIM THIS NEWS.
THE NINJA ARE PLANNING THEIR OWN DOOM!

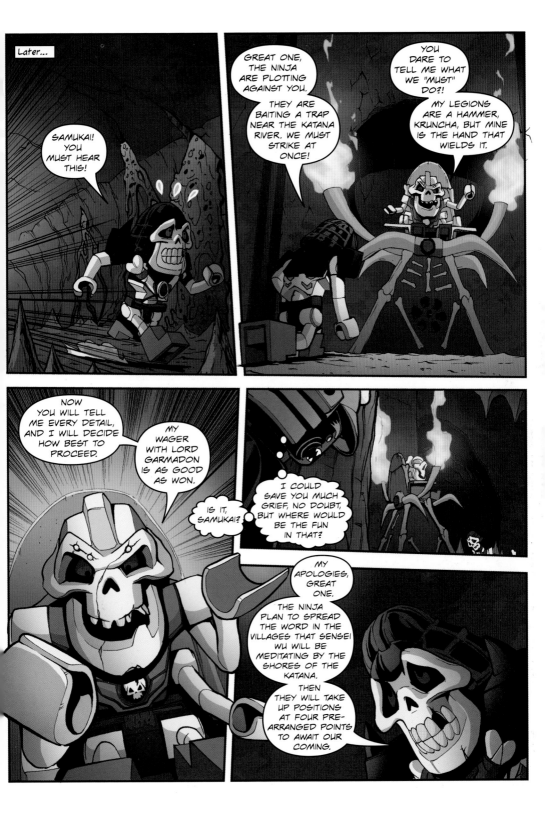

Later...

SAMUKAI! YOU MUST HEAR THIS!

GREAT ONE, THE NINJA ARE PLOTTING AGAINST YOU.

THEY ARE BAITING A TRAP NEAR THE KATANA RIVER. WE MUST STRIKE AT ONCE!

YOU DARE TO TELL ME WHAT WE "MUST" DO?!

MY LEGIONS ARE A HAMMER, KRUNCHA, BUT MINE IS THE HAND THAT WIELDS IT.

NOW YOU WILL TELL ME EVERY DETAIL, AND I WILL DECIDE HOW BEST TO PROCEED.

MY WAGER WITH LORD GARMADON IS AS GOOD AS WON.

IS IT, SAMUKAI?

I COULD SAVE YOU MUCH GRIEF, NO DOUBT, BUT WHERE WOULD BE THE FUN IN THAT?

MY APOLOGIES, GREAT ONE.

THE NINJA PLAN TO SPREAD THE WORD IN THE VILLAGES THAT SENSEI WU WILL BE MEDITATING BY THE SHORES OF THE KATANA.

THEN THEY WILL TAKE UP POSITIONS AT FOUR PRE-ARRANGED POINTS TO AWAIT OUR COMING.

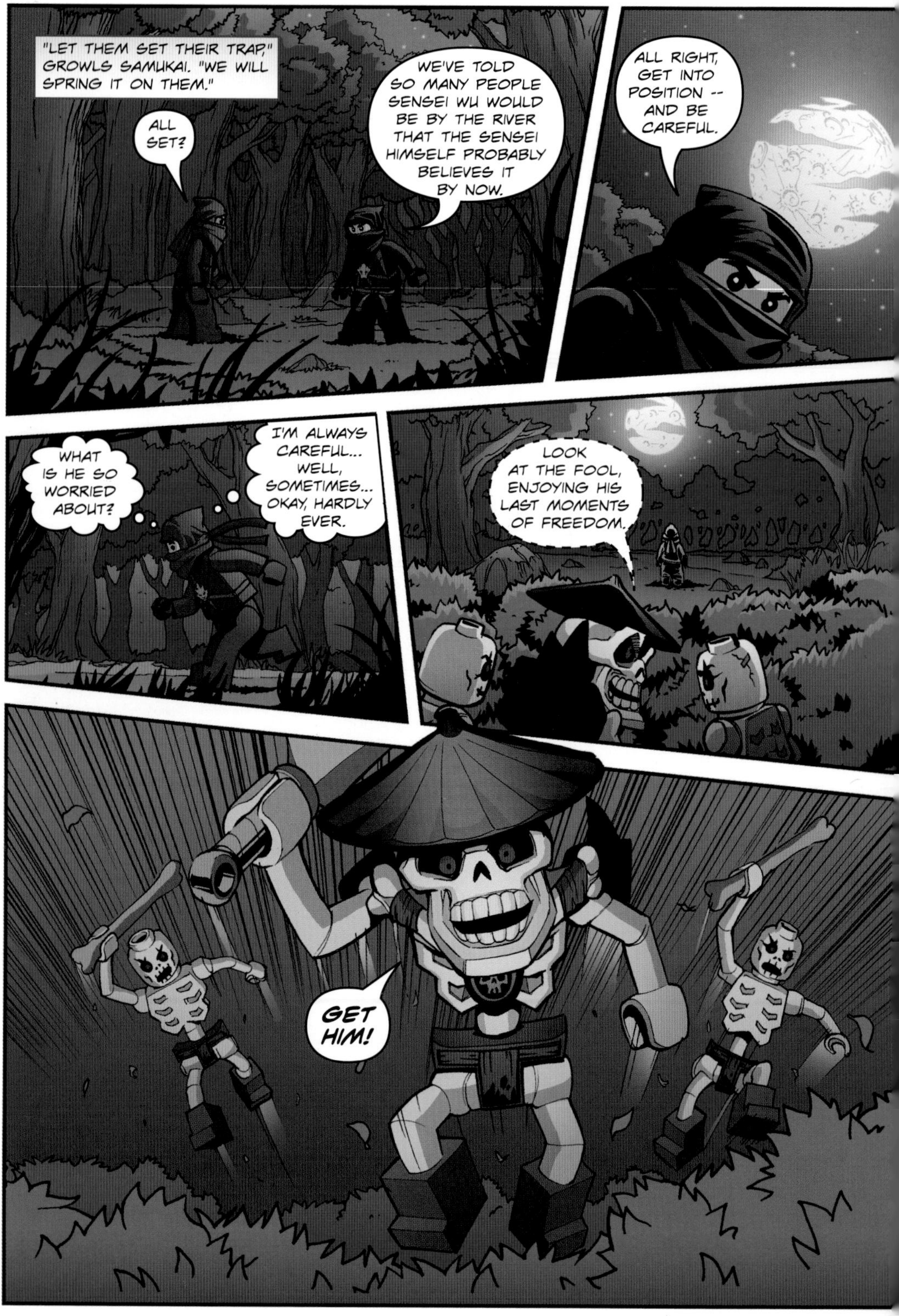
"LET THEM SET THEIR TRAP," GROWLS SAMUKAI. "WE WILL SPRING IT ON THEM."
ALL SET?
WE'VE TOLD SO MANY PEOPLE SENSEI WU WOULD BE BY THE RIVER THAT THE SENSEI HIMSELF PROBABLY BELIEVES IT BY NOW.
ALL RIGHT, GET INTO POSITION -- AND BE CAREFUL.
WHAT IS HE SO WORRIED ABOUT?
I'M ALWAYS CAREFUL... WELL, SOMETIMES... OKAY, HARDLY EVER.
LOOK AT THE FOOL, ENJOYING HIS LAST MOMENTS OF FREEDOM.
GET HIM!

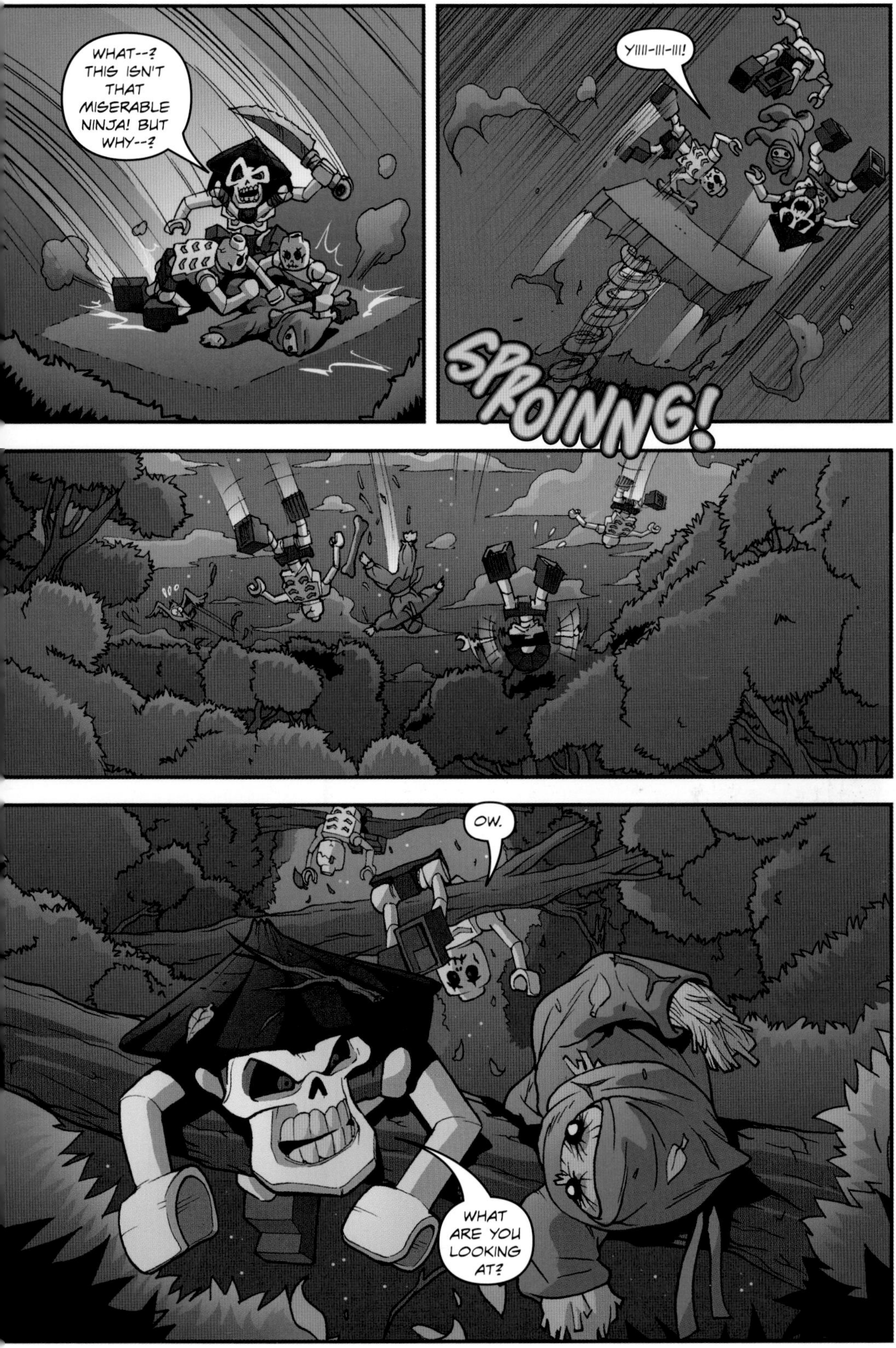
WHAT--? THIS ISN'T THAT MISERABLE NINJA! BUT WHY--?
YIIII-III-III!
SPROINNG!
OW.
WHAT ARE YOU LOOKING AT?

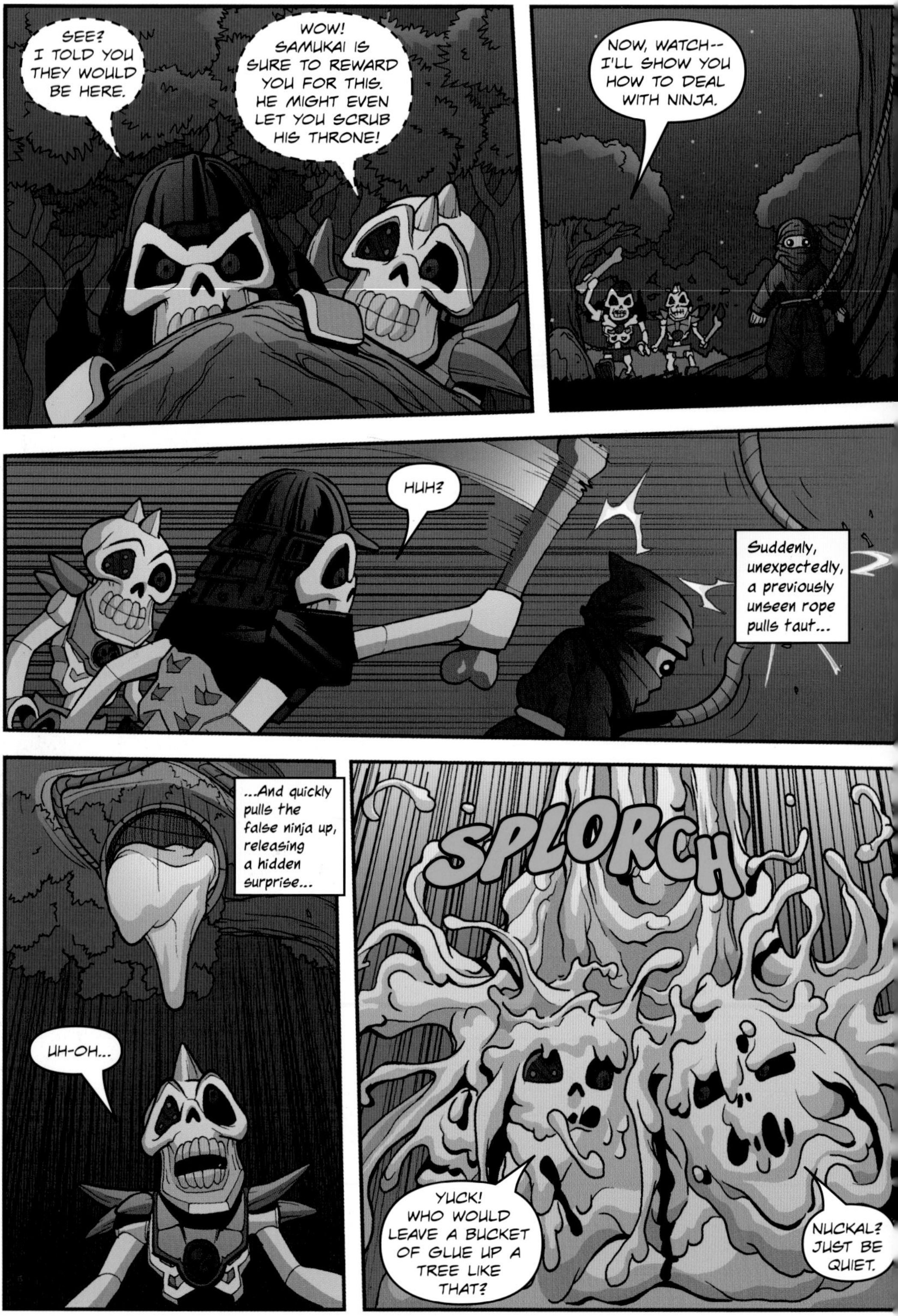
SEE? I TOLD YOU THEY WOULD BE HERE.
WOW! SAMUKAI IS SURE TO REWARD YOU FOR THIS. HE MIGHT EVEN LET YOU SCRUB HIS THRONE!
NOW, WATCH-- I'LL SHOW YOU HOW TO DEAL WITH NINJA.
HUH?
Suddenly, unexpectedly, a previously unseen rope pulls taut...
...And quickly pulls the false ninja up, releasing a hidden surprise...
UH-OH...
SPLORCH
YUCK! WHO WOULD LEAVE A BUCKET OF GLUE UP A TREE LIKE THAT?
NUCKAL? JUST BE QUIET.

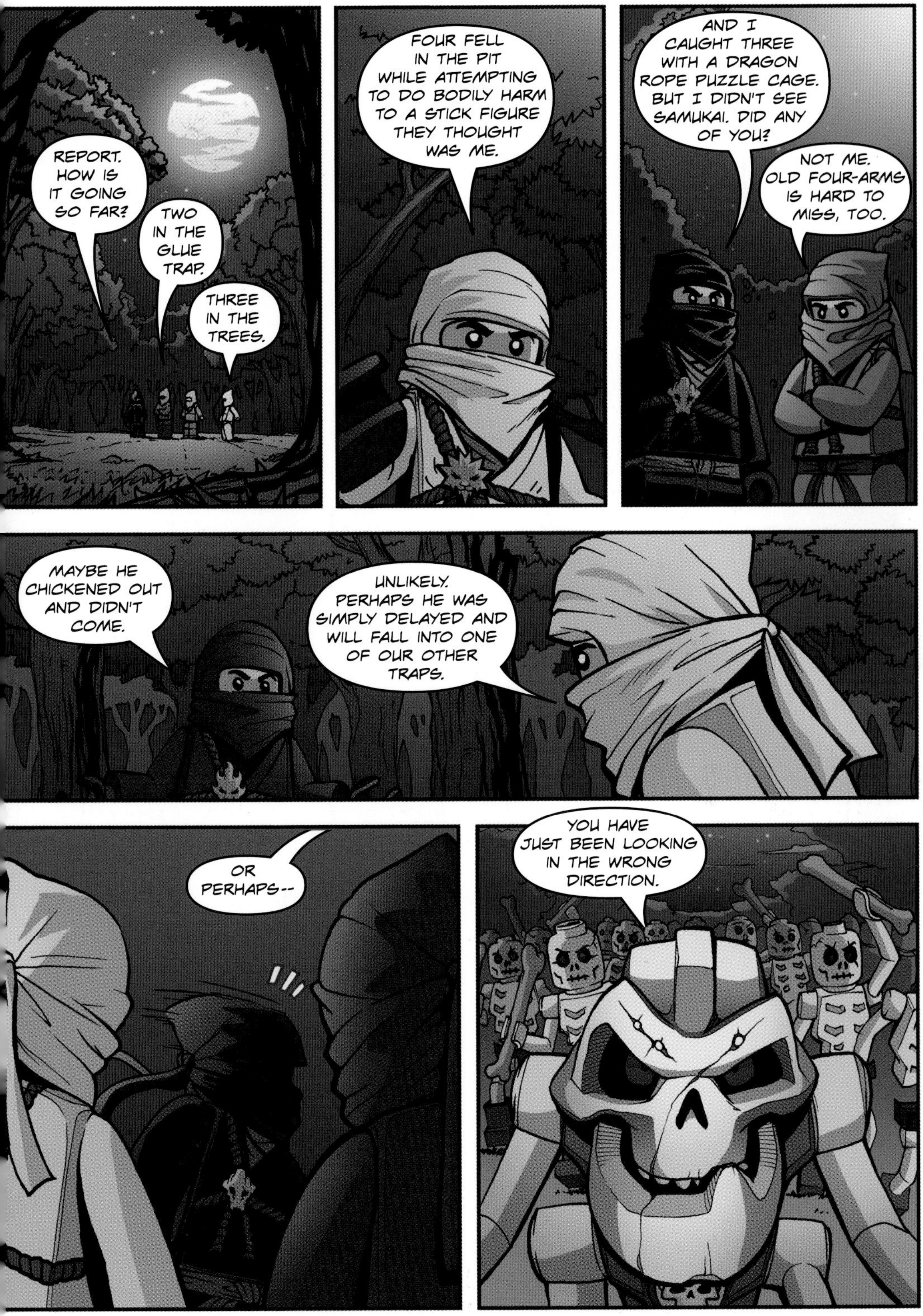
REPORT. HOW IS IT GOING SO FAR?
TWO IN THE GLUE TRAP.
THREE IN THE TREES.
FOUR FELL IN THE PIT WHILE ATTEMPTING TO DO BODILY HARM TO A STICK FIGURE THEY THOUGHT WAS ME.
AND I CAUGHT THREE WITH A DRAGON ROPE PUZZLE CAGE. BUT I DIDN'T SEE SAMUKAI. DID ANY OF YOU?
NOT ME. OLD FOUR-ARMS IS HARD TO MISS, TOO.
MAYBE HE CHICKENED OUT AND DIDN'T COME.
UNLIKELY. PERHAPS HE WAS SIMPLY DELAYED AND WILL FALL INTO ONE OF OUR OTHER TRAPS.
OR PERHAPS--
YOU HAVE JUST BEEN LOOKING IN THE WRONG DIRECTION.

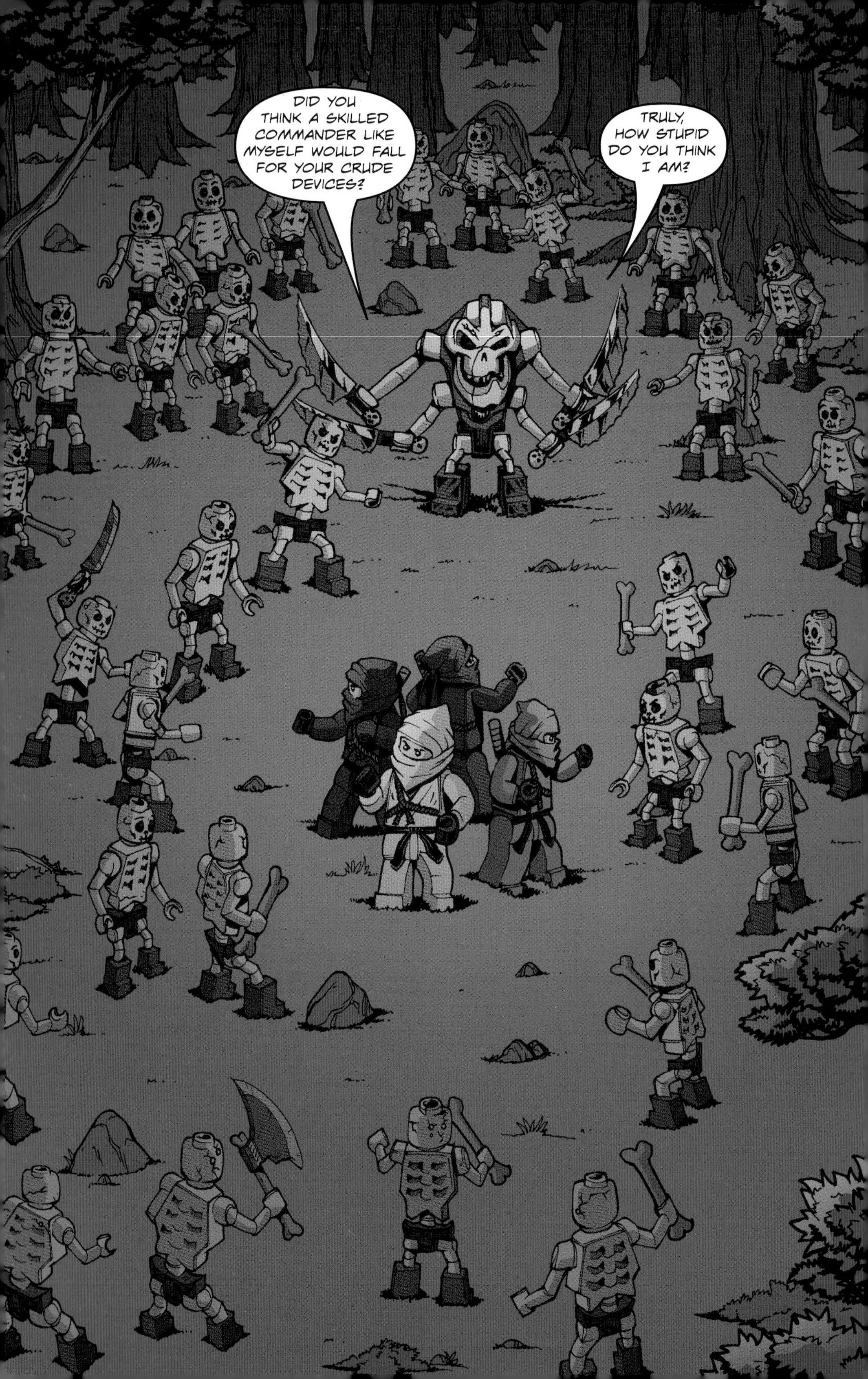
DID YOU THINK A SKILLED COMMANDER LIKE MYSELF WOULD FALL FOR YOUR CRUDE DEVICES?
TRULY, HOW STUPID DO YOU THINK I AM?

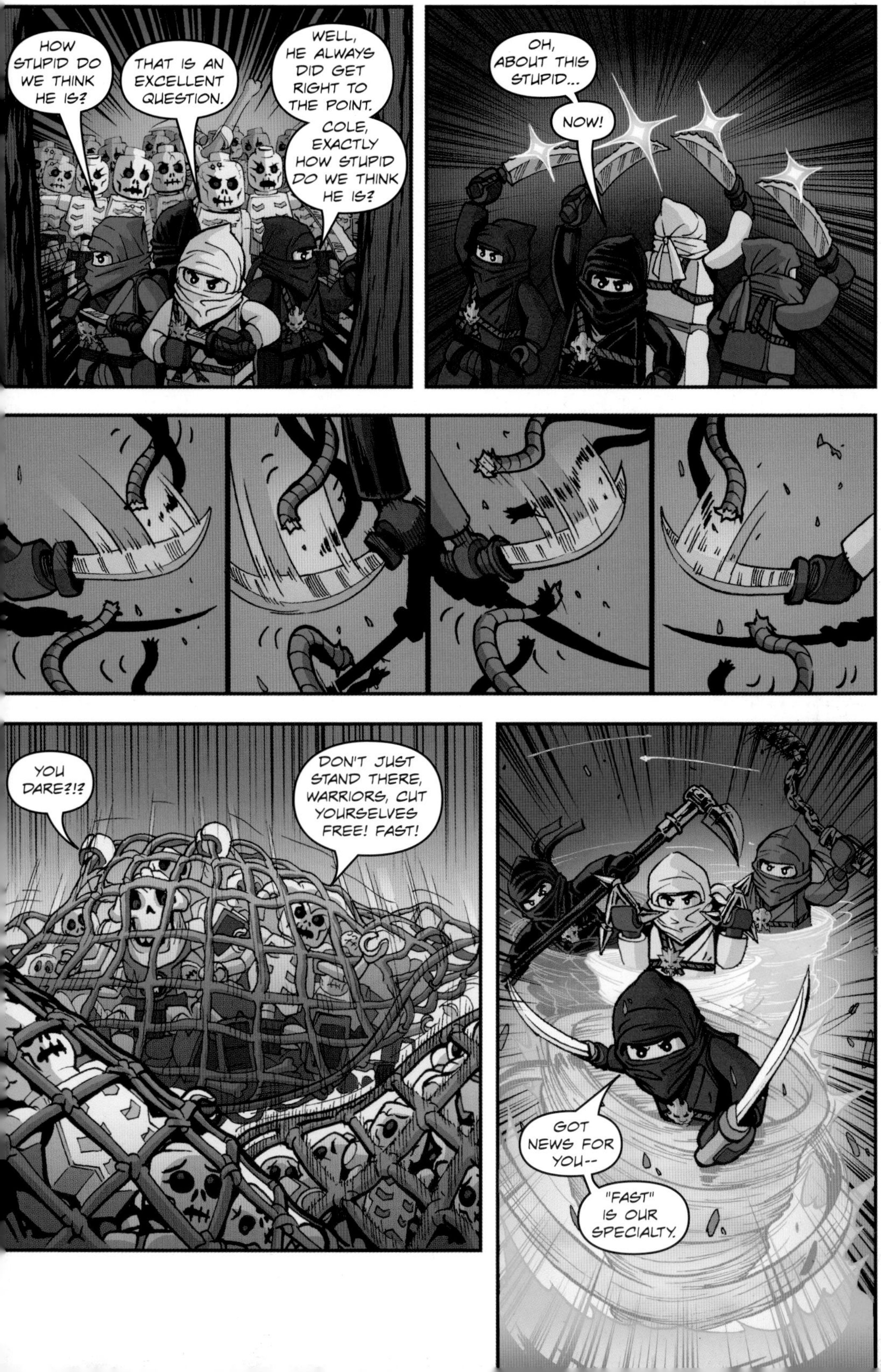
HOW STUPID DO WE THINK HE IS?
THAT IS AN EXCELLENT QUESTION.
WELL, HE ALWAYS DID GET RIGHT TO THE POINT.
COLE, EXACTLY HOW STUPID DO WE THINK HE IS?
OH, ABOUT THIS STUPID...
NOW!
YOU DARE?!?
DON'T JUST STAND THERE, WARRIORS, CUT YOURSELVES FREE! FAST!
GOT NEWS FOR YOU--
"FAST" IS OUR SPECIALTY.

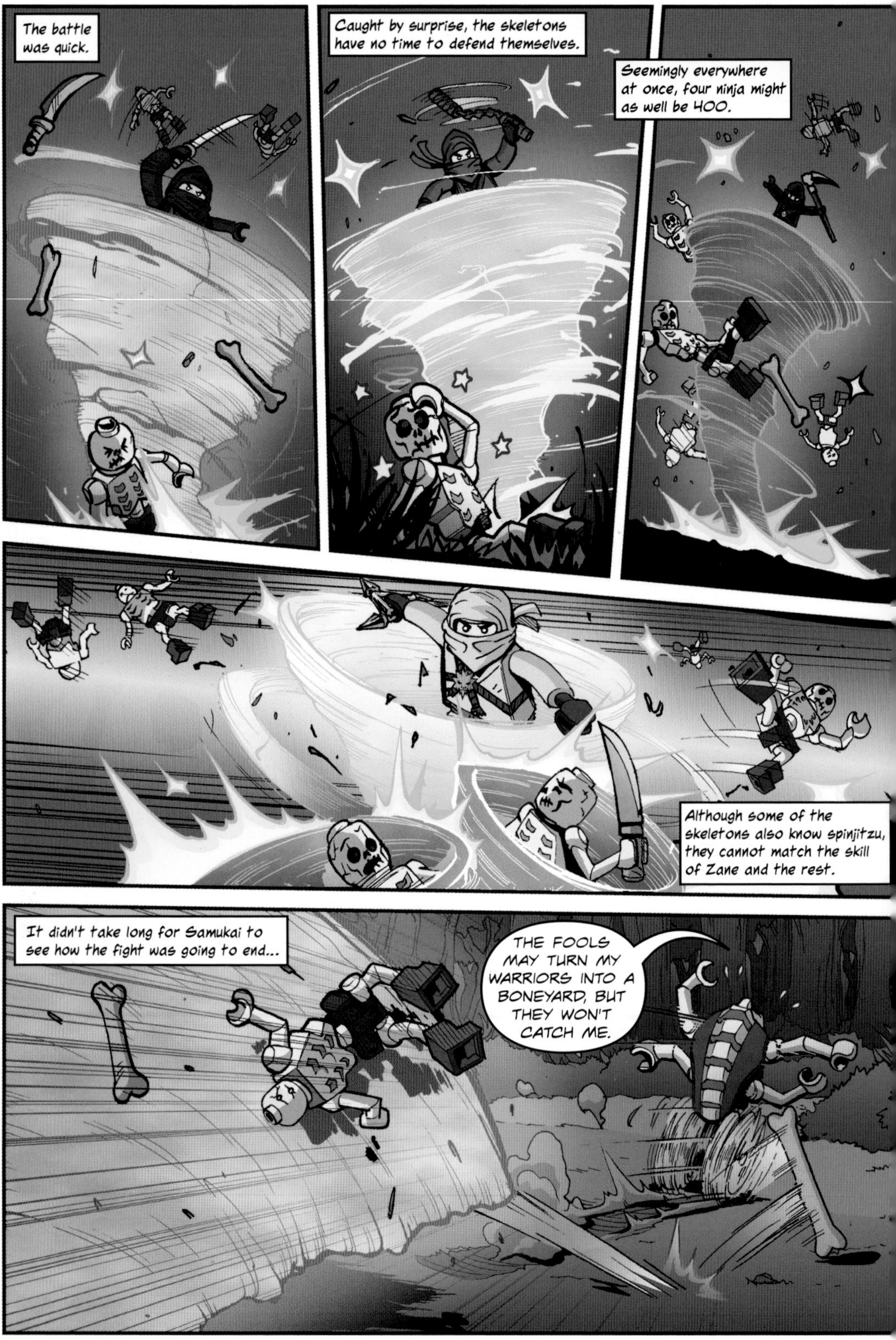

The battle was quick.
Caught by surprise, the skeletons have no time to defend themselves.
Seemingly everywhere at once, four ninja might as well be 400.
Although some of the skeletons also know spinjitzu, they cannot match the skill of Zane and the rest.
It didn't take long for Samukai to see how the fight was going to end...
THE FOOLS MAY TURN MY WARRIORS INTO A BONEYARD, BUT THEY WON'T CATCH ME.

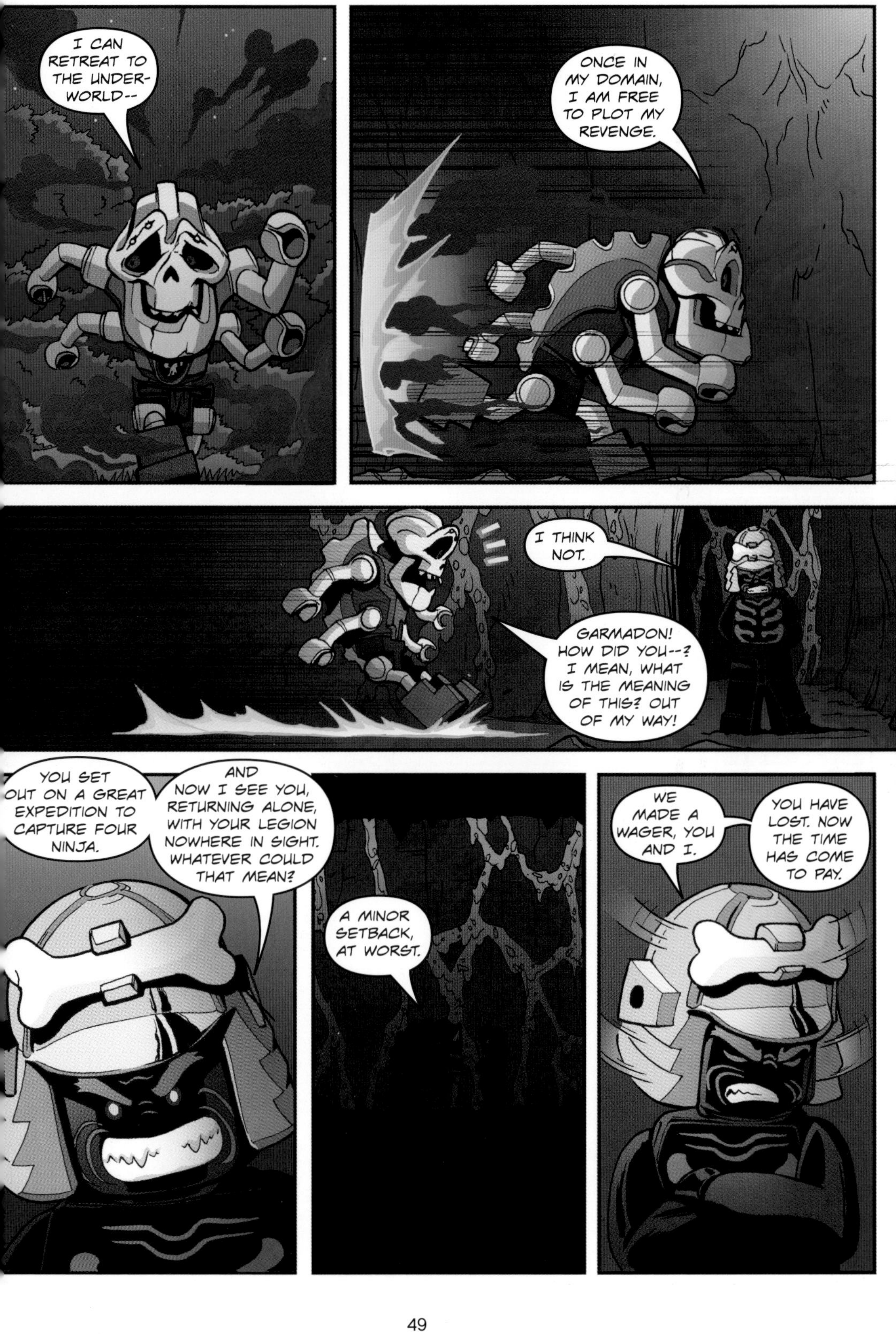
I CAN RETREAT TO THE UNDER-WORLD--
ONCE IN MY DOMAIN, I AM FREE TO PLOT MY REVENGE.
I THINK NOT.
GARMADON! HOW DID YOU--? I MEAN, WHAT IS THE MEANING OF THIS? OUT OF MY WAY!
YOU SET OUT ON A GREAT EXPEDITION TO CAPTURE FOUR NINJA.
AND NOW I SEE YOU, RETURNING ALONE, WITH YOUR LEGION NOWHERE IN SIGHT. WHATEVER COULD THAT MEAN?
A MINOR SETBACK, AT WORST.
WE MADE A WAGER, YOU AND I.
YOU HAVE LOST. NOW THE TIME HAS COME TO PAY.

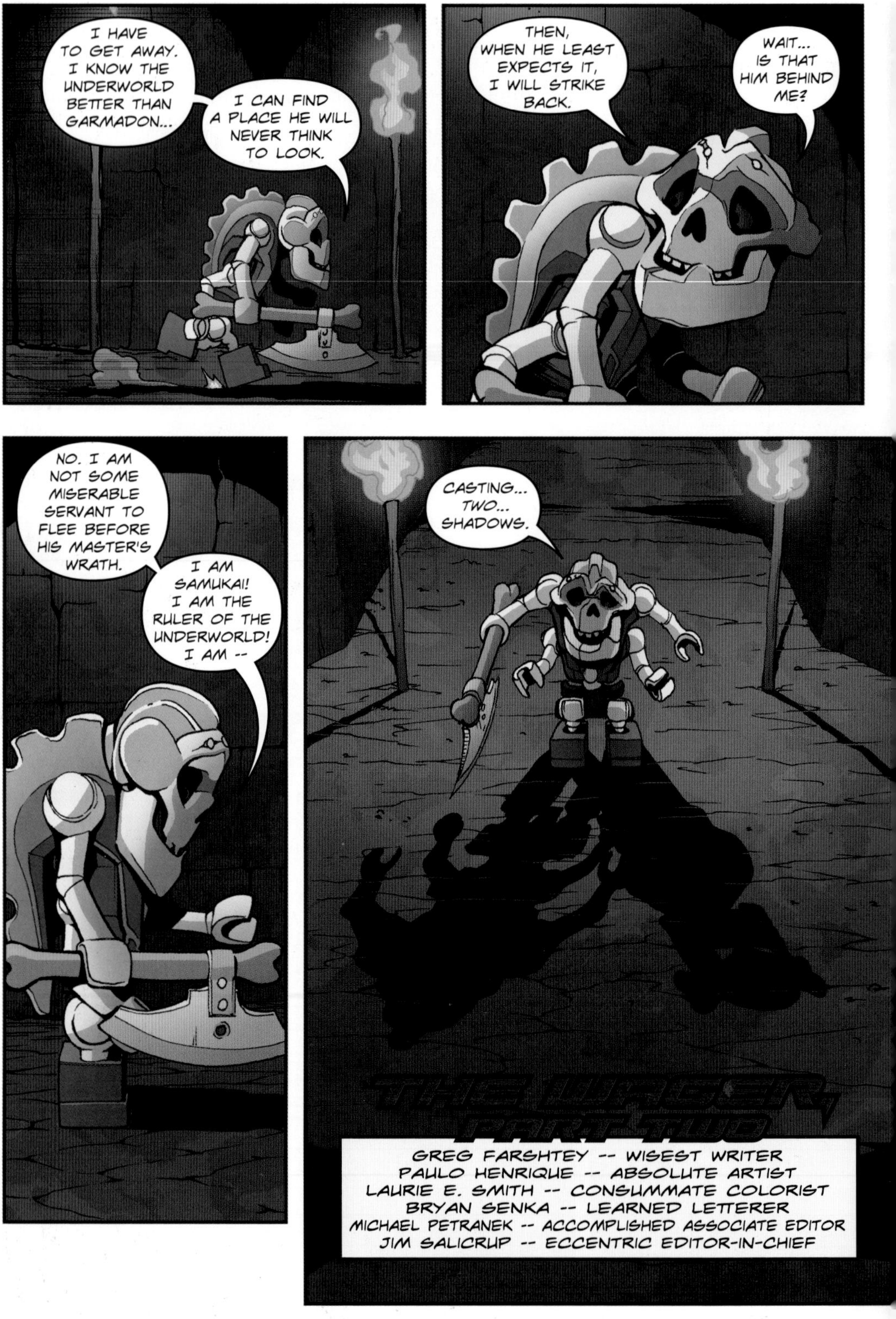
I HAVE TO GET AWAY. I KNOW THE UNDERWORLD BETTER THAN GARMADON...
I CAN FIND A PLACE HE WILL NEVER THINK TO LOOK.
THEN, WHEN HE LEAST EXPECTS IT, I WILL STRIKE BACK.
WAIT... IS THAT HIM BEHIND ME?
NO. I AM NOT SOME MISERABLE SERVANT TO FLEE BEFORE HIS MASTER'S WRATH.
I AM SAMUKAI! I AM THE RULER OF THE UNDERWORLD! I AM --
CASTING... TWO... SHADOWS.
THE WAGER, PART TWO
GREG FARSHTEY -- WISEST WRITER
PAULO HENRIQUE -- ABSOLUTE ARTIST
LAURIE E. SMITH -- CONSUMMATE COLORIST
BRYAN SENKA -- LEARNED LETTERER
MICHAEL PETRANEK -- ACCOMPLISHED ASSOCIATE EDITOR
JIM SALICRUP -- ECCENTRIC EDITOR-IN-CHIEF

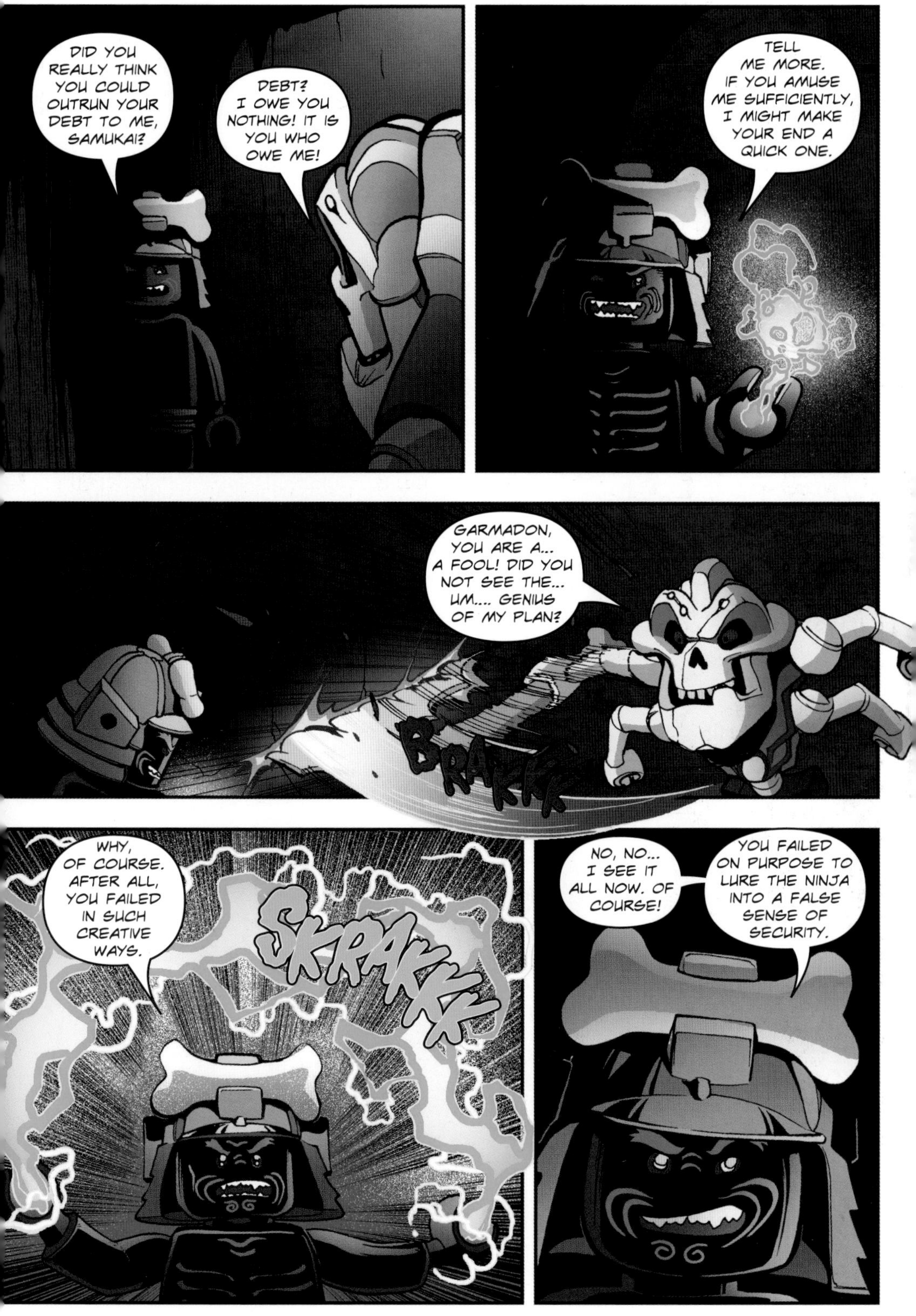
DID YOU REALLY THINK YOU COULD OUTRUN YOUR DEBT TO ME, SAMUKAI?
DEBT? I OWE YOU NOTHING! IT IS YOU WHO OWE ME!
TELL ME MORE. IF YOU AMUSE ME SUFFICIENTLY, I MIGHT MAKE YOUR END A QUICK ONE.
GARMADON, YOU ARE A... A FOOL! DID YOU NOT SEE THE... UM.... GENIUS OF MY PLAN?
BRAKKK
WHY, OF COURSE. AFTER ALL, YOU FAILED IN SUCH CREATIVE WAYS.
SKRAKKK
NO, NO... I SEE IT ALL NOW. OF COURSE!
YOU FAILED ON PURPOSE TO LURE THE NINJA INTO A FALSE SENSE OF SECURITY.

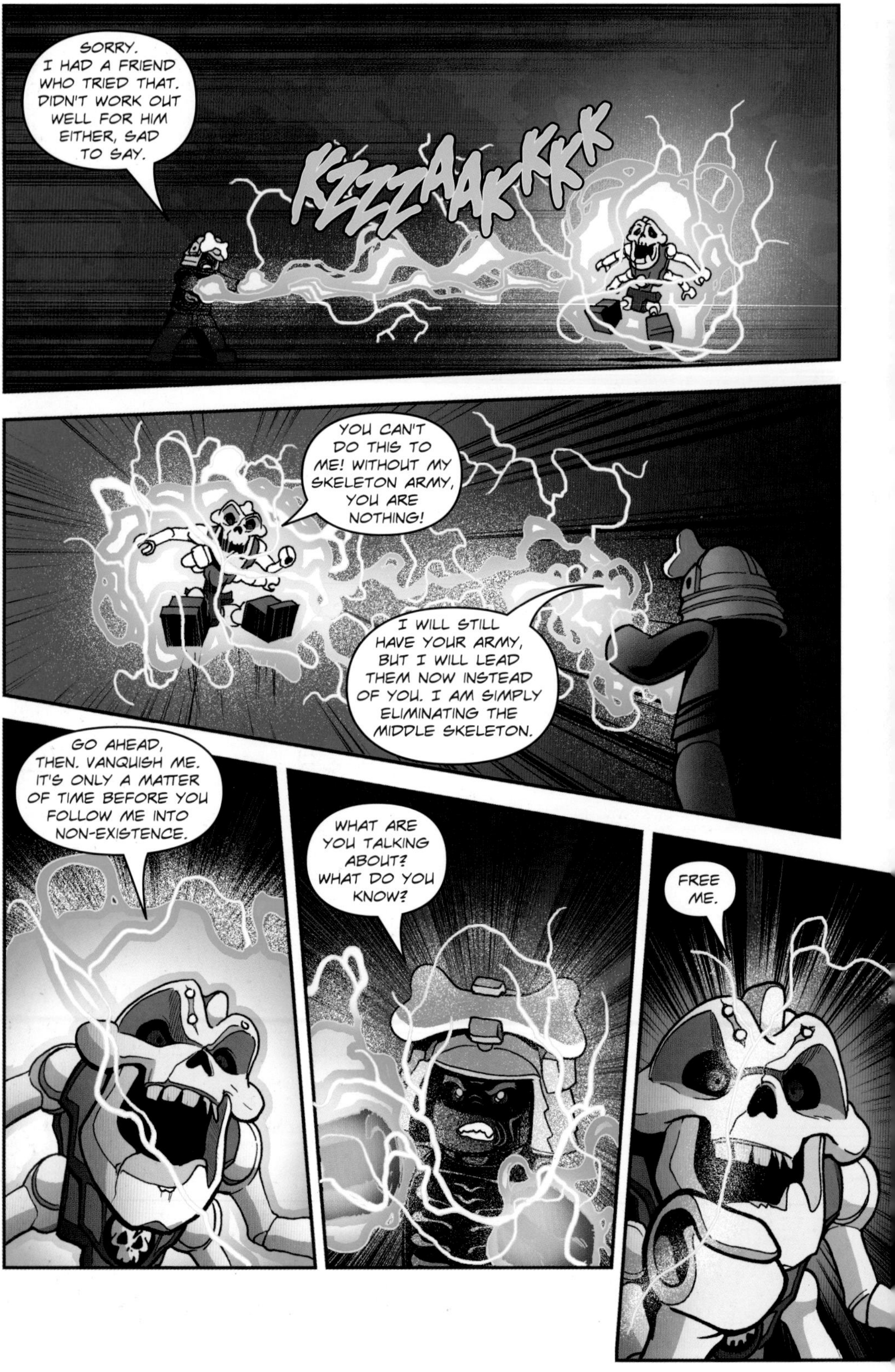
SORRY. I HAD A FRIEND WHO TRIED THAT. DIDN'T WORK OUT WELL FOR HIM EITHER, SAD TO SAY.
KZZZAAKKKK
YOU CAN'T DO THIS TO ME! WITHOUT MY SKELETON ARMY, YOU ARE NOTHING!
I WILL STILL HAVE YOUR ARMY, BUT I WILL LEAD THEM NOW INSTEAD OF YOU. I AM SIMPLY ELIMINATING THE MIDDLE SKELETON.
GO AHEAD, THEN. VANQUISH ME. IT'S ONLY A MATTER OF TIME BEFORE YOU FOLLOW ME INTO NON-EXISTENCE.
WHAT ARE YOU TALKING ABOUT? WHAT DO YOU KNOW?
FREE ME.

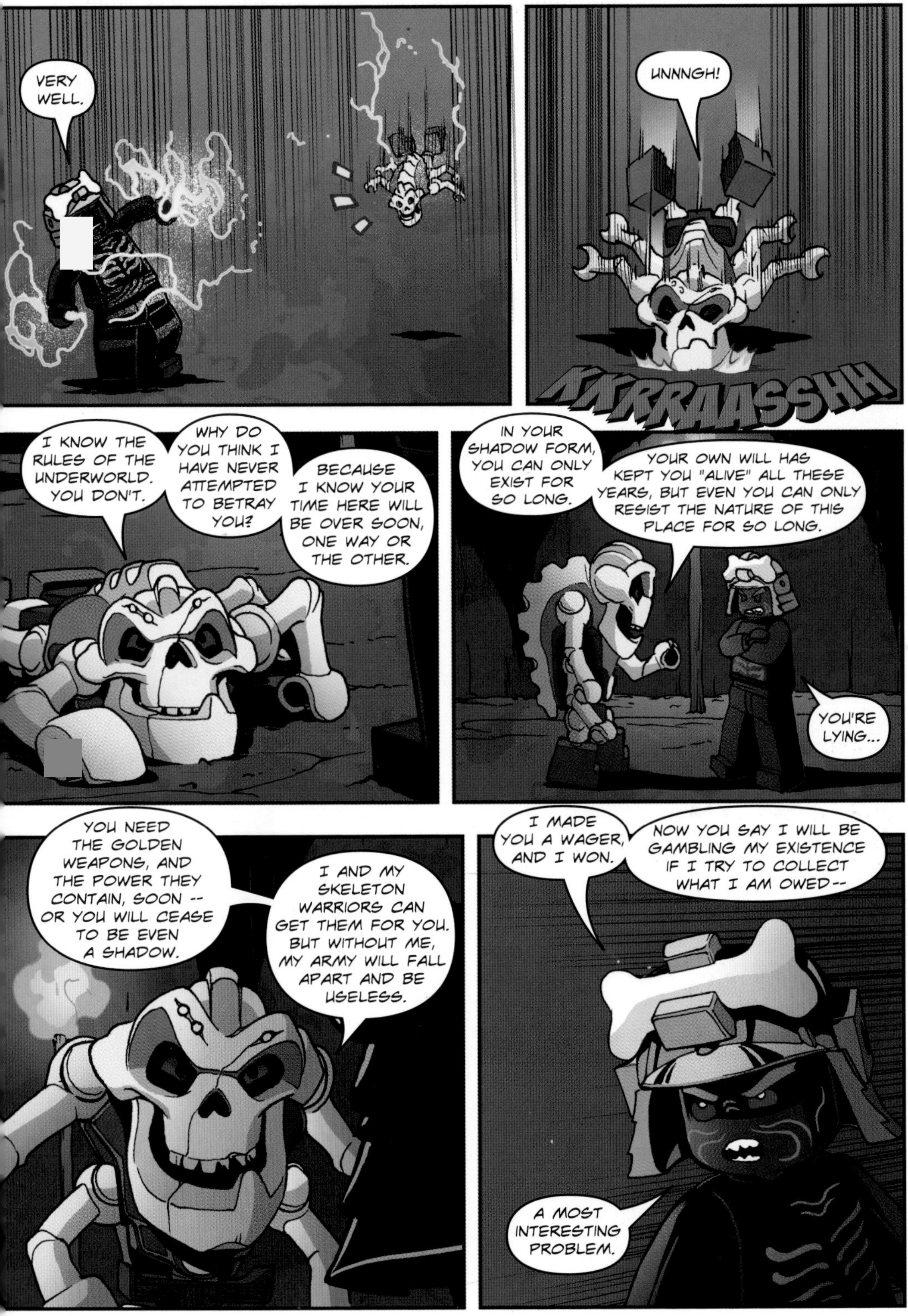
VERY WELL.
UNNNGH!
KKRRAASSHH
I KNOW THE RULES OF THE UNDERWORLD. YOU DON'T.
WHY DO YOU THINK I HAVE NEVER ATTEMPTED TO BETRAY YOU?
BECAUSE I KNOW YOUR TIME HERE WILL BE OVER SOON, ONE WAY OR THE OTHER.
IN YOUR SHADOW FORM, YOU CAN ONLY EXIST FOR SO LONG.
YOUR OWN WILL HAS KEPT YOU "ALIVE" ALL THESE YEARS, BUT EVEN YOU CAN ONLY RESIST THE NATURE OF THIS PLACE FOR SO LONG.
YOU'RE LYING...
YOU NEED THE GOLDEN WEAPONS, AND THE POWER THEY CONTAIN, SOON -- OR YOU WILL CEASE TO BE EVEN A SHADOW.
I AND MY SKELETON WARRIORS CAN GET THEM FOR YOU. BUT WITHOUT ME, MY ARMY WILL FALL APART AND BE USELESS.
I MADE YOU A WAGER, AND I WON.
NOW YOU SAY I WILL BE GAMBLING MY EXISTENCE IF I TRY TO COLLECT WHAT I AM OWED--
A MOST INTERESTING PROBLEM.

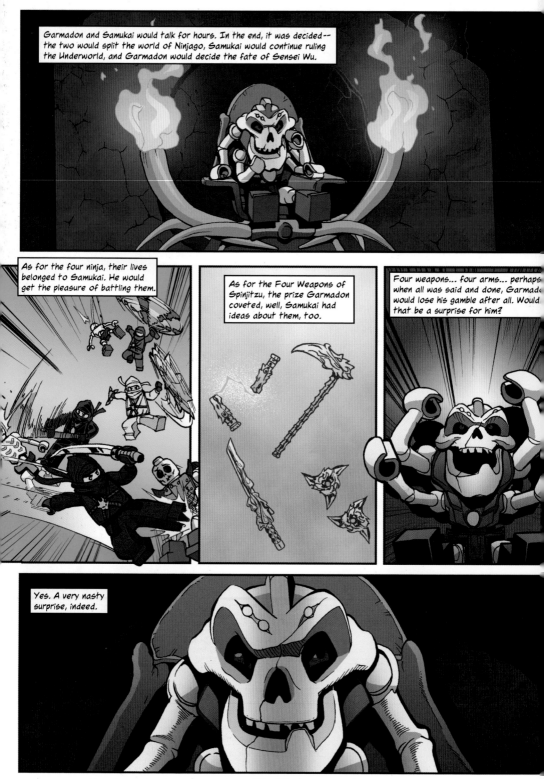

Garmadon and Samukai would talk for hours. In the end, it was decided-- the two would split the world of Ninjago, Samukai would continue ruling the Underworld, and Garmadon would decide the fate of Sensei Wu.

As for the four ninja, their lives belonged to Samukai. He would get the pleasure of battling them.

As for the Four Weapons of Spinjitzu, the prize Garmadon coveted, well, Samukai had ideas about them, too.

Four weapons... four arms... perhaps when all was said and done, Garmado would lose his gamble after all. Would that be a surprise for him?

Yes. A very nasty surprise, indeed.

The End

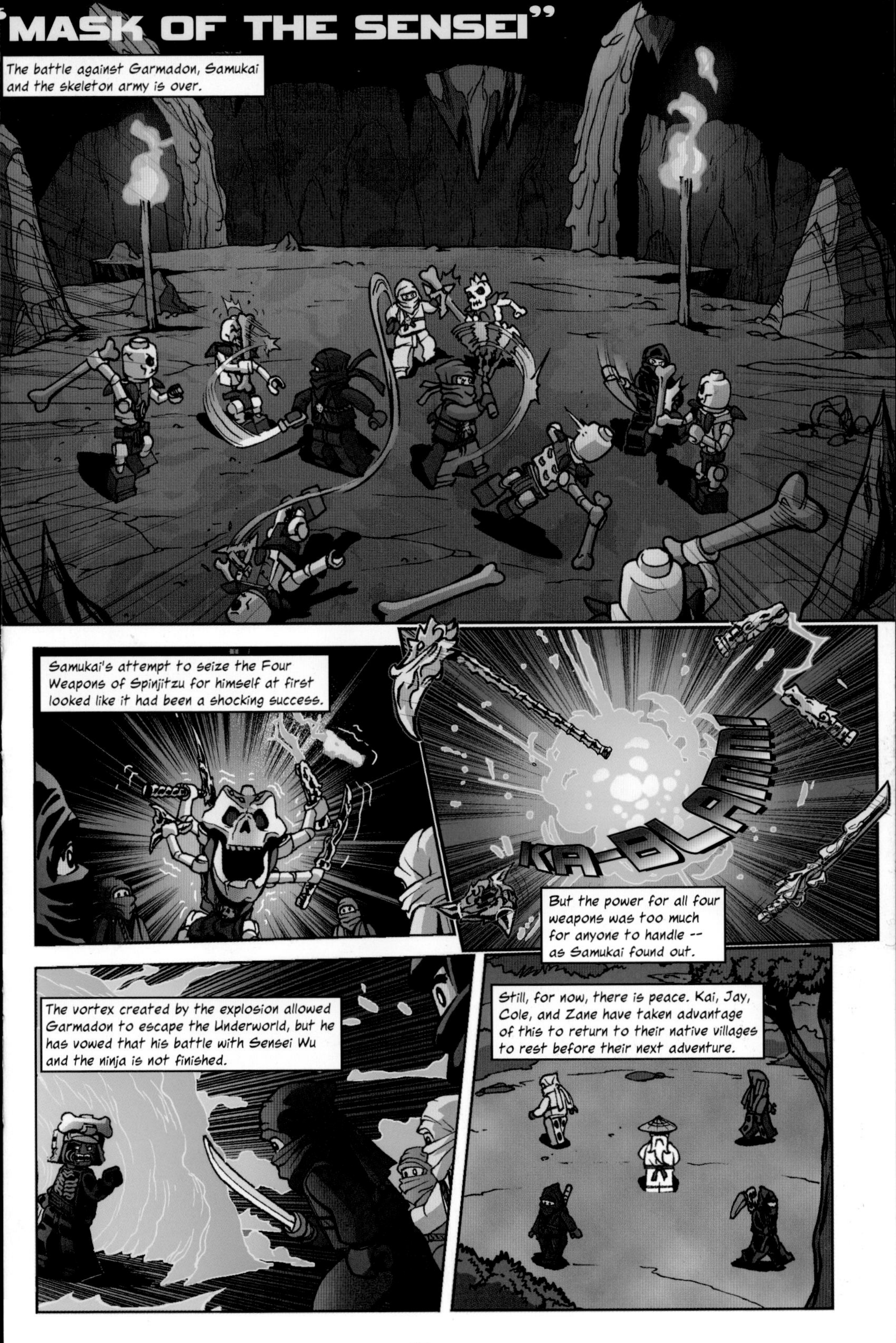
"MASK OF THE SENSEI"
The battle against Garmadon, Samukai and the skeleton army is over.
Samukai's attempt to seize the Four Weapons of Spinjitzu for himself at first looked like it had been a shocking success.
KA-BLAM!
But the power for all four weapons was too much for anyone to handle -- as Samukai found out.
The vortex created by the explosion allowed Garmadon to escape the Underworld, but he has vowed that his battle with Sensei Wu and the ninja is not finished.
Still, for now, there is peace. Kai, Jay, Cole, and Zane have taken advantage of this to return to their native villages to rest before their next adventure.

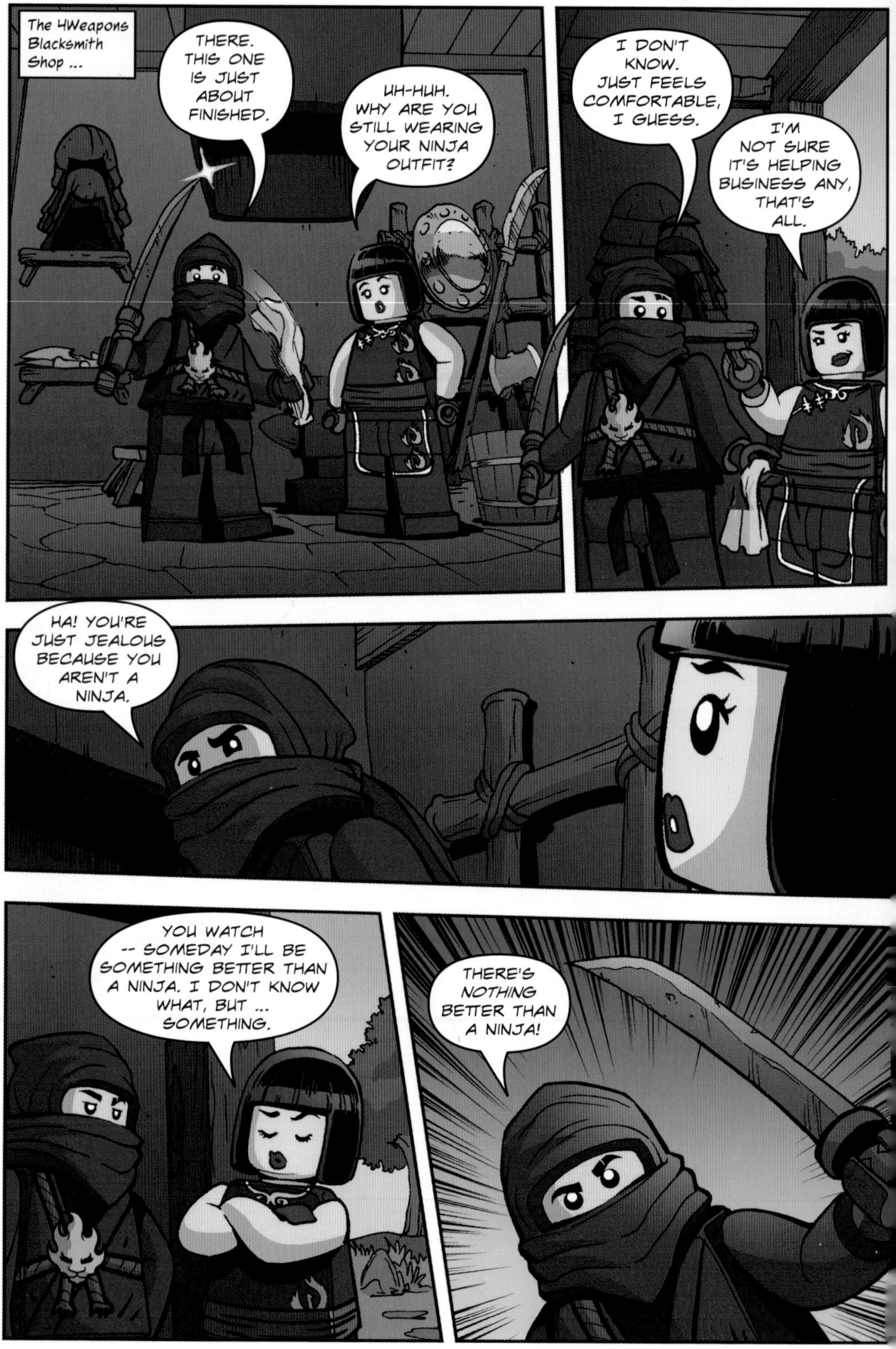

The 4Weapons Blacksmith Shop ...
THERE. THIS ONE IS JUST ABOUT FINISHED.
UH-HUH. WHY ARE YOU STILL WEARING YOUR NINJA OUTFIT?
I DON'T KNOW. JUST FEELS COMFORTABLE, I GUESS.
I'M NOT SURE IT'S HELPING BUSINESS ANY, THAT'S ALL.
HA! YOU'RE JUST JEALOUS BECAUSE YOU AREN'T A NINJA.
YOU WATCH -- SOMEDAY I'LL BE SOMETHING BETTER THAN A NINJA. I DON'T KNOW WHAT, BUT ... SOMETHING.
THERE'S NOTHING BETTER THAN A NINJA!

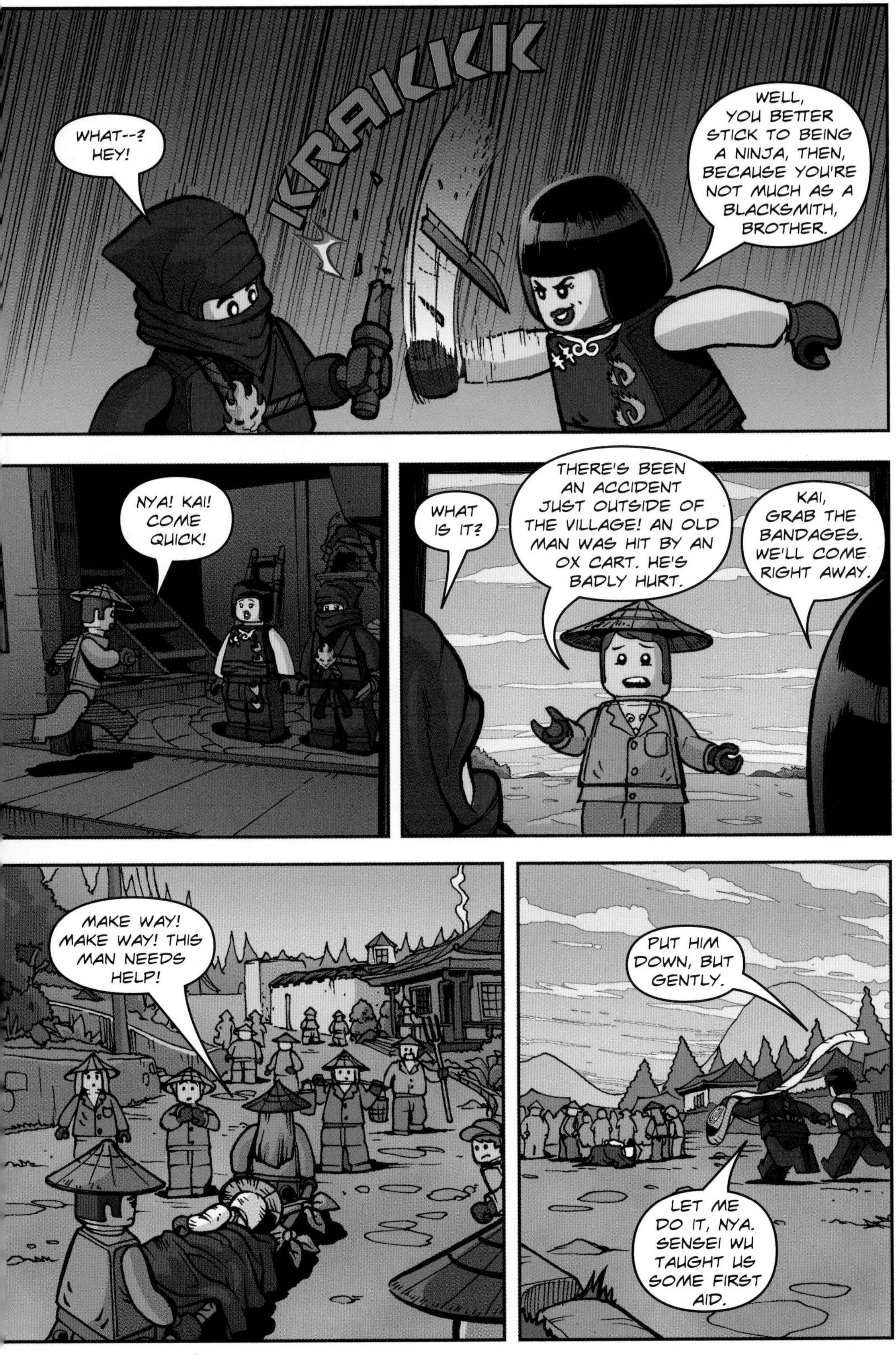
KRAKKK
WHAT--? HEY!
WELL, YOU BETTER STICK TO BEING A NINJA, THEN, BECAUSE YOU'RE NOT MUCH AS A BLACKSMITH, BROTHER.
NYA! KAI! COME QUICK!
WHAT IS IT?
THERE'S BEEN AN ACCIDENT JUST OUTSIDE OF THE VILLAGE! AN OLD MAN WAS HIT BY AN OX CART. HE'S BADLY HURT.
KAI, GRAB THE BANDAGES. WE'LL COME RIGHT AWAY.
MAKE WAY! MAKE WAY! THIS MAN NEEDS HELP!
PUT HIM DOWN, BUT GENTLY.
LET ME DO IT, NYA. SENSEI WU TAUGHT US SOME FIRST AID.

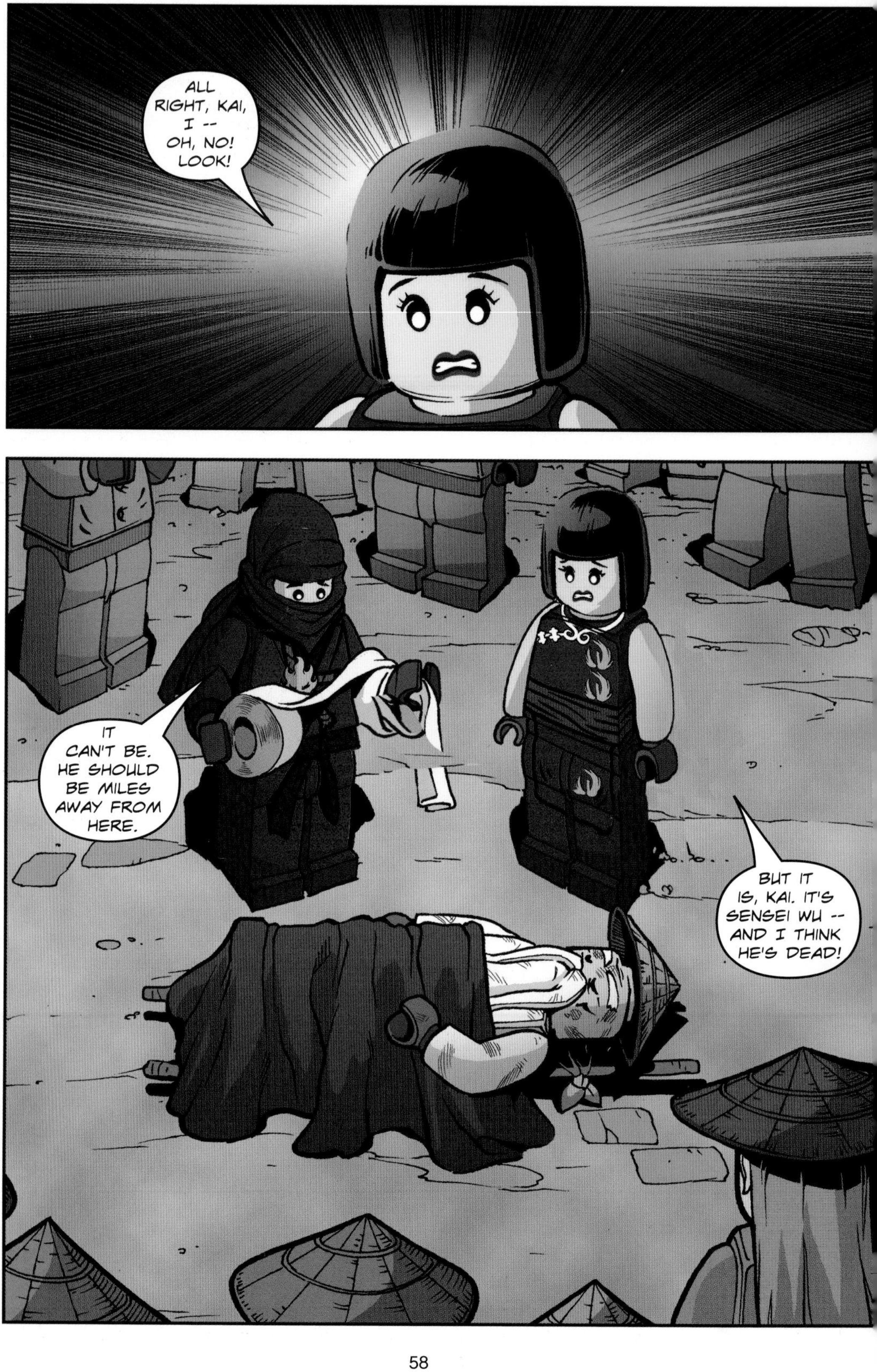
ALL RIGHT, KAI, I -- OH, NO! LOOK!
IT CAN'T BE. HE SHOULD BE MILES AWAY FROM HERE.
BUT IT IS, KAI. IT'S SENSEI WU -- AND I THINK HE'S DEAD!

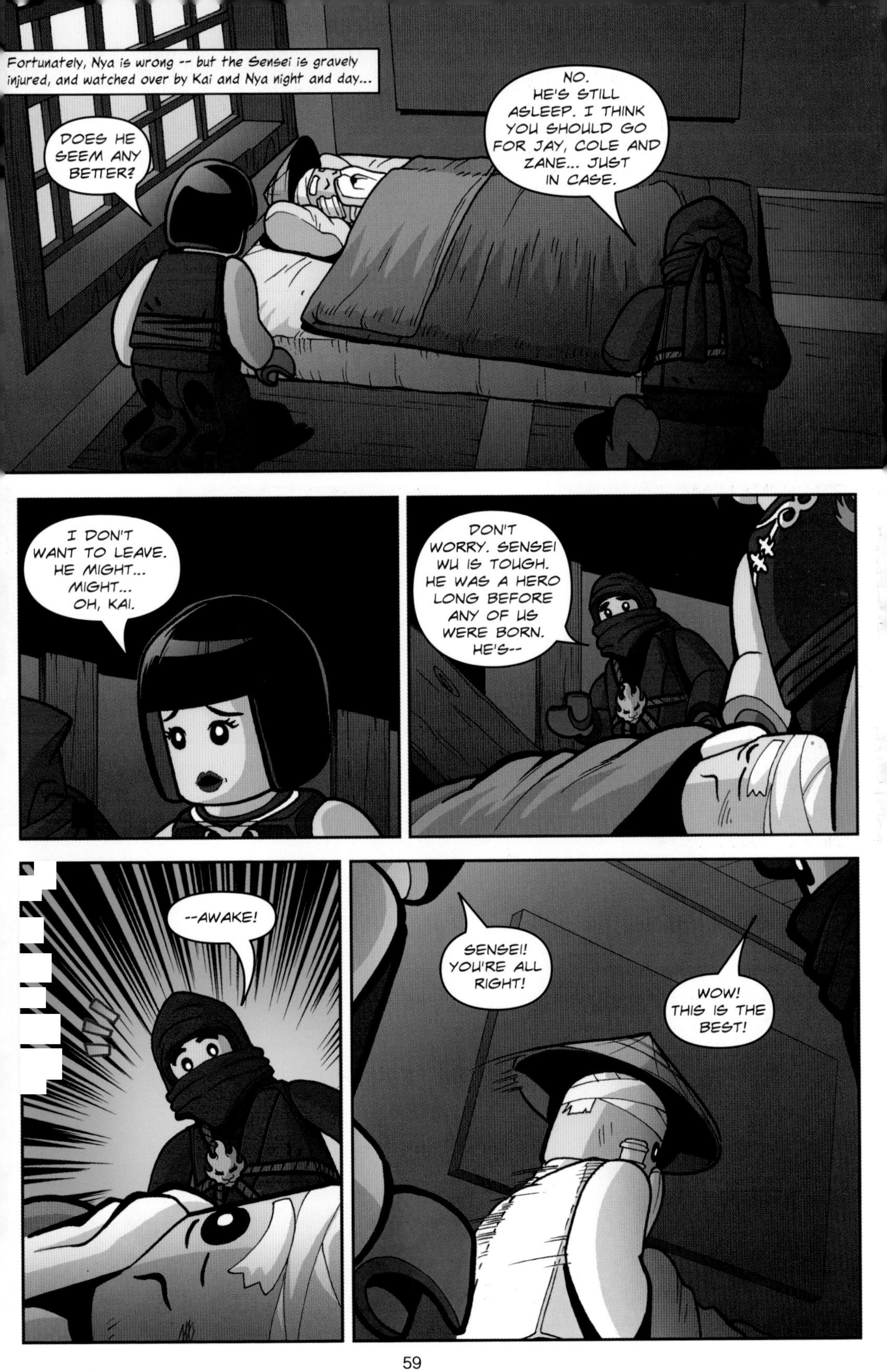
Fortunately, Nya is wrong -- but the Sensei is gravely injured, and watched over by Kai and Nya night and day...
DOES HE SEEM ANY BETTER?
NO. HE'S STILL ASLEEP. I THINK YOU SHOULD GO FOR JAY, COLE AND ZANE... JUST IN CASE.
I DON'T WANT TO LEAVE. HE MIGHT... MIGHT... OH, KAI.
DON'T WORRY. SENSEI WU IS TOUGH. HE WAS A HERO LONG BEFORE ANY OF US WERE BORN. HE'S--
--AWAKE!
SENSEI! YOU'RE ALL RIGHT!
WOW! THIS IS THE BEST!

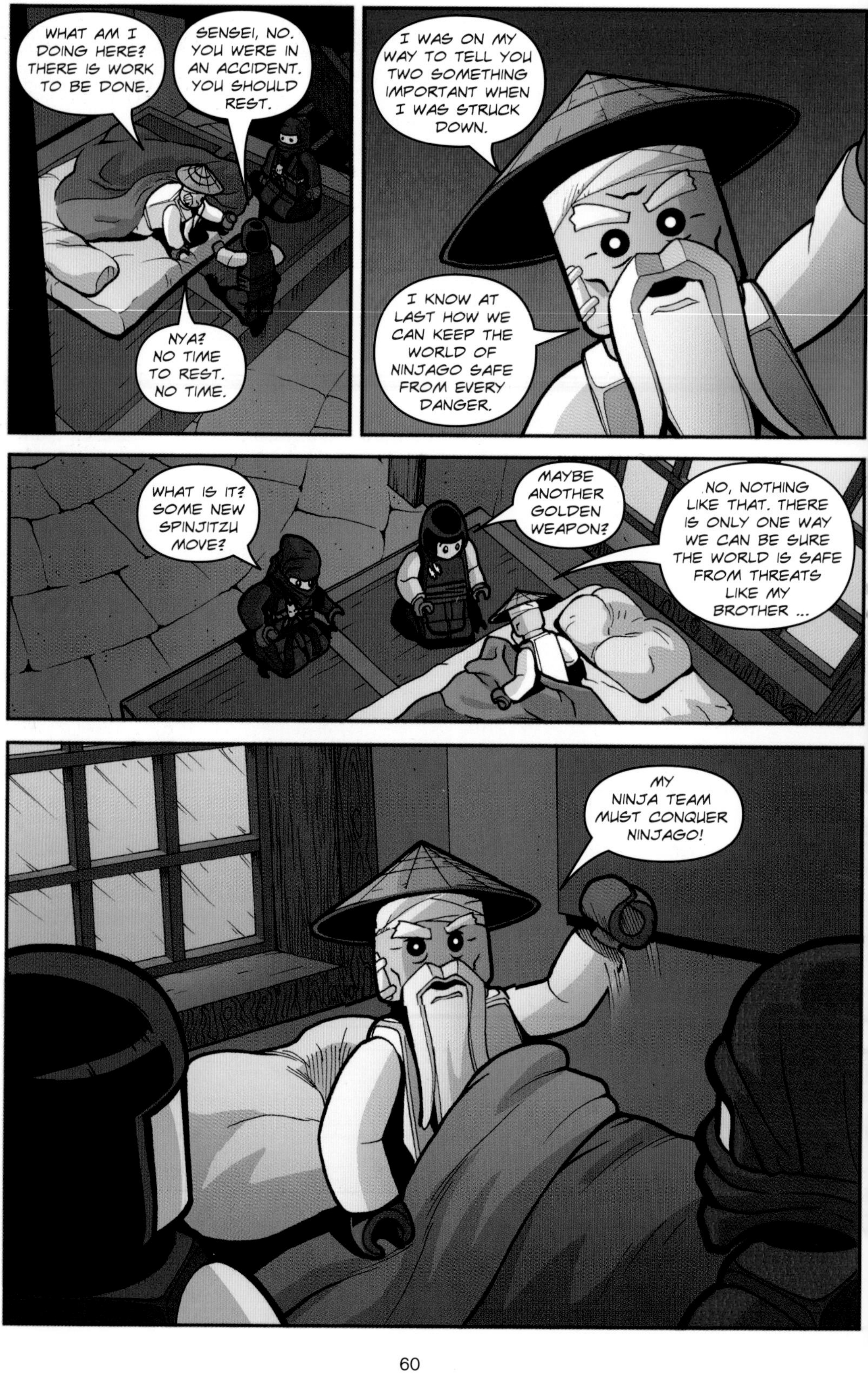
WHAT AM I DOING HERE? THERE IS WORK TO BE DONE.
SENSEI, NO. YOU WERE IN AN ACCIDENT. YOU SHOULD REST.
NYA? NO TIME TO REST. NO TIME.
I WAS ON MY WAY TO TELL YOU TWO SOMETHING IMPORTANT WHEN I WAS STRUCK DOWN.
I KNOW AT LAST HOW WE CAN KEEP THE WORLD OF NINJAGO SAFE FROM EVERY DANGER.
WHAT IS IT? SOME NEW SPINJITZU MOVE?
MAYBE ANOTHER GOLDEN WEAPON?
NO, NOTHING LIKE THAT. THERE IS ONLY ONE WAY WE CAN BE SURE THE WORLD IS SAFE FROM THREATS LIKE MY BROTHER ...
MY NINJA TEAM MUST CONQUER NINJAGO!

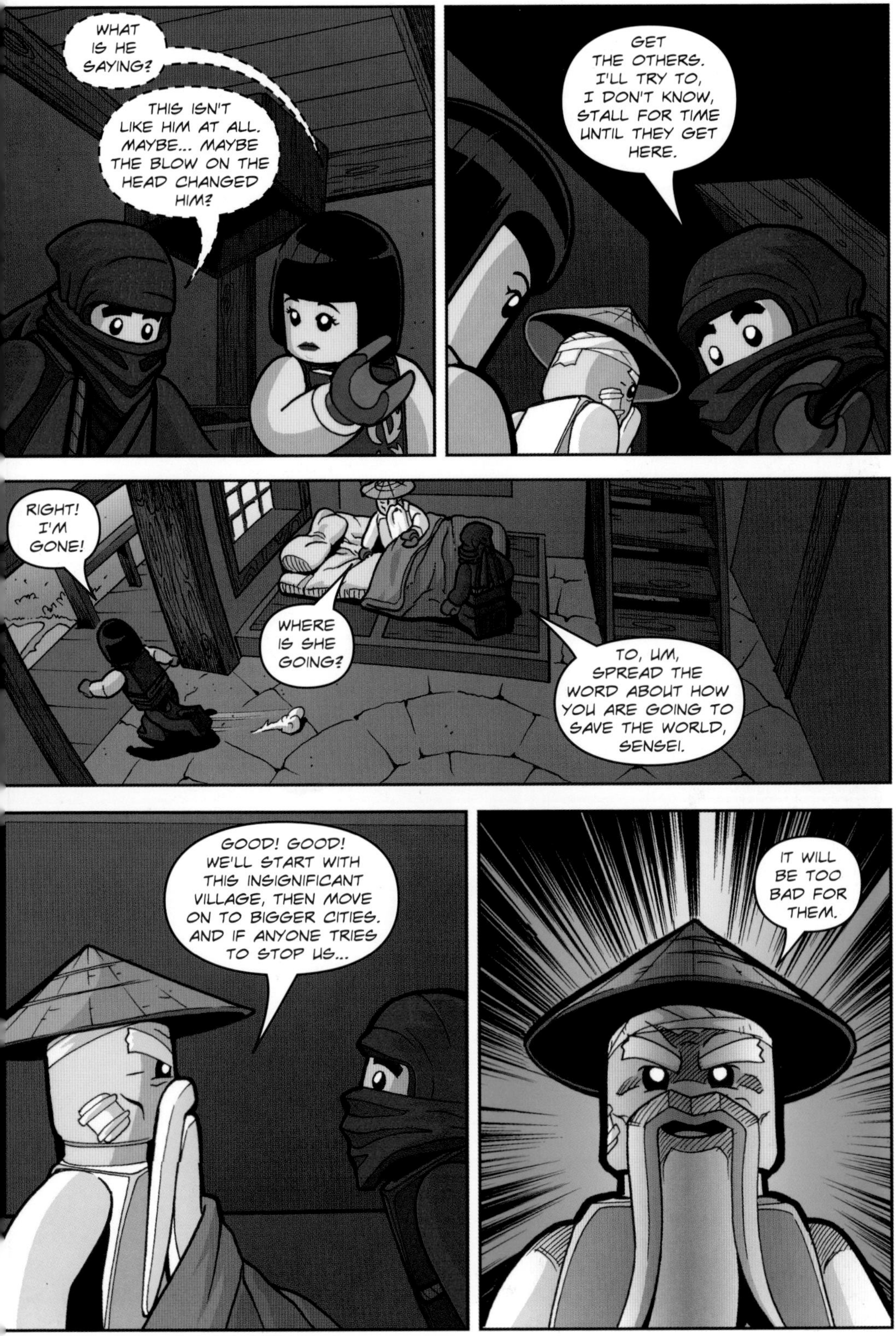
WHAT IS HE SAYING?
THIS ISN'T LIKE HIM AT ALL. MAYBE... MAYBE THE BLOW ON THE HEAD CHANGED HIM?
GET THE OTHERS. I'LL TRY TO, I DON'T KNOW, STALL FOR TIME UNTIL THEY GET HERE.
RIGHT! I'M GONE!
WHERE IS SHE GOING?
TO, UM, SPREAD THE WORD ABOUT HOW YOU ARE GOING TO SAVE THE WORLD, SENSEI.
GOOD! GOOD! WE'LL START WITH THIS INSIGNIFICANT VILLAGE, THEN MOVE ON TO BIGGER CITIES. AND IF ANYONE TRIES TO STOP US...
IT WILL BE TOO BAD FOR THEM.

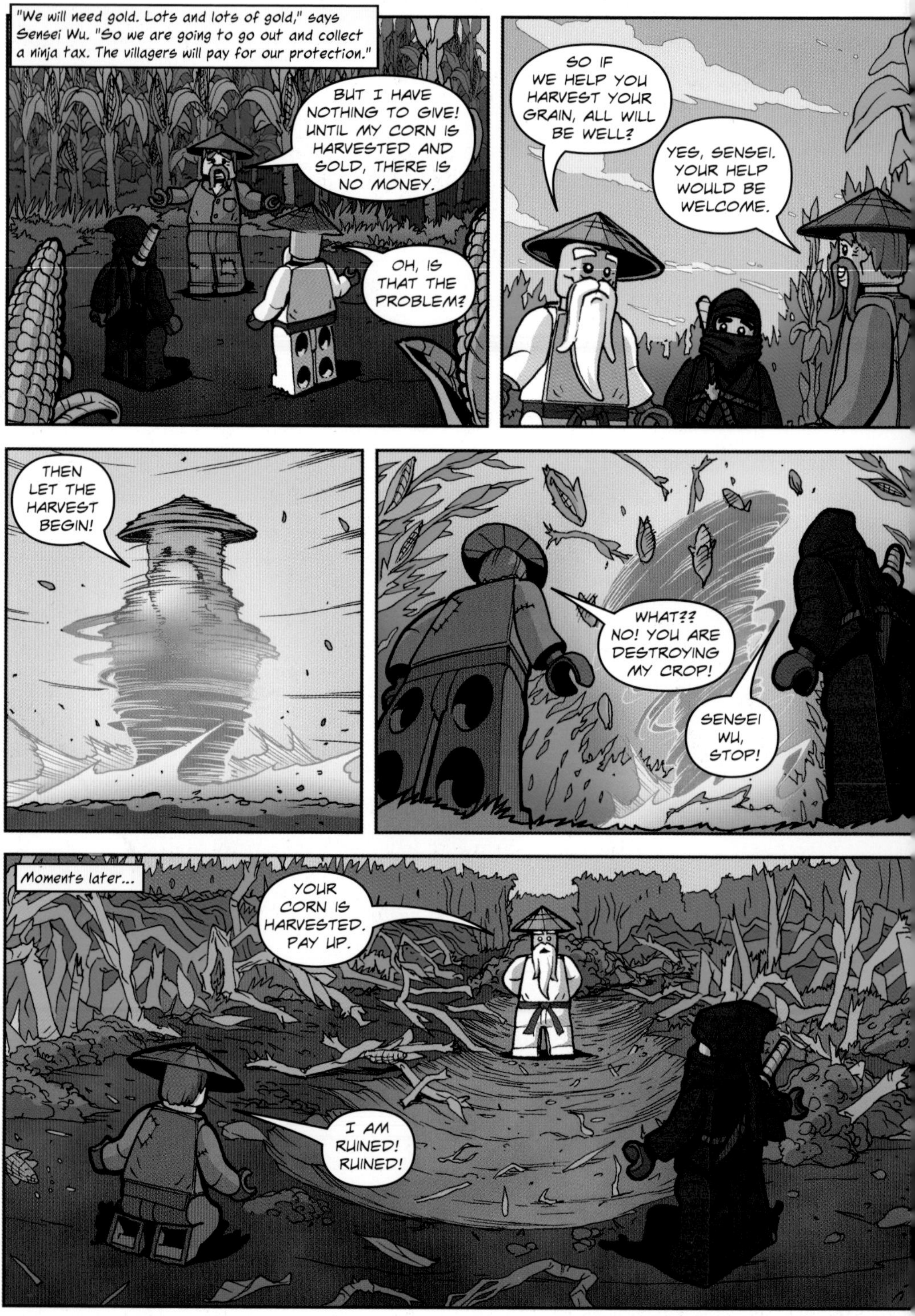
"We will need gold. Lots and lots of gold," says Sensei Wu. "So we are going to go out and collect a ninja tax. The villagers will pay for our protection."
BUT I HAVE NOTHING TO GIVE! UNTIL MY CORN IS HARVESTED AND SOLD, THERE IS NO MONEY.
OH, IS THAT THE PROBLEM?
SO IF WE HELP YOU HARVEST YOUR GRAIN, ALL WILL BE WELL?
YES, SENSEI. YOUR HELP WOULD BE WELCOME.
THEN LET THE HARVEST BEGIN!
WHAT?? NO! YOU ARE DESTROYING MY CROP!
SENSEI WU, STOP!
Moments later...
YOUR CORN IS HARVESTED. PAY UP.
I AM RUINED! RUINED!

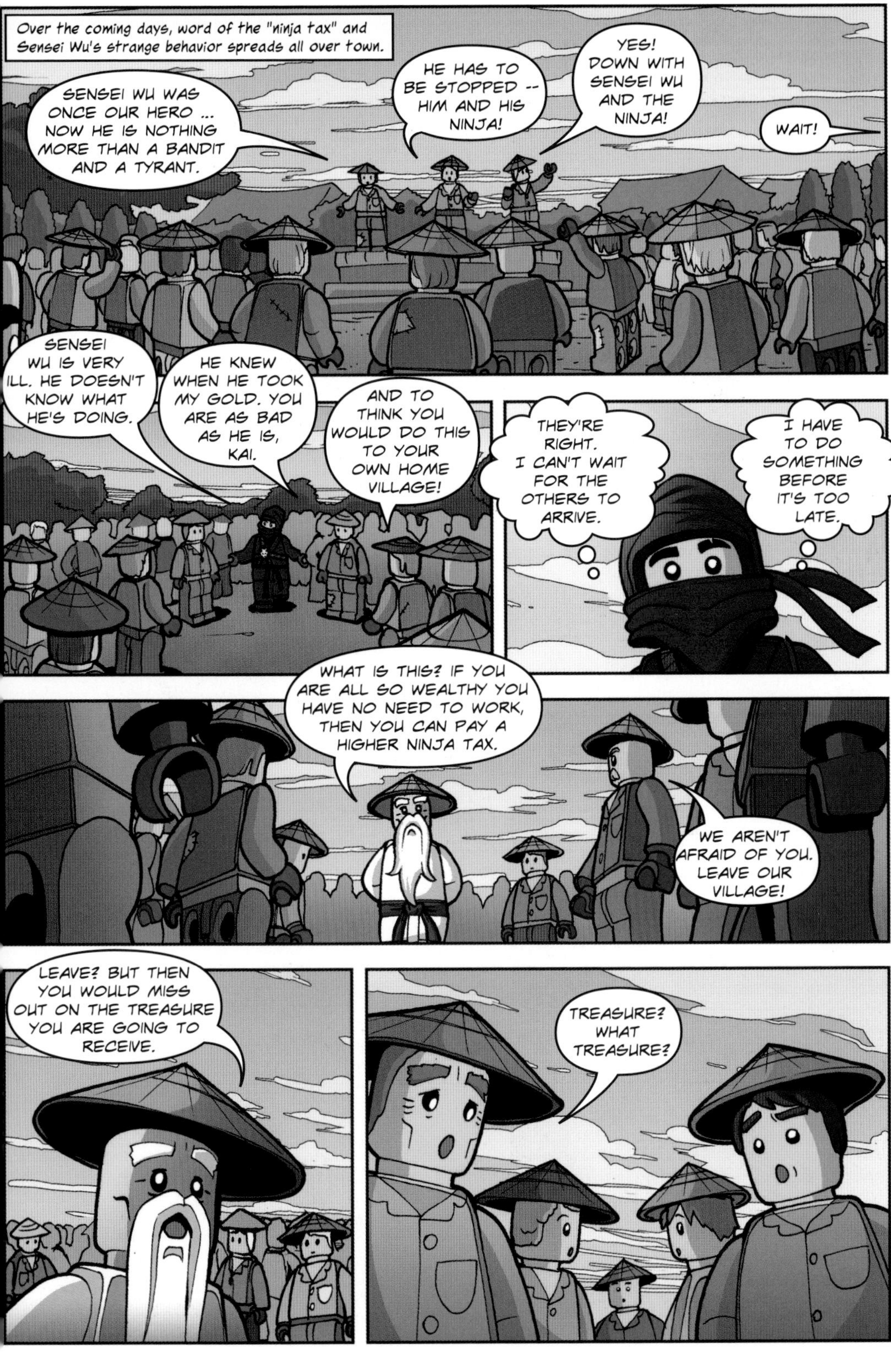
Over the coming days, word of the "ninja tax" and Sensei Wu's strange behavior spreads all over town.
SENSEI WU WAS ONCE OUR HERO ... NOW HE IS NOTHING MORE THAN A BANDIT AND A TYRANT.
HE HAS TO BE STOPPED -- HIM AND HIS NINJA!
YES! DOWN WITH SENSEI WU AND THE NINJA!
WAIT!
SENSEI WU IS VERY ILL. HE DOESN'T KNOW WHAT HE'S DOING.
HE KNEW WHEN HE TOOK MY GOLD. YOU ARE AS BAD AS HE IS, KAI.
AND TO THINK YOU WOULD DO THIS TO YOUR OWN HOME VILLAGE!
THEY'RE RIGHT. I CAN'T WAIT FOR THE OTHERS TO ARRIVE.
I HAVE TO DO SOMETHING BEFORE IT'S TOO LATE.
WHAT IS THIS? IF YOU ARE ALL SO WEALTHY YOU HAVE NO NEED TO WORK, THEN YOU CAN PAY A HIGHER NINJA TAX.
WE AREN'T AFRAID OF YOU. LEAVE OUR VILLAGE!
LEAVE? BUT THEN YOU WOULD MISS OUT ON THE TREASURE YOU ARE GOING TO RECEIVE.
TREASURE? WHAT TREASURE?

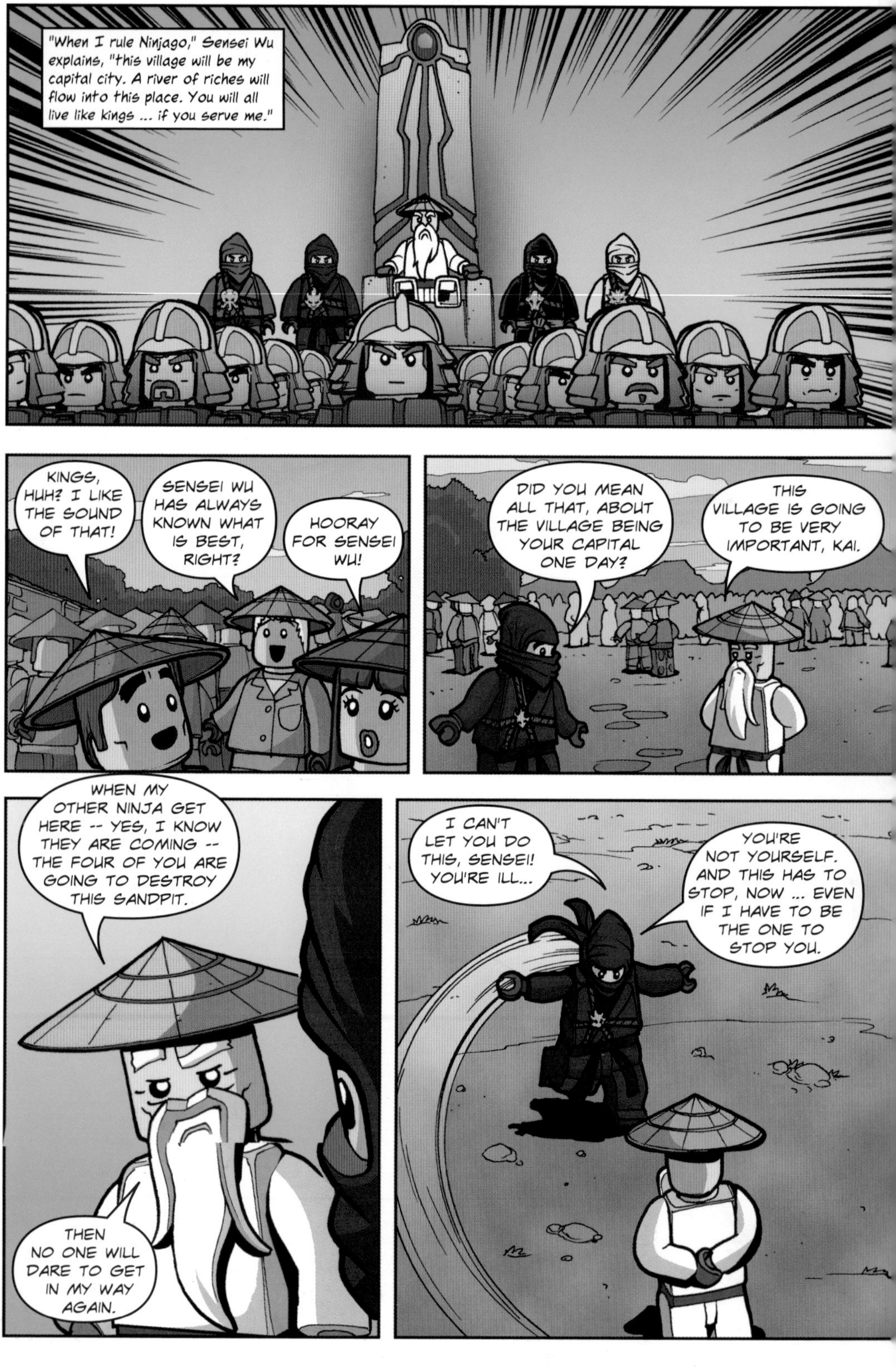
"When I rule Ninjago," Sensei Wu explains, "this village will be my capital city. A river of riches will flow into this place. You will all live like kings ... if you serve me."
KINGS, HUH? I LIKE THE SOUND OF THAT!
SENSEI WU HAS ALWAYS KNOWN WHAT IS BEST, RIGHT?
HOORAY FOR SENSEI WU!
DID YOU MEAN ALL THAT, ABOUT THE VILLAGE BEING YOUR CAPITAL ONE DAY?
THIS VILLAGE IS GOING TO BE VERY IMPORTANT, KAI.
WHEN MY OTHER NINJA GET HERE -- YES, I KNOW THEY ARE COMING -- THE FOUR OF YOU ARE GOING TO DESTROY THIS SANDPIT.
THEN NO ONE WILL DARE TO GET IN MY WAY AGAIN.
I CAN'T LET YOU DO THIS, SENSEI! YOU'RE ILL...
YOU'RE NOT YOURSELF. AND THIS HAS TO STOP, NOW ... EVEN IF I HAVE TO BE THE ONE TO STOP YOU.

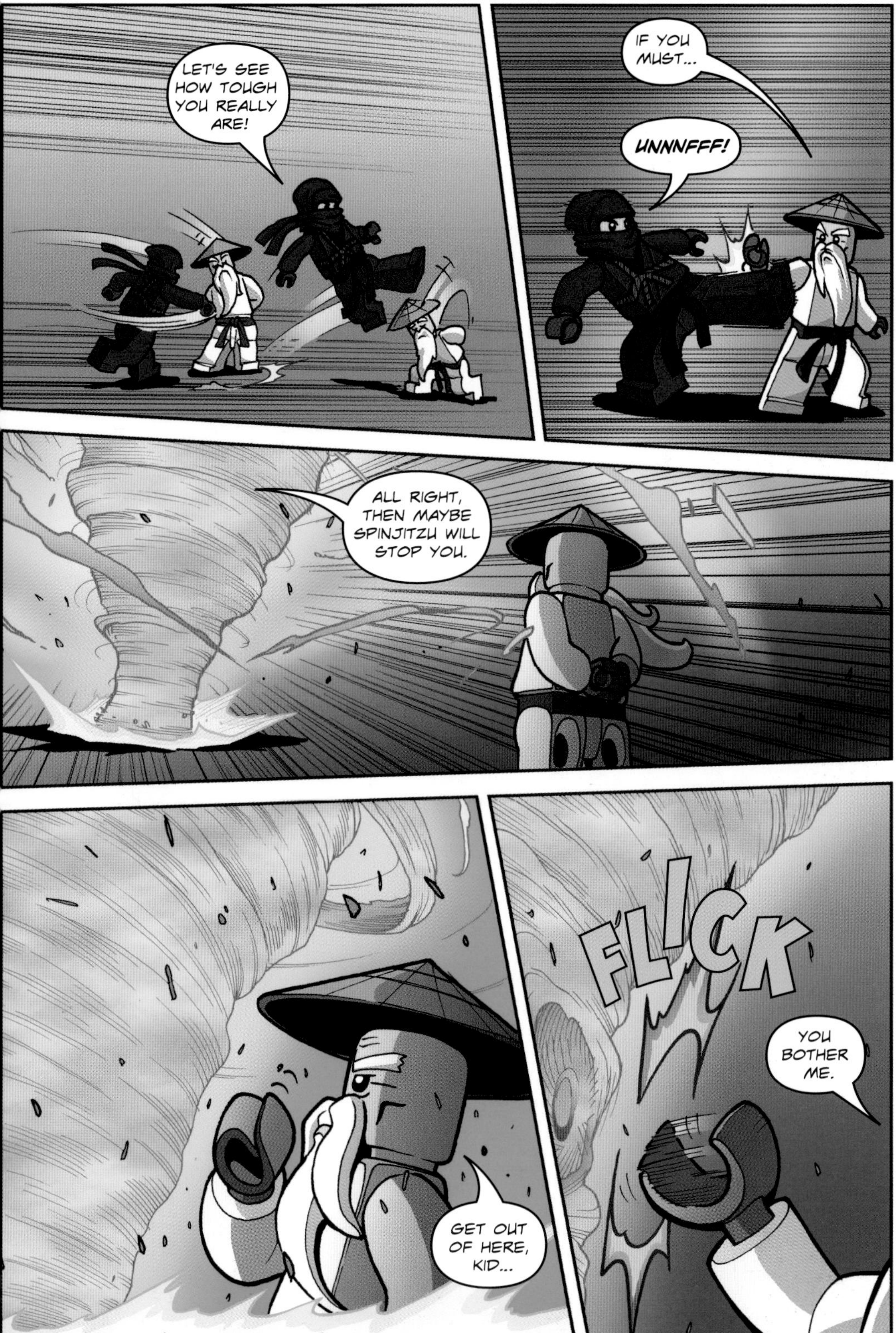
LET'S SEE HOW TOUGH YOU REALLY ARE!
IF YOU MUST...
UNNNFFF!
ALL RIGHT, THEN MAYBE SPINJITZU WILL STOP YOU.
GET OUT OF HERE, KID...
FLICK
YOU BOTHER ME.

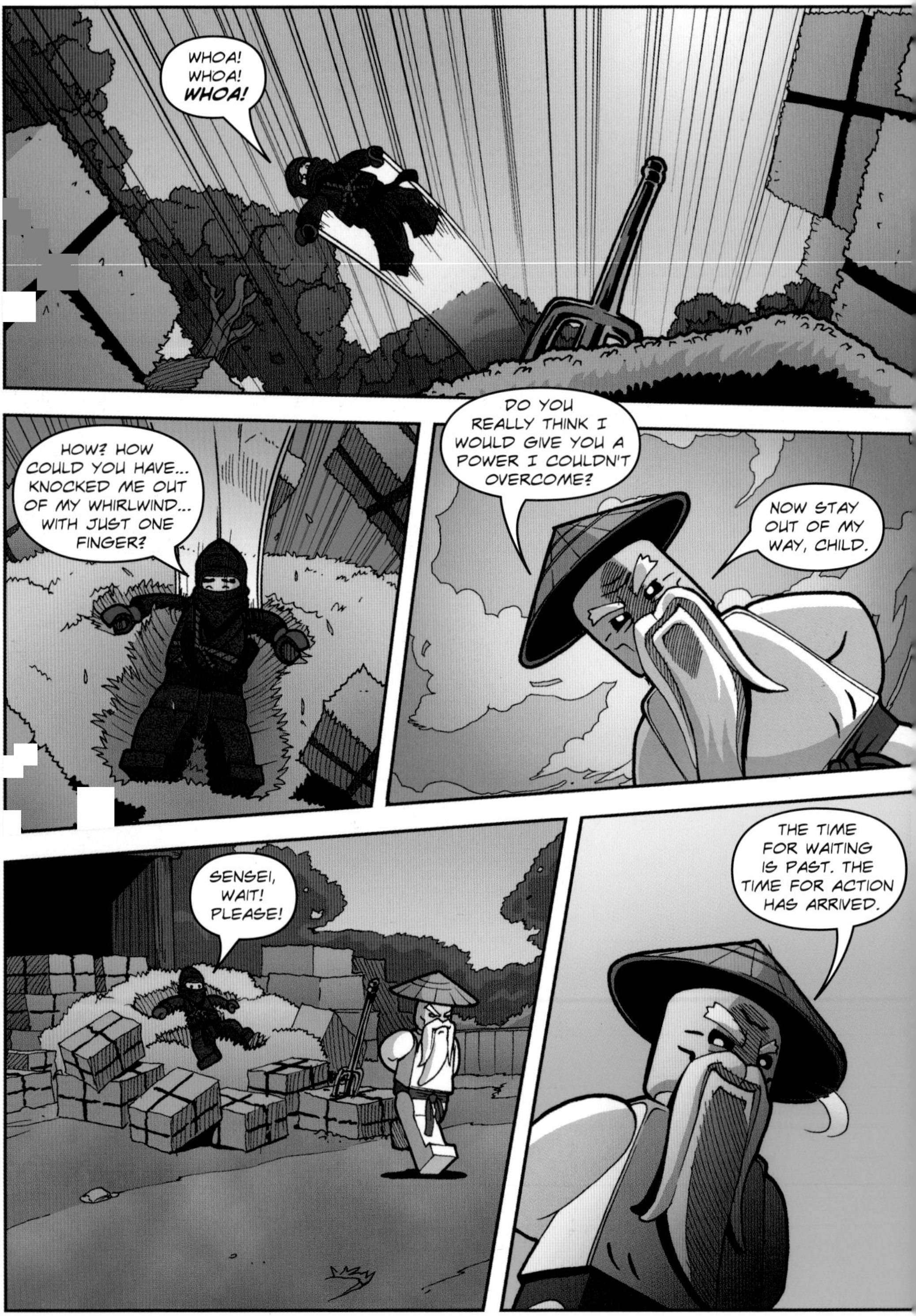
WHOA! WHOA! WHOA!
HOW? HOW COULD YOU HAVE... KNOCKED ME OUT OF MY WHIRLWIND... WITH JUST ONE FINGER?
DO YOU REALLY THINK I WOULD GIVE YOU A POWER I COULDN'T OVERCOME?
NOW STAY OUT OF MY WAY, CHILD.
SENSEI, WAIT! PLEASE!
THE TIME FOR WAITING IS PAST. THE TIME FOR ACTION HAS ARRIVED.

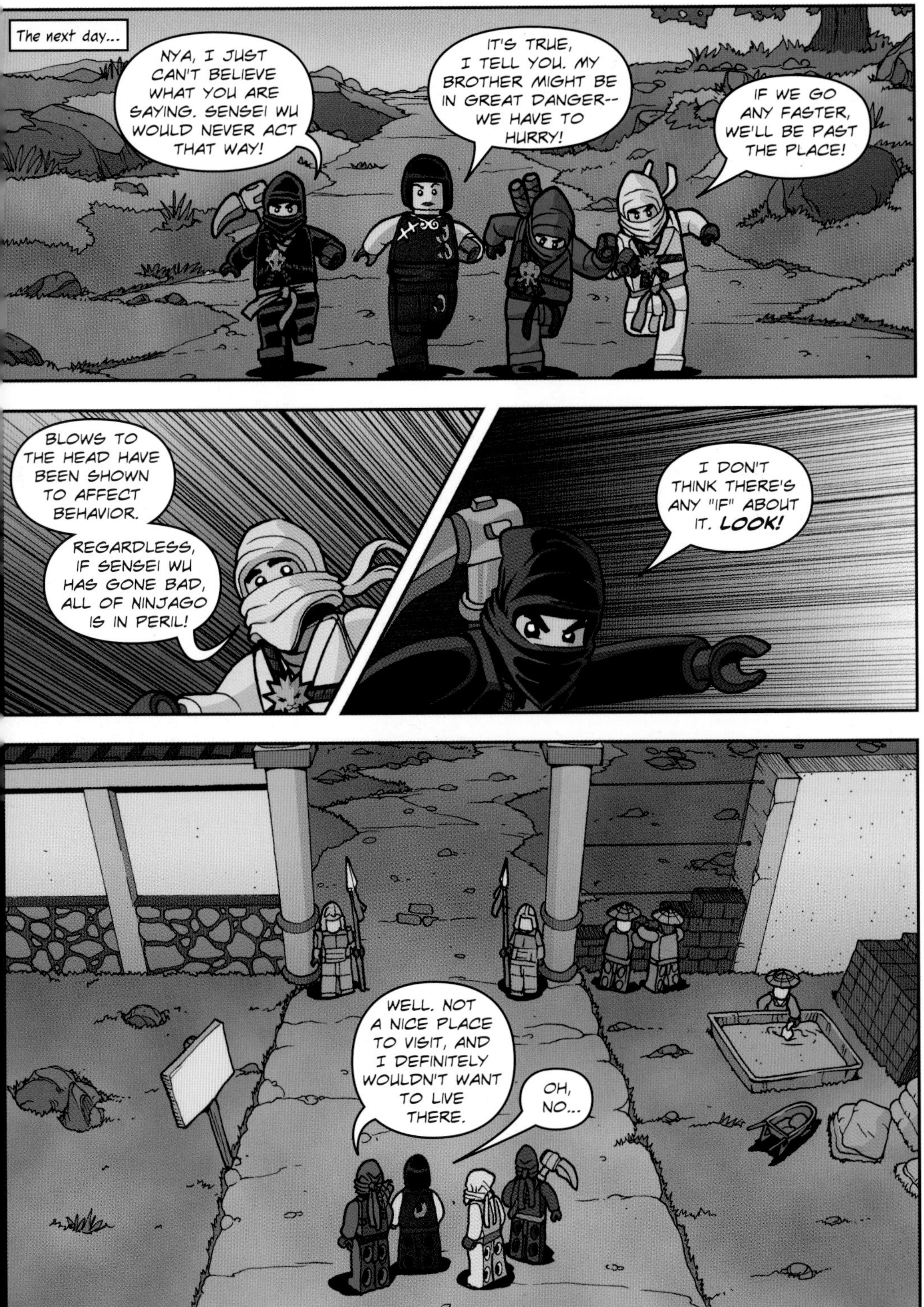
The next day...
NYA, I JUST CAN'T BELIEVE WHAT YOU ARE SAYING. SENSEI WU WOULD NEVER ACT THAT WAY!
IT'S TRUE, I TELL YOU. MY BROTHER MIGHT BE IN GREAT DANGER-- WE HAVE TO HURRY!
IF WE GO ANY FASTER, WE'LL BE PAST THE PLACE!
BLOWS TO THE HEAD HAVE BEEN SHOWN TO AFFECT BEHAVIOR.
REGARDLESS, IF SENSEI WU HAS GONE BAD, ALL OF NINJAGO IS IN PERIL!
I DON'T THINK THERE'S ANY "IF" ABOUT IT. **LOOK!**
WELL. NOT A NICE PLACE TO VISIT, AND I DEFINITELY WOULDN'T WANT TO LIVE THERE.
OH, NO...

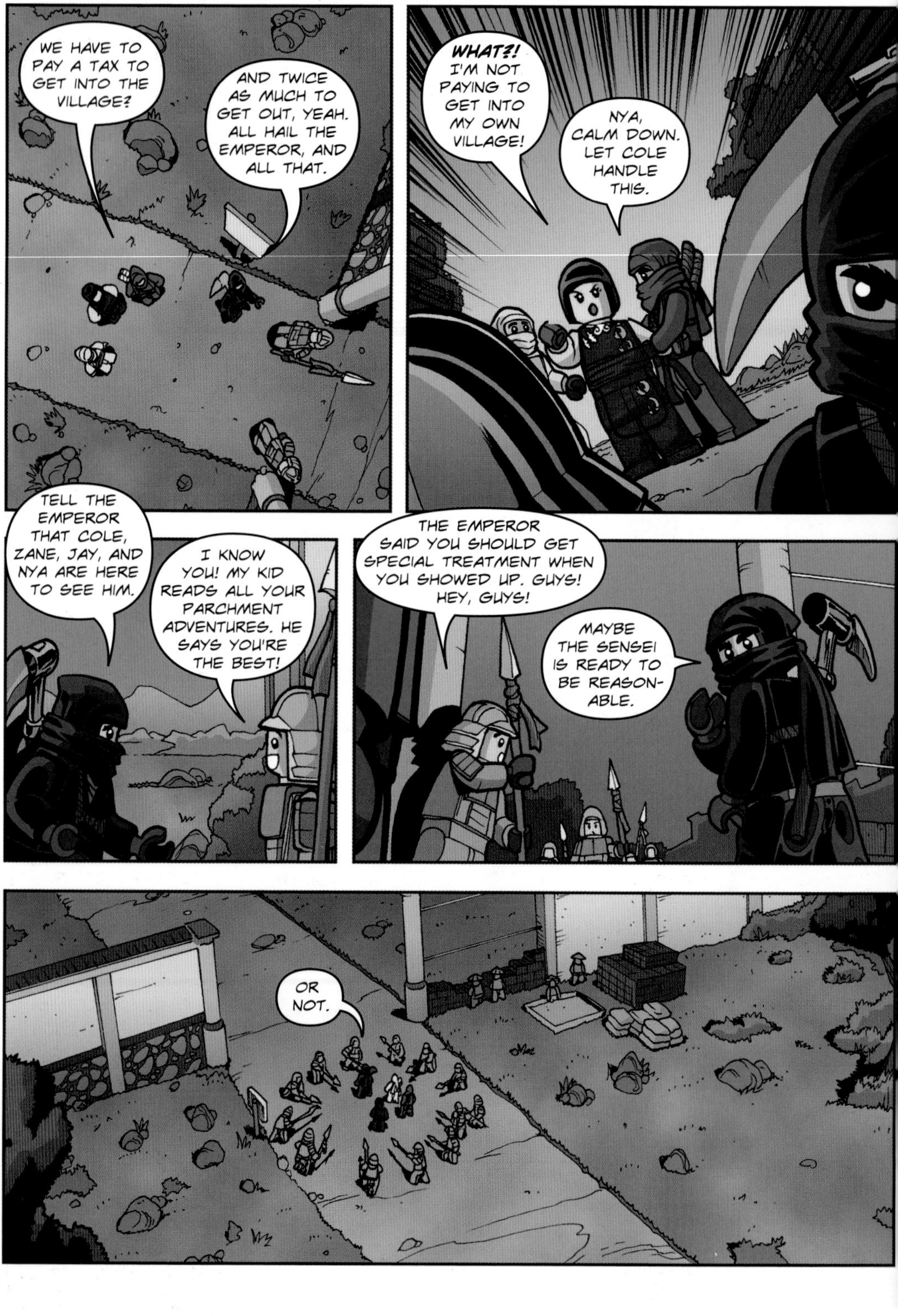
WE HAVE TO PAY A TAX TO GET INTO THE VILLAGE?
AND TWICE AS MUCH TO GET OUT, YEAH. ALL HAIL THE EMPEROR, AND ALL THAT.
WHAT?! I'M NOT PAYING TO GET INTO MY OWN VILLAGE!
NYA, CALM DOWN. LET COLE HANDLE THIS.
TELL THE EMPEROR THAT COLE, ZANE, JAY, AND NYA ARE HERE TO SEE HIM.
I KNOW YOU! MY KID READS ALL YOUR PARCHMENT ADVENTURES. HE SAYS YOU'RE THE BEST!
THE EMPEROR SAID YOU SHOULD GET SPECIAL TREATMENT WHEN YOU SHOWED UP. GUYS! HEY, GUYS!
MAYBE THE SENSEI IS READY TO BE REASON-ABLE.
OR NOT.

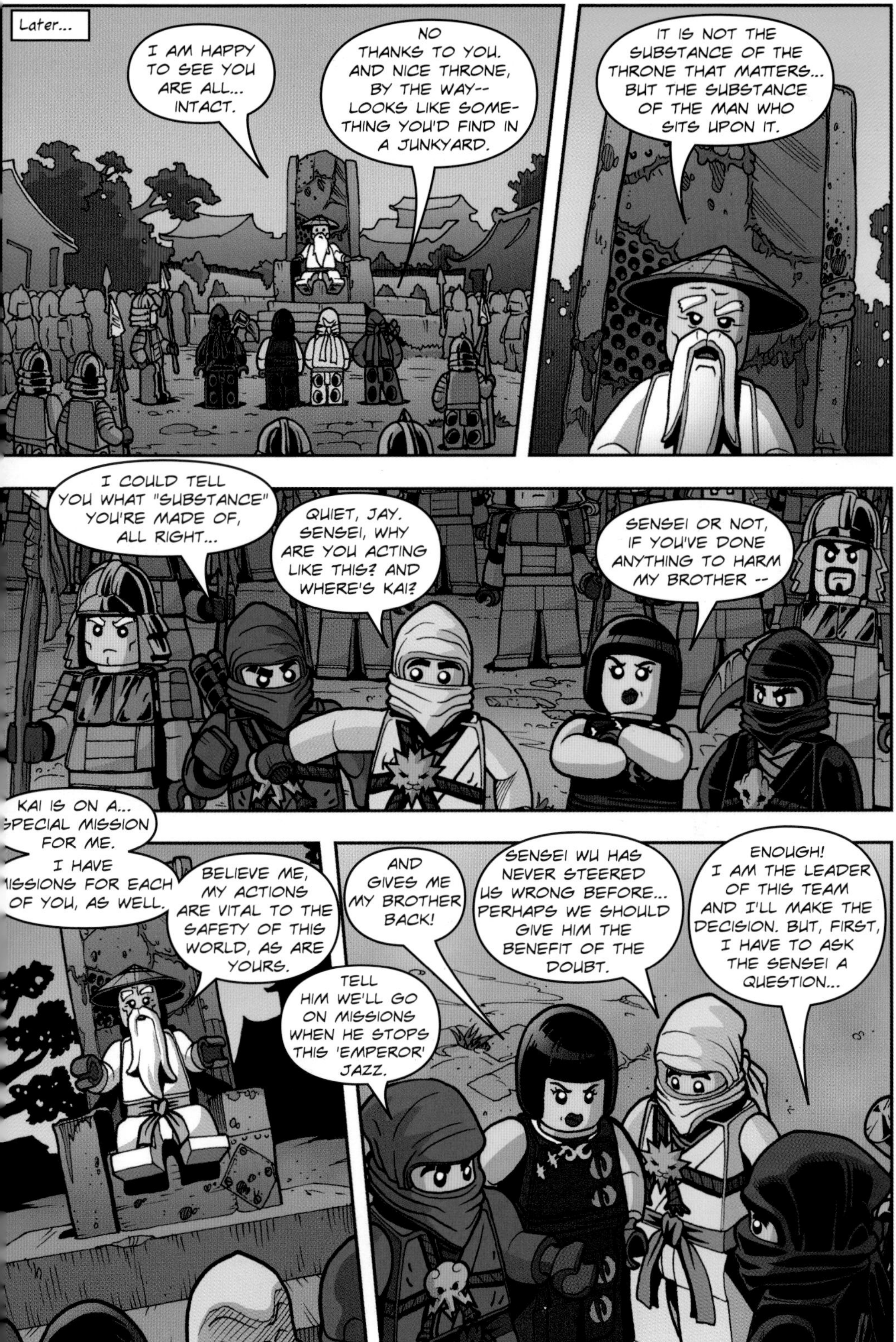
Later...
I AM HAPPY TO SEE YOU ARE ALL... INTACT.
NO THANKS TO YOU. AND NICE THRONE, BY THE WAY-- LOOKS LIKE SOME-THING YOU'D FIND IN A JUNKYARD.
IT IS NOT THE SUBSTANCE OF THE THRONE THAT MATTERS... BUT THE SUBSTANCE OF THE MAN WHO SITS UPON IT.
I COULD TELL YOU WHAT "SUBSTANCE" YOU'RE MADE OF, ALL RIGHT...
QUIET, JAY. SENSEI, WHY ARE YOU ACTING LIKE THIS? AND WHERE'S KAI?
SENSEI OR NOT, IF YOU'VE DONE ANYTHING TO HARM MY BROTHER --
KAI IS ON A... SPECIAL MISSION FOR ME.
I HAVE MISSIONS FOR EACH OF YOU, AS WELL.
BELIEVE ME, MY ACTIONS ARE VITAL TO THE SAFETY OF THIS WORLD, AS ARE YOURS.
TELL HIM WE'LL GO ON MISSIONS WHEN HE STOPS THIS 'EMPEROR' JAZZ.
AND GIVES ME MY BROTHER BACK!
SENSEI WU HAS NEVER STEERED US WRONG BEFORE... PERHAPS WE SHOULD GIVE HIM THE BENEFIT OF THE DOUBT.
ENOUGH! I AM THE LEADER OF THIS TEAM AND I'LL MAKE THE DECISION. BUT, FIRST, I HAVE TO ASK THE SENSEI A QUESTION...

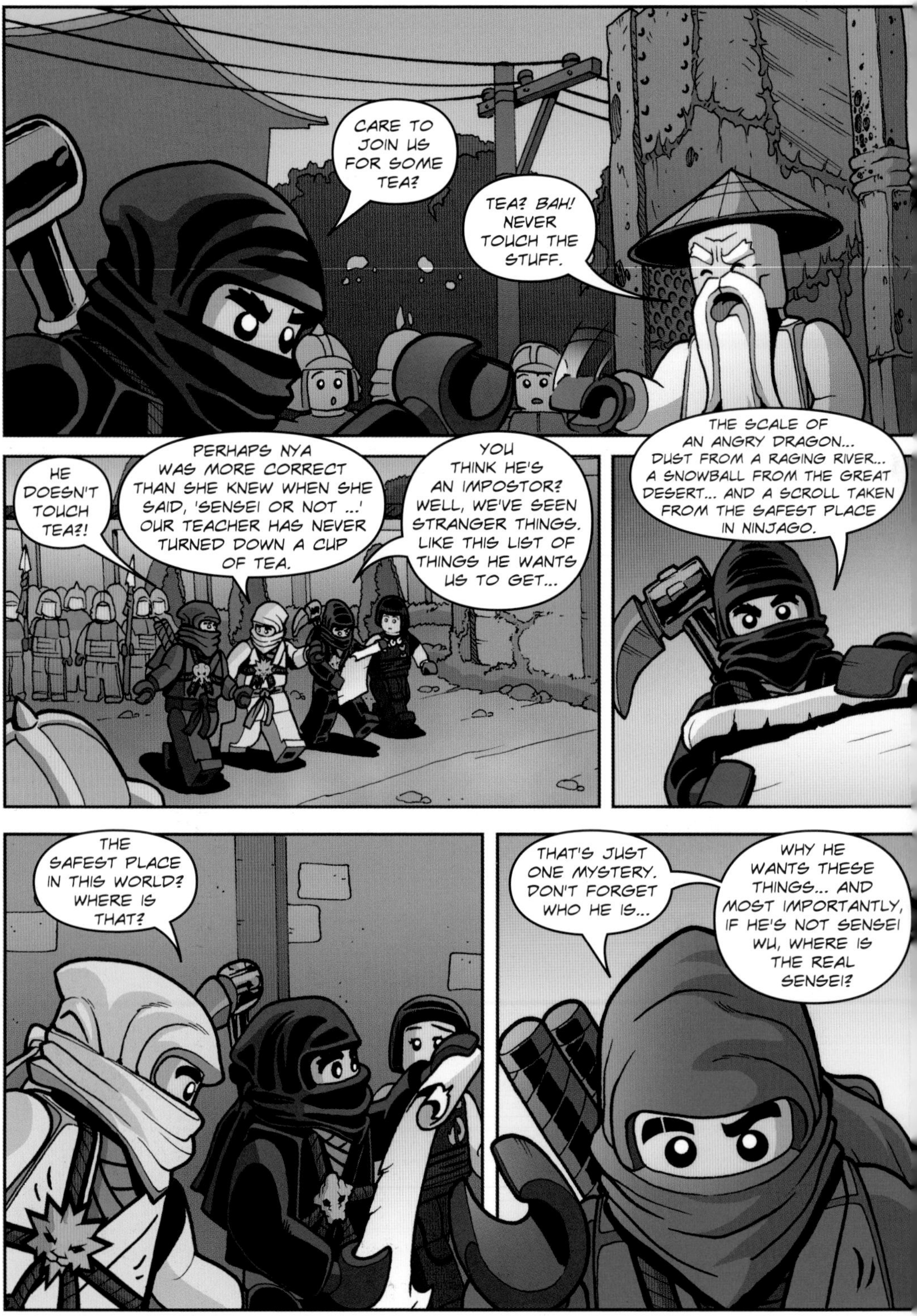
CARE TO JOIN US FOR SOME TEA?
TEA? BAH! NEVER TOUCH THE STUFF.
HE DOESN'T TOUCH TEA?!
PERHAPS NYA WAS MORE CORRECT THAN SHE KNEW WHEN SHE SAID, 'SENSEI OR NOT ...' OUR TEACHER HAS NEVER TURNED DOWN A CUP OF TEA.
YOU THINK HE'S AN IMPOSTOR? WELL, WE'VE SEEN STRANGER THINGS. LIKE THIS LIST OF THINGS HE WANTS US TO GET...
THE SCALE OF AN ANGRY DRAGON... DUST FROM A RAGING RIVER... A SNOWBALL FROM THE GREAT DESERT... AND A SCROLL TAKEN FROM THE SAFEST PLACE IN NINJAGO.
THE SAFEST PLACE IN THIS WORLD? WHERE IS THAT?
THAT'S JUST ONE MYSTERY. DON'T FORGET WHO HE IS...
WHY HE WANTS THESE THINGS... AND MOST IMPORTANTLY, IF HE'S NOT SENSEI WU, WHERE IS THE REAL SENSEI?

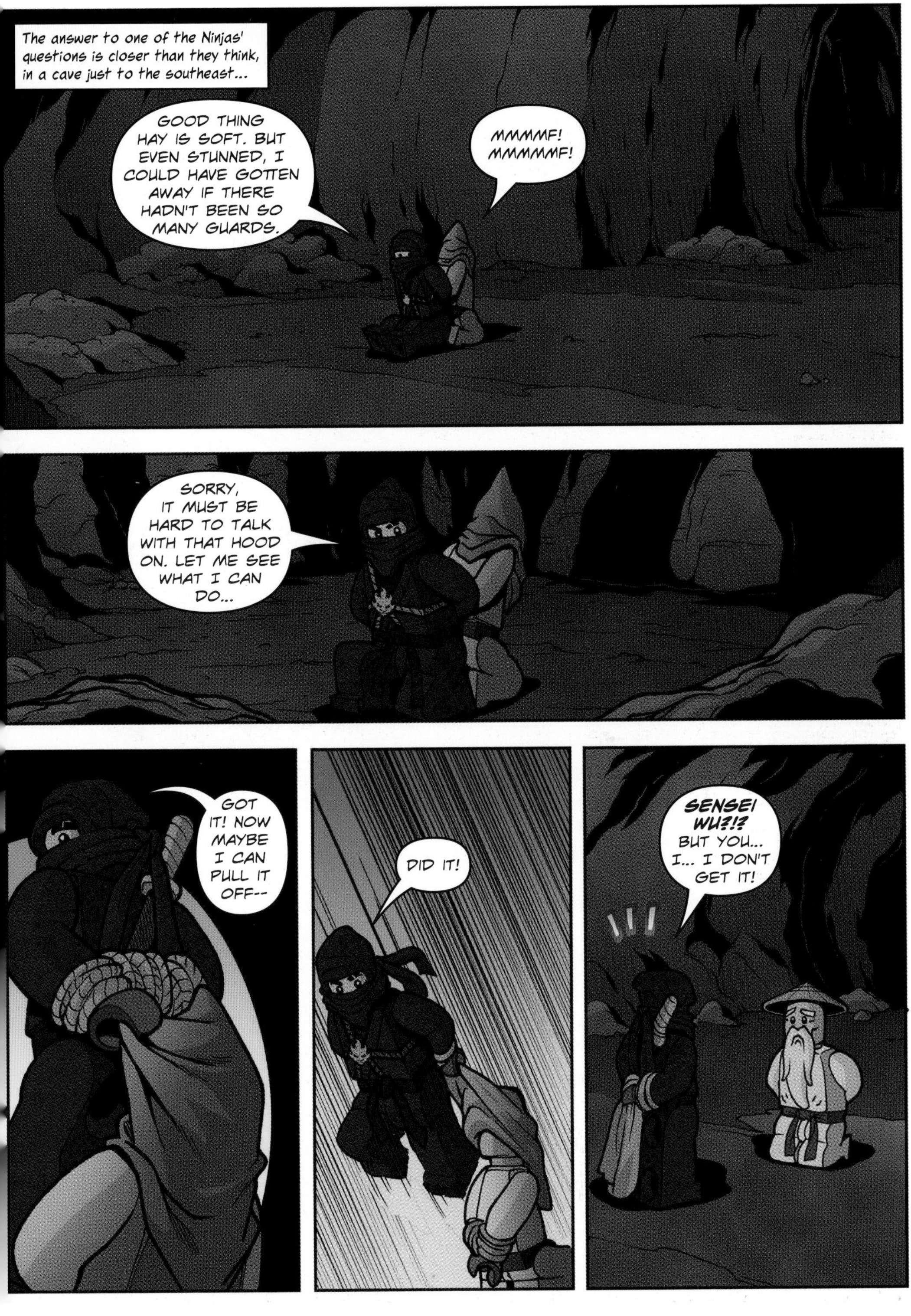
The answer to one of the Ninjas' questions is closer than they think, in a cave just to the southeast...
GOOD THING HAY IS SOFT. BUT EVEN STUNNED, I COULD HAVE GOTTEN AWAY IF THERE HADN'T BEEN SO MANY GUARDS.
MMMMF! MMMMMF!
SORRY, IT MUST BE HARD TO TALK WITH THAT HOOD ON. LET ME SEE WHAT I CAN DO...
GOT IT! NOW MAYBE I CAN PULL IT OFF--
DID IT!
SENSEI WU?!? BUT YOU... I... I DON'T GET IT!

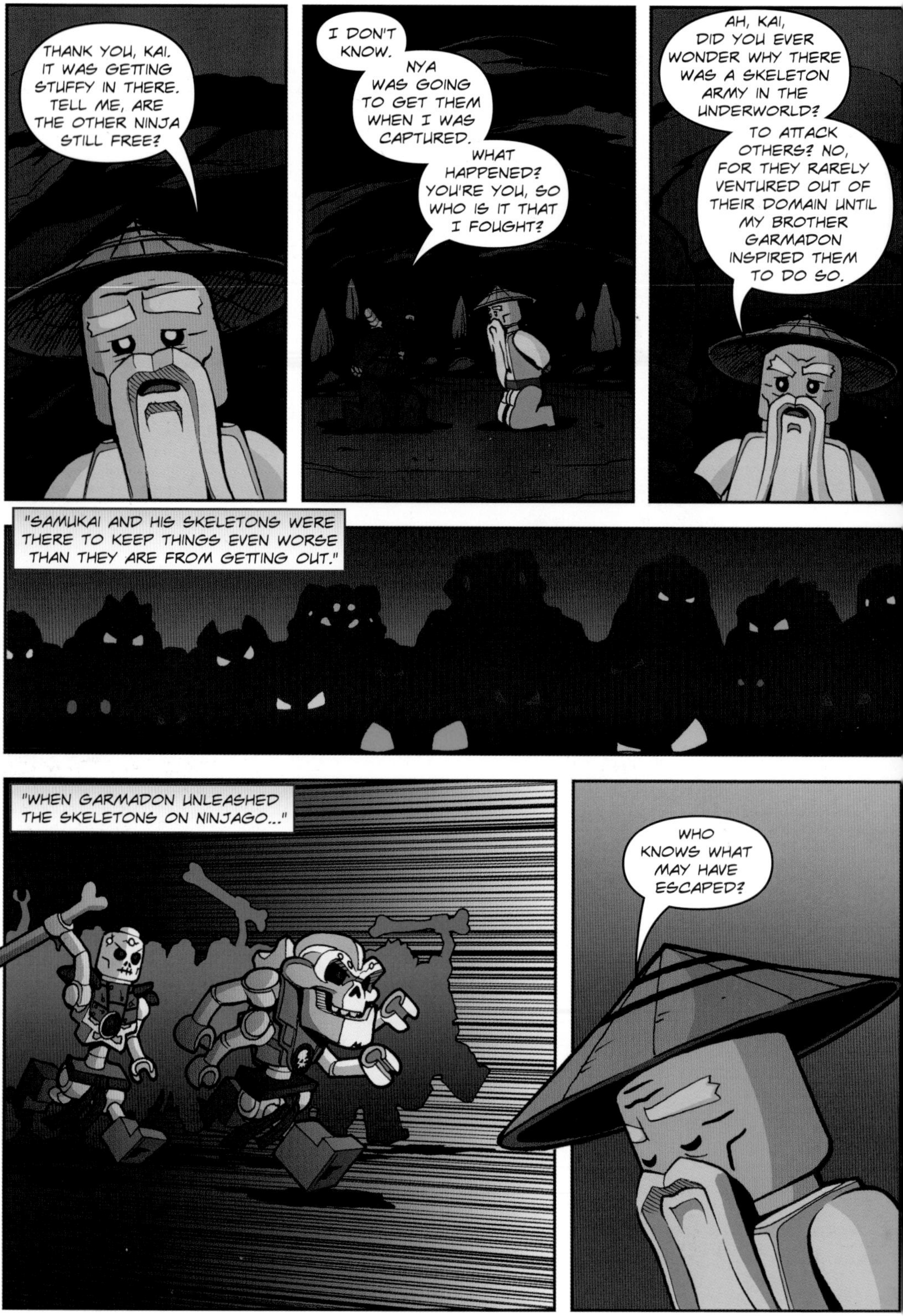
THANK YOU, KAI. IT WAS GETTING STUFFY IN THERE. TELL ME, ARE THE OTHER NINJA STILL FREE?
I DON'T KNOW.
NYA WAS GOING TO GET THEM WHEN I WAS CAPTURED.
WHAT HAPPENED? YOU'RE YOU, SO WHO IS IT THAT I FOUGHT?
AH, KAI, DID YOU EVER WONDER WHY THERE WAS A SKELETON ARMY IN THE UNDERWORLD?
TO ATTACK OTHERS? NO, FOR THEY RARELY VENTURED OUT OF THEIR DOMAIN UNTIL MY BROTHER GARMADON INSPIRED THEM TO DO SO.
"SAMUKAI AND HIS SKELETONS WERE THERE TO KEEP THINGS EVEN WORSE THAN THEY ARE FROM GETTING OUT."
"WHEN GARMADON UNLEASHED THE SKELETONS ON NINJAGO..."
WHO KNOWS WHAT MAY HAVE ESCAPED?

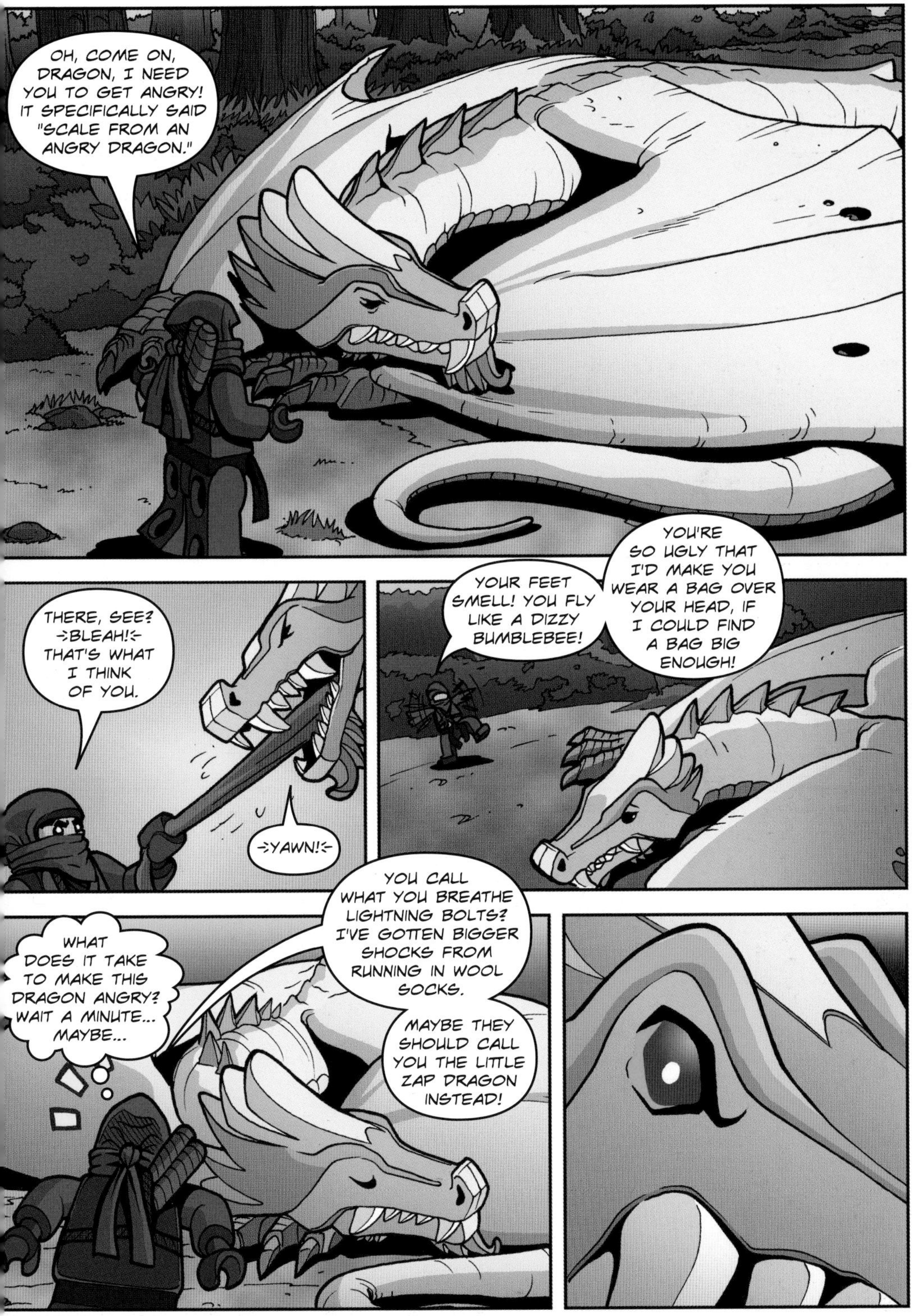
OH, COME ON, DRAGON, I NEED YOU TO GET ANGRY! IT SPECIFICALLY SAID "SCALE FROM AN ANGRY DRAGON."
THERE, SEE? ⇝BLEAH!⇜ THAT'S WHAT I THINK OF YOU.
⇝YAWN!⇜
YOUR FEET SMELL! YOU FLY LIKE A DIZZY BUMBLEBEE!
YOU'RE SO UGLY THAT I'D MAKE YOU WEAR A BAG OVER YOUR HEAD, IF I COULD FIND A BAG BIG ENOUGH!
WHAT DOES IT TAKE TO MAKE THIS DRAGON ANGRY? WAIT A MINUTE... MAYBE...
YOU CALL WHAT YOU BREATHE LIGHTNING BOLTS? I'VE GOTTEN BIGGER SHOCKS FROM RUNNING IN WOOL SOCKS.
MAYBE THEY SHOULD CALL YOU THE LITTLE ZAP DRAGON INSTEAD!

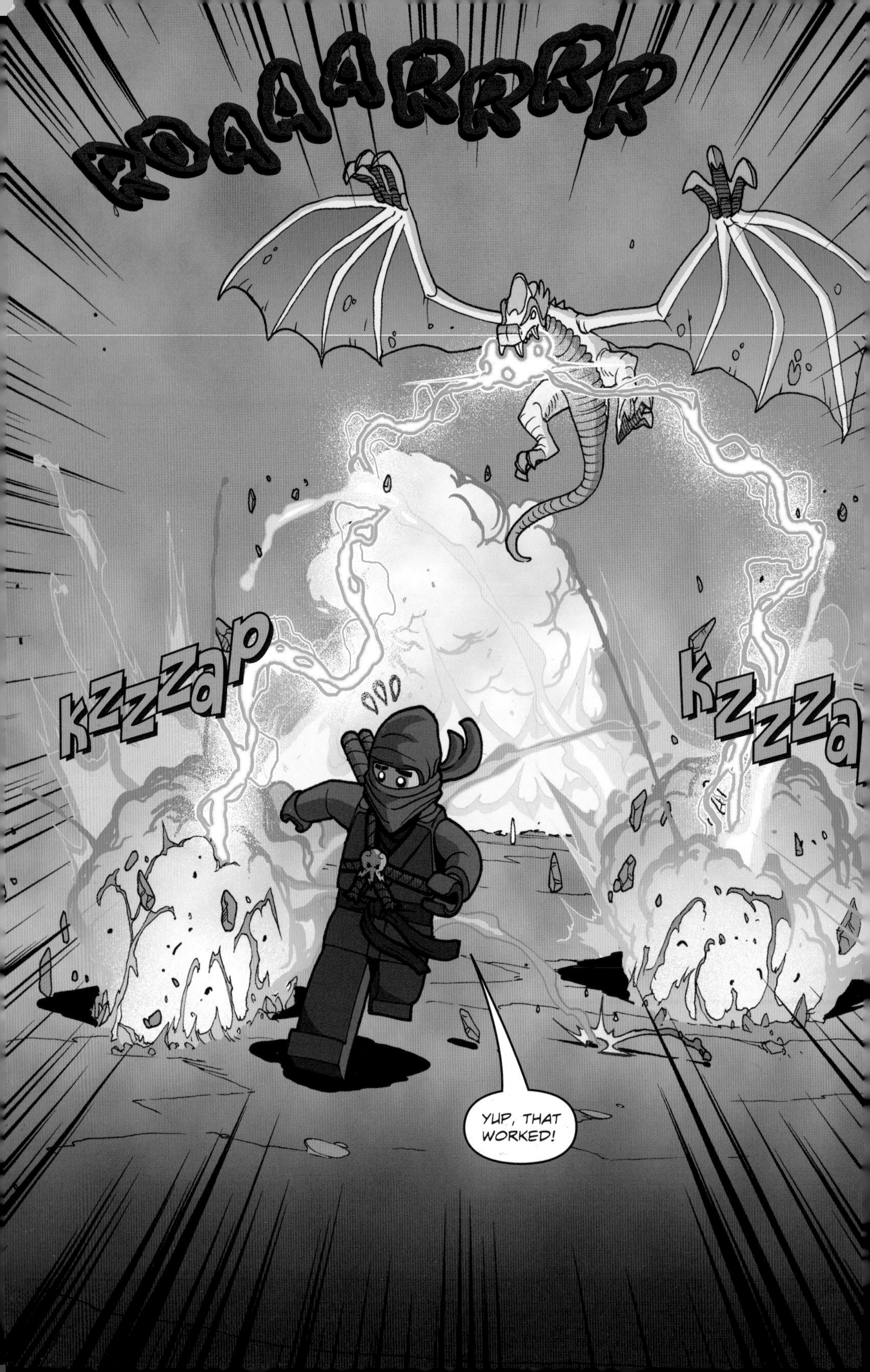
ROOAAARRRRR
KZZZZAP
KZZZZA
YUP, THAT WORKED!

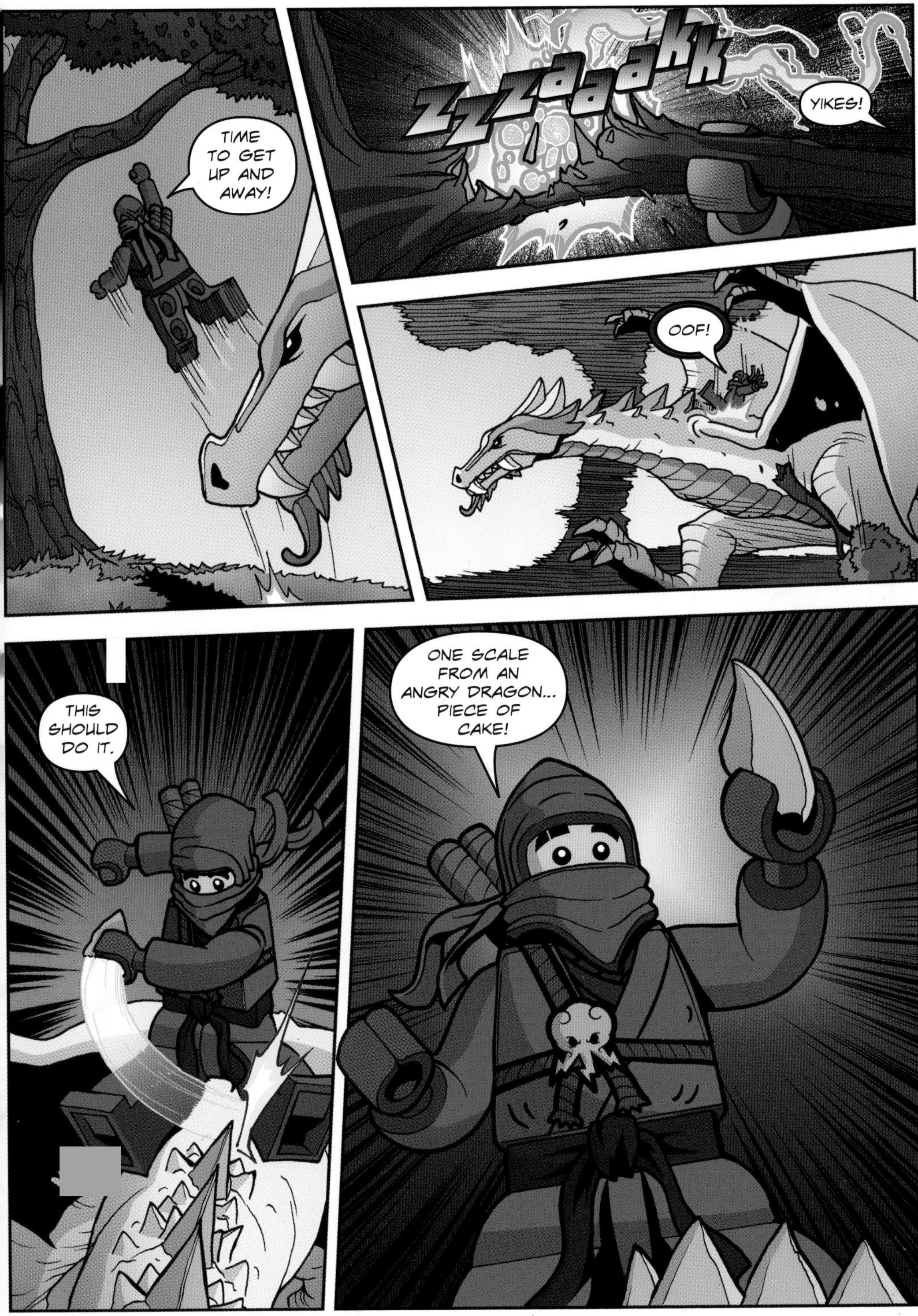
TIME TO GET UP AND AWAY!
ZZZAAAKK
YIKES!
OOF!
THIS SHOULD DO IT.
ONE SCALE FROM AN ANGRY DRAGON... PIECE OF CAKE!

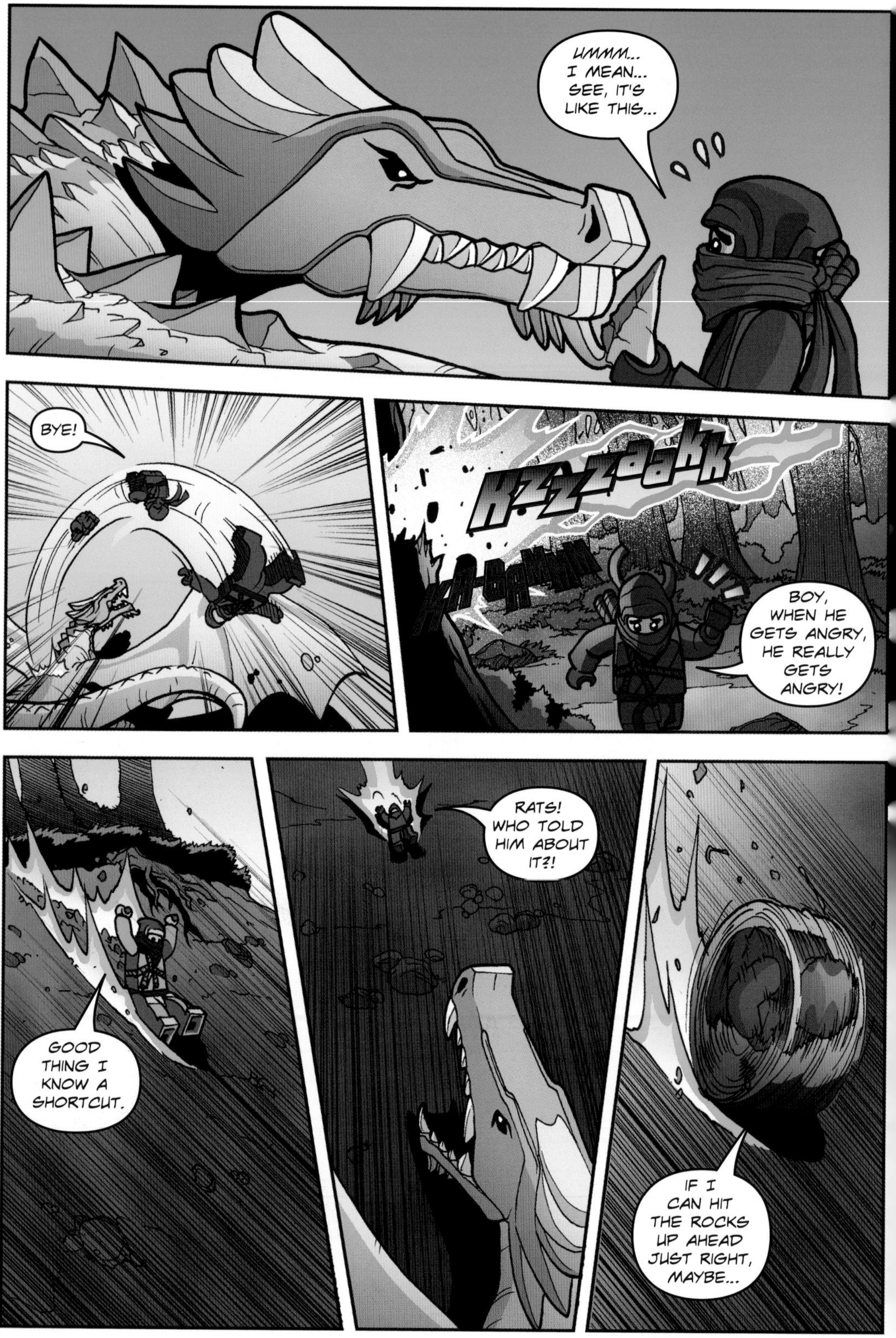
UMMM... I MEAN... SEE, IT'S LIKE THIS...
BYE!
KZZZAAKK
KA-BAMMM
BOY, WHEN HE GETS ANGRY, HE REALLY GETS ANGRY!
GOOD THING I KNOW A SHORTCUT.
RATS! WHO TOLD HIM ABOUT IT?!
IF I CAN HIT THE ROCKS UP AHEAD JUST RIGHT, MAYBE...

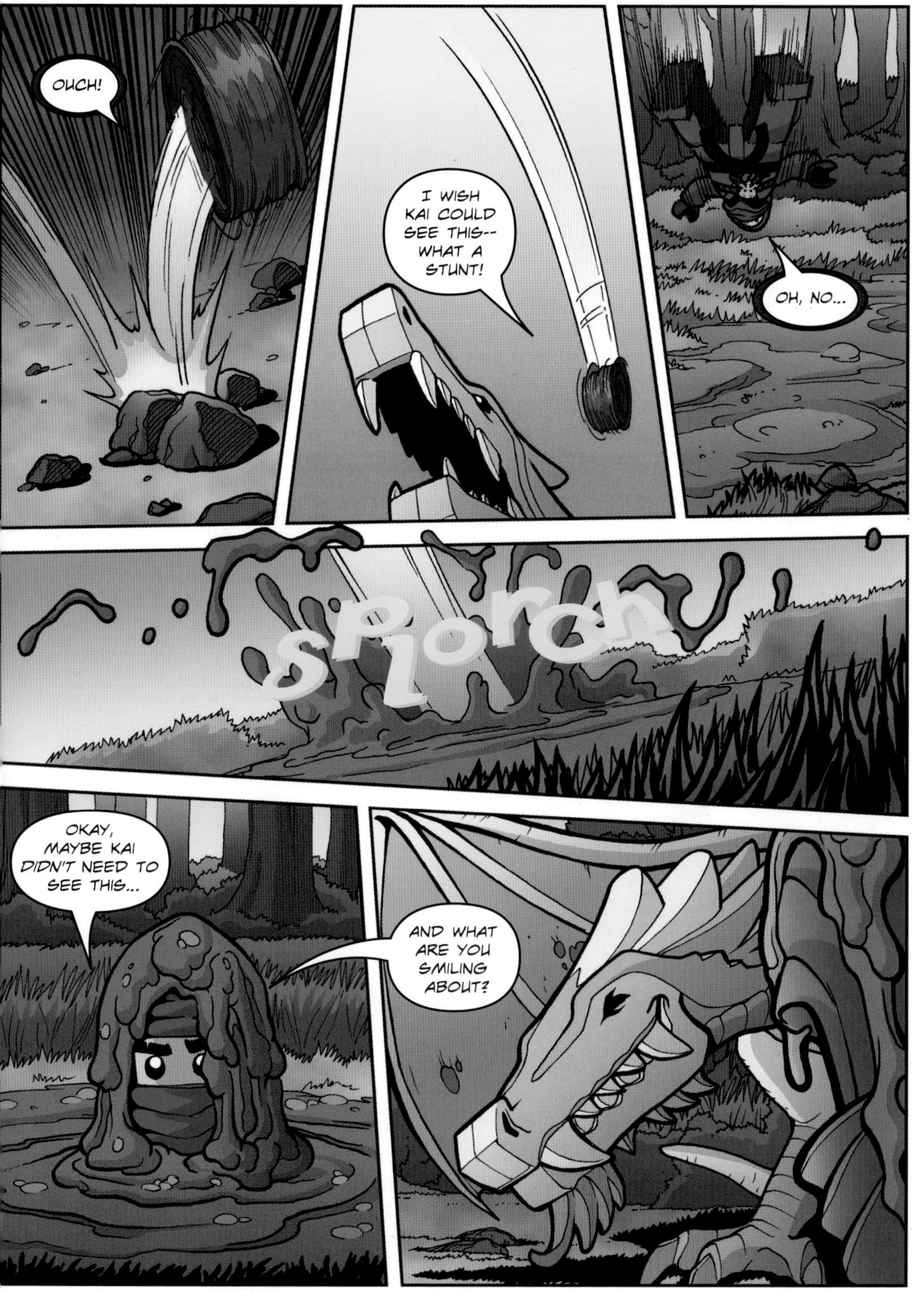
OUCH!
I WISH KAI COULD SEE THIS-- WHAT A STUNT!
OH, NO...
SPLORCH
OKAY, MAYBE KAI DIDN'T NEED TO SEE THIS...
AND WHAT ARE YOU SMILING ABOUT?

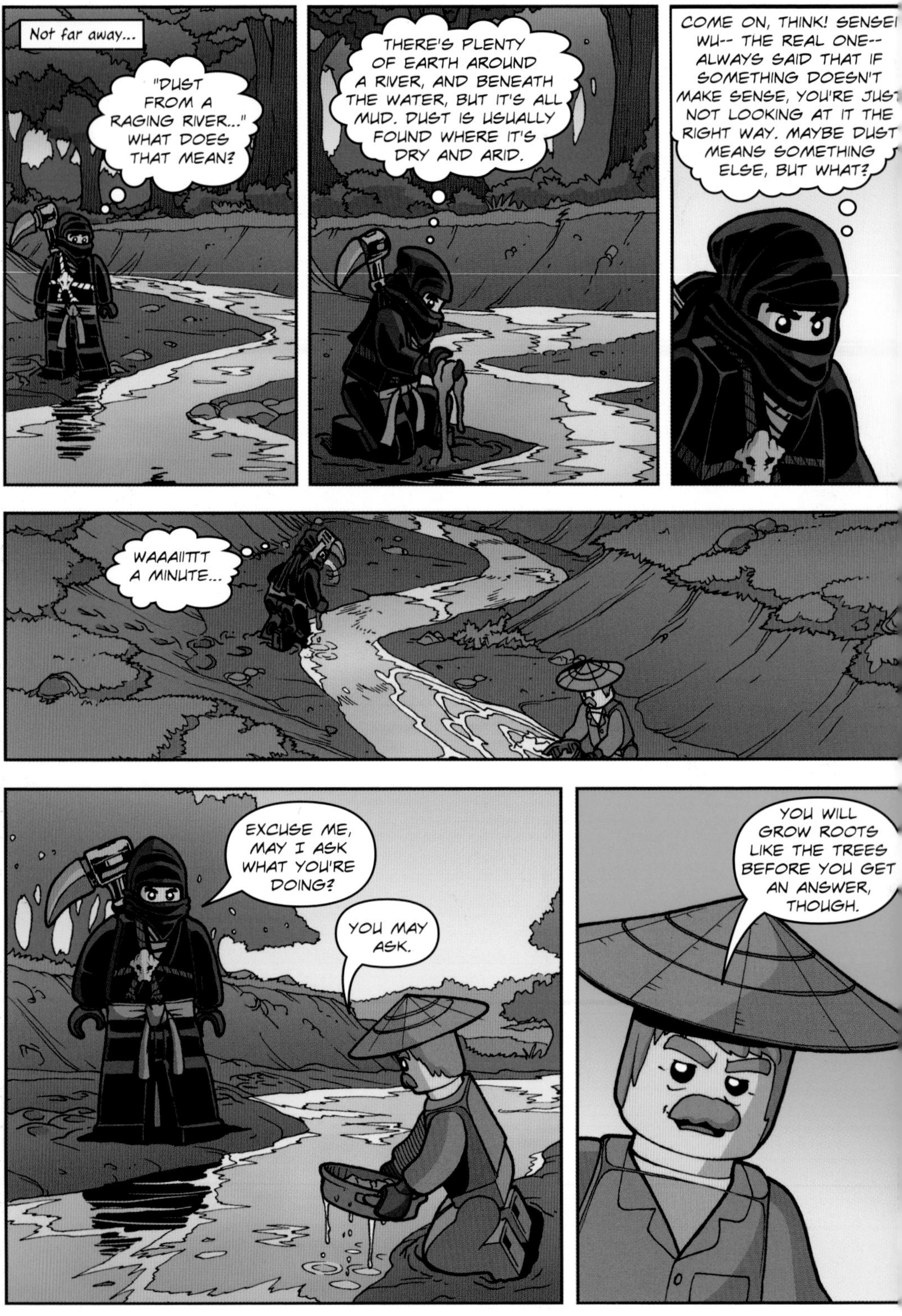
Not far away...
"DUST FROM A RAGING RIVER..." WHAT DOES THAT MEAN?
THERE'S PLENTY OF EARTH AROUND A RIVER, AND BENEATH THE WATER, BUT IT'S ALL MUD. DUST IS USUALLY FOUND WHERE IT'S DRY AND ARID.
COME ON, THINK! SENSEI WU-- THE REAL ONE-- ALWAYS SAID THAT IF SOMETHING DOESN'T MAKE SENSE, YOU'RE JUST NOT LOOKING AT IT THE RIGHT WAY. MAYBE DUST MEANS SOMETHING ELSE, BUT WHAT?
WAAAIITTT A MINUTE...
EXCUSE ME, MAY I ASK WHAT YOU'RE DOING?
YOU MAY ASK.
YOU WILL GROW ROOTS LIKE THE TREES BEFORE YOU GET AN ANSWER, THOUGH.

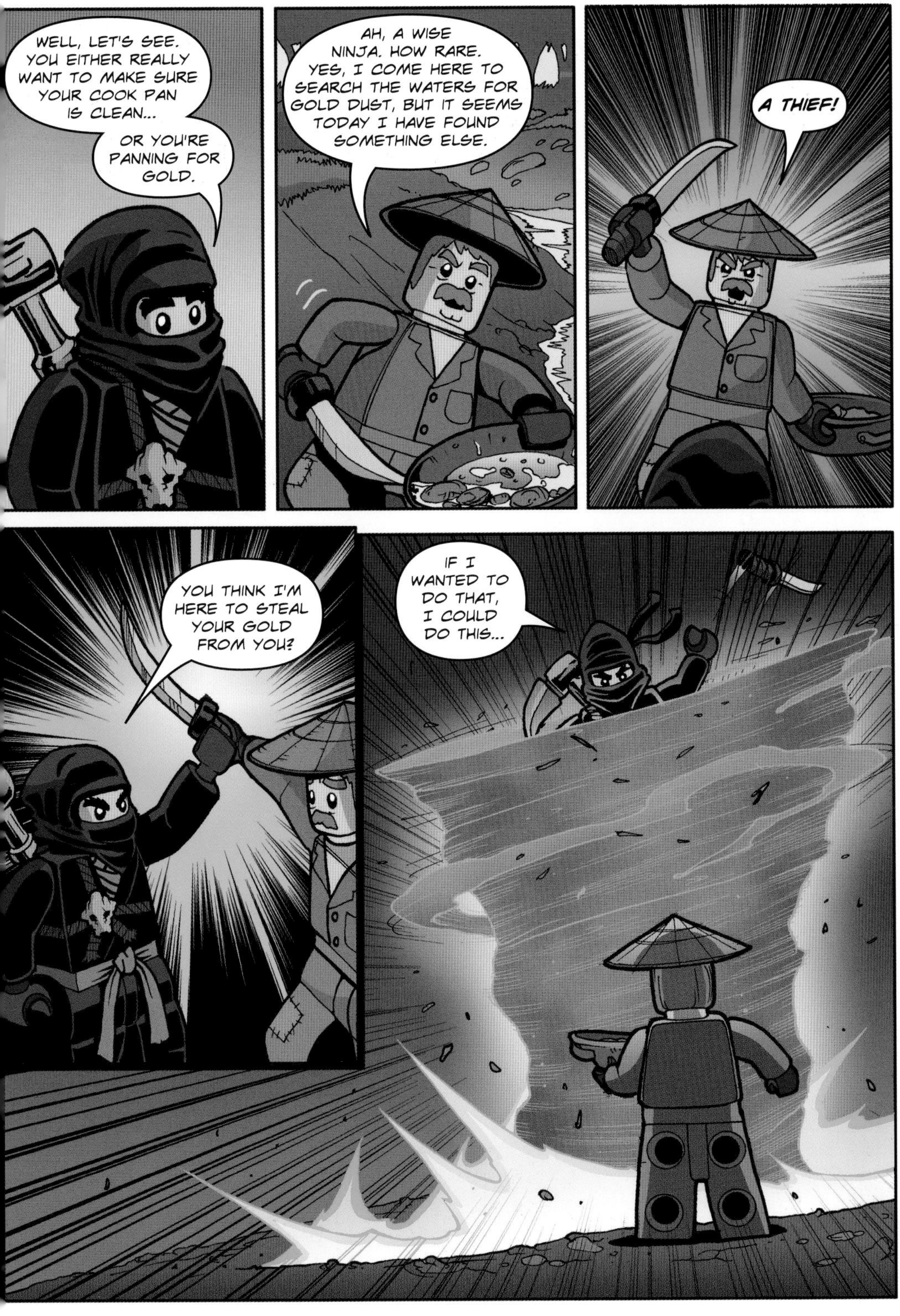
WELL, LET'S SEE. YOU EITHER REALLY WANT TO MAKE SURE YOUR COOK PAN IS CLEAN...
OR YOU'RE PANNING FOR GOLD.
AH, A WISE NINJA. HOW RARE. YES, I COME HERE TO SEARCH THE WATERS FOR GOLD DUST, BUT IT SEEMS TODAY I HAVE FOUND SOMETHING ELSE.
A THIEF!
YOU THINK I'M HERE TO STEAL YOUR GOLD FROM YOU?
IF I WANTED TO DO THAT, I COULD DO THIS...

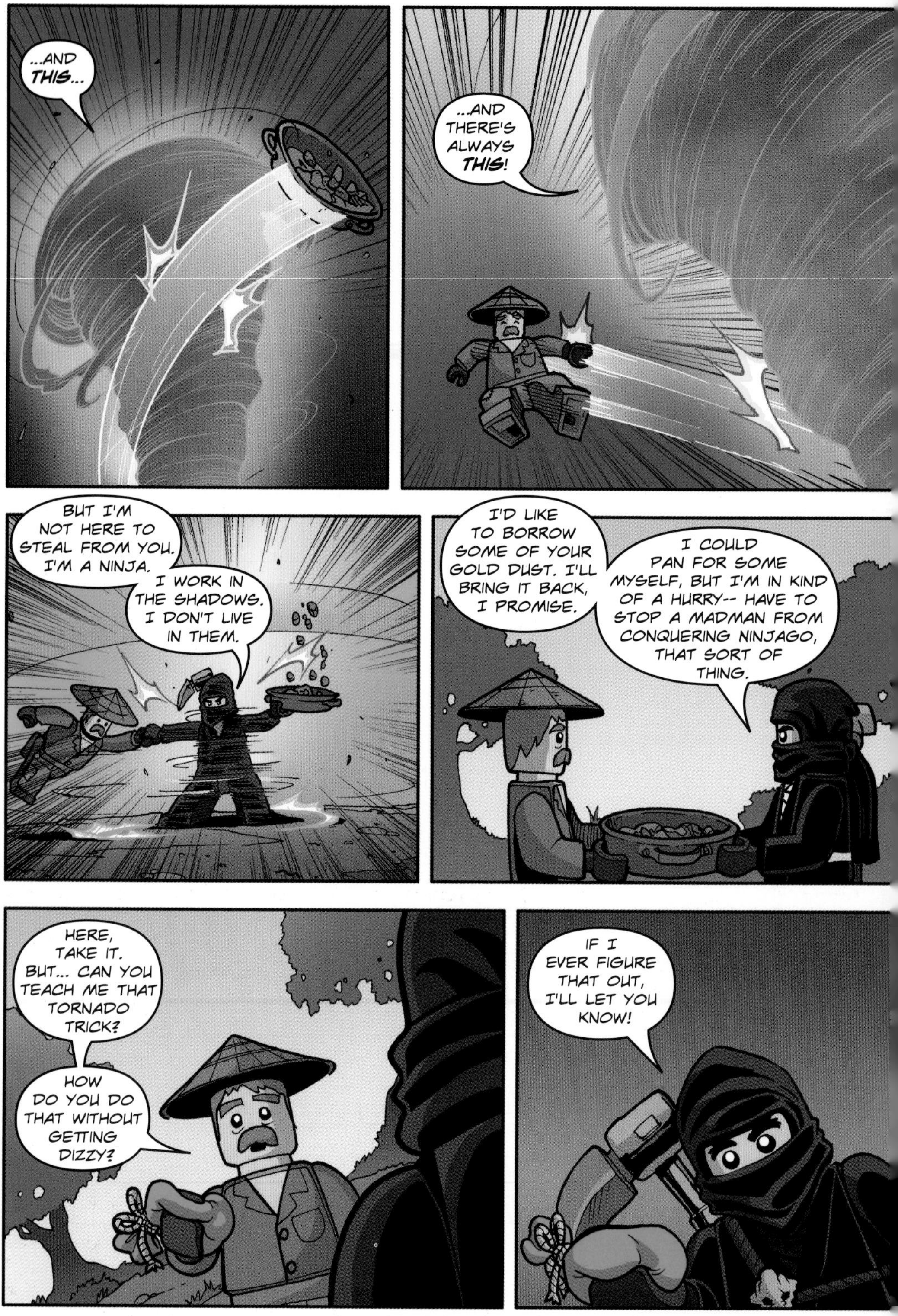
...AND THIS...
...AND THERE'S ALWAYS THIS!
BUT I'M NOT HERE TO STEAL FROM YOU. I'M A NINJA.
I WORK IN THE SHADOWS. I DON'T LIVE IN THEM.
I'D LIKE TO BORROW SOME OF YOUR GOLD DUST. I'LL BRING IT BACK, I PROMISE.
I COULD PAN FOR SOME MYSELF, BUT I'M IN KIND OF A HURRY-- HAVE TO STOP A MADMAN FROM CONQUERING NINJAGO, THAT SORT OF THING.
HERE, TAKE IT. BUT... CAN YOU TEACH ME THAT TORNADO TRICK?
HOW DO YOU DO THAT WITHOUT GETTING DIZZY?
IF I EVER FIGURE THAT OUT, I'LL LET YOU KNOW!

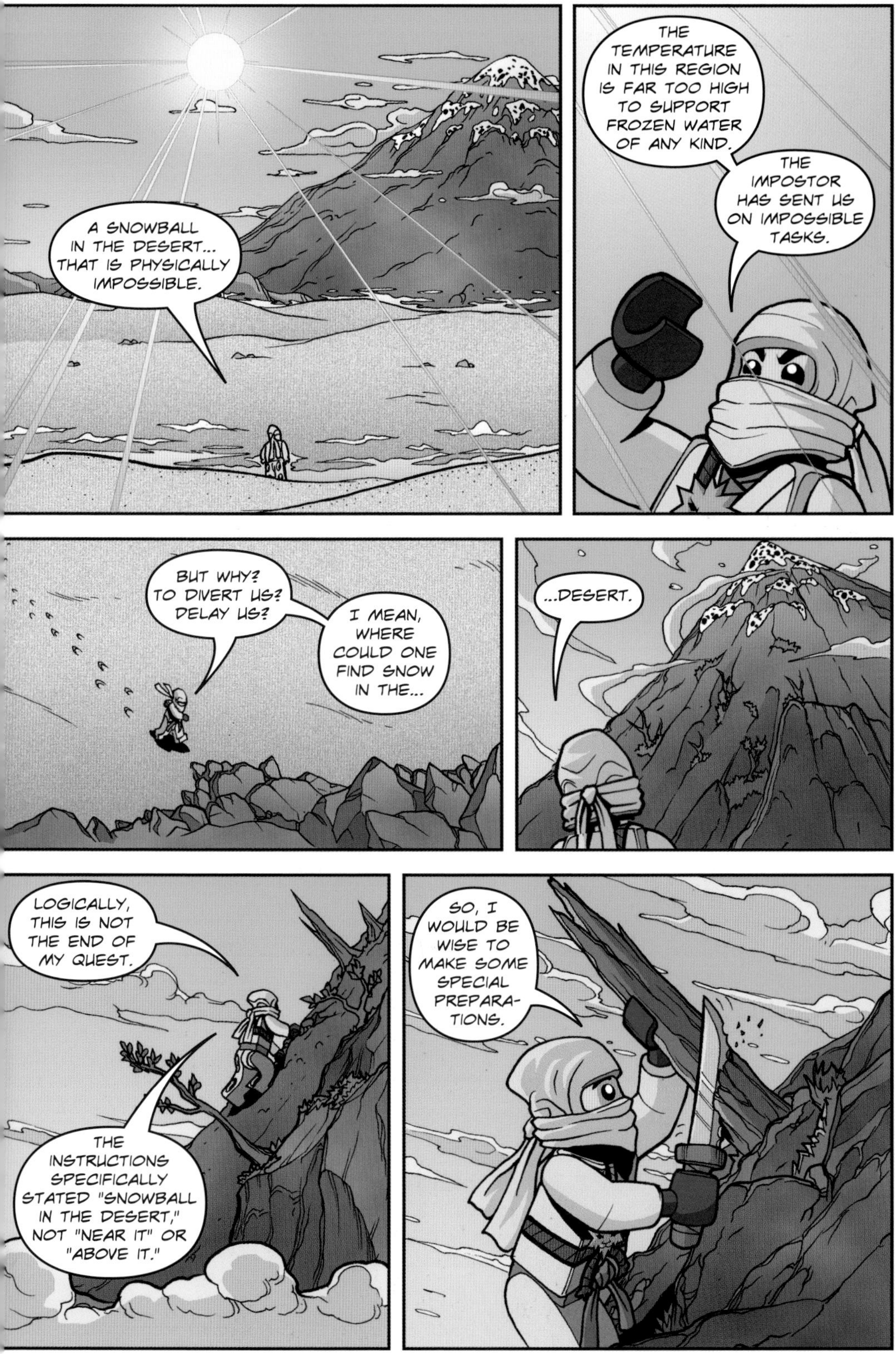
A SNOWBALL IN THE DESERT... THAT IS PHYSICALLY IMPOSSIBLE.
THE TEMPERATURE IN THIS REGION IS FAR TOO HIGH TO SUPPORT FROZEN WATER OF ANY KIND.
THE IMPOSTOR HAS SENT US ON IMPOSSIBLE TASKS.
BUT WHY? TO DIVERT US? DELAY US?
I MEAN, WHERE COULD ONE FIND SNOW IN THE...
...DESERT.
LOGICALLY, THIS IS NOT THE END OF MY QUEST.
THE INSTRUCTIONS SPECIFICALLY STATED "SNOWBALL IN THE DESERT," NOT "NEAR IT" OR "ABOVE IT."
SO, I WOULD BE WISE TO MAKE SOME SPECIAL PREPARA-TIONS.

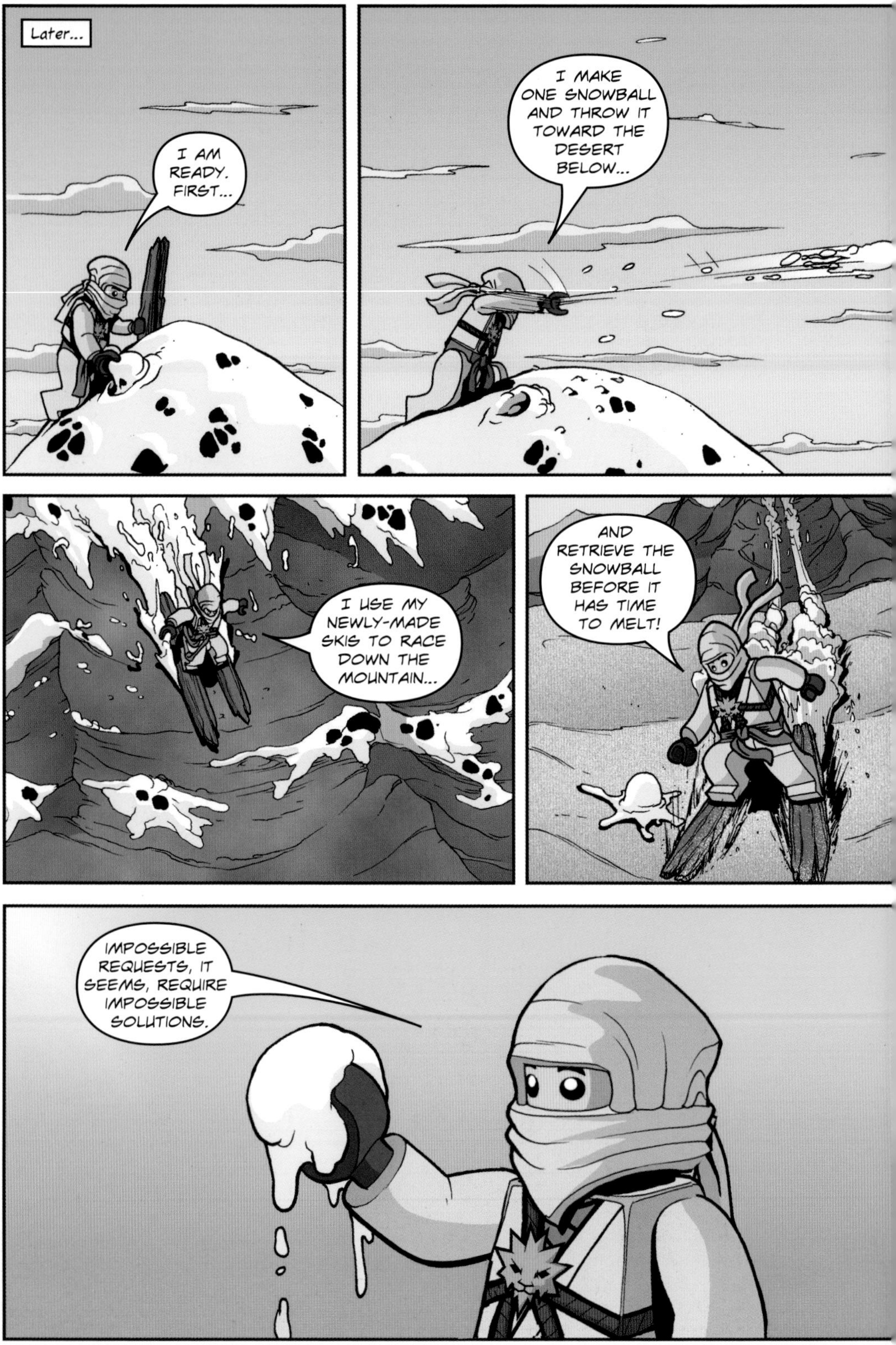
Later...
I AM READY. FIRST...
I MAKE ONE SNOWBALL AND THROW IT TOWARD THE DESERT BELOW...
I USE MY NEWLY-MADE SKIS TO RACE DOWN THE MOUNTAIN...
AND RETRIEVE THE SNOWBALL BEFORE IT HAS TIME TO MELT!
IMPOSSIBLE REQUESTS, IT SEEMS, REQUIRE IMPOSSIBLE SOLUTIONS.

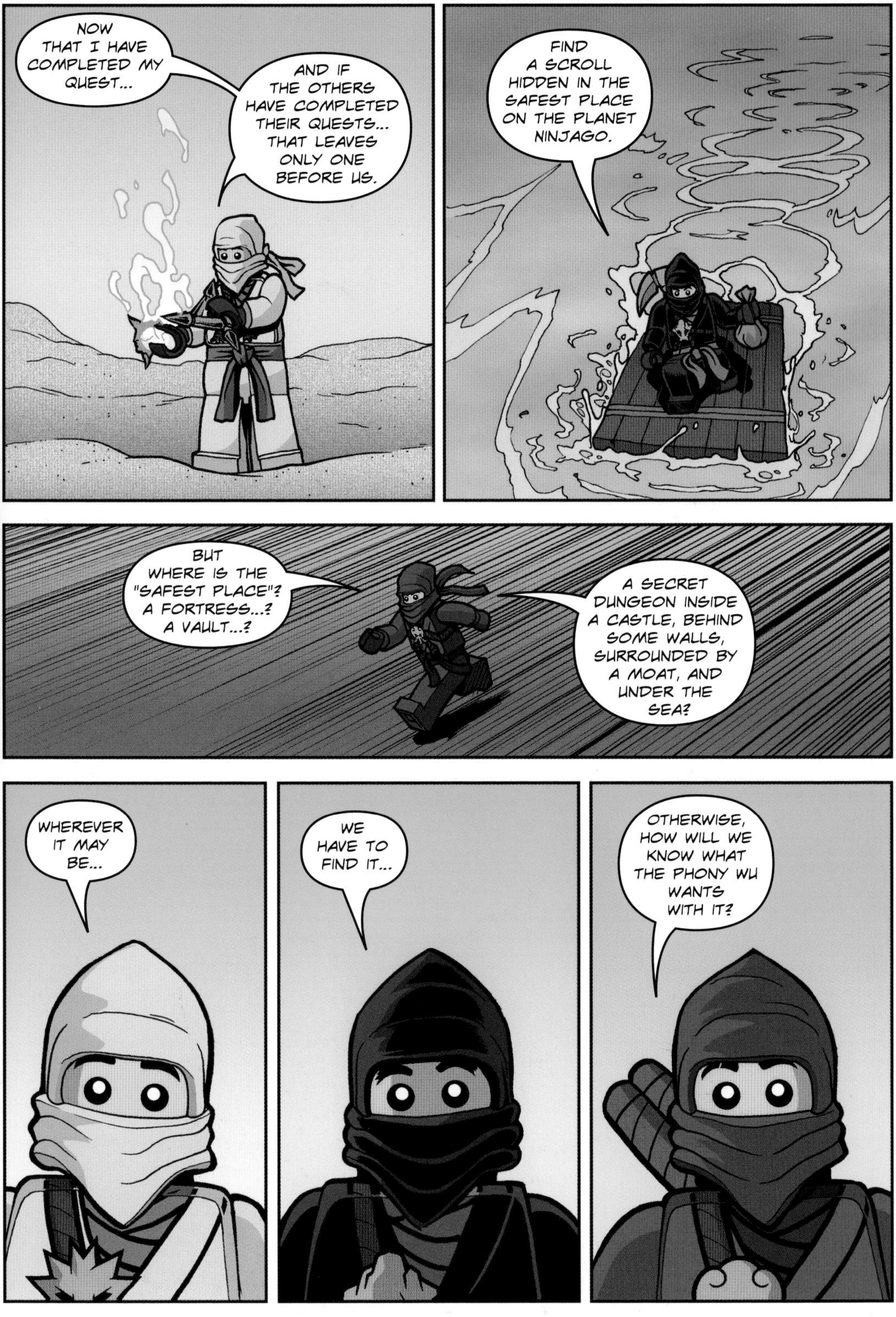
NOW THAT I HAVE COMPLETED MY QUEST...
AND IF THE OTHERS HAVE COMPLETED THEIR QUESTS... THAT LEAVES ONLY ONE BEFORE US.
FIND A SCROLL HIDDEN IN THE SAFEST PLACE ON THE PLANET NINJAGO.
BUT WHERE IS THE "SAFEST PLACE"? A FORTRESS...? A VAULT...?
A SECRET DUNGEON INSIDE A CASTLE, BEHIND SOME WALLS, SURROUNDED BY A MOAT, AND UNDER THE SEA?
WHEREVER IT MAY BE...
WE HAVE TO FIND IT...
OTHERWISE, HOW WILL WE KNOW WHAT THE PHONY WU WANTS WITH IT?

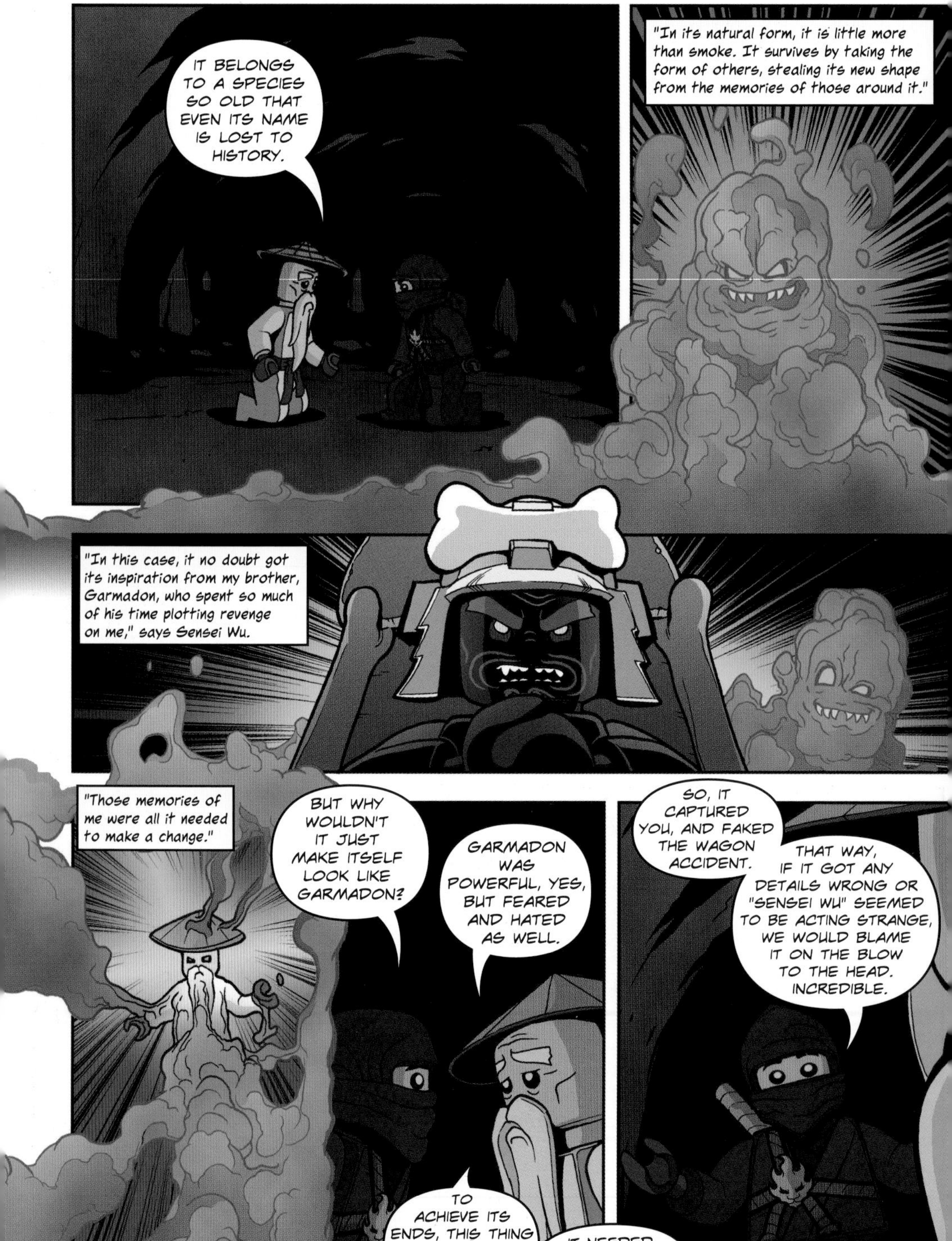
IT BELONGS TO A SPECIES SO OLD THAT EVEN ITS NAME IS LOST TO HISTORY.
"In its natural form, it is little more than smoke. It survives by taking the form of others, stealing its new shape from the memories of those around it."
"In this case, it no doubt got its inspiration from my brother, Garmadon, who spent so much of his time plotting revenge on me," says Sensei Wu.
"Those memories of me were all it needed to make a change."
BUT WHY WOULDN'T IT JUST MAKE ITSELF LOOK LIKE GARMADON?
GARMADON WAS POWERFUL, YES, BUT FEARED AND HATED AS WELL.
TO ACHIEVE ITS ENDS, THIS THING NEEDS TO BE HONORED AND ADMIRED.
IT NEEDED TO BECOME SOMEONE OTHERS WOULD TRUST.
SO, IT CAPTURED YOU, AND FAKED THE WAGON ACCIDENT.
THAT WAY, IF IT GOT ANY DETAILS WRONG OR "SENSEI WU" SEEMED TO BE ACTING STRANGE, WE WOULD BLAME IT ON THE BLOW TO THE HEAD. INCREDIBLE.

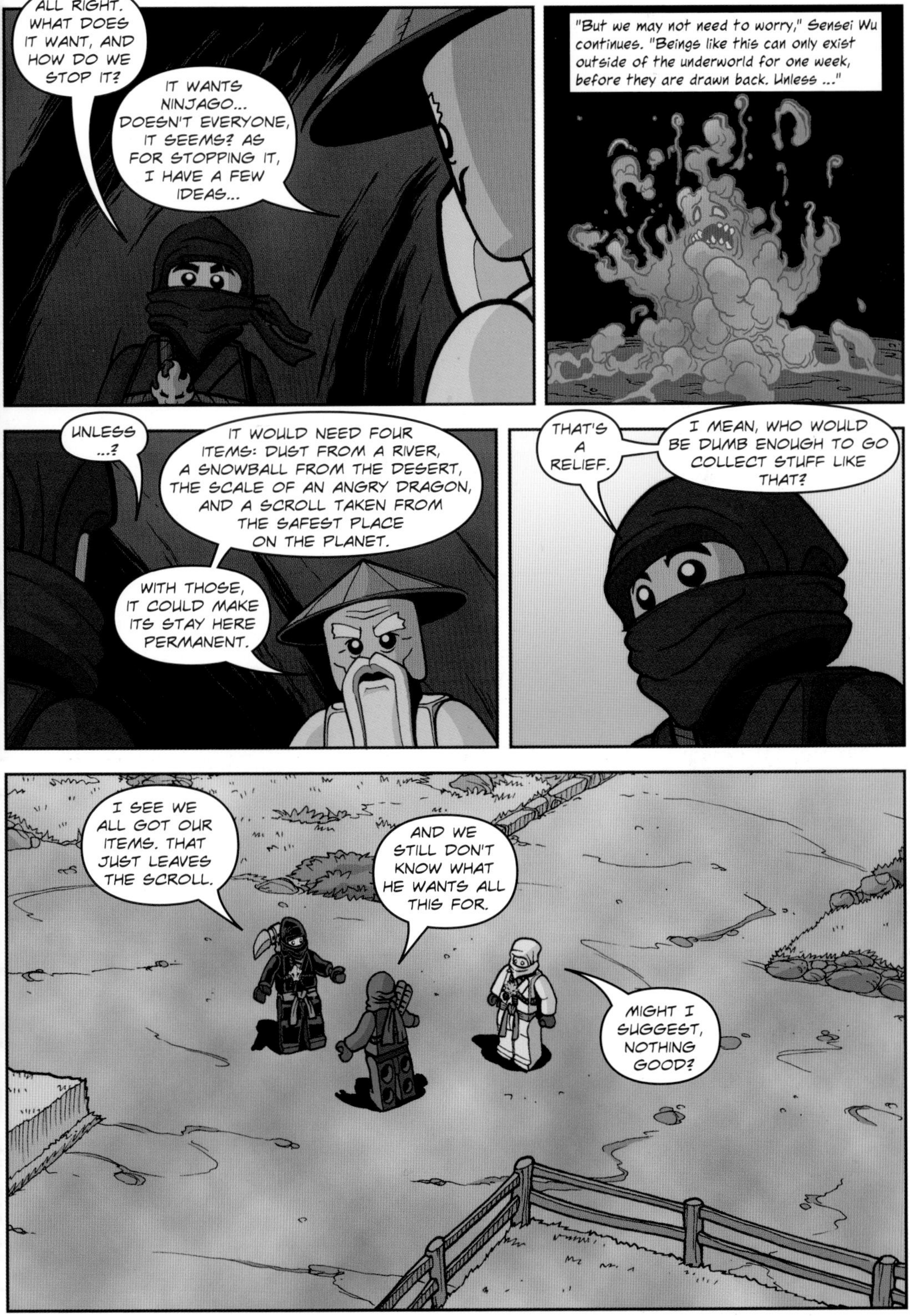
ALL RIGHT. WHAT DOES IT WANT, AND HOW DO WE STOP IT?
IT WANTS NINJAGO... DOESN'T EVERYONE, IT SEEMS? AS FOR STOPPING IT, I HAVE A FEW IDEAS...
"But we may not need to worry," Sensei Wu continues. "Beings like this can only exist outside of the underworld for one week, before they are drawn back. Unless ..."
UNLESS ...?
IT WOULD NEED FOUR ITEMS: DUST FROM A RIVER, A SNOWBALL FROM THE DESERT, THE SCALE OF AN ANGRY DRAGON, AND A SCROLL TAKEN FROM THE SAFEST PLACE ON THE PLANET.
WITH THOSE, IT COULD MAKE ITS STAY HERE PERMANENT.
THAT'S A RELIEF.
I MEAN, WHO WOULD BE DUMB ENOUGH TO GO COLLECT STUFF LIKE THAT?
I SEE WE ALL GOT OUR ITEMS. THAT JUST LEAVES THE SCROLL.
AND WE STILL DON'T KNOW WHAT HE WANTS ALL THIS FOR.
MIGHT I SUGGEST, NOTHING GOOD?

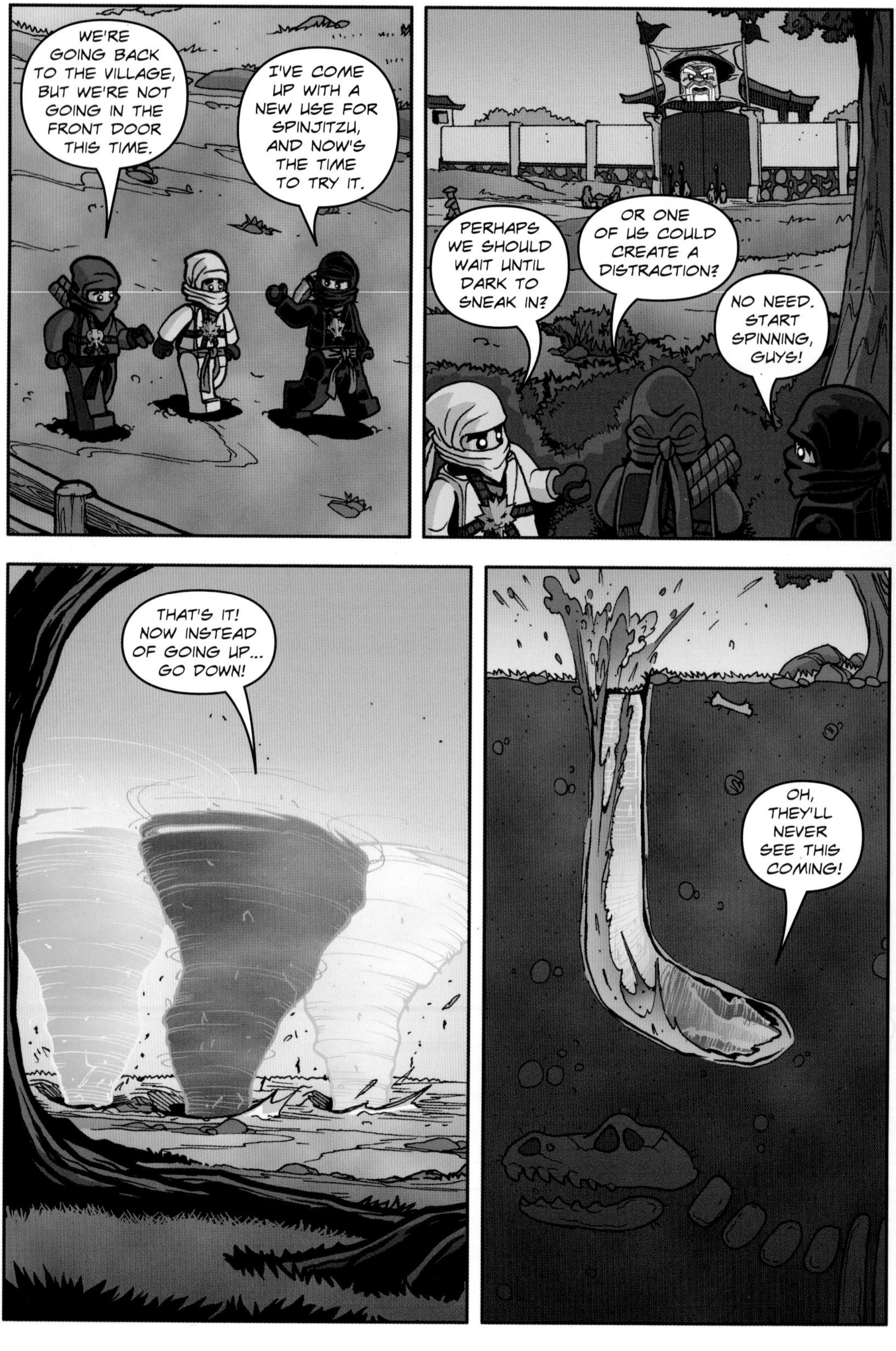
WE'RE GOING BACK TO THE VILLAGE, BUT WE'RE NOT GOING IN THE FRONT DOOR THIS TIME.
I'VE COME UP WITH A NEW USE FOR SPINJITZU, AND NOW'S THE TIME TO TRY IT.
PERHAPS WE SHOULD WAIT UNTIL DARK TO SNEAK IN?
OR ONE OF US COULD CREATE A DISTRACTION?
NO NEED. START SPINNING, GUYS!
THAT'S IT! NOW INSTEAD OF GOING UP... GO DOWN!
OH, THEY'LL NEVER SEE THIS COMING!

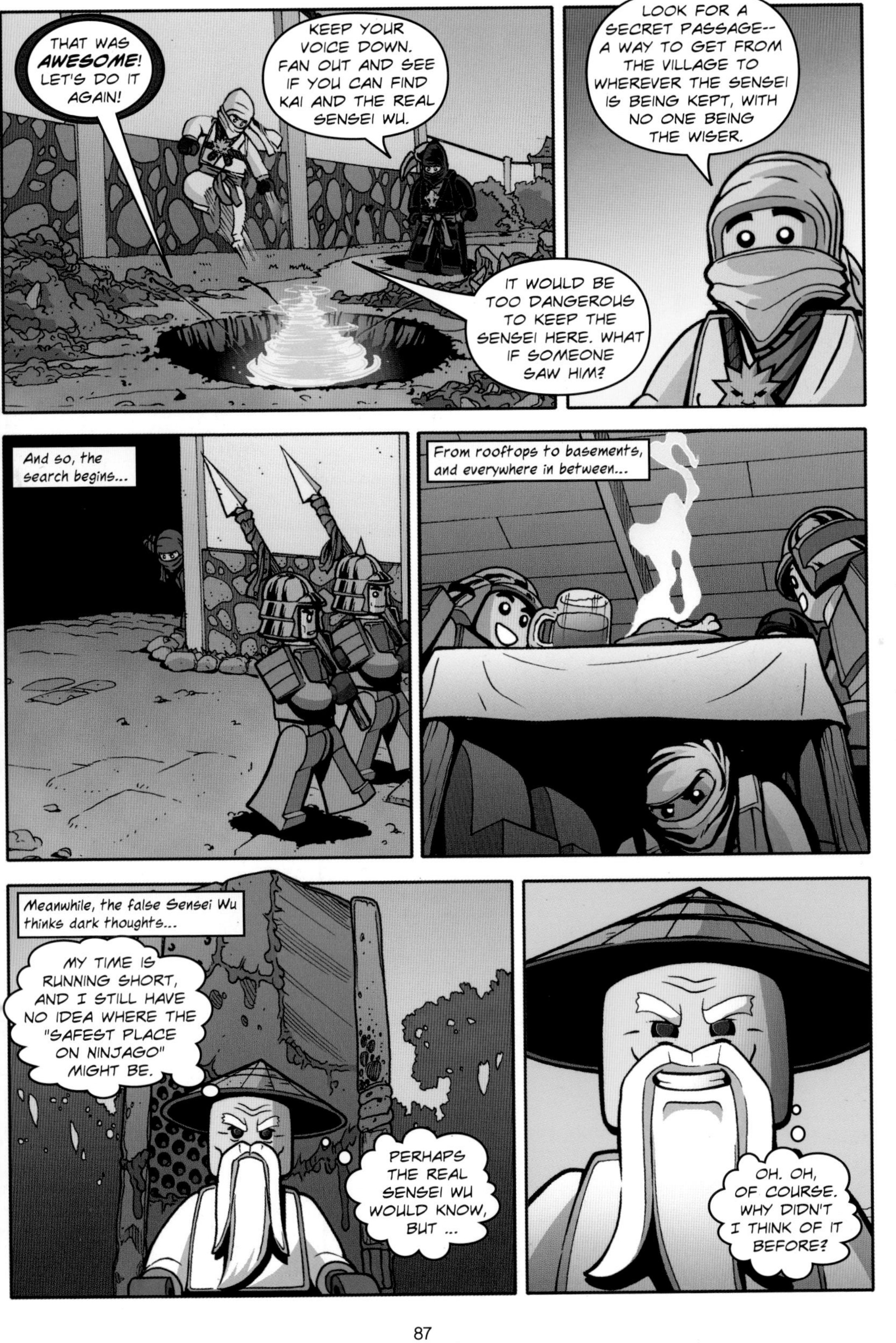
THAT WAS **AWESOME**! LET'S DO IT AGAIN!
KEEP YOUR VOICE DOWN. FAN OUT AND SEE IF YOU CAN FIND KAI AND THE REAL SENSEI WU.
IT WOULD BE TOO DANGEROUS TO KEEP THE SENSEI HERE. WHAT IF SOMEONE SAW HIM?
LOOK FOR A SECRET PASSAGE-- A WAY TO GET FROM THE VILLAGE TO WHEREVER THE SENSEI IS BEING KEPT, WITH NO ONE BEING THE WISER.
And so, the search begins...
From rooftops to basements, and everywhere in between...
Meanwhile, the false Sensei Wu thinks dark thoughts...
MY TIME IS RUNNING SHORT, AND I STILL HAVE NO IDEA WHERE THE "SAFEST PLACE ON NINJAGO" MIGHT BE.
PERHAPS THE REAL SENSEI WU WOULD KNOW, BUT ...
OH. OH, OF COURSE. WHY DIDN'T I THINK OF IT BEFORE?

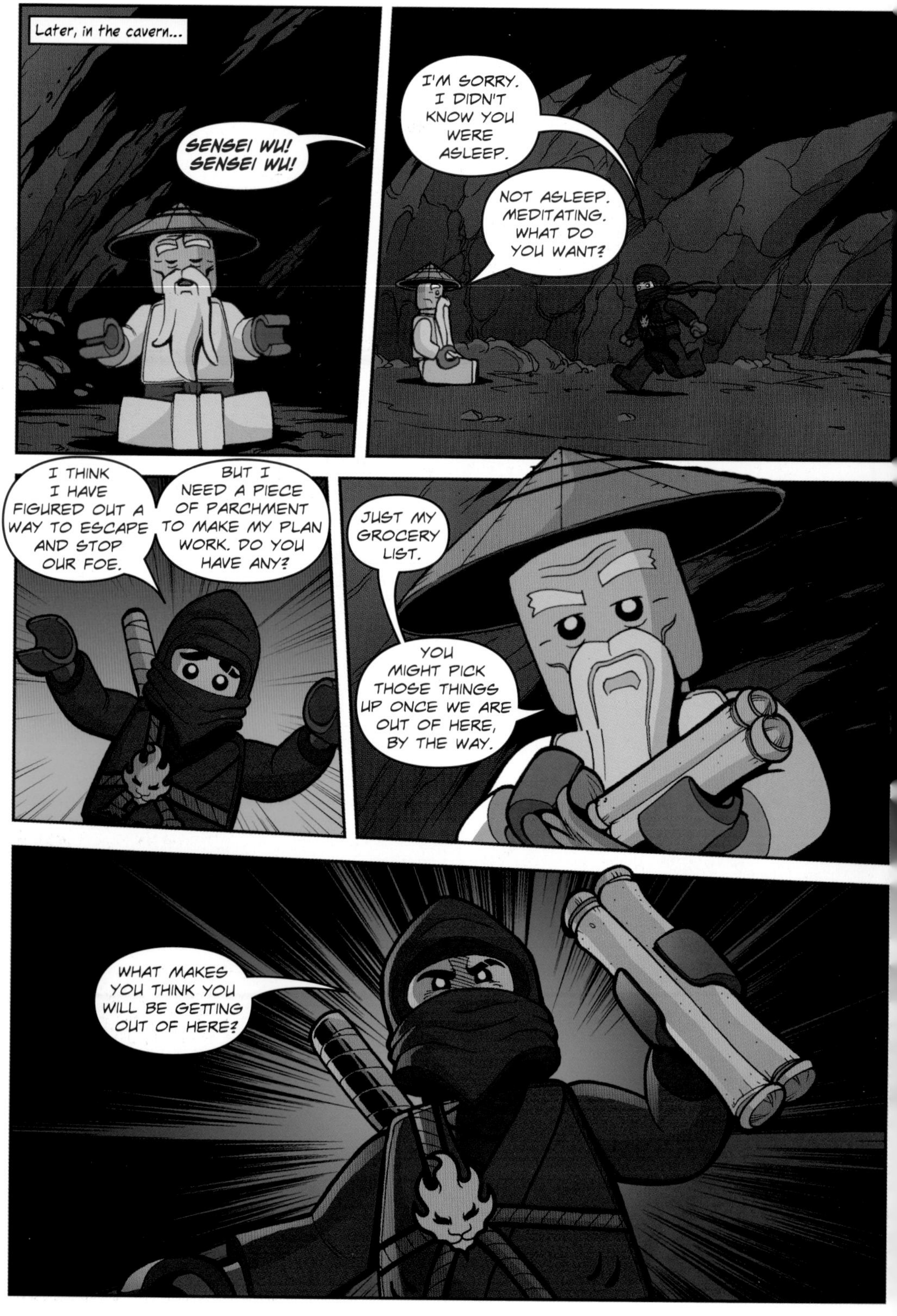
Later, in the cavern...
SENSEI WU! SENSEI WU!
I'M SORRY. I DIDN'T KNOW YOU WERE ASLEEP.
NOT ASLEEP. MEDITATING. WHAT DO YOU WANT?
I THINK I HAVE FIGURED OUT A WAY TO ESCAPE AND STOP OUR FOE.
BUT I NEED A PIECE OF PARCHMENT TO MAKE MY PLAN WORK. DO YOU HAVE ANY?
JUST MY GROCERY LIST.
YOU MIGHT PICK THOSE THINGS UP ONCE WE ARE OUT OF HERE, BY THE WAY.
WHAT MAKES YOU THINK YOU WILL BE GETTING OUT OF HERE?

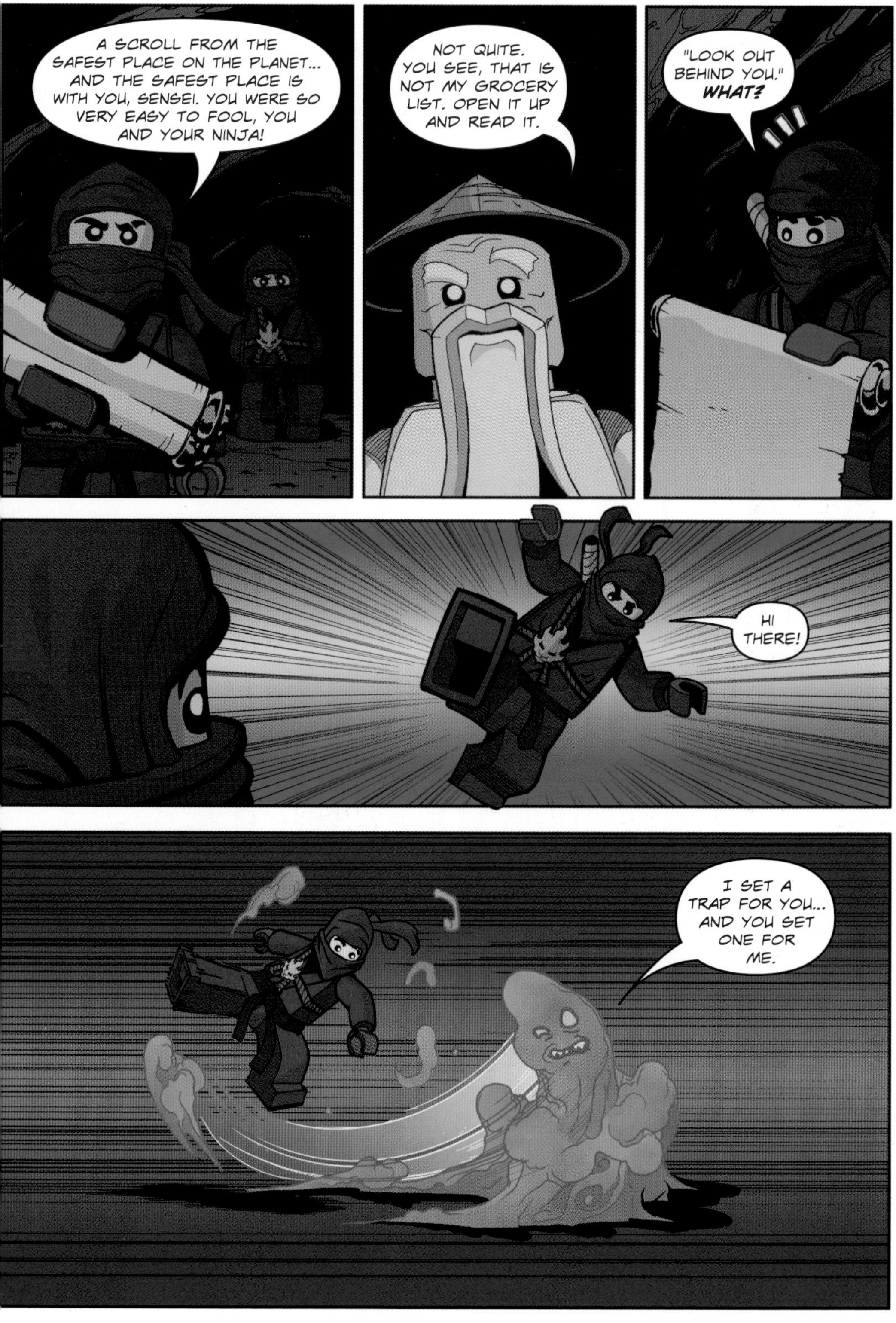
A SCROLL FROM THE SAFEST PLACE ON THE PLANET... AND THE SAFEST PLACE IS WITH YOU, SENSEI. YOU WERE SO VERY EASY TO FOOL, YOU AND YOUR NINJA!
NOT QUITE. YOU SEE, THAT IS NOT MY GROCERY LIST. OPEN IT UP AND READ IT.
"LOOK OUT BEHIND YOU." **WHAT?**
HI THERE!
I SET A TRAP FOR YOU... AND YOU SET ONE FOR ME.

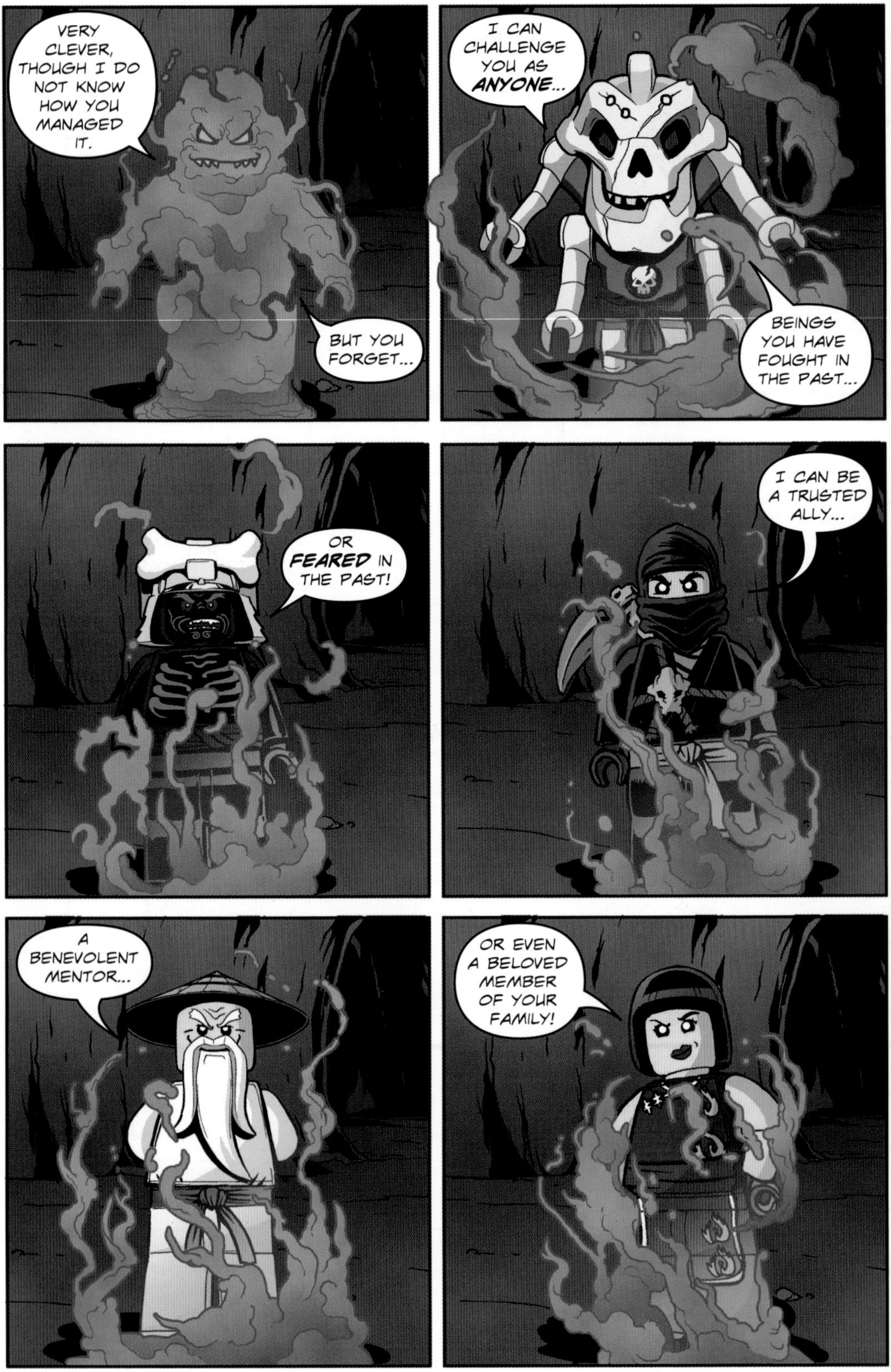
VERY CLEVER, THOUGH I DO NOT KNOW HOW YOU MANAGED IT.
BUT YOU FORGET...
I CAN CHALLENGE YOU AS ANYONE...
BEINGS YOU HAVE FOUGHT IN THE PAST...
OR FEARED IN THE PAST!
I CAN BE A TRUSTED ALLY...
A BENEVOLENT MENTOR...
OR EVEN A BELOVED MEMBER OF YOUR FAMILY!

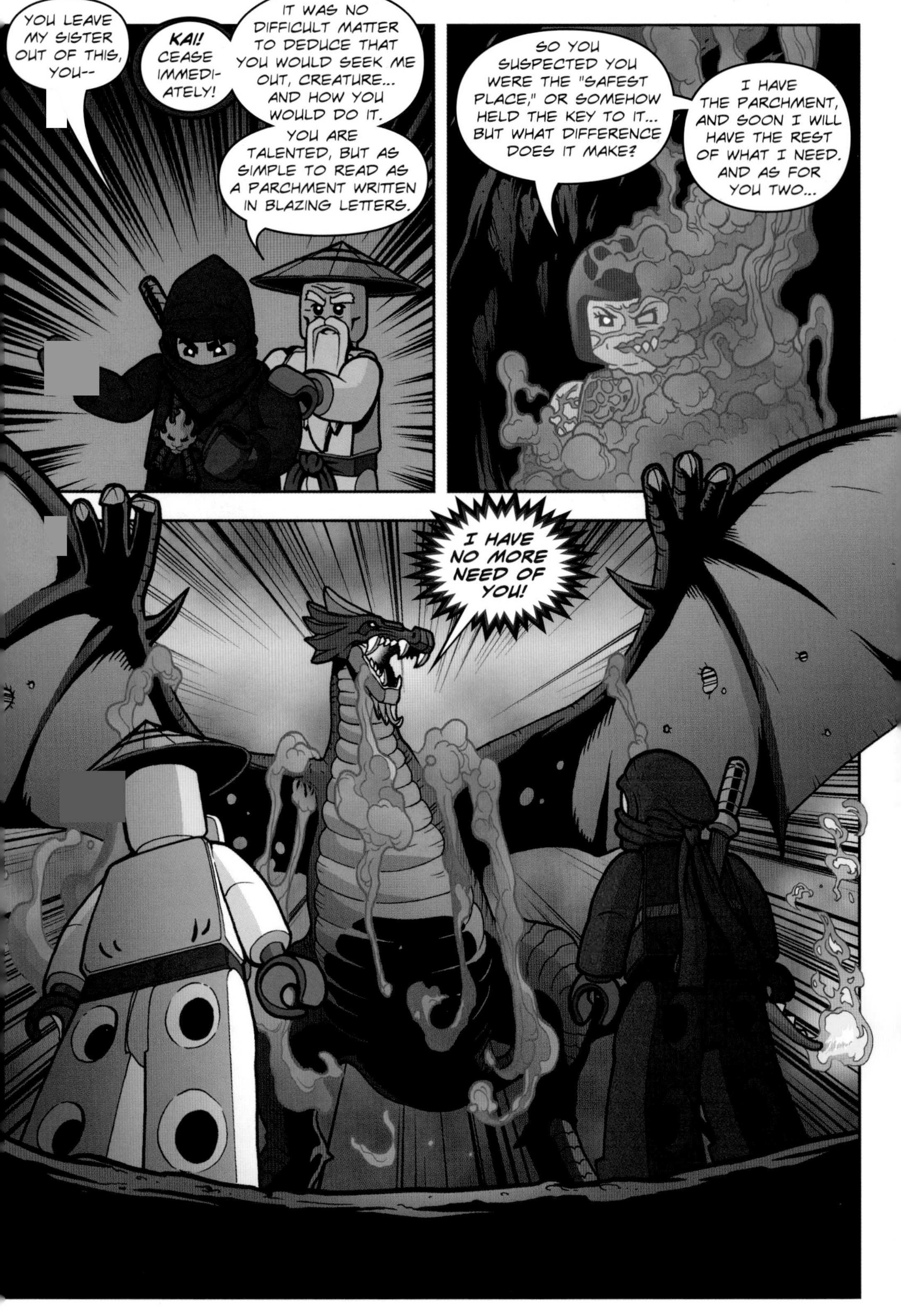
YOU LEAVE MY SISTER OUT OF THIS, YOU--
KAI! CEASE IMMEDI-ATELY!
IT WAS NO DIFFICULT MATTER TO DEDUCE THAT YOU WOULD SEEK ME OUT, CREATURE... AND HOW YOU WOULD DO IT.
YOU ARE TALENTED, BUT AS SIMPLE TO READ AS A PARCHMENT WRITTEN IN BLAZING LETTERS.
SO YOU SUSPECTED YOU WERE THE "SAFEST PLACE," OR SOMEHOW HELD THE KEY TO IT... BUT WHAT DIFFERENCE DOES IT MAKE?
I HAVE THE PARCHMENT, AND SOON I WILL HAVE THE REST OF WHAT I NEED. AND AS FOR YOU TWO...
I HAVE NO MORE NEED OF YOU!

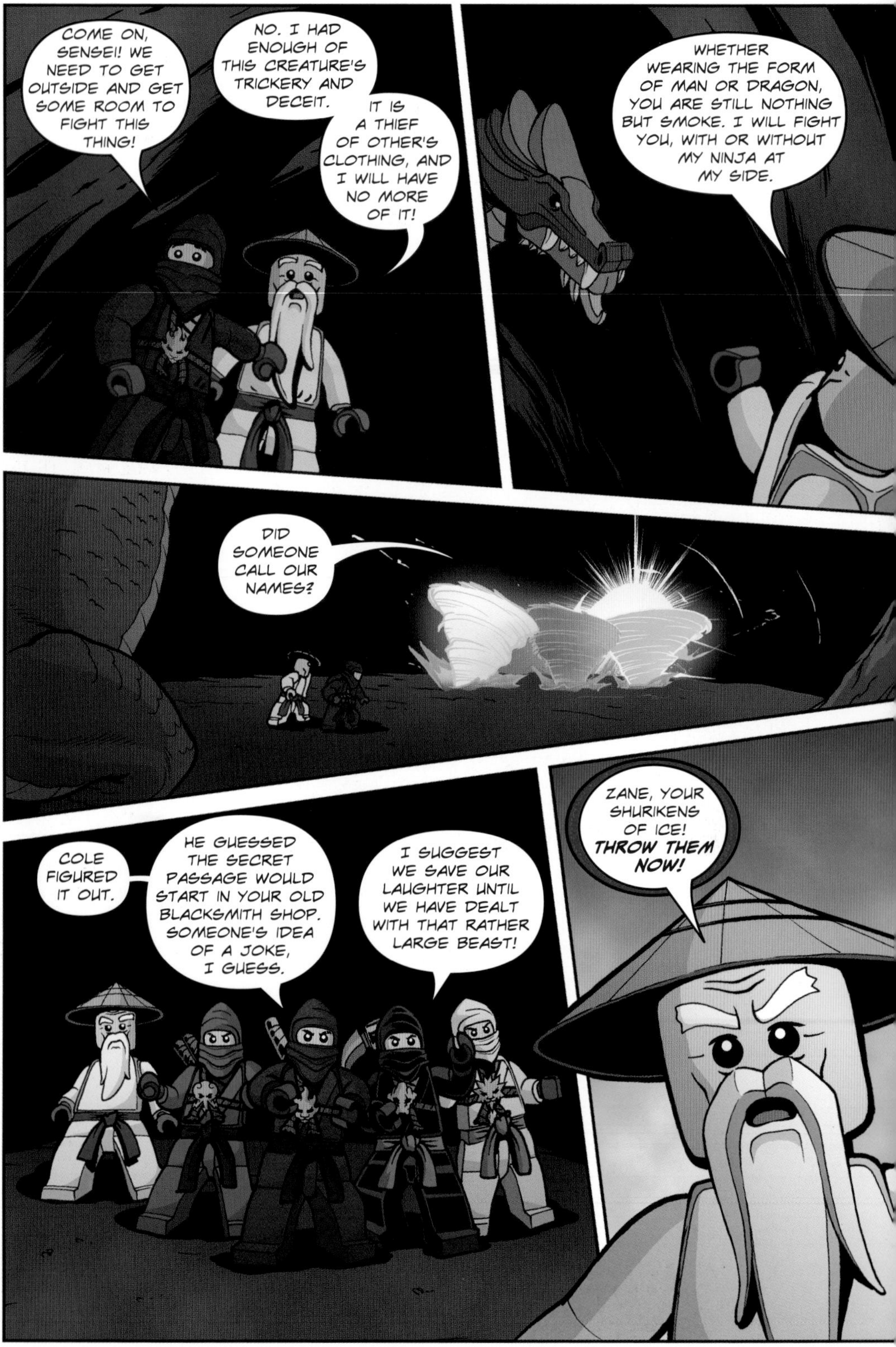
COME ON, SENSEI! WE NEED TO GET OUTSIDE AND GET SOME ROOM TO FIGHT THIS THING!
NO. I HAD ENOUGH OF THIS CREATURE'S TRICKERY AND DECEIT.
IT IS A THIEF OF OTHER'S CLOTHING, AND I WILL HAVE NO MORE OF IT!
WHETHER WEARING THE FORM OF MAN OR DRAGON, YOU ARE STILL NOTHING BUT SMOKE. I WILL FIGHT YOU, WITH OR WITHOUT MY NINJA AT MY SIDE.
DID SOMEONE CALL OUR NAMES?
COLE FIGURED IT OUT.
HE GUESSED THE SECRET PASSAGE WOULD START IN YOUR OLD BLACKSMITH SHOP. SOMEONE'S IDEA OF A JOKE, I GUESS.
I SUGGEST WE SAVE OUR LAUGHTER UNTIL WE HAVE DEALT WITH THAT RATHER LARGE BEAST!
ZANE, YOUR SHURIKENS OF ICE! **THROW THEM NOW!**

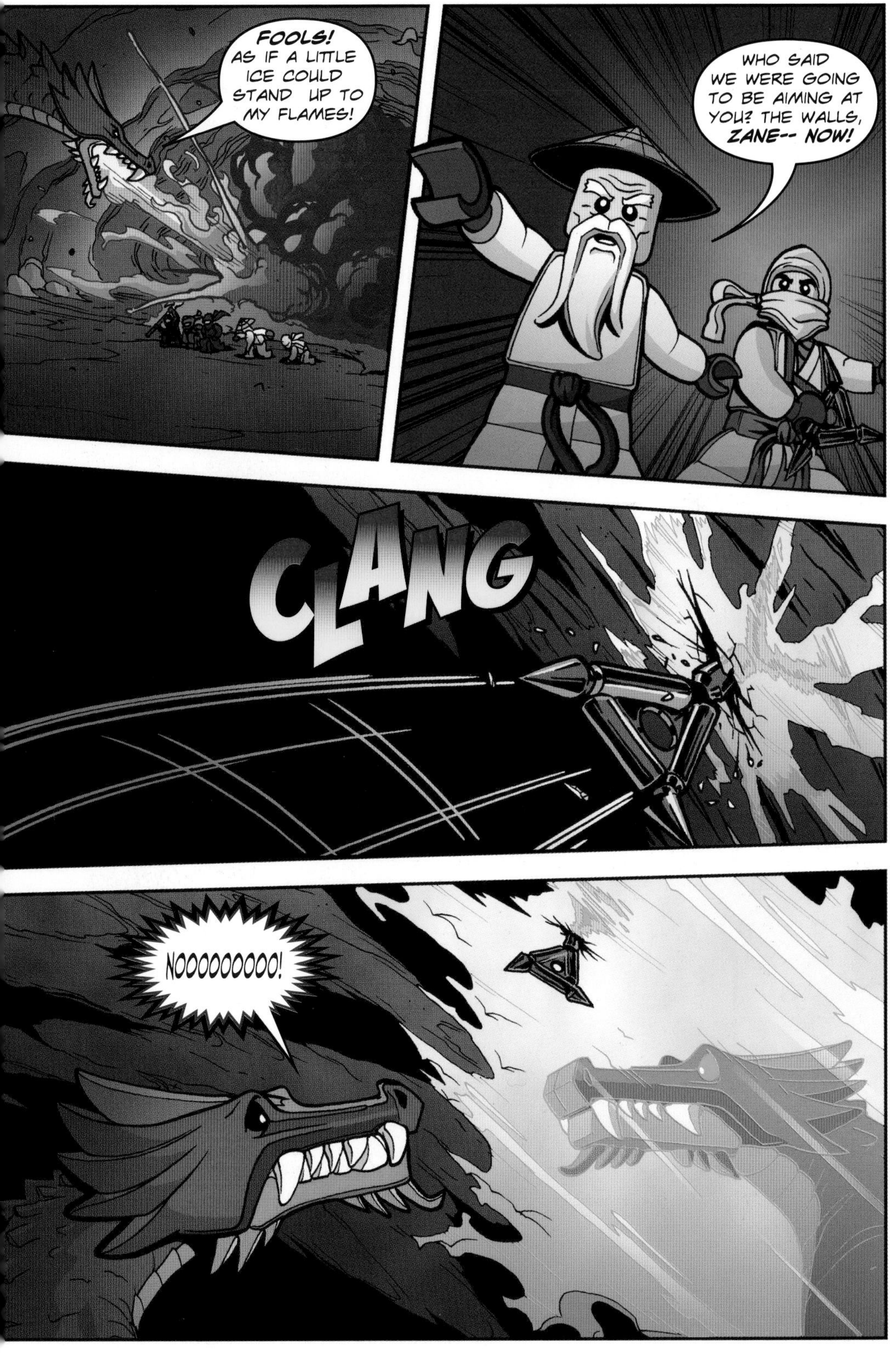
FOOLS! AS IF A LITTLE ICE COULD STAND UP TO MY FLAMES!
WHO SAID WE WERE GOING TO BE AIMING AT YOU? THE WALLS, ZANE-- NOW!
CLANG
NOOOOOOOOO!

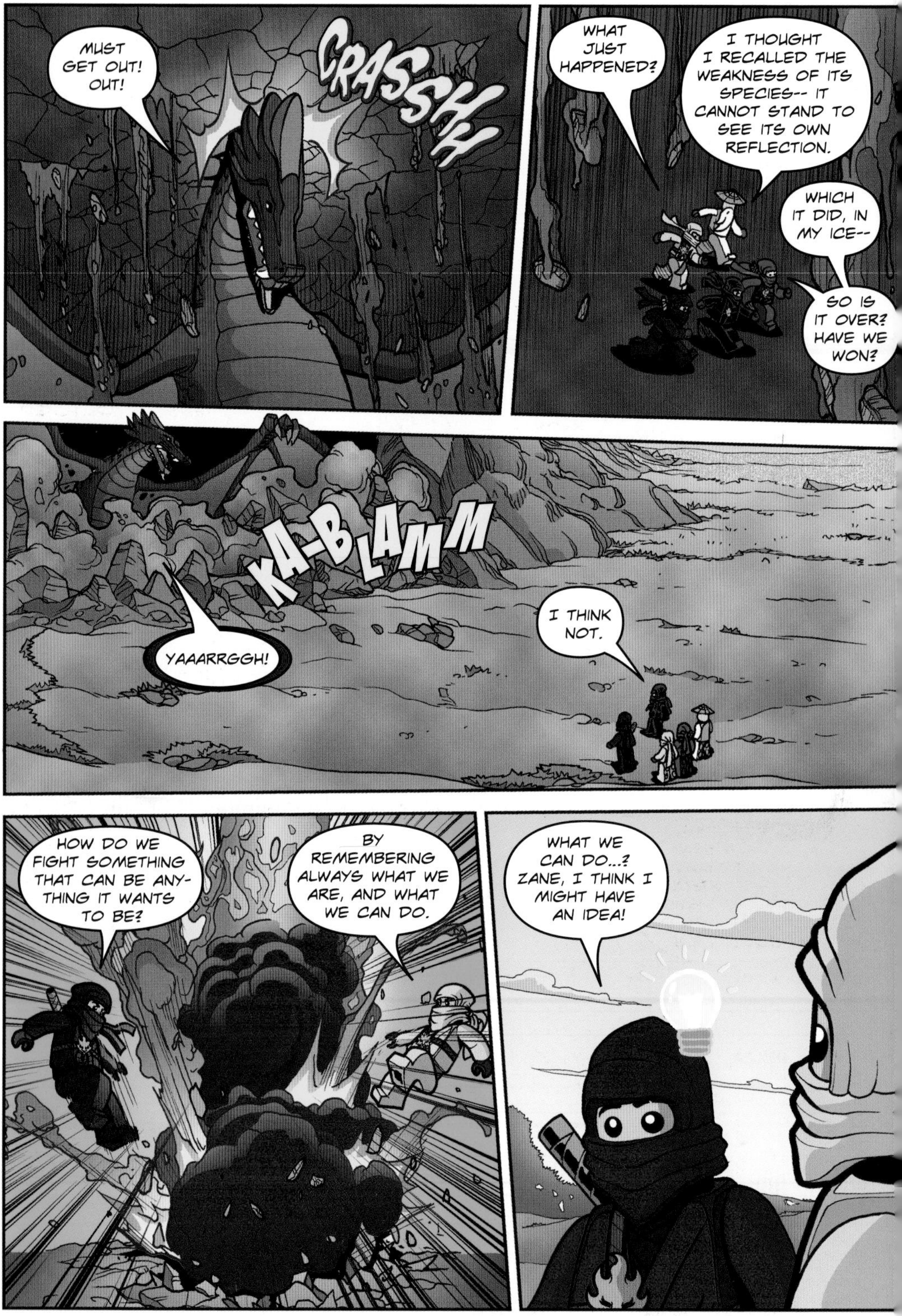
MUST GET OUT! OUT!
CRASSHH
WHAT JUST HAPPENED?
I THOUGHT I RECALLED THE WEAKNESS OF ITS SPECIES-- IT CANNOT STAND TO SEE ITS OWN REFLECTION.
WHICH IT DID, IN MY ICE--
SO IS IT OVER? HAVE WE WON?
KA-BLAMM
YAAARRGGH!
I THINK NOT.
HOW DO WE FIGHT SOMETHING THAT CAN BE ANY-THING IT WANTS TO BE?
BY REMEMBERING ALWAYS WHAT WE ARE, AND WHAT WE CAN DO.
WHAT WE CAN DO...? ZANE, I THINK I MIGHT HAVE AN IDEA!

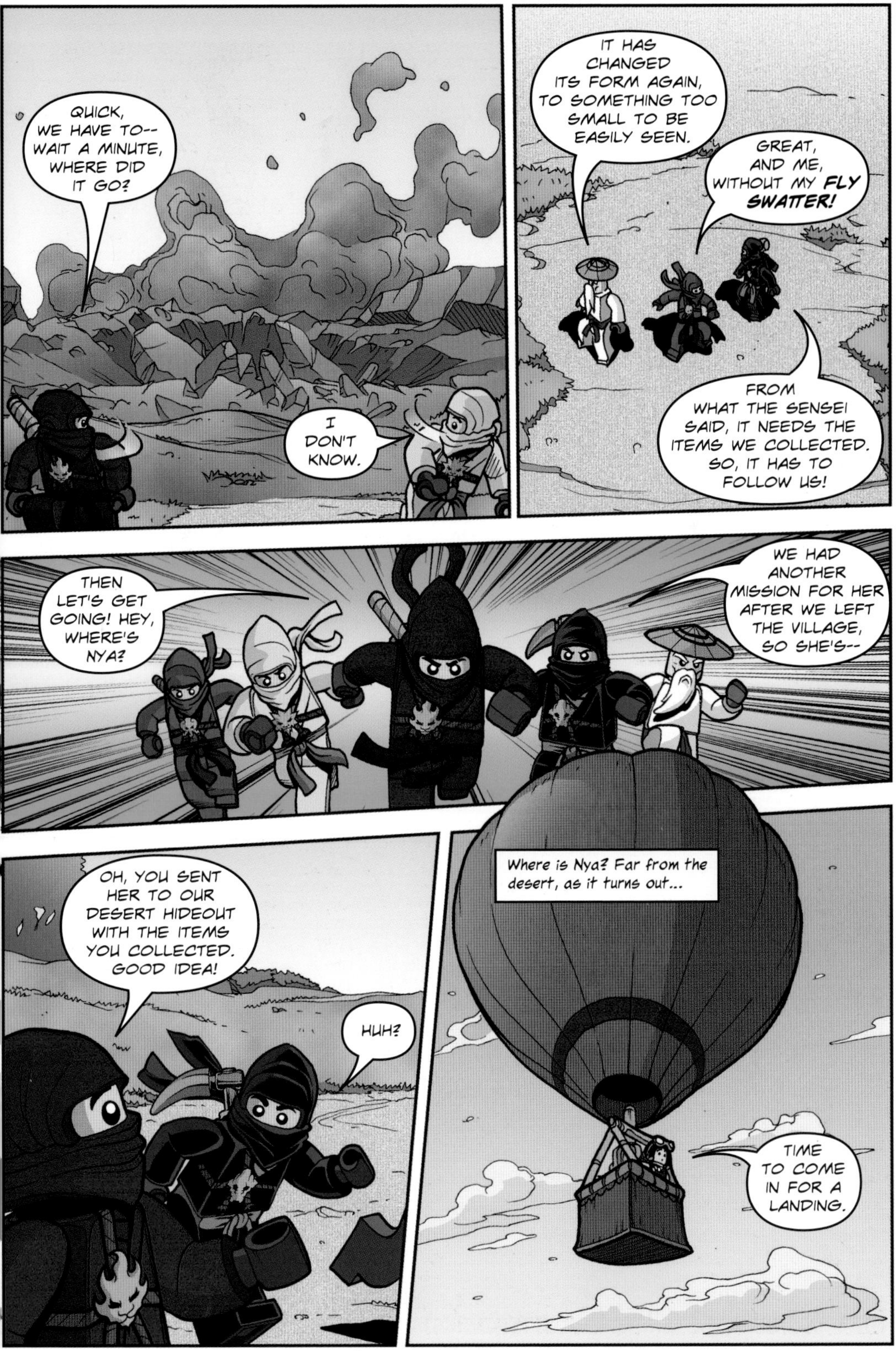
QUICK, WE HAVE TO-- WAIT A MINUTE, WHERE DID IT GO?
I DON'T KNOW.
IT HAS CHANGED ITS FORM AGAIN, TO SOMETHING TOO SMALL TO BE EASILY SEEN.
GREAT, AND ME, WITHOUT MY **FLY SWATTER!**
FROM WHAT THE SENSEI SAID, IT NEEDS THE ITEMS WE COLLECTED. SO, IT HAS TO FOLLOW US!
THEN LET'S GET GOING! HEY, WHERE'S NYA?
WE HAD ANOTHER MISSION FOR HER AFTER WE LEFT THE VILLAGE, SO SHE'S--
OH, YOU SENT HER TO OUR DESERT HIDEOUT WITH THE ITEMS YOU COLLECTED. GOOD IDEA!
HUH?
Where is Nya? Far from the desert, as it turns out...
TIME TO COME IN FOR A LANDING.

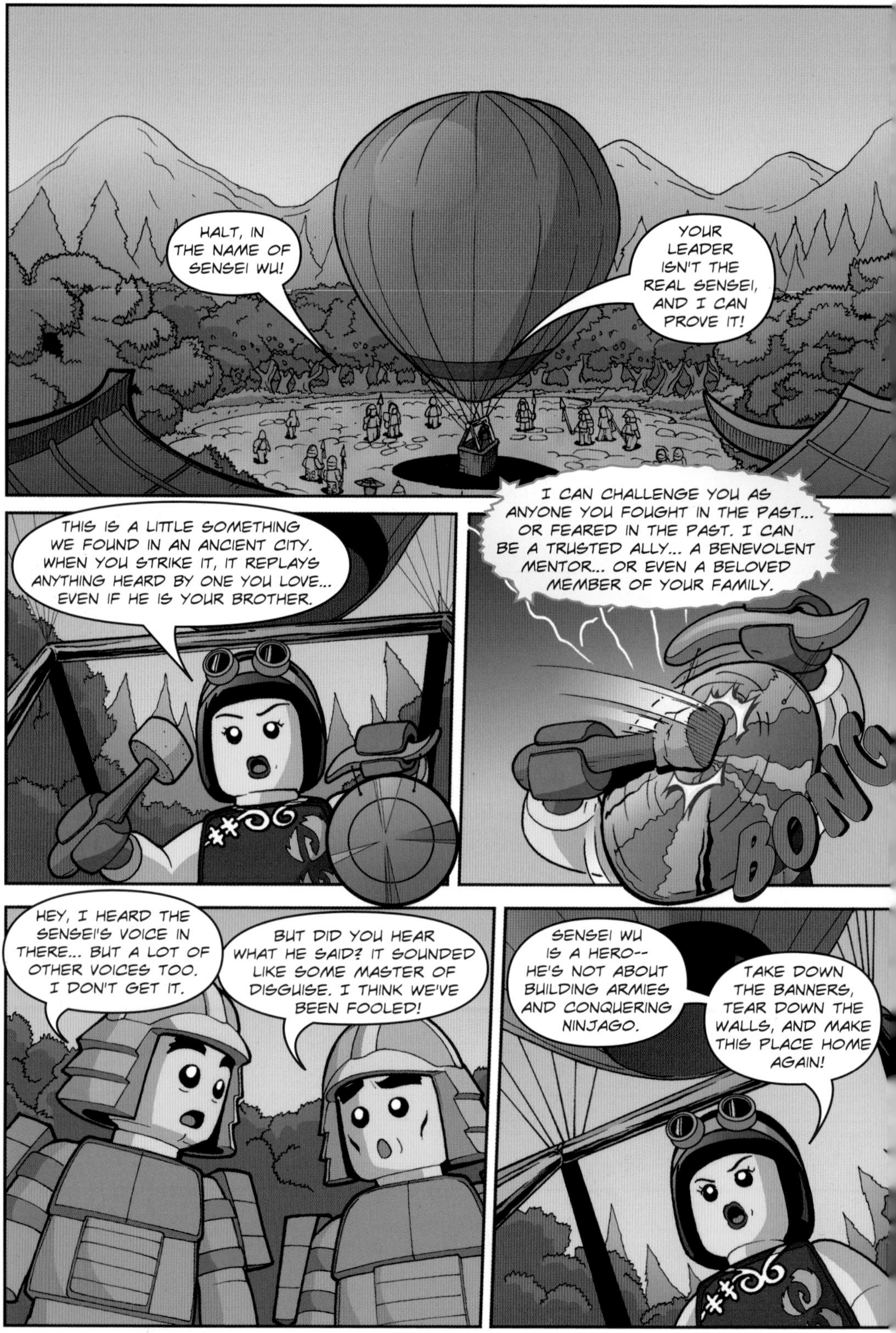
HALT, IN THE NAME OF SENSEI WU!
YOUR LEADER ISN'T THE REAL SENSEI, AND I CAN PROVE IT!
THIS IS A LITTLE SOMETHING WE FOUND IN AN ANCIENT CITY. WHEN YOU STRIKE IT, IT REPLAYS ANYTHING HEARD BY ONE YOU LOVE... EVEN IF HE IS YOUR BROTHER.
I CAN CHALLENGE YOU AS ANYONE YOU FOUGHT IN THE PAST... OR FEARED IN THE PAST. I CAN BE A TRUSTED ALLY... A BENEVOLENT MENTOR... OR EVEN A BELOVED MEMBER OF YOUR FAMILY.
BONG
HEY, I HEARD THE SENSEI'S VOICE IN THERE... BUT A LOT OF OTHER VOICES TOO. I DON'T GET IT.
BUT DID YOU HEAR WHAT HE SAID? IT SOUNDED LIKE SOME MASTER OF DISGUISE. I THINK WE'VE BEEN FOOLED!
SENSEI WU IS A HERO-- HE'S NOT ABOUT BUILDING ARMIES AND CONQUERING NINJAGO.
TAKE DOWN THE BANNERS, TEAR DOWN THE WALLS, AND MAKE THIS PLACE HOME AGAIN!

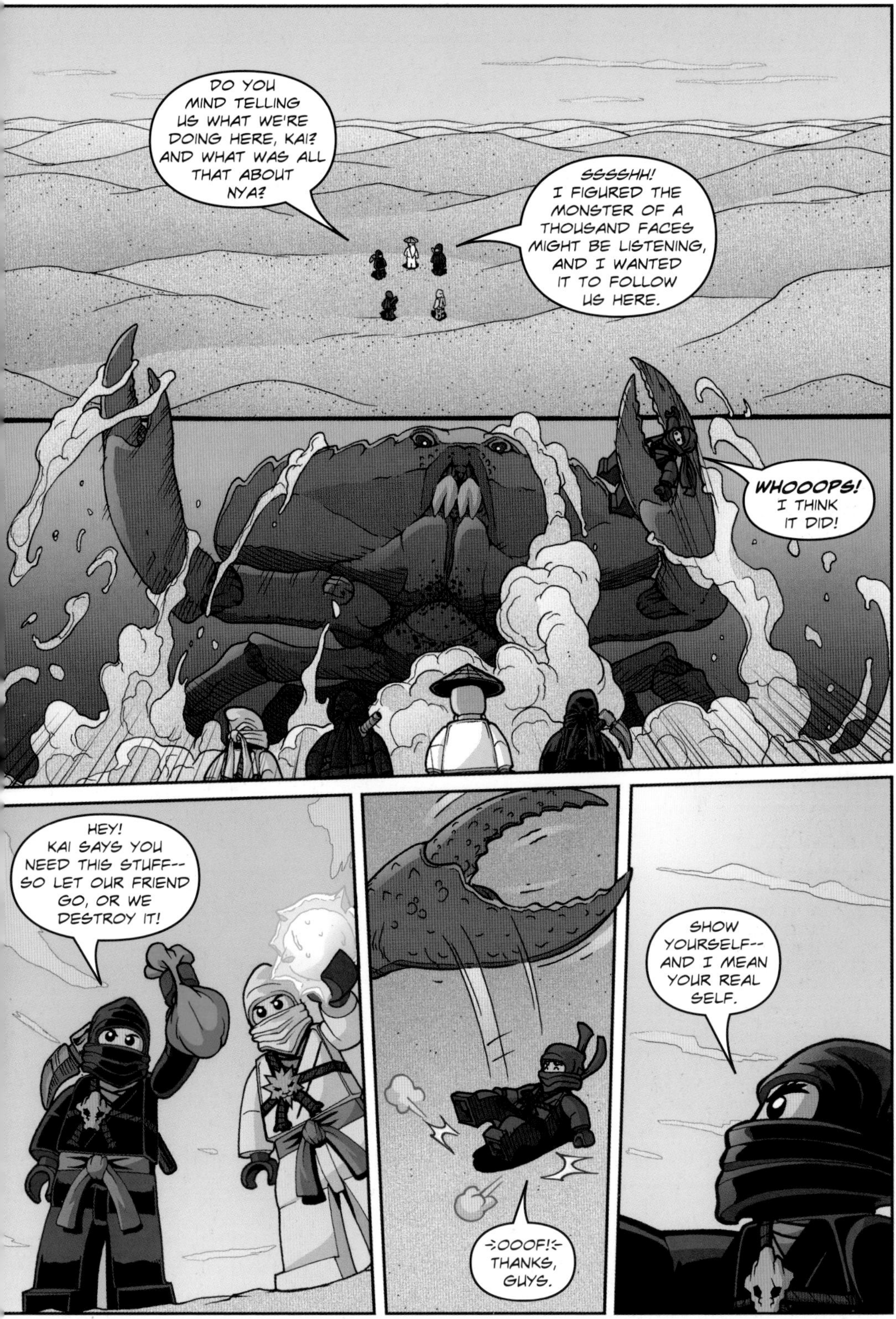
DO YOU MIND TELLING US WHAT WE'RE DOING HERE, KAI? AND WHAT WAS ALL THAT ABOUT NYA?
SSSSHH! I FIGURED THE MONSTER OF A THOUSAND FACES MIGHT BE LISTENING, AND I WANTED IT TO FOLLOW US HERE.
WHOOOPS! I THINK IT DID!
HEY! KAI SAYS YOU NEED THIS STUFF-- SO LET OUR FRIEND GO, OR WE DESTROY IT!
OOOF! THANKS, GUYS.
SHOW YOURSELF-- AND I MEAN YOUR REAL SELF.

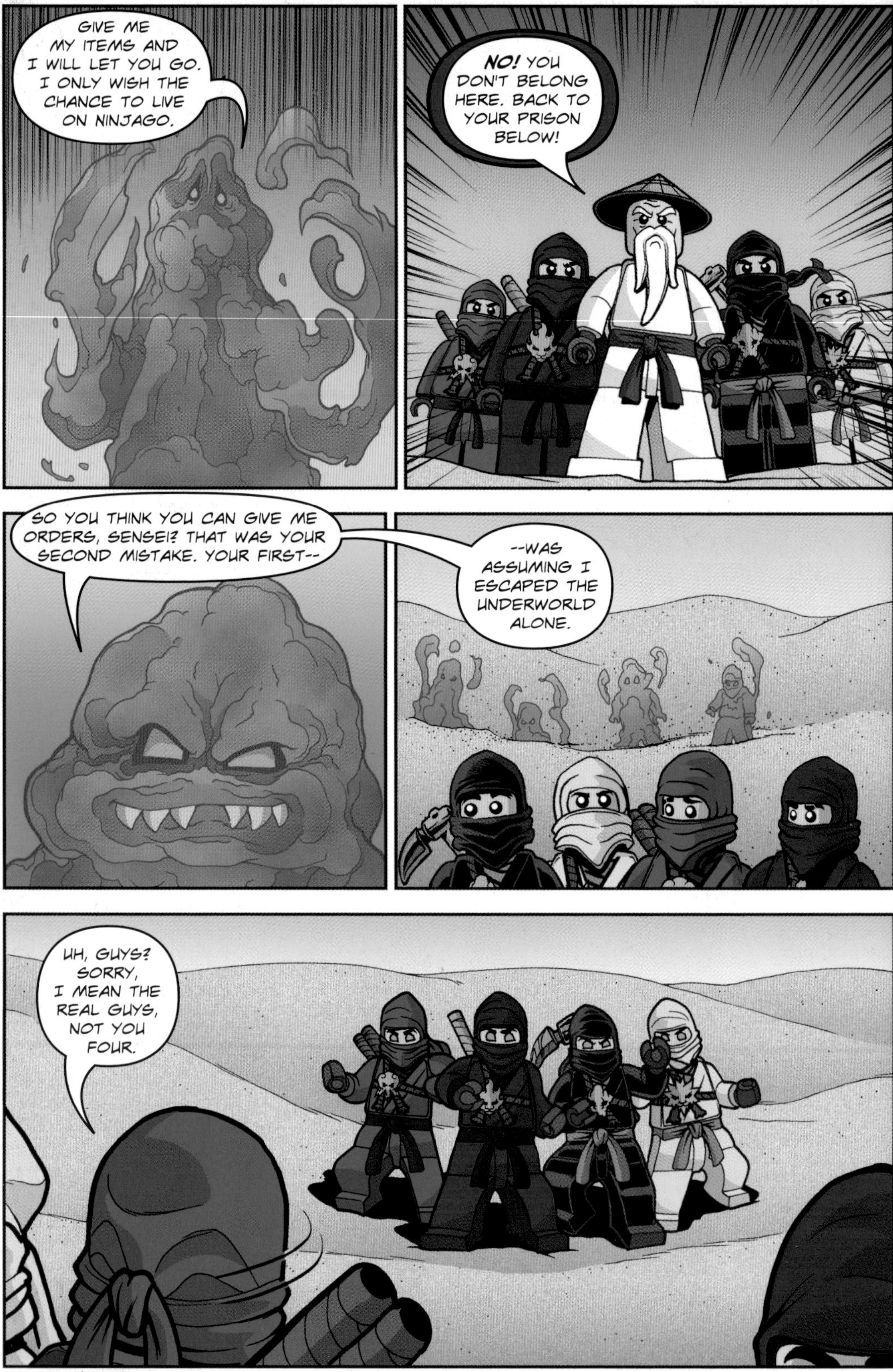
GIVE ME MY ITEMS AND I WILL LET YOU GO. I ONLY WISH THE CHANCE TO LIVE ON NINJAGO.
NO! YOU DON'T BELONG HERE. BACK TO YOUR PRISON BELOW!
SO YOU THINK YOU CAN GIVE ME ORDERS, SENSEI? THAT WAS YOUR SECOND MISTAKE. YOUR FIRST--
--WAS ASSUMING I ESCAPED THE UNDERWORLD ALONE.
UH, GUYS? SORRY, I MEAN THE REAL GUYS, NOT YOU FOUR.

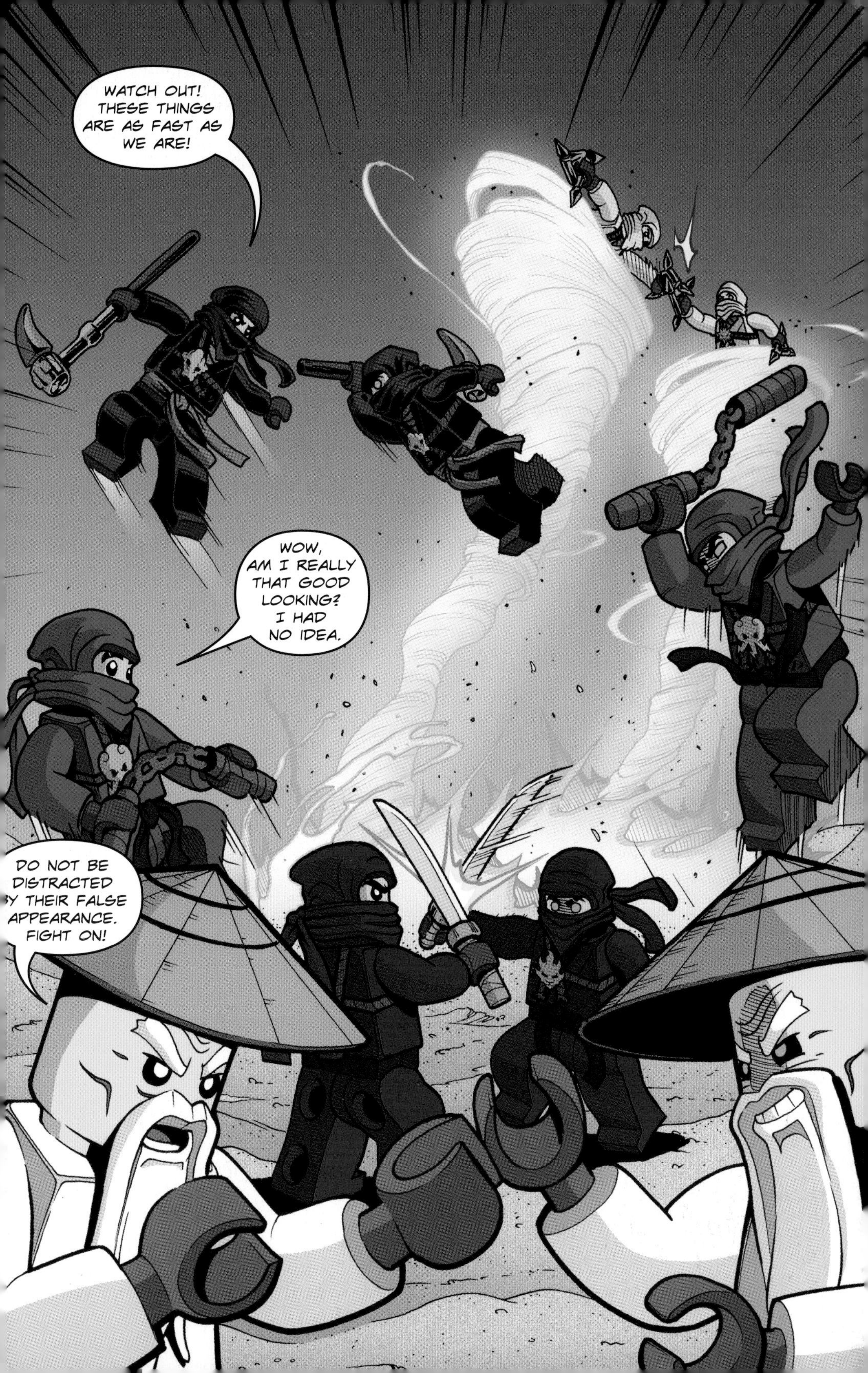
WATCH OUT! THESE THINGS ARE AS FAST AS WE ARE!
WOW, AM I REALLY THAT GOOD LOOKING? I HAD NO IDEA.
DO NOT BE DISTRACTED BY THEIR FALSE APPEARANCE. FIGHT ON!

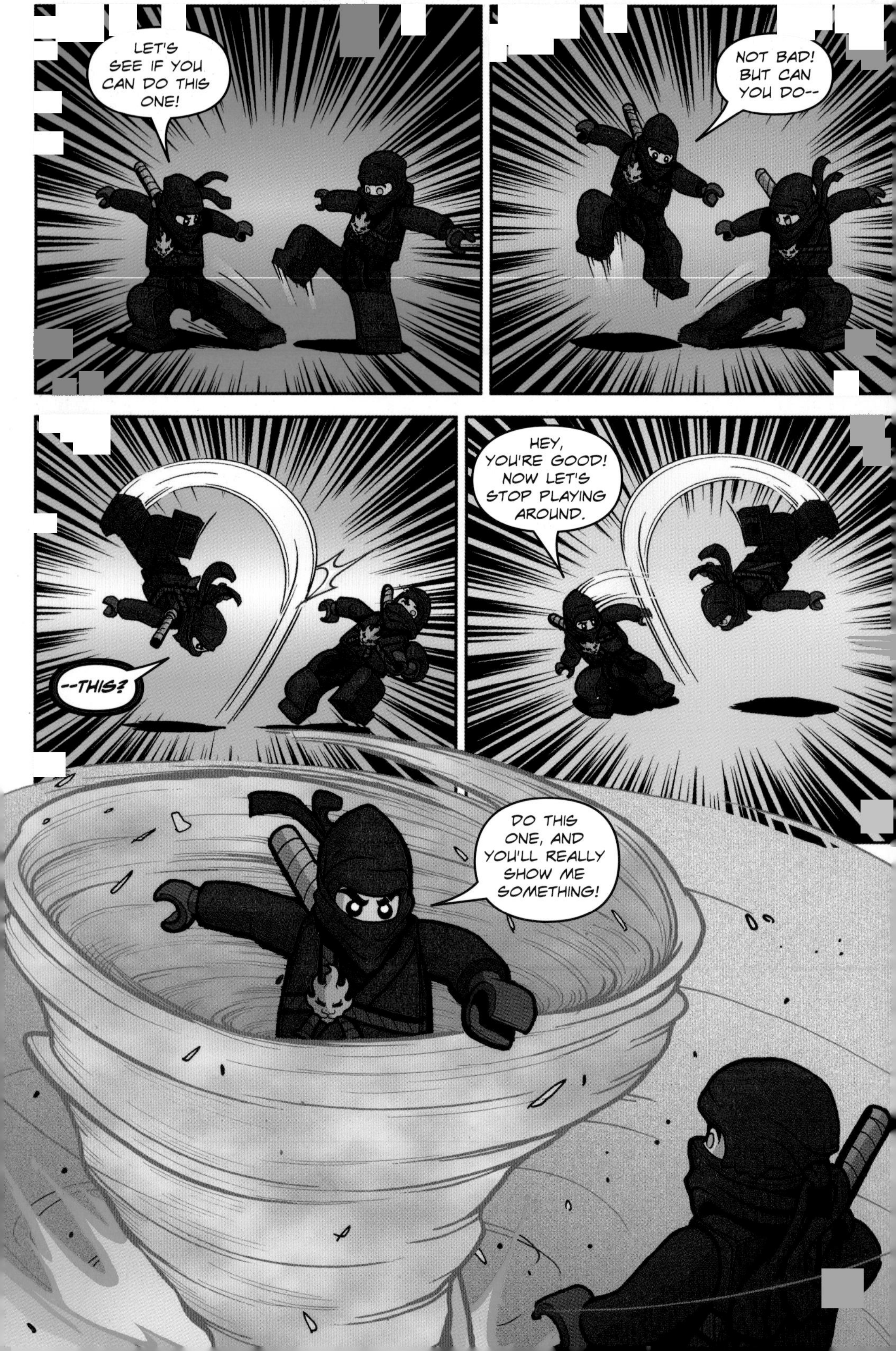
LET'S SEE IF YOU CAN DO THIS ONE!
NOT BAD! BUT CAN YOU DO--
--THIS?
HEY, YOU'RE GOOD! NOW LET'S STOP PLAYING AROUND.
DO THIS ONE, AND YOU'LL REALLY SHOW ME SOMETHING!

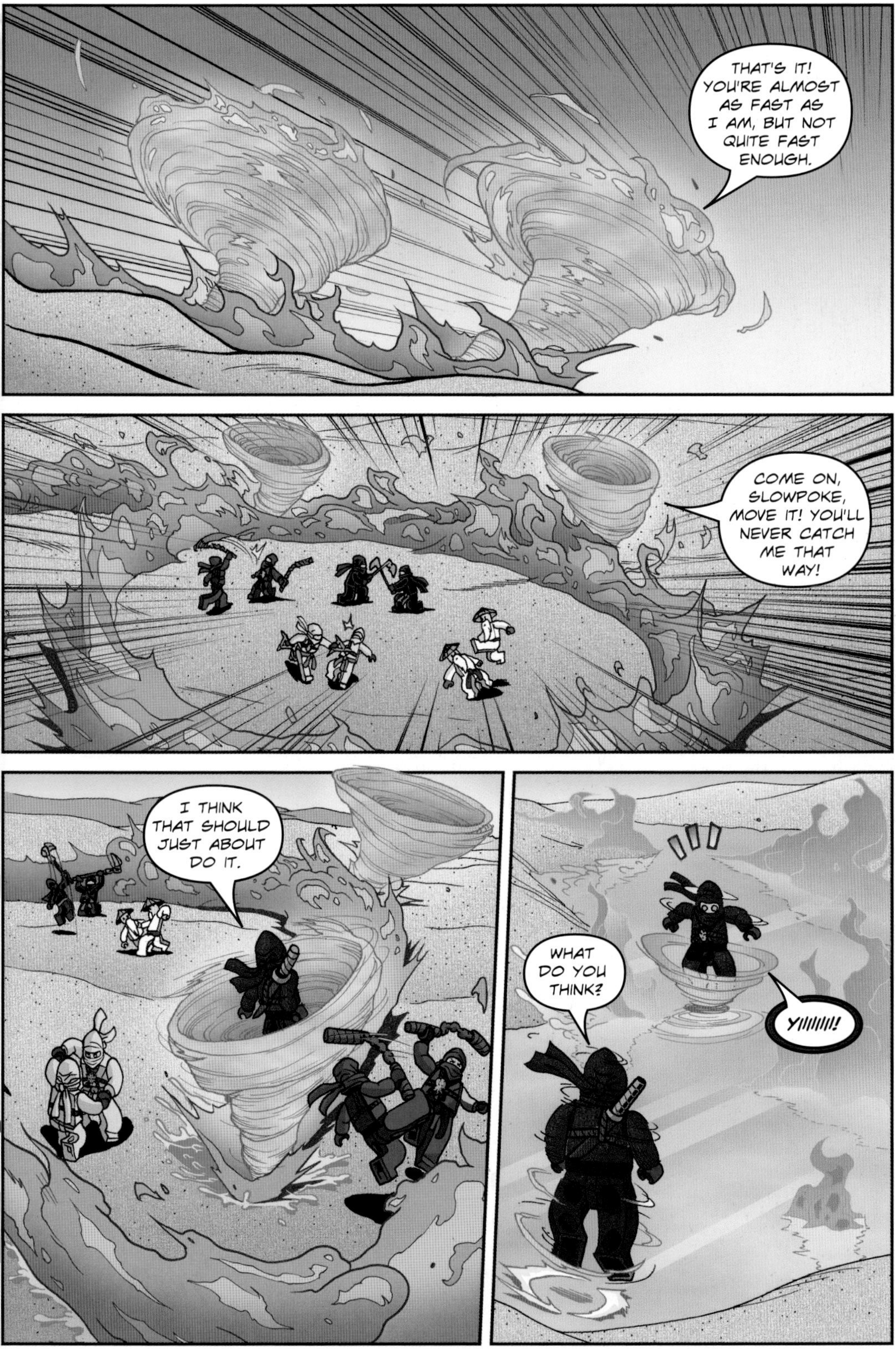
THAT'S IT! YOU'RE ALMOST AS FAST AS I AM, BUT NOT QUITE FAST ENOUGH.
COME ON, SLOWPOKE, MOVE IT! YOU'LL NEVER CATCH ME THAT WAY!
I THINK THAT SHOULD JUST ABOUT DO IT.
WHAT DO YOU THINK?
YIIIIIII!

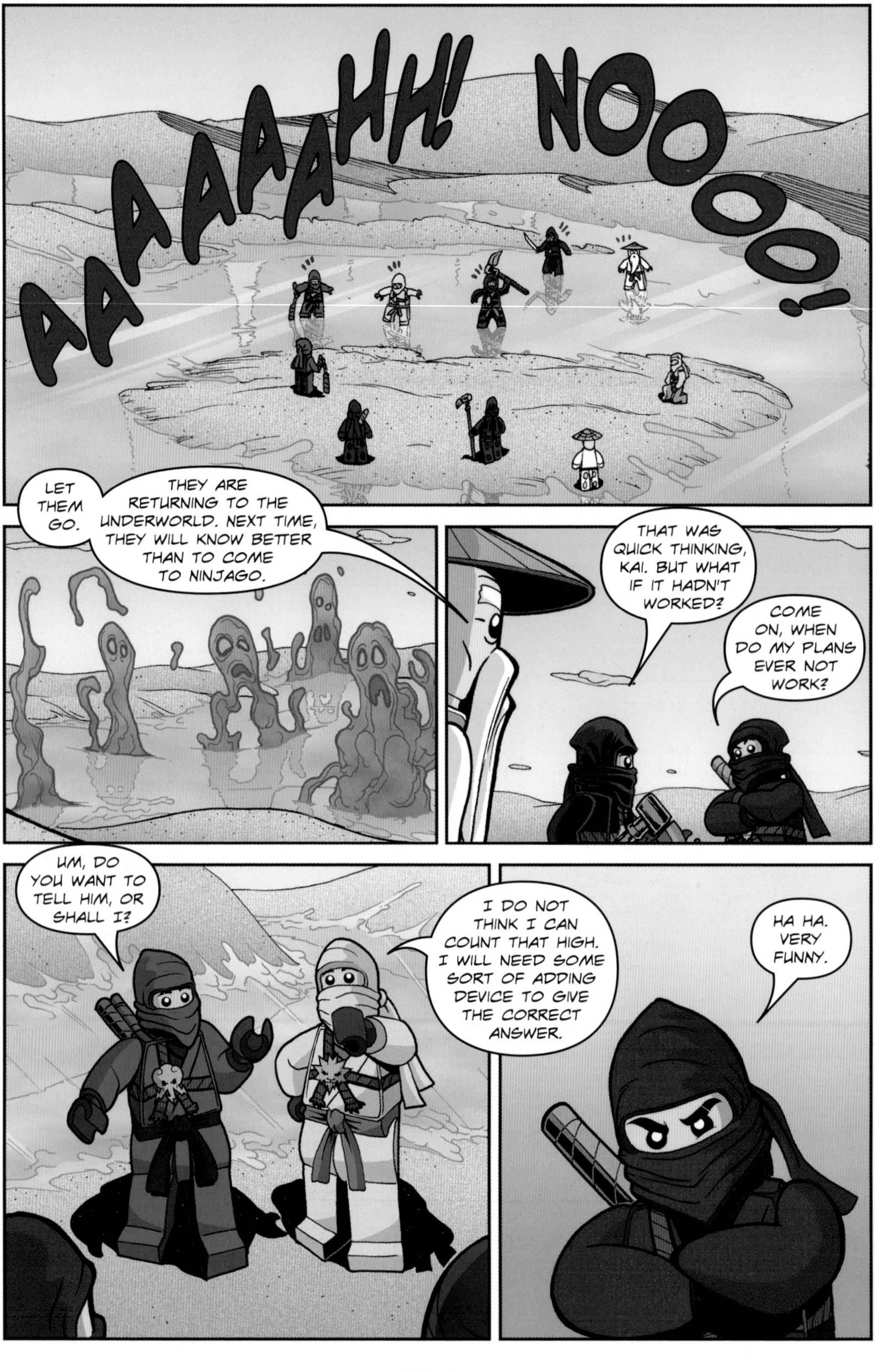
AAAAAAHH! NOOOOO!
LET THEM GO.
THEY ARE RETURNING TO THE UNDERWORLD. NEXT TIME, THEY WILL KNOW BETTER THAN TO COME TO NINJAGO.
THAT WAS QUICK THINKING, KAI. BUT WHAT IF IT HADN'T WORKED?
COME ON, WHEN DO MY PLANS EVER NOT WORK?
UM, DO YOU WANT TO TELL HIM, OR SHALL I?
I DO NOT THINK I CAN COUNT THAT HIGH. I WILL NEED SOME SORT OF ADDING DEVICE TO GIVE THE CORRECT ANSWER.
HA HA. VERY FUNNY.

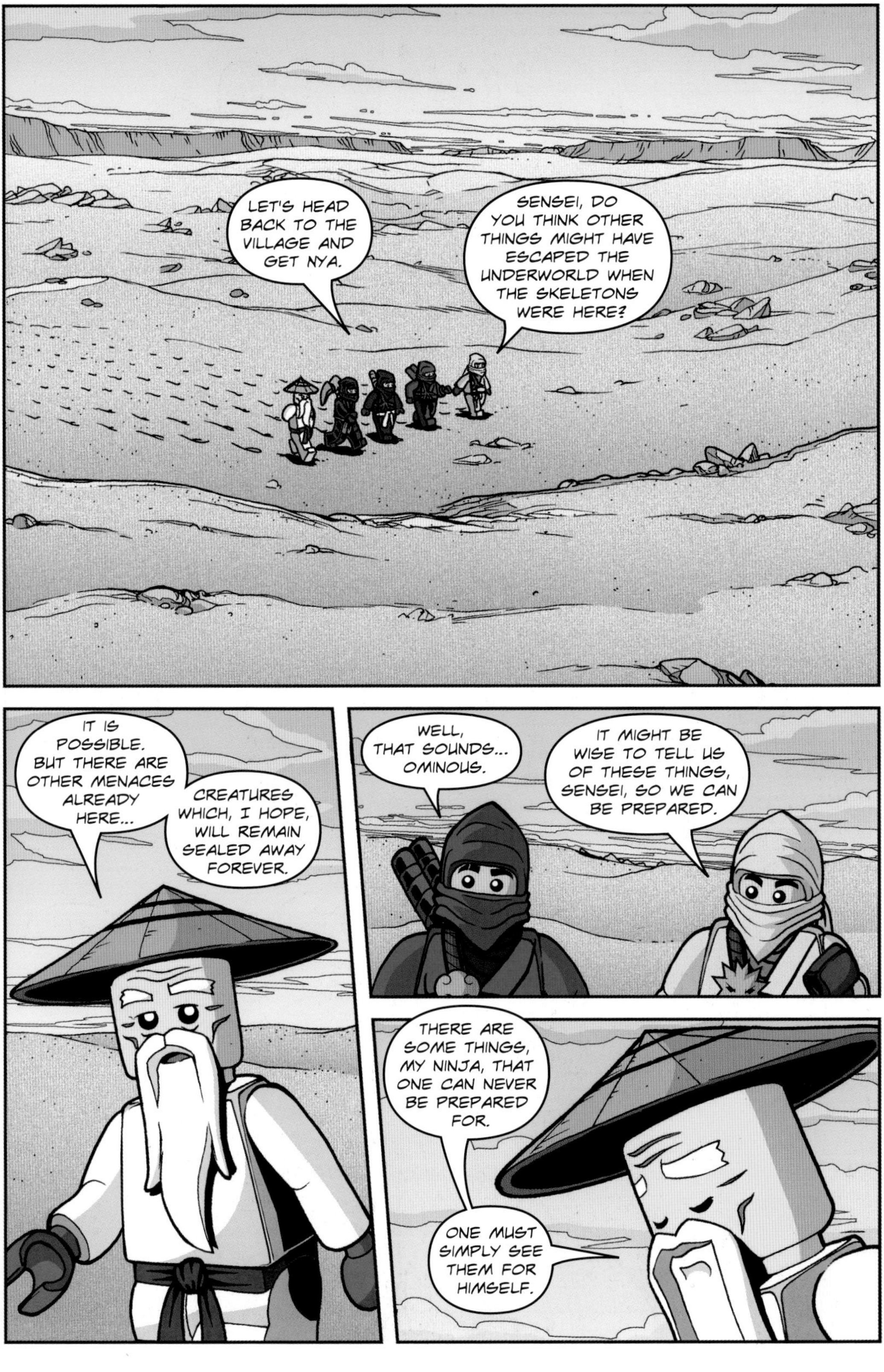
LET'S HEAD BACK TO THE VILLAGE AND GET NYA.
SENSEI, DO YOU THINK OTHER THINGS MIGHT HAVE ESCAPED THE UNDERWORLD WHEN THE SKELETONS WERE HERE?
IT IS POSSIBLE. BUT THERE ARE OTHER MENACES ALREADY HERE...
CREATURES WHICH, I HOPE, WILL REMAIN SEALED AWAY FOREVER.
WELL, THAT SOUNDS... OMINOUS.
IT MIGHT BE WISE TO TELL US OF THESE THINGS, SENSEI, SO WE CAN BE PREPARED.
THERE ARE SOME THINGS, MY NINJA, THAT ONE CAN NEVER BE PREPARED FOR.
ONE MUST SIMPLY SEE THEM FOR HIMSELF.

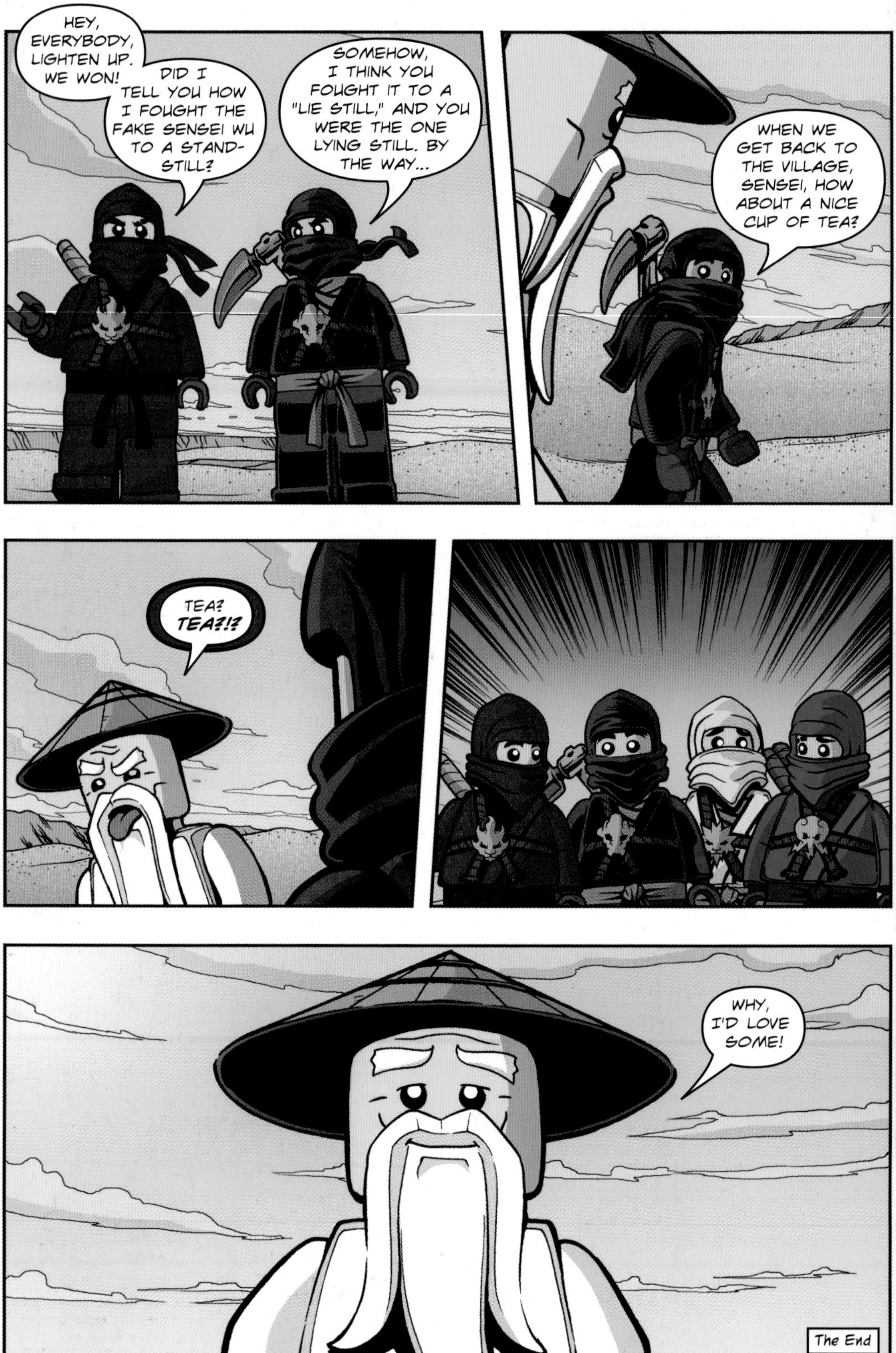
HEY, EVERYBODY, LIGHTEN UP. WE WON!
DID I TELL YOU HOW I FOUGHT THE FAKE SENSEI WU TO A STAND-STILL?
SOMEHOW, I THINK YOU FOUGHT IT TO A "LIE STILL," AND YOU WERE THE ONE LYING STILL. BY THE WAY...
WHEN WE GET BACK TO THE VILLAGE, SENSEI, HOW ABOUT A NICE CUP OF TEA?
TEA? TEA?!?
WHY, I'D LOVE SOME!
The End

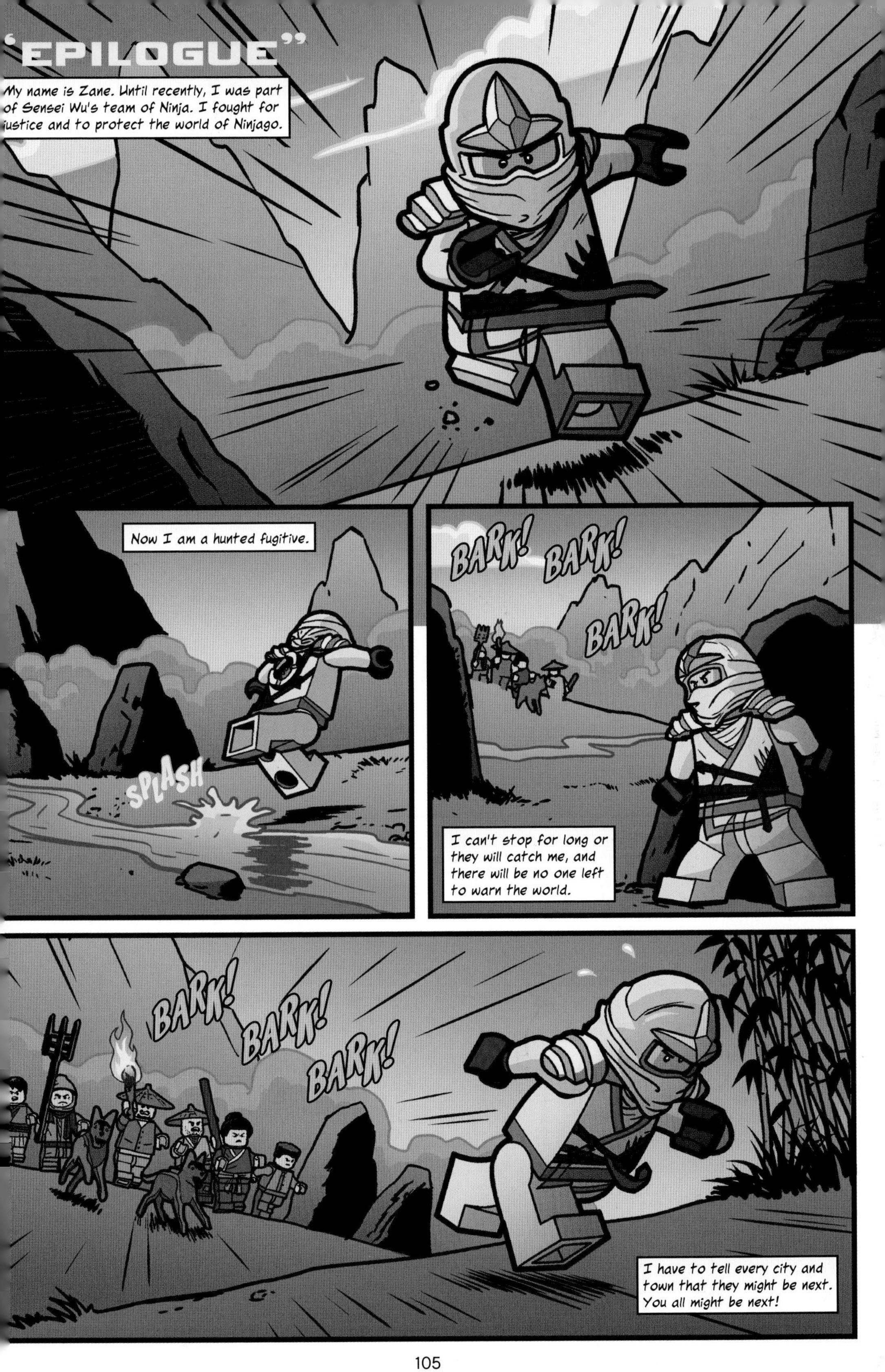
"EPILOGUE"
My name is Zane. Until recently, I was part of Sensei Wu's team of Ninja. I fought for justice and to protect the world of Ninjago.
Now I am a hunted fugitive.
SPLASH
BARK! BARK!
BARK!
I can't stop for long or they will catch me, and there will be no one left to warn the world.
BARK!
BARK!
BARK!
I have to tell every city and town that they might be next. You all might be next!

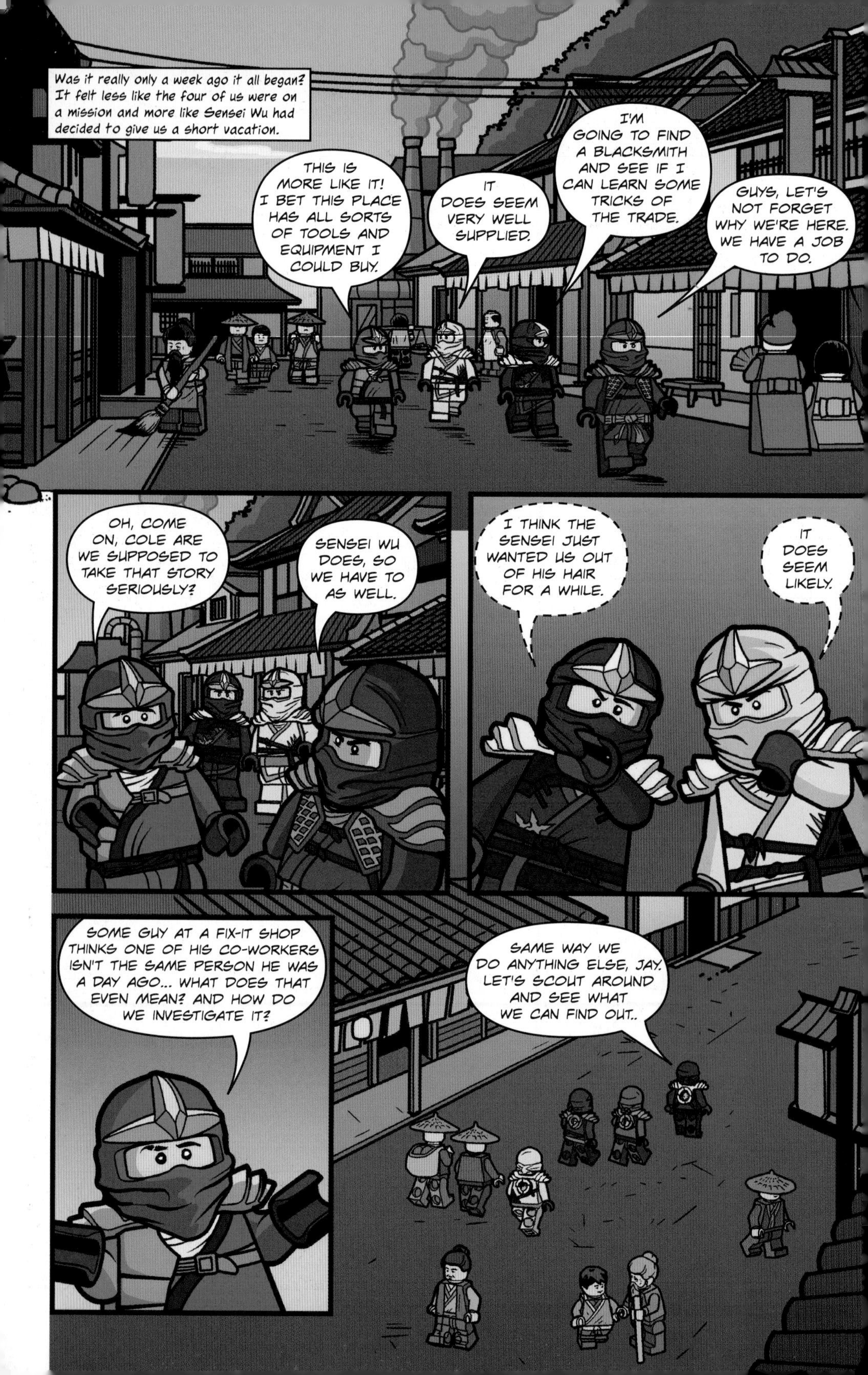
Was it really only a week ago it all began? It felt less like the four of us were on a mission and more like Sensei Wu had decided to give us a short vacation.
THIS IS MORE LIKE IT! I BET THIS PLACE HAS ALL SORTS OF TOOLS AND EQUIPMENT I COULD BUY.
IT DOES SEEM VERY WELL SUPPLIED.
I'M GOING TO FIND A BLACKSMITH AND SEE IF I CAN LEARN SOME TRICKS OF THE TRADE.
GUYS, LET'S NOT FORGET WHY WE'RE HERE. WE HAVE A JOB TO DO.
OH, COME ON, COLE ARE WE SUPPOSED TO TAKE THAT STORY SERIOUSLY?
SENSEI WU DOES, SO WE HAVE TO AS WELL.
I THINK THE SENSEI JUST WANTED US OUT OF HIS HAIR FOR A WHILE.
IT DOES SEEM LIKELY.
SOME GUY AT A FIX-IT SHOP THINKS ONE OF HIS CO-WORKERS ISN'T THE SAME PERSON HE WAS A DAY AGO... WHAT DOES THAT EVEN MEAN? AND HOW DO WE INVESTIGATE IT?
SAME WAY WE DO ANYTHING ELSE, JAY. LET'S SCOUT AROUND AND SEE WHAT WE CAN FIND OUT..

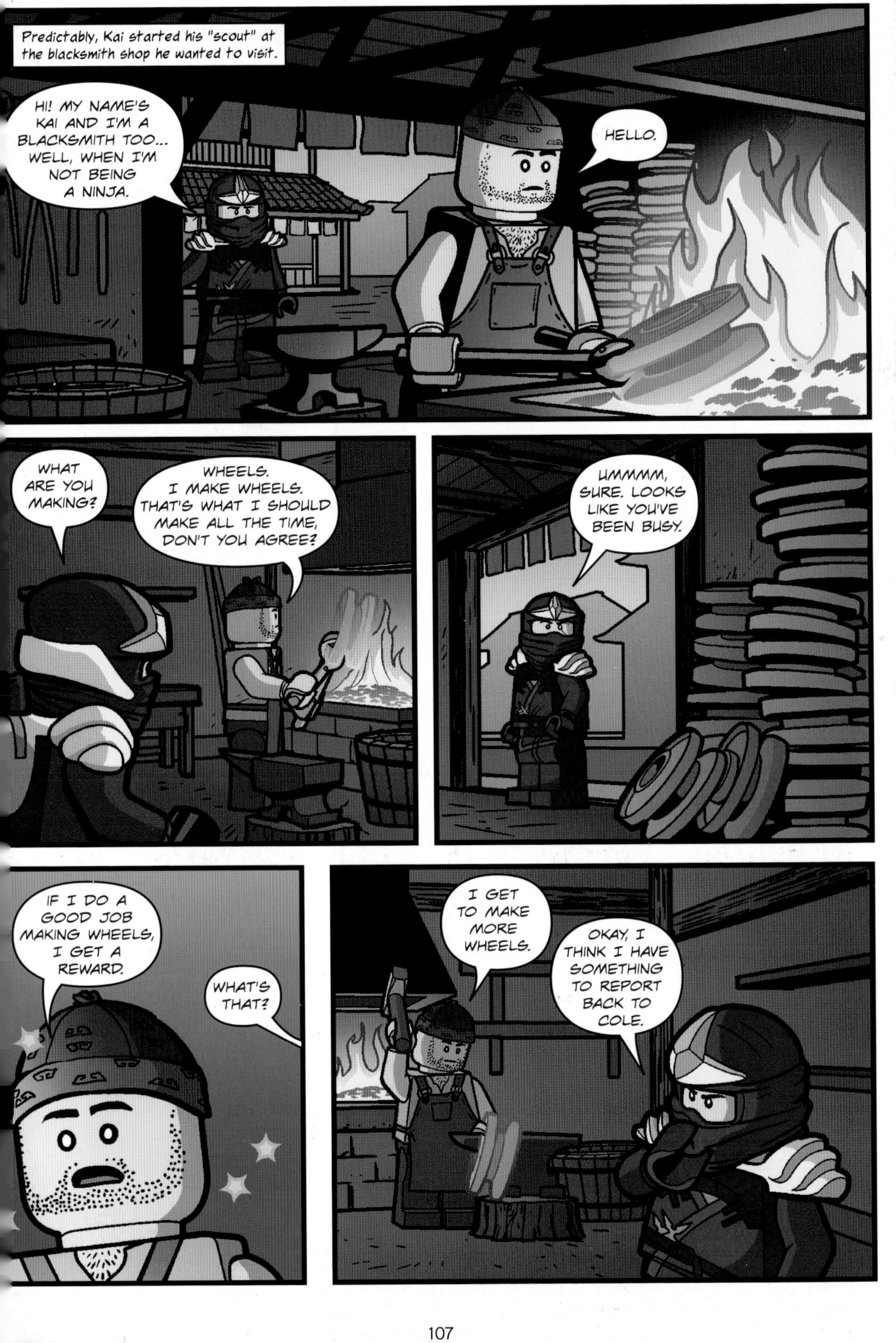
Predictably, Kai started his "scout" at the blacksmith shop he wanted to visit.
HI! MY NAME'S KAI AND I'M A BLACKSMITH TOO... WELL, WHEN I'M NOT BEING A NINJA.
HELLO.
WHAT ARE YOU MAKING?
WHEELS. I MAKE WHEELS. THAT'S WHAT I SHOULD MAKE ALL THE TIME, DON'T YOU AGREE?
UMMMM, SURE. LOOKS LIKE YOU'VE BEEN BUSY.
IF I DO A GOOD JOB MAKING WHEELS, I GET A REWARD.
WHAT'S THAT?
I GET TO MAKE MORE WHEELS.
OKAY, I THINK I HAVE SOMETHING TO REPORT BACK TO COLE.

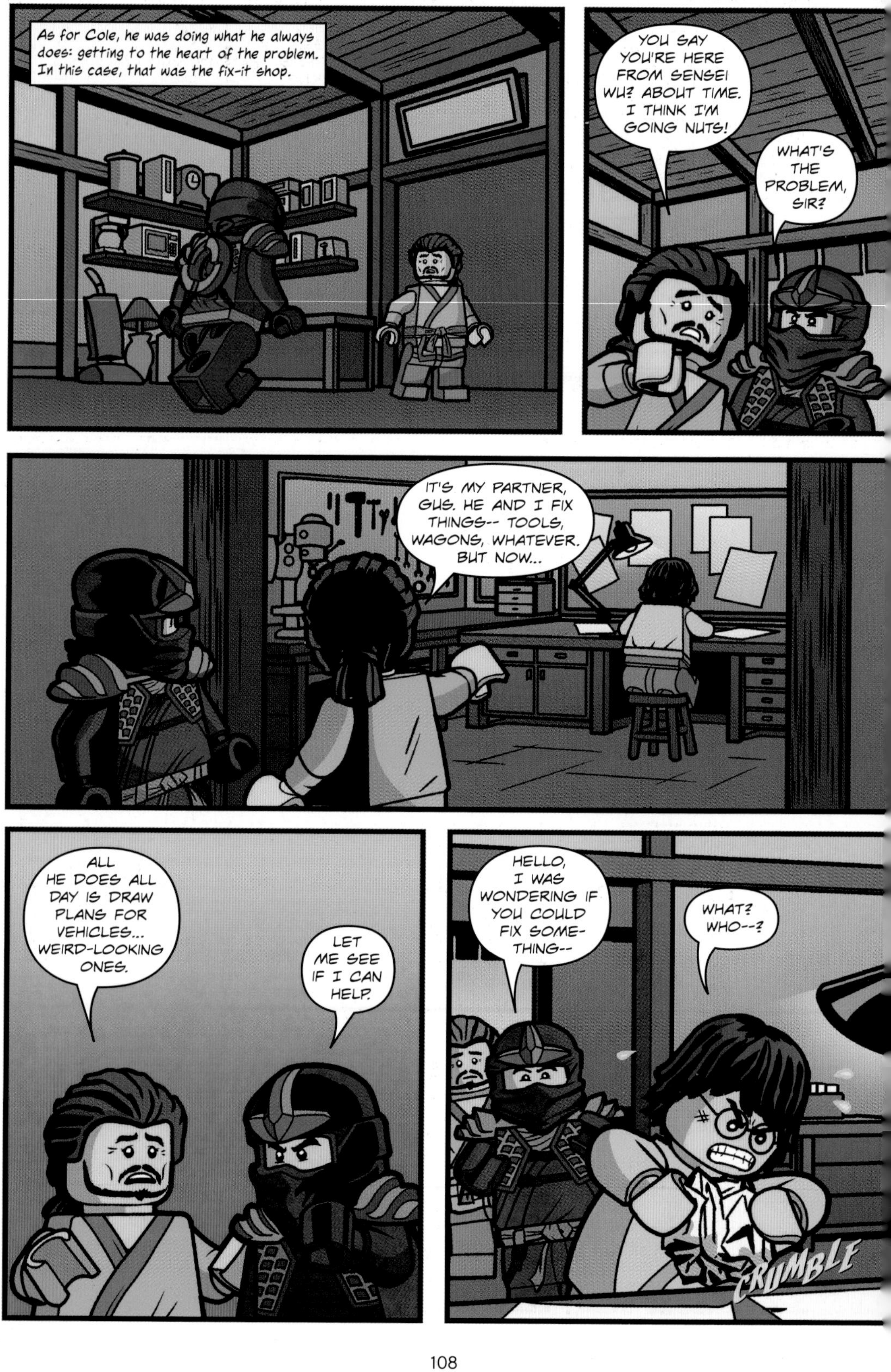
As for Cole, he was doing what he always does: getting to the heart of the problem. In this case, that was the fix-it shop.
YOU SAY YOU'RE HERE FROM SENSEI WU? ABOUT TIME. I THINK I'M GOING NUTS!
WHAT'S THE PROBLEM, SIR?
IT'S MY PARTNER, GUS. HE AND I FIX THINGS-- TOOLS, WAGONS, WHATEVER. BUT NOW...
ALL HE DOES ALL DAY IS DRAW PLANS FOR VEHICLES... WEIRD-LOOKING ONES.
LET ME SEE IF I CAN HELP.
HELLO, I WAS WONDERING IF YOU COULD FIX SOME-THING--
WHAT? WHO--?
CRUMBLE

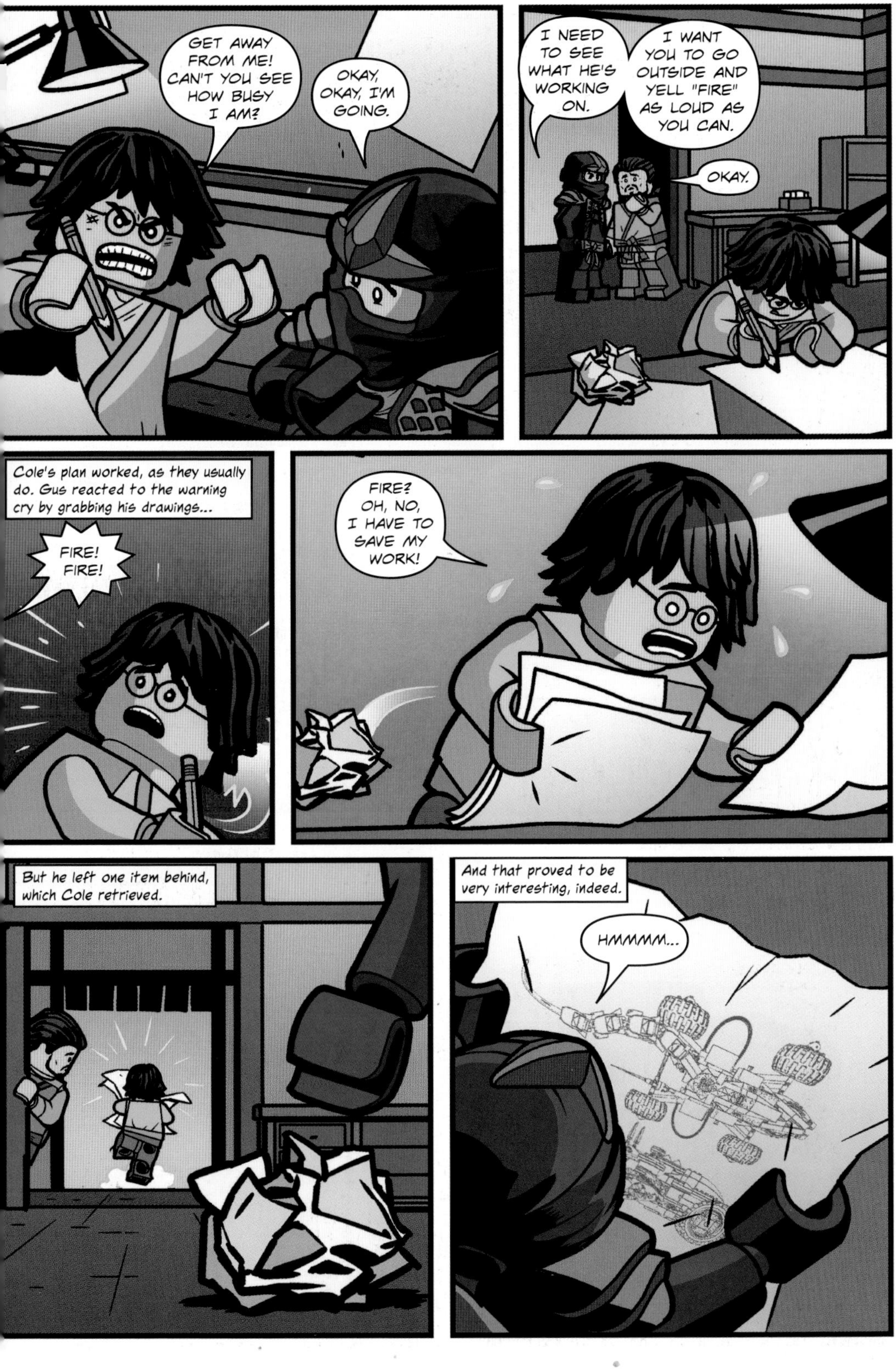
GET AWAY FROM ME! CAN'T YOU SEE HOW BUSY I AM?
OKAY, OKAY, I'M GOING.
I NEED TO SEE WHAT HE'S WORKING ON.
I WANT YOU TO GO OUTSIDE AND YELL "FIRE" AS LOUD AS YOU CAN.
OKAY.
Cole's plan worked, as they usually do. Gus reacted to the warning cry by grabbing his drawings...
FIRE! FIRE!
FIRE? OH, NO, I HAVE TO SAVE MY WORK!
But he left one item behind, which Cole retrieved.
And that proved to be very interesting, indeed.
HMMMM...

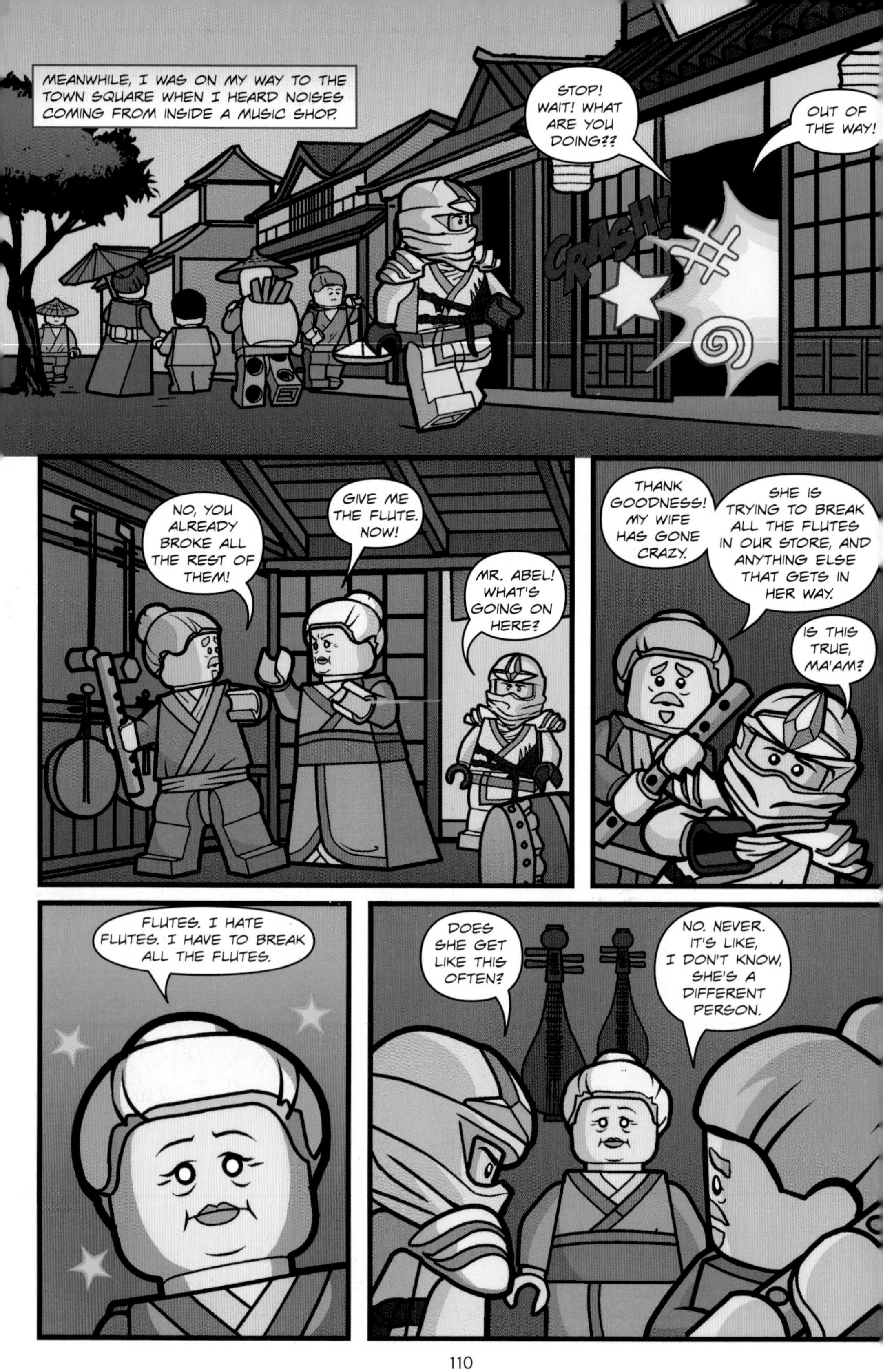
MEANWHILE, I WAS ON MY WAY TO THE TOWN SQUARE WHEN I HEARD NOISES COMING FROM INSIDE A MUSIC SHOP.
STOP! WAIT! WHAT ARE YOU DOING??
OUT OF THE WAY!
CRASH!
NO, YOU ALREADY BROKE ALL THE REST OF THEM!
GIVE ME THE FLUTE. NOW!
MR. ABEL! WHAT'S GOING ON HERE?
THANK GOODNESS! MY WIFE HAS GONE CRAZY.
SHE IS TRYING TO BREAK ALL THE FLUTES IN OUR STORE, AND ANYTHING ELSE THAT GETS IN HER WAY.
IS THIS TRUE, MA'AM?
FLUTES. I HATE FLUTES. I HAVE TO BREAK ALL THE FLUTES.
DOES SHE GET LIKE THIS OFTEN?
NO. NEVER. IT'S LIKE, I DON'T KNOW, SHE'S A DIFFERENT PERSON.

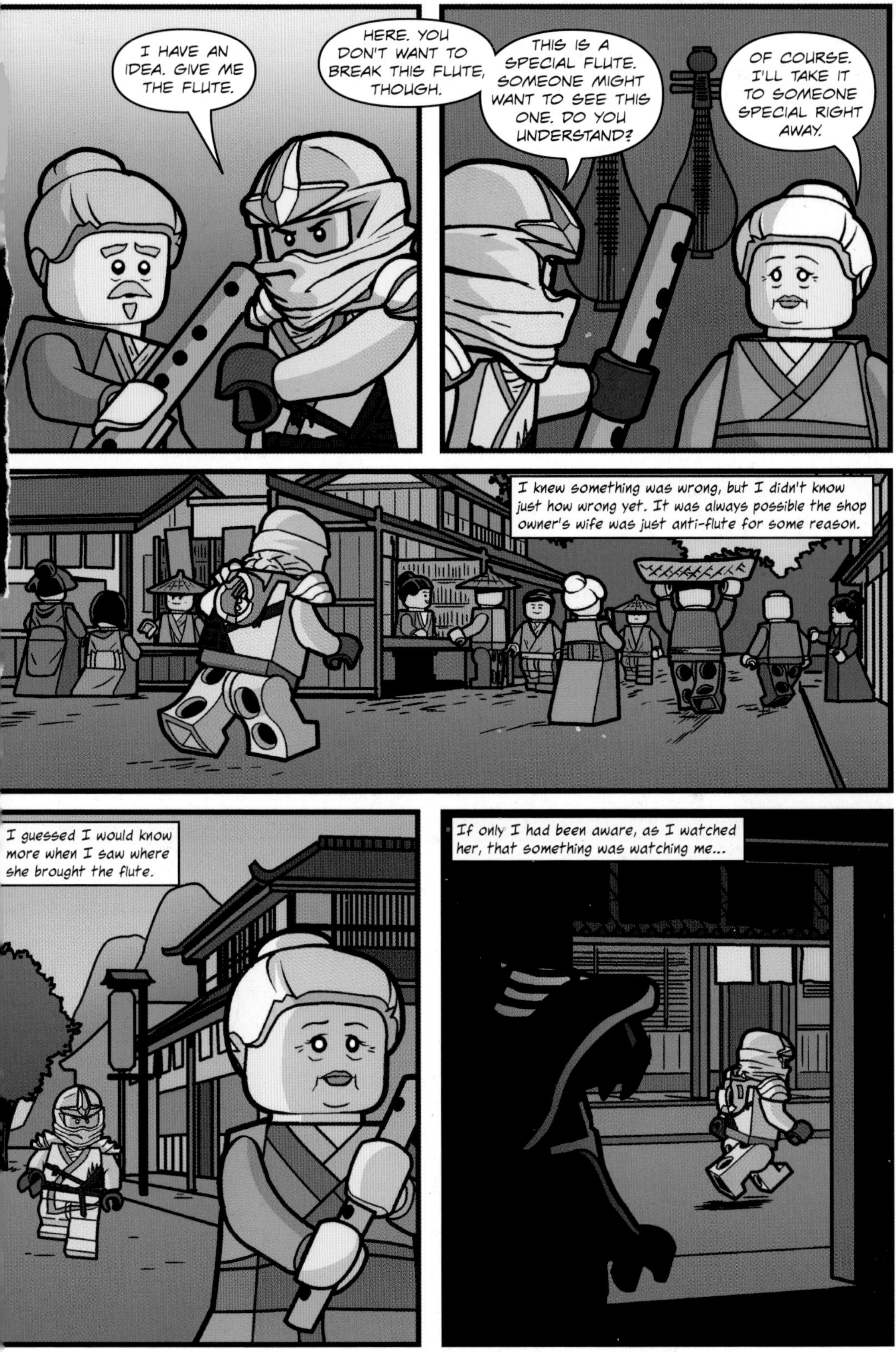
I HAVE AN IDEA. GIVE ME THE FLUTE.
HERE. YOU DON'T WANT TO BREAK THIS FLUTE, THOUGH.
THIS IS A SPECIAL FLUTE. SOMEONE MIGHT WANT TO SEE THIS ONE. DO YOU UNDERSTAND?
OF COURSE. I'LL TAKE IT TO SOMEONE SPECIAL RIGHT AWAY.
I knew something was wrong, but I didn't know just how wrong yet. It was always possible the shop owner's wife was just anti-flute for some reason.
I guessed I would know more when I saw where she brought the flute.
If only I had been aware, as I watched her, that something was watching me...

TO BE CONTINUED IN NINJAGO #3 "RISE OF THE SERPENTINE"

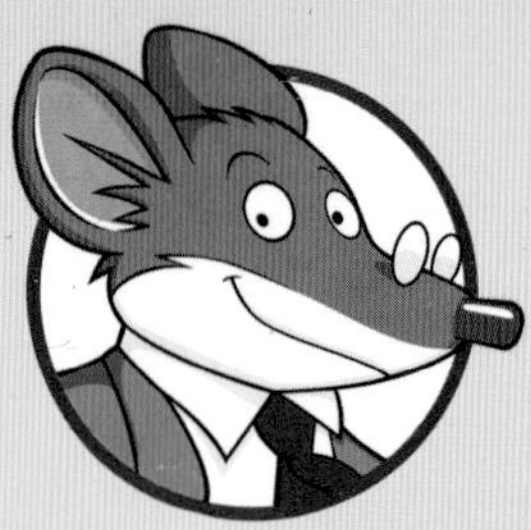

Geronimo Stilton

Graphic Novels Available Now:

#1 "The Discovery of America"
ISBN: 978-1-59707-158-1

#2 "The Secret of the Sphinx"
ISBN: 978-1-59707-159-8

#3 "The Coliseum Con"
ISBN: 978-1-59707-172-7

#4 "Following the Trail of Marco Polo"
ISBN: 978-1-59707-188-8

#5 "The Great Ice Age"
ISBN: 978-1-59707-202-1

#6 "Who Stole the Mona Lisa?"
ISBN: 978-1-59707-221-2

#7 "Dinosaurs in Action"
ISBN: 978-1-59707-239-7

#8 "Play it Again, Mozart!"
ISBN: 978-1-59707-276-2

#9 "The Weird Book Machine"
ISBN: 978-1-59707-295-3

#10 "Geronimo Stilton Saves the Olympics"
ISBN: 978-1-59707-317-2

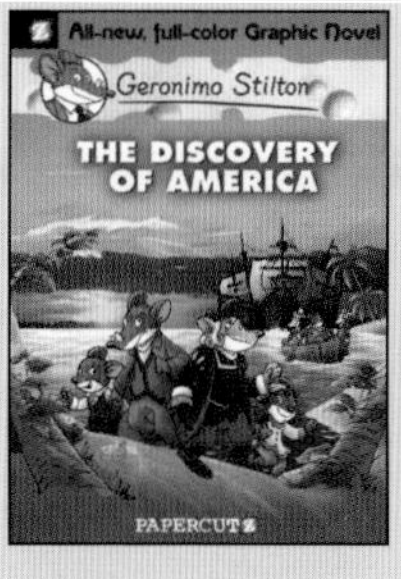
All-new, full-color Graphic Novel
Geronimo Stilton
THE DISCOVERY OF AMERICA
PAPERCUTZ

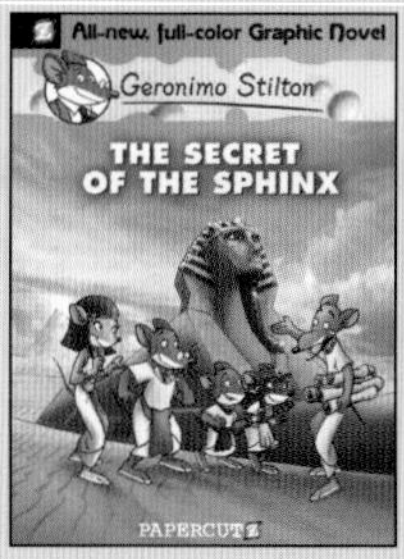
All-new, full-color Graphic Novel
Geronimo Stilton
THE SECRET OF THE SPHINX
PAPERCUTZ

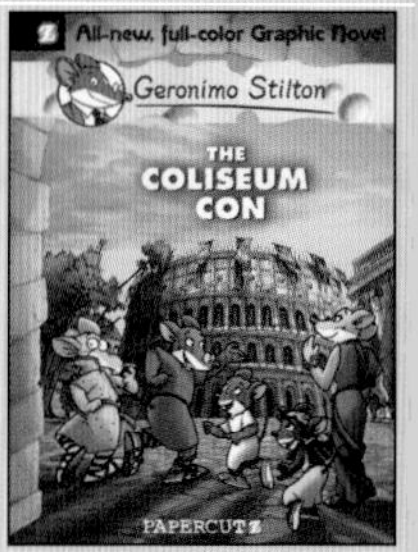
All-new, full-color Graphic Novel
Geronimo Stilton
THE COLISEUM CON
PAPERCUTZ

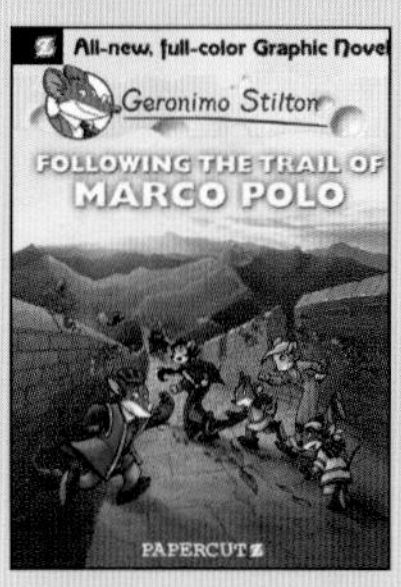
All-new, full-color Graphic Novel
Geronimo Stilton
FOLLOWING THE TRAIL OF MARCO POLO
PAPERCUTZ

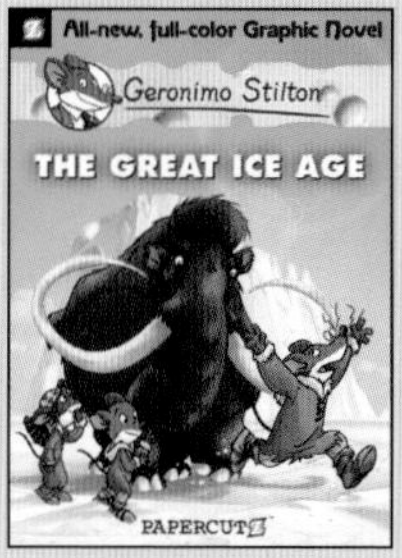
All-new, full-color Graphic Novel
Geronimo Stilton
THE GREAT ICE AGE
PAPERCUTZ

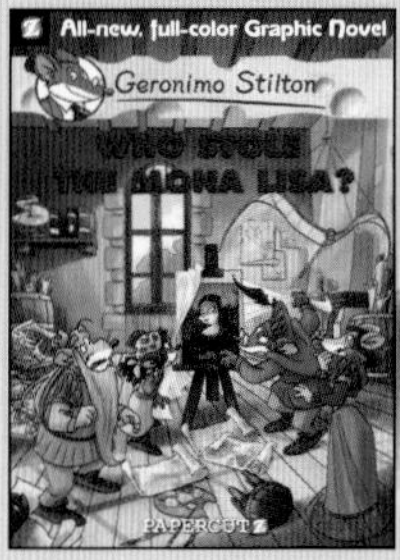
All-new, full-color Graphic Novel
Geronimo Stilton
WHO STOLE THE MONA LISA?
PAPERCUTZ

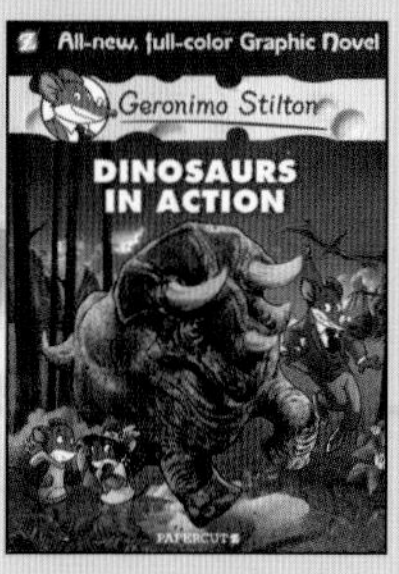
All-new, full-color Graphic Novel
Geronimo Stilton
DINOSAURS IN ACTION
PAPERCUTZ

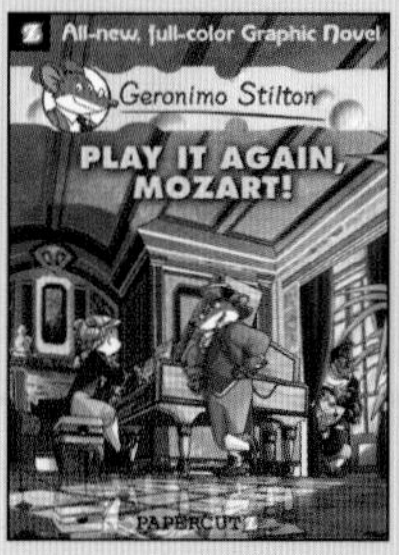
All-new, full-color Graphic Novel
Geronimo Stilton
PLAY IT AGAIN, MOZART!
PAPERCUTZ

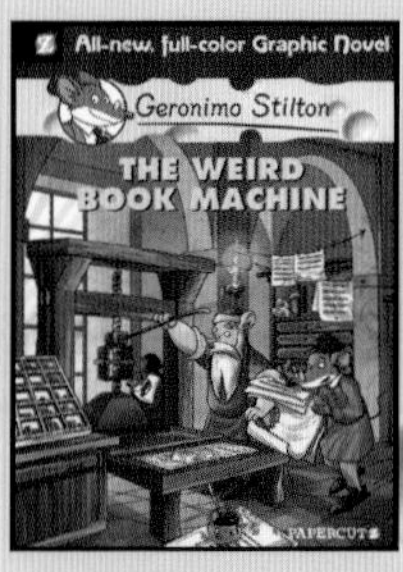
All-new, full-color Graphic Novel
Geronimo Stilton
THE WEIRD BOOK MACHINE
PAPERCUTZ

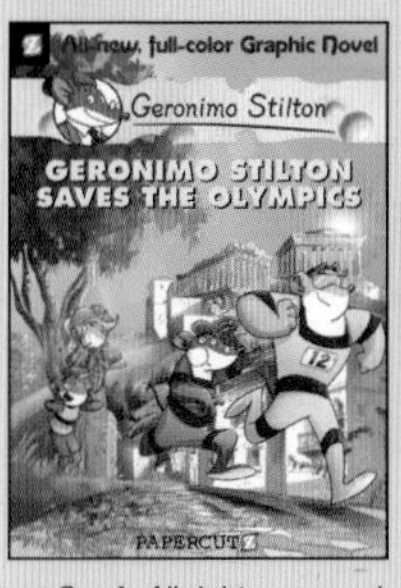
All-new, full-color Graphic Novel
Geronimo Stilton
GERONIMO STILTON SAVES THE OLYMPICS
PAPERCUTZ

GERONIMO STILTON graphic novels are available at booksellers everywhere. GERONIMO STILTON is available in hardcover only for $9.99 each. Or order from us: please add $4.00 for postage and handling for first book, add $1.00 for each additional book. Please make check payable to NBM Publishing.
Send to: Papercutz 160 Broadway, Suite 700, East Wing, New York, NY 10038. 1-800-886-1223

www.papercutz.com